PUPPET MASTER

Puppet Master

by

Barry T Hawkins

Gotham Books

30 N Gould St.
Ste. 20820, Sheridan, WY 82801
https://gothambooksinc.com/

Phone: 1 (307) 464-7800

© 2025 *Barry T Hawkins*. All rights reserved.

No part of this book may be reproduced, stored in a retrieval system, or transmitted by any means without the written permission of the author.

Published by Gotham Books (June 13, 2025)

ISBN: 979-8-3484-9434-6 (H)
ISBN: 979-8-3484-9432-2 (P)
ISBN: 979-8-3484-9433-9 (E)

Because of the dynamic nature of the Internet, any web addresses or links contained in this book may have changed since publication and may no longer be valid.

The views expressed in this work are solely those of the author and do not necessarily reflect the views of the publisher, and the publisher hereby disclaims any responsibility for them.

Contents

Chapter 1 1
Chapter 2 7
Chapter 3 15
Chapter 4 21
Chapter 5 27
Chapter 6 31
Chapter 7 33
Chapter 8 38
Chapter 9 43
Chapter 10 51
Chapter 11 57
Chapter 12 61
Chapter 13 71
Chapter 14 80
Chapter 15 85
Chapter 16 91
Chapter 17 106
Chapter 18 114
Chapter 19 121
Chapter 20 133
Chapter 21 140
Chapter 22 144
Chapter 23 146
Chapter 24 153
Chapter 25 160
Chapter 26 173
Chapter 27 187
Chapter 28 191
Chapter 29 193

Chapter	Page
Chapter 30	196
Chapter 31	203
Chapter 32	207
Chapter 33	216
Chapter 34	218
Chapter 35	223
Chapter 36	233
Chapter 37	242
Chapter 38	245
Chapter 39	251
Chapter 40	255
Chapter 41	261
Chapter 42	265
Chapter 43	270
Chapter 44	272
Chapter 45	283
Chapter 46	285
Chapter 47	291
Chapter 48	293
Chapter 49	301
Chapter 50	304
Chapter 51	315
Chapter 52	322

Chapter I

Saturday, 6:27 pm, Manhattan, NY

The day had a taste of honey and vinegar. The sweetness came with an edge of bitterness. There was no way she could ever get back the wasted year, but this was one hell of a great day. Meredith Granger had just dropped off a final copy of her master's thesis at the post office, registered mail, return receipt requested. She hoped this copy would now work its way through the mysteries of the postal service system to her faculty advisor in Babylon, Long Island. She had paid for an official-looking green tag to ward off careless destruction of the document in some monstrous mail masher or accidental derailment to an abandoned siding in Sheboygan. Not that Meredith was willing to trust that no mishaps would occur to this bloodied monument of her effort. Trust was not easy these days. Complete copies were stashed in both her apartment and a safe deposit box at the local branch of Chemical Bank. Hard experience had made her ready to go to extravagant lengths to protect the product of her work.

The master's degree she would earn in sociology at New York University would represent twice the amount of effort normally required. Her first academic advisor left his job in the middle of Meredith's initial year to take a faculty position at the distant University of Hawaii. That was hard enough to accept, as it produced feelings of both abandonment and envy— Hawaii, for God's sake! It also set back her project by at least half-a-year.

No quitter, this petite bundle of energy perpetually dressed in Lycra and sneakers was determined to finish. She set out to overcome the obstacles by sheer will power. She was used to overcoming apparently insurmountable obstacles. When you are less than four and a half feet tall, and weigh eighty pounds, there are many apparently insurmountable obstacles. Some people complain if they get asked for proof of age when they are two or three years older than the minimum drinking age. Meredith even had trouble getting into adult movies. It wasn't unusual for one of her boyfriends to be asked what "your daughter wants" at a restaurant. Some people seemed to take a perverse pleasure in toying with her, like she was a child. Men were always hoisting her up into the air, pleased with themselves that they appeared so strong, and completely oblivious to the helplessness and humiliation she experienced. A few classes in Tai Kwan Do had given her some simple moves that were designed to dislodge someone's grip, before they could lift her into the air, even disable them if necessary. So far, she hadn't had the nerve to use the moves in a real situation.

The worst of it was not the physical problem of her size, but the way people tended to discount her as a person. She reacted to this size discrimination with perseverance and energy. After twenty-seven years of scrapping, clawing, and pummeling her way through a world where she was at best three-quarter size, she was not going to give up just because of a little delay. What she didn't know then, was that delay would grow to be much more than a little.

She dutifully went through the difficult process of finding a new mentor, but ten months later, the replacement advisor took a sudden leave of absence. Meredith's inquiries were ignored for a series of vague reasons, until it was too late to finish her thesis that year. Finally, she learned that this second mentor was fighting a form of lymphatic cancer that would debilitate him for an extended period. In fact, he might not survive at all. She found it hard to be angry at someone with such a tragic development, but her frustration was almost unbearable. Her immediate impulse was to give up the whole program, but Meredith had never yet failed to reach a goal she had set for herself, and she wasn't going to quit now. So, she stormed the administrative offices and managed to talk Dean Wynter into assigning a multiple-person advisory team to her. That way, if another advisor was lost there were still three to maintain continuity.

A full two years late, Meredith had finally typed the last few words of the thesis' conclusion on her discount laptop, the final document adding up to one hundred twelve pages. She carried it on a flash drive as if it were a winning lottery ticket. That was handed over at the Ginko office where it could be printed. After storing safe copies, she took a hard copy to the college print shop, where it would be copied again and bound into book form for placement in the university library.

With trembling hands, she surrendered it to a clerk she had identified as helpful and considerate in past encounters. She watched as he placed it under an arm and went into a back room, staring after him like a mother who had just seen her child off on a train. Then she walked home, lost in a kind of numb disbelief.

She sat on the threadbare sofa bed for a few minutes in her personal fog. But soon the first spark of understanding sent a thrill of adrenalin shrieking into her limbs.

Sitting time was over.

It was time to move.

It was time to jump, to shout, to run. Out her apartment door, down the two flights of stairs in about five leaps, and quickly onto the street—horizontal flight of a Stinger missile.

Look out, here I come!

One block, two, three—across West Ninth Street, then down Broadway to Astor Place, past the big black cube sculpture by Rosenthal placed during the Lindsey administration. It was titled "ALAMO," as if making a last stand against the hordes of city dwellers who threatened. She passed it on the fly, taking comfort in its familiarity and permanence. She paralleled Cooper Union, dodging the street vendors and assorted hustlers like she was doing a downhill slalom. As she sped south on Bowery, she began to feel her energy waning. She turned left onto Houston, wondering for the hundredth time, why it was pronounced "How-stun" in New York and "Hew-stun" in Texas.

Finally, glowing and puffing, she slowed, now more than a mile from home. There was still a lilt in her step, and a euphoric cloud around her. She didn't notice the figure hidden in the shadows of the overgrown vacant lot—one of those strange open areas in the midst of the massive city structures, where a few small plots of vegetables had been planted in contemporary imitation of the victory gardens of a previous generation. Now wilted by early frosts and urban smog, the cooperative gardens vied for space with the street bums' makeshift shelters and furtively dumped garbage, human and non-human refuse intermingling in various states of decay.

A man was watching. Dressed in loose-fitting army fatigues and jackboots. In a long side pocket was a curved woodcarver's blade, about four inches long, with a rounded hardwood handle darkened by the sweat of much handling. The inner edge of the claw-like blade was honed to razor sharpness. His index finger slid rhythmically along the back side of the knife, as he followed the young woman's progress. He stroked the carving tool in time to her steps, feeling a stirring between his legs. The blade tip penetrated the cloth of his pocket and bit lightly into his well-muscled thigh. A drop of blood welled from the minute puncture. Sensing the wetness, he felt his excitement grow.

He whispered to himself.

"You would never look at me, would you, bitch? You are the kind that would stare right through me, as if I don't exist."

His face did not reflect the violent wash of emotion suggested by the words. Flat, wooden, unanimated, even the lips did not move during the jerky rushes of guttural sound.

"To you I am just a piece of wood, a papier mâché figure, a mannequin. Where are you dancing to, my little cunt? To entertain your sugar daddy? To one of many? To whoever will shove his pole into you? I have a pole, too and I will fill you. I will fill you with thoughts of beauty from my head, and words of wit from my mouth, and movement from my hand, and life from my pole. First, I will empty you, and then I will fill you."

Cold eyes tracked her movement.

Scuttling, spiderlike, on an intersecting tangent that would bring them together just beside the foul-smelling green dumpster near the overgrown corner of the lot, he gave little yips of feral anticipation.

Perhaps she sensed something of the tracking, or just became spooked by the darkness, mugginess, and distance from home, but Meredith stopped celebrating and started shivering. She began to wonder what the hell she was doing, out alone in a poorly lit, high crime area. It was getting late. Shadows of the city buildings were helping to diminish the little remaining light. She tried to mentally suppress childish fears of the dark and wild things in the night, but a primitive knowledge of her vulnerability squeezed up juices of panic and dark cramps. She went over Tai Kwon Do movements in her mind. She walked faster.

Now she had the choice of going all the way back the route she had come, or cutting over to Avenue C, and up three blocks to Greg's apartment. Just as she was telling herself she would be damned if she had to run to a man for protection, she ran into damnation. First, it was a hand on her throat, then an arm under hers and up behind her head. For a moment everything came to a stop—her legs, her thoughts, her heart. There was no thought of martial arts techniques, no thought at all ... no time. With a crash of pain, a knee drove into her back and she went down. Her knees hit the sidewalk, then her chest, and finally her face smacked into the hard surface.

With ripping force, a heavy cloth bag slipped over her head, rasping over the scrapes her face had received in the tackling assault. Intellect would say that air can enter cloth, but intellect was only the batboy here. Her primal fear of suffocation fused with the pain of being dragged over concrete into scrabbly stubble and the punishing jabs and scratches of bramble bushes. Brutal yanks brought her arms together behind her back while what felt like wire gouged into her wrists, as it was lashed around and around. She had a clarity that she might not have maintained, had she not already ridden her emotions on a wild ride. Her system had gotten used to the adrenalin high of overwork, too much caffeine and emotional rollercoasters. Like an addict who could operate on doses that would stun others, she maintained a surprising level of functioning. Despite the nylon over her head, every sound, every touch came unscreened into her consciousness. The pressure on her back eased but she heard with pricked-up ears the dreaded, yet predictable sound of a zipper. Then weight and warmth at her back, and a silky pushing against her hands, followed by squirts of warm liquid.

Conflicting emotions fought for the upper hand. Vast sickening helplessness, as she sensed her absolute lack of power. Disgust and anger at being fouled. Relief, that the creature had apparently spent himself without entering her.

The last thought was premature.

Soon he entered her.

It was done with his knife.

Chapter 2

Sunday, 8:45 a.m.

Steam from the shower misted part of the bathroom mirror, especially near the top, so Gil's reflection seemed a strange headless form, seen through a dreamy fog. Or was it more nightmarish than dreamlike? He paused, viewing this body that he used so much, but seldom chose to really look at. The scars had faded to white dots and dashes. His chest was a human Morse code exhibit. Some of the knife wounds had healed into slot-shaped marks that reminded him of those on data entry cards. "Run me through a computer and you'd get one hell of a printout," he mumbled, wryly.

The few who had seen him with his shirt off and dared to ask, had usually accepted the stories he had made up to explain the pattern of violence on his skin. Sometimes lies seem more believable than the truth. Still, one time, a little drunk and curious about the possible reactions, he had tested out that theory, and told a girlfriend the real story.

"My mother tried to kill me when I was four years old."

His companion assumed he was joking, so responded in kind.

"Yeah, my Dad tried to teach me to swim by tossing me in a lake, tied up in a bag full of rocks!"

Gil didn't press the point. Most of the time it was better not to think about it. He gave his date some polite laughter, and trotted out one of his fictional versions. It was the one about heroic war exploits that usually helped get the female listener closer to bed. He had several other stories ready to use as necessary, including an attack by crazed drug dealers during a bust that went wrong. When he wanted to hide his identity as a cop, he used the one about an industrial accident too grim to talk about.

No one really wanted to believe a mother could be so lacking in maternal instinct, so hostile, as to try to destroy the product of her own womb. In reality, it happens often. Without even getting into the old issues about abortion, Gil knew from his years in the N.Y.P.D. that hundreds of children were maimed and killed by their mothers every year. Thousands more were just lucky enough that the thrown knife missed, the bush under the window broke the fall, the mother was too drunk to complete the choke hold or she missed with the bat. In his head he knew he wasn't unique. Dealing with the feelings wasn't quite as easy.

There was always the big question: "What kind of person is so terrible, even his mother wants him dead?" Gil normally didn't let that one surface Almost thirty-five years had gone into not thinking about it. Actually, he remembered very little of his childhood. He knew that his mother had walked out of a psychiatric hospital less than a year after she had been placed there by the authorities. The inpatient stay followed an incident that Gil was glad he didn't remember, the one that had almost cost him his life. She committed suicide a few months later in a typically bizarre manner, walking naked into the local sewage treatment plant and jumping into a mechanical waste processor. If there was some symbolic significance to her choice of means, he didn't want to know about it.

His father just disappeared after that, right before Gil's sixth birthday. No calls, no letters, no trace. A few years ago, as an adult, Gil had gone through a brief period of depression and tried to deal with it by tracking down his old man. But despite the resources of the Police Department, intervening years had washed away the spoor.

It took almost six months before the boy was discharged from the hospital. After that, references to childhood usually conjured up images of white uniforms and the smell of antiseptic. He had been adopted by his maternal grandparents, and his name changed from Gdnewski to Beccarelli. As an adult, he changed the Beccarelli to Beach, and Gordon to Gil. Gordy Beccarelli became Gil Beach. That way he didn't have to get rid of his monogrammed luggage, not that he actually had any.

He couldn't get rid of the scars ... or the dreams.

Gil turned away from the mirror, and moved to the window, draping the large bath towel around himself like a toga, ... or a shroud.

He decided that he must be lonely. It wasn't that he felt the emotion as such, but everything pointed that way. When he went to select some music, there was the choice of the somber Rimsky-Korsakov recording, a push-away-the-darkness type of music, instead of the more upbeat Vivaldi. Then he caught himself staring out the back window at the children playing on a decrepit jungle gym. Yes, the signs were there ... like talking to the cat.

"It's the news media that does it," he explained to his neurotic Calico. He had named her "Pepper" because of her habit of sniffing dust balls, then sneezing.

"They did it with crack cocaine. Now they've done it with crystal meth."

He grabbed the newspaper, with a headline featuring the newest raid on an "Ice" production laboratory in South Jamaica, Queens.

"Sure, they would have been popular drugs anyway, but the media made them fads, and then epidemics. They tell everybody about this incredible new drug that everybody wants and give it a cooler than cool nickname. Its not drugs, its 'ecstasy.' Suddenly a million heads want to find out about this stuff. A million new customers! Lo and behold, it's the terrible scourge the media said it was going to be. Only they didn't mention that they helped make it happen by giving it a snappy name and advertising it!"

Pepper narrowed her eyes and shifted her position on the windowsill, looking away from him to the ledge outside the window where birds often paraded, protected by the glass, knowing they were safe for the moment from her claws.

"Yeah, right. You don't care either."

Definitely lonely.

Gil knew the signs. He had been living alone for several years. Unlike the relationships of many cops, the marriage of Gil and Diane Beach had endured the shift work and long absences, the secretiveness and jealousies. But some evil cosmic joker had decided that two wasn't a proper number. If neither Gil nor Diane would turn to another lover, this Grand Trickster would make a triangle anyway. Gil spent eighteen months competing with her cancer. Finally, like a woman drawn compulsively to a drifter passing through town, she summoned Gil to say goodbye. She said she didn't want to leave, but it was the end. He had fought for her, but the competition was over, and he had lost.

That was when he stopped believing in God. It was easier than hating a being who had absolute and arbitrary power over everything you cared about.

Friends encouraged him to get rid of the house after Diane went into the hospital for the last time. But he knew that would be another loss, and he had lost too much already. For two years after her death, Gil saw a psychotherapist—Dr. Abraham Brenkowski, a guy with a big practice, a big office, and a big fee. Sometimes Gil wanted to talk about the dreams, but Brenkowski kept putting that aside and coming back to ideas about merger, or fusion, or other things Gil didn't understand. Eventually, Gil realized that the shrink was telling him that his feelings for Diane were unhealthy.

"You see, your relationship had become a substitute for a fuller life," the therapist suggested with a slight smirk, as if letting Gil in on a secret he had been saving for a long time, and wasn't he smart to know all this. Brenkowski lifted one fuzzy eyebrow.

"Your childhood made you quite incapable of an intimate relationship with a person of the opposite sex. Only in memory is it so wonderful. I think you need to look at the fact that you are idealizing a relationship that was really pathologically dependent."

That was the first time the anger had surfaced.

Nothing seemed to happen for a moment, then there was a creaking sound from the pressure of the Detective's arms against the chair. His body began to rise from its seat, an eerie levitation that became a leap toward the surprised doctor. Only the fact that Gil slipped on a throw rug during his lunge had saved the therapist. As it was, the office didn't escape the destruction aimed at Brenkowski. The repair bill was twenty-seven hundred, which Gil eventually paid. He never saw if the restoration was worth it, because he never returned. But the anger did.

A few months later he had been suspended from the Force. He was working the Sixth Precinct Robbery Team. That was when they were calling them R.I.P. Units. Making a collar on a two-bit robbery suspect, Gil had suddenly found his fellow detectives pulling him off a bloody mess that looked vaguely like a human being. It took a while before he realized that the lumpy red mound was the suspect, and that he, Gilmore A. Beach, respected officer of the law, was responsible for the wreckage.

The man was a "Bug," with no apparent redeeming human qualities. His primitive animal-like behavior may have been something of an advantage in the criminal life. On the street, sometimes nastiness was self- protective like the bad taste of an insect that made it unpalatable to predators. It was not an advantage in dealing with Gil.

"Why don'tcha go pick up some whores?" the bug had complained. "Your wife might like to see ya."

Gil's normal ability to dismiss a wise ass's comments didn't work this time. When the scum added, "She's probably ready for you, the horse is finished with her," the Detective lost control. It was like a blackout. He had no memory of what he did until he felt the hands of other officers pulling him off the man.

The slimy character of the suspect, along with a few well-placed lies by his team had kept him from being convicted of assault or being permanently booted from the Job, but it didn't prevent him from being suspended for three months, demoted and transferred to the South Bronx for a year. The moment he walked away from the broken human being that had been the force of his violence, he knew life was not going to be the same. He knew he was going to have to get himself under control.

Memories clutched at him with images of that long ago day of rage and purging. For a moment he was back there.

"You crazy stupid bastard. You really fucked up this time," he berated himself." You stupid idiot! You dummy!"

He had barely been conscious of his surroundings. He had ripped himself away from the restraining hands and pushed out into the street. The perp was lying in a pool of blood, while Gil was drowning in feelings he couldn't even identify. The focus of his anger had moved inward from the punk to himself. If he had come to a bridge first, he might have just gone over the side and ended up a floater for the M.E.'s office to deal with. But instead of a bridge, he came to the stadium of a local high school. He turned through a gap in the cyclone fence, hunkered down in a fighter's stance with rigid, bunched muscles, fighting an inner demon. Tensed to hold his insides together, he felt his turmoil pushing him forward in a jog, then faster, into a run.

As he rounded the first turn of the track, he sighted an open entrance to the stadium seats. A series of staircases led up to the top. He leaped up the first three stairs, and took the next dozen, two at a time. Then he pounded up four more stories to the rim of the stadium, step by step. Later, he learned that there were sixty-five steps from the track to the rim, which doesn't sound like so many until you try shoving a hundred and seventy pounds up each of them.

That first time, he reached the top with legs like gelatin. A chain link barrier stopped him. He paused, gasping, for a few seconds, then tried to go back down. His legs wouldn't cooperate. Despite his police training, Gil's body was not ready for this assault, and he felt himself collapsing. He managed to grab seats to each side, preventing a serious fall. It wasn't that he cared about being injured, he just wasn't through yet. By the time he had managed to descend, his legs were beginning to work better, so he turned and started up again. He only made it halfway this time. He collapsed, smashing a knee and elbow into the concrete. Tears of pain mixed with those of his rage finally gave way to the despair underlying it all. He lay crumpled beneath the weight of his human limitations and the crushing burden of so many losses. It was a long time before he got up. When he did, the weight no longer seemed unbearable. Something had been expelled, flushed out, released.

Gil shook his head, bringing himself back to the present. He padded back to the bathroom, where he splashed cold water on his face. Then he vigorously toweled down, the cold water and rough rubbing making him feel more alert. But he needed more than that to drive out the old images and feelings. He pulled on a warm-up suit and his New Balance Utility training shoes. Pepper gave a plaintive mew.

"Back in a flash, Pepperkins."

The cat blinked a couple of times, and started licking itself, with the disregard cat fanciers seem to interpret as independence.

Gil slipped out into the early morning fustiness. There were three cars in the garage. A late model Plymouth sedan, which he used most often, a 1980 M.G. midget that he drove for fun, when it wasn't broken down or in the middle of significant tinkering effort, and a '47 Studebaker that he meant to restore, but never quite got around to working on, except a day or two annually when he took some vacation. The Studebaker didn't run, but it was worth the garage space just in fantasy power, not to mention reminiscences of double dates in a jalopy just like it, when he was a teenager. Today he took the M.G. Another sign. He was definitely lonely.

Beach no longer did his discipline at the high school. He had only returned a half dozen times before he found another stadium located nearer his house in the hills of Staten Island. This one had a roof that made it accessible year-round. He didn't mind the effect of cold weather on his body, but ice made the steps at the High School almost unnegotiable, and the routine had become essential for him to cope with the toxic waste that accumulated in his gut.

Wagner College was a small private college on Staten Island, with a serious football program and a Howard Avenue campus located only five minutes from his Grymes Hill address. When he discovered the stadium, he made a deal to "patrol it now and then" if the college gave him a key to the gate. The college's security conscious administrators were happy to have a cop around, especially when it cost them nothing. Now he went three or four times a week.

He had stopped counting the stairs. Up flight after flight, he pushed himself to the top, around the upper walkway to the next aisle, then down. A punishing lap of the quarter-mile track, then up the stairs again. Most times he lapsed into a kind of coma, blankly passing through time and space, though an observer might- have seen something much more intense. He would come to his senses, an hour or more later, when at some point the forty-year-old legs refused to work any longer, and he found himself sunken to the ground, completely spent.

Today followed the usual pattern. It was almost an hour and a half before he reached his limits. Not that he acknowledged them. He finally collapsed but maintained a sense of incompleteness. Since he didn't feel finished, he felt like he must not have done enough. It was never enough.

CHAPTER 3

Monday, 7:53 a.m.

"Yo, Gabby. What did ya do on yer day off? Sleep in a cement mixer?"

Wilson, the Desk Officer, always greeted Gil with some wisecrack. The nickname was habit within the Detective Division. Wilson was exercising a familiarity he could not really claim, but Beach had learned to tolerate the man's frequent lapses of savvy. There wasn't much social skill in Wilson's repertoire.

"Gabby" was both a play on his initials, G.A.B., and a dig. Gil was anything but talkative. So, the handle stuck. He didn't mind. It was clear to him that nicknames were a sign of being accepted—at least as long as they said them to your face. There was no room for fragile flowers in this business. Anybody who couldn't take a little ribbing couldn't be trusted in the trenches. There were worse fates in the locker room, or the muster room he was now crossing.

Gil passed the length of the desk, a massive structure running nearly a length of the large room at shoulder height, with a scuffed brass rail providing a protective fence around it. He pushed through the double swinging doors to the rear hall and took the stairway up the second-floor squad room of the Precinct Detective Unit.

His desk was on the east side of the P.D.U. office, catching the early sun, so the spider plant on his file cabinet was waterfalling all the way to the floor. His work space was a massive clutter. Anyone who sized him up by the jumble on his desk would have misunderstood one of Gil's greatest gifts. Despite some messiness in other parts of his life, Gil Beach could bring order out of chaos in the only realm that counted to the Job. He could find purpose within insanity, direction within confusion, reason within absurdity. To himself, he figured that he had experienced so much disorder in life that he was at home with it, so could move through chaos undaunted, like a pro fullback pushing through a high school defensive line. Maybe not a touchdown each time, but always forward, always a gain.

Treadwell was at the coffee pot. Dress shirt stained with sweat, shoulder holster browned by years of intimate contact, he was planning retirement within a year. His sagging shoulders and belly spoke of the emotional weight the job had added to his life. Gil winced inwardly. Treadwell had a detached, tentative manner, as if he had already half begun the separation he both anticipated and dreaded from the N.Y.P.D. The stresses of police work and personal tragedy had taken away his spirit. But that had left him with only the badge as an identity. Beach had seen others like this—no longer able to do the Job ... nothing without it.

"How old is it?" Gil asked, nodding toward the coffee.

"It's brown and it's hot. What more do you want? Besides, all the spoons are still here, so it can't be that bad."

"Unless they've been stirring with pencils, in which case, we're in a lot of trouble."

"Speaking of trouble, we caught a good one over the weekend, while you were off fooling around."

Gil smiled at the use of the inclusive "we." He knew that if it was any real trouble, it would end up on his desk. As he moved over to his clutter, he saw that it was already there.

A packet of glossy photos sat on top of the other accumulated debris. He slid them out of the envelope. They showed what was left of a body after some heavy cutting. There was a headless torso, gutted out like a dressed deer. It was hard to think that the body was once a human being. It was more like a pig carcass in a butcher store. Gil remembered once stumbling in on an autopsy, where he saw for the first time, the disemboweled corpse at midpoint in the procedure. It changed his whole attitude about the human body. Nothing very dramatic, just a loss of mystery. It was less sacred now. Just a thing that could be taken apart, like a radio, or a turkey.

"Kinda different, eh?" Treadwell raised graying eyebrows.

"Yeah, if somebody's going to gut someone, they usually go in from the front. This one looks like it was from the back."

"Who did the post?"

"Your buddy, Krispy Kritters."

Gil waited. He didn't like Treadwell's sense of humor. The nickname was a reference to the pathologist's specialty, burn victims. Ever since he had worked for three months on the carcasses of several men involved in a military accident with napalm, Anton Krispnick had increasingly been called on to make sense of the charred remains of fire victims. Earlier, in a well-publicized case, a much disliked attorney had made the wrong conclusion when he saw the fighting stance of a burned body. He tried to use that as evidence the deceased had been attacking someone. Krispnick had blown the shyster's case, when he explained in court that this was a typical pose of fire victims, caused by the action of heat on muscles and tendons, not a combative activity at the time of death. Although pathologists often were proud of their ability to remain unmoved by the worst carnage, Gil had seen tears in Anton's eyes after that first multiple victim fire disaster, and had seen them since.

Treadwell filled the silence, reading from his ever-present notebook.

"Not too committal. Cause of death, exsanguination. Time of death, somewhere between nine and midnight Saturday. The perp used a short blade. Drug screen says the girl had been using speed."

Gil made a mental note to talk to Anton. The forensic pathologist always had something he didn't put in the official autopsy report, the stuff that he suspected but didn't want to defend should he ever be called as a witness in court.

"What else do we have on her?"

"Not a lot at this point. Stuff from her purse was scattered around the scene, so we didn't have any trouble making her, even without the head. Name's Meredith Granger. Twenty-seven years old. She's a graduate student. A real one, not one of those campus whores. Her student I.D. included a thumb print that matched the body. We checked her address. Neighbors say she lives alone, except when she stays with her boyfriend, over in Alphabet-land. Family is mostly in the Detroit area. Parents are flying in today."

"Don't let them see the body," Gil quickly interjected.

"What about the positive I.D.?

"The prints should be enough for now. If the head shows up, we can use the boyfriend to identify it."

Treadwell nodded. He probably didn't understand the difference between losing someone you had known or even loved for just a short time and losing your child. Gil understood.

His older brother had died in Viet Nam. After that the grandparents who raised them both had never been the same. At least they had the comfort that Craig had died in the service of his country. Gil had lost that, too. Three years after the man in full dress uniform had come to the door with his awful news, another man had come to the door while Gil's grandparents were out at a Rotary Club dinner. He was not in uniform, and he was drunk. He said his name was Eugene. Eugene claimed to have been with Craig when he died, but according to his memory, it wasn't the heroic firefight the service records described.

The man confessed in a beery blubber of guilt, that the squad had gotten wasted on opium. There had been an argument and the combination of distorted emotions, drug-deadened inhibitions, and weapons at hand had led to a tragedy. One of the guys had grabbed his weapon and jerked the trigger. Dozens of bullets spewed out of the automatic rifle. Craig was one of those hit by the fusillade. Two died, another was injured. The others, shocked into sobriety, faked an ambush to cover the insanity. Eugene seemed to be seeking some kind of absolution. What he needed was detoxification. Gil couldn't give him either. He lied to the man, telling him they already knew about the incident. It was the only way he could think to keep the drunk from coming back to tell his grandparents the same story. They would never know, he decided. But he hated the man who had forced him to carry this new burden of shame, broken illusions, and secrecy. Another loss.

Gil walked over to the window. The view matched his mood—bleak and melancholy. Dribbles of rain ran down the window, making tracks in the sooty layer of filth. Across the street, he could see the deserted playground of the school a block over. A fading sign listed "Park Rules," as if there were a lovely grassy picnic area, instead of cracked, litter-strewn concrete and rusted netless basketball hoops, sandwiched between cinderblock buildings and a police impound lot filled with old autos in various states of disrepair. The sight brought images of broken human bodies to mind, painted in colors of pain.

No one in the room suspected what was going on within him. Only a lover or a close friend might have noted the slight tensing of his body, the minute increase in the set of his shoulders. But no one was watching, and few knew Gil that well. They never got close enough.

Tonight, he would do the stairs.

Knowing that, he was able to turn back to his desk.

He leafed through the initial reports of the killing, as well as the ongoing investigations of two other homicides—a wino found strangled in an alley and a pretty clear-cut love triangle killing with a very guilty looking ex-boyfriend. Part of him wished they were all "Grounders," routine and easy to solve, but he knew there was another part of him – the part that felt summoned, the part that felt called.

All the other cases were important, but they were just preparation, a rehearsal for the other kind– the dark ones, the evil ones, like the unexplained slaughter of this young girl. At a deep level, Gil sensed a very personified evil roaming the city. Not a religious person, he didn't go much further than that. But sometimes he sensed something calling him to a contest. This was below the level of language for him, just a quickening, like the chess master who plays with little enthusiasm until he hears a rumor of a newcomer with an Eastern European name, who was observed making an unusual series of chess moves. Beach was hardly aware that the tune he whistled under his breath, as he grabbed his topcoat and headed down the stairs, was "Mack the Knife."

CHAPTER 4

Monday, 11:05 a.m.

For those handy with a pocketknife there is an old craft, often taught to children by granddads, that involves carving a face into a fresh apple. If the apple is then dried, it slowly shrinks and discolors to look like a weathered, aged person. The brow drops, the cheeks pull in, and wrinkles appear all over the surface. The final product looks like a wizened old native in miniature, or perhaps a shrunken head. Gil was reminded of such a face, every time he saw the security guard outside M.E. Anton Krispnick's office.

The Medical Examiner's office was on First Avenue, at Thirtieth Street. Gil pulled the M.G. into a reserved parking spot, tossed his identification card on to the dashboard, and lurched out the car door, trying with only partial success to step over a massive puddle blocking his exit. The elderly guard waiting outside labored to push open the door to the building. The man was of an indeterminate age, anywhere from sixty to a hundred. His tiny, crinkled head perched on a stick-like neck. The paramilitary uniform hung on him like he was one of those stick figure mannequins used in the stylish boutiques, not intended to fill out the clothes, but merely provide a minimal support in order not to detract from the display of tailoring. It was always hard for Gil to imagine what protective role such fragile creatures in guard costumes could provide. In truth, it always provoked a childish impulse to go push one of them over and demonstrate how insubstantial they were. But the thought brought a twinge of shame. He would never act on such a childish fancy. That is what separates normal people from maniacs.

The truth was that he sympathized with the needy elderly—needy for identity and activity as much as for money. He felt another twinge of guilt when the old man gave him a sprightly nod and wink. Maybe these workers purpose was a more humane than protective one, he speculated, making the city a little more personable, a bit more friendly. If so, the minuscule salaries of the job were probably well spent. This city could use some softening.

Anton was in his cluttered office. Maybe that was one of the first things that linked him to Gil Beach. Neither was a neatnik. Anton was saved from total disorganization by a secretary that fussed and bothered over him. But she had been completely unsuccessful in trying to invade the pathologist's inner office. Cardboard boxes with ripped seams were stacked in disorderly piles. Sheaves of paper, manila envelopes, books, binders, and assorted folders covered every surface. Rumpled lab coats, Styrofoam cups, and bits of electronic gadgetry peeked out here and there from the mounds of paper. Dozens of pens and pencils, most missing caps or erasers, were scattered like colored sprinkles on a giant ice cream sundae. Gil felt right at home.

"Didn't take you long to get here," a wheezy voice rasped, the rotund figure of the doctor wheeling about in an ancient swivel chair. He pushed his wire-framed glasses up a notch on his nose, gave a porcine snort, and shoved a pile of papers to the side in apparent disregard of their order, or whether they mixed with a stack of unopened mail and several slightly soiled napkins from Burger King. The expression on his lumpy Slovak face implied annoyance at being interrupted, but all the body language spoke of relief and readiness to push aside the bureaucracy for as long as necessary—or longer. One bristly eyebrow elevated itself.

"I can't guess which one you want to know about. Initial report not good enough, eh?"

"Oh sure, the initial report. As I read it, the major conclusion was that the victim was dead, right?"

"What more does a cop need to know, anyway? I suppose you want me to solve another one for you. I can't figure out why the city doesn't just pay us real detectives double salaries and get rid of you guys anyway. It might speed things up a lot, and we'd have a lot of side benefits, like more parking places."

"Anton, you're so full of shit, they could give you a laxative and only have a skin for your assistants to autopsy," Gil laughed.

"Nice to see you too, sport," the pathologist answered with a grin. There was much of a personal nature that the detective did not and would not reveal to the stubby genius, but he was about as close as Gil Beach got to a friend.

"So, am I going to have to pump you, or what?" Gil snorted.

"Oh, this one is different, all right." Anton went on, "The guy who did it had something special in mind. This was not random hack job. Some of the cutting looks ritualistic. In one spot a rectangle was cut in the dorsal skin surface, before he began the deep work. There are divisions marked at the wrists, ankles, and neck, with serial punctures. It looked almost like fake stitches, you know, like when they try to make somebody up to look like Frankenstein. Then I realized that was because she was tied up with barbed wire. The evenly spaced puncture marks would be consistent. You want to take a look?"

Gil wanted to say, "No," but acknowledged he had to see her. Much investigative work is boring, routine labor. It is done with the brain, for the most part, i.e., the intellect. But there is another part, the part Gil knew made the difference between the detectives who were clerks and the ones who were hunters. You could call it intuition, or instinct, or some two-bit psychological term. Whatever you called it, Gil suspected that the good detectives were like method actors. They lived the scenes of crimes like they were their own lives. Once the world of the killer and the killed came alive, the investigator could then project this new level of awareness into areas not obvious when looking only at the hard data and visible evidence. To do that, Gil knew he had to see the victim, see the victimization.

The city morgue is located beneath the M.E.'s offices on thirtieth street. The elevator let the two men out into a waiting room furnished like a comfortable lounge. Was there a compassionate soul somewhere who recognized the horror that wives would experience when they came to identify their broken husbands, parents their overdosed children, lovers their charred loves? Beach doubted it, but was glad the furnishings weren't too bleak.

They walked through swinging double doors, reminiscent of an operating room, down a short hallway and through another set of doors, into the green-tiled storage room. Several gurney carts were arranged against the wall. Gil recalled his college fraternity days, and a party they had produced at their frat house, called the "Embalmer's Ball. "To highlight the theme, girls had been picked up from their dorms by a rented hearse, and the fraternity brothers had been waiting, lying under sheets, with tags tied to their toes to be matched with the party invitations. At the time he had thought it quite hilarious. After a few visits to the real thing, he didn't think he would have found it so funny.

His primary impression today wasn't from his eyes, but from his nose. The cloying smell of disinfectant, gaseous wastes, and other unidentifiable odors mixed for a characteristic atmosphere that stayed with him for hours after leaving the morgue. Unlike the flower scents and perfumes of an undertaker's parlor, this basement carnal house held the undisguised face of death—the bloated, dripping, desiccating cadavers that were desperately trying to return to their elemental components. Later, many of the corpses would receive purging and cosmetic treatments, so that well-meaning relatives would sincerely comment "He looks so natural, just like he was still alive." In this basement workplace there was no confusion about that. The bodies lay in stark naturalism, bloodless and flaccid, without question wholly and incontrovertibly dead.

One cart seemed almost empty. The disposable plastic sheet was hardly displaced by the small mound underneath. Anton slipped it off quickly, in a practiced flip of his hands. Despite his familiarity with corpses and mutilated remains, Gil still found himself taken aback.

"My God, she's so small!"

We estimate her actual height at about four-foot-five. Even with spike heels and a bouffant, she wouldn't make five feet."

"A child."

"Not really. Her biological age matches the twenty-seven years we have down on paper. We make her as having had at least one pregnancy already. She's had a tubal ligation. Even some gray hairs hidden here and there. She's small, but she's a woman."

Despite how different he was from the victim, Beach was beginning to feel that intuitive connection already. A nascent sense of familiarity. The facts would be important, but there was a smell of something other than the morgue that his hunter sense was sniffing. He kept his thoughts to himself, but he trusted his instincts, or whatever whispered in his inner heart. And that voice murmured that for the killer, it was not a woman but a child who had been killed here.

Krispnick's voice broke through his reverie.

"There was no semen in the vagina, though there was something that might be traces of it externally, samples went to the lab— no evidence of sexual penetration. That is, he didn't use his cock. She was, however, apparently skewered with an object of some sort. Tests on that aren't complete. This is a sick one, Gilligan. We did find some of the head."

The pathologist's voice had slowly grown softer as he spoke.

"Some?" the detective pressed, frowning.

"We found the eyes—gouged out, apparently. And some mashed up cerebral tissue. Somehow the guy scooped out her brain."

Gil considered this information, and tried to picture the man... or thing, that would so mutilate a delicate little woman.

Chapter 5

Monday, 1:50 p.m.

You always know when you have an audience in your grasp. They stop all the fidgeting and moving around. No sound, not a whisper. A thousand eyes on invisible threads attached to your lips. The performer pitied people who had never known the power. It was like wearing a vast cape, that you could swirl and flap at will. Every twitch of a wrist, reflected in waves and undulations. A shift of the shoulder and the watchers would rear forward, a changed facial expression and they would sag into their seats. For a time, you were the leader, the Fuhrer, the King, the God. Once they gave themselves to you, there was no holding back. He knew that if he asked them to, they would raise their hands in salute, or stand-up, or applaud.

It was a form of hypnotism, the performance. Mass capitulation, renunciation of the will. Once that barrier was crossed, there was no resistance. He could mold them and move them with ludicrous ease. He would perform a simple double-take, and they would burst out in laughter as if waiting a month for someone to release this pent-up energy. A lifted eyebrow and dozens would collapse in howls of mirth.

This audience was tough. They sat like they were dead. The performer lifted the vent figure onto his knee. It was a female figure with red hair. He hadn't used this one before, and he wasn't as sure of his movements as he usually was. He started with a standard piece of "business," a sight gag. First, he set it up with a quick intro.

"Say hello to the folks, Sally."

"Uh, uh." (Shaking her head negatively) The ventriloquist thought of having her say "Nope," but decided to avoid the "P" sound for now. He might have used the more difficult word, but he was still fighting this audience, and didn't want to give them anything they could use to dismiss him, even if it was a muffled word. Later, when they were on his side, he would grandstand some carefully practiced phrases supposedly difficult for ventriloquists to pull off, like "bread and butter."

"Are you going to be difficult tonight, Sally?"

"Well, how come you get to tell me what to do? I'm no DUMMY you know."

The ventriloquist didn't assume that everybody caught the pun, despite its complete lack of subtlety. He usually aimed at a third-grade level humor, and still the adults loved it. So he reinforced the wordplay with his physical reaction. A lift of his eyes, and a Jack Benny head tilt.

"Oh, is that right? Well, what would you be without me?"

"Famous!"

"Oh, come on, Sally. You couldn't do anything without me."

"I can do lots of things. I can do things you can't even do."

"Oh yeah? Like what?" (A superior smirk from the performer was designed to set up the audience. Everyone hates a pompous ass, so they were more likely to hope for his deflation.)

"Well, for one thing, I got better vision!" The wooden mouth clacked open in perfect synchronization with the words. The head rotated slowly to the right, as if the puppet was scanning the distance.

"Better vision?" Now the figure did a slow visual pan to the left, the ventriloquist matching exactly the figure's movement.

"Yeah! Mine's three hundred and sixty degrees!" The figure's head panned right again, only this time the rotation continued, so the head spun completely around on the torso.

It was old, it was corny, but it always worked. The dummy had made the big arrogant guy look stupid. It was a guaranteed laugh. If that didn't get 'em, you might as well pack it in and go home.

Rows of faces stared passively up from the seats. Still. No laughter, no smiles, no response at all.

The performer began to perspire. It must be the new figure. She was too pretty. Not enough of the ludicrous in her features. And the wiring wasn't working right. The mouth hung slack and flipped gobbets of red onto his shirt when he pulled the mouth lever. The paint must not yet be dry. Maybe it was the name. Sally was too common ... should have made her either a cutesy, like "Binky," or a corny name, like "Brunhilde."

He began to feel the old feelings. The shame, the helplessness. Contempt wafted over him from the rows of frozen faces. Disgust. Rejection. Judgment.

"It's not ME," he pleaded, "It's HER. I am the smart one—SHE is the dummy!" Tone of voice rising, into almost a feminine range. "I am NOT stupid. I am NOT stupid. I am NOT STUPID!"

His body shaking now, features mottled, veins bulging.

"I am not the dummy. I AM NOT THE DUMMY!"

Dozens of blank stares shot lances into the performer's chest and groin. His speech lost coherence, and the words merged into a high keening wail.

"Immmmmnnnnottttheeeeduuuummmmmmm-MMMMMEEEEEEEEEEE! "

He kicked over the chair he had been sitting on, and stood in rabid frenzy, jerking and twitching, until the muscle fibers in his limbs could not be triggered by nerve impulses any longer. He held for a moment longer in a state of vibrating agony, then collapsed on the floor, the sound echoing in the dark and empty loft where he had his stage. The figure he had been holding fell from his grasp. The head part separated from the wood and fabric torso. Meredith Granger's mutilated skull fell heavily to the floor.

There was no one to react. Rows of inanimate figures - severed heads on sticks, and propped up dead animals continued to stare in silent disregard. Only the flies moved, buzzing around the lifeless audience.

CHAPTER 6

A flag snapped wetly in the intermittent wind. It's hoisting cable whacked against the metal pole with a slow bonging sound, like a slender bell, tolling lost souls of distant wars. A figure strode heavily through the deteriorating park, carrying the clouds like weighted duffle bags over his shoulders. As the dampness seeped into his winter-weight uniform, officer C.L. Weigert felt twenty-five pounds heavier than usual. Weigert was no lightweight to begin with. His spreading waistline had already prompted a couple of punk colleagues in the Precinct to nickname him "Officer Wide Girth." Thank God they didn't know that the C. in his name stood for Clyde. They would have had a great time with that!

Other people's humor was mostly a source of confusion to Weigert. He tried to fit in with the crowd by laughing when they did, though often he knew that he was the butt of the laughter. So he continued trying to understand, listening carefully to the conversation at Nick and Annie's, a cop's bar on the West Side. He spent an hour or two there every Friday, tucked into the smoke and atmosphere of camaraderie, watching the other cop's apparently easy conversation, feeling like an alien studying the habits of another life form. He never was completely comfortable at the bar, but stopped by regularly, to make it seem he fit in with everyone else.

Weigert sniffed, ferret like, at the soupy air. His thoughts were mostly about the smell of his clothing, a musty thickness hinting of dead meat and overexertion. He knew he should have the uniform cleaned, but when it was a choice between the cost of a dry cleaner and the price of a satisfying lunch at Casa Maria, he usually chose the lunch. Wrapped as he was into the coat and self-pity, he almost didn't see the entrails.

Any number of other damp citizens, civil service or not, would have ignored the partially crushed box of tissues, welded soggily to the lip of the park walkway, and what looked like a red jump rope lying in a tangle. But much of the self-esteem officer Weigert had experienced during his thirty-three years of life had been a direct reward for his methodical need to keep things in order. Weigert could no more walk past that pulpy mess slopped over the tangled red rope, than a ten-year-old boy could walk past a good climbing tree. There are some things placed in your path that you must act on.

So Clyde Lucius Weigert slipped on a pair of latex gloves from the pouch on his belt, hiked-up his Sam Brown belt, then puffed down into a labored squat to scoop up the soggy mess. His hand jerked back, when he realized that what had appeared to be a red rope was actually loops of bloody intestine, and the whitish mass, spilling from a tissue box. appeared to be a brain. Too large for a dog or cat, yet smaller than a man, it seemed it could have come from a large monkey ... or a human child.

CHAPTER 7

Monday, 2:07 p.m.

In a different part of town, Gil Beach returned to the precinct to find a compact, dark-haired officer slumped in his desk chair. The man jumped up at Gil's approach.

"Oops. Hope you don't mind my using your desk," he offered apologetically. "I had a message for you, and figured I'd use the phone while I was here."

The man was Frank Terranova, a patrolman who was apparently winning a battle with the bottle. After being caught drinking on duty several times and ramming his R.M.P. into a parked garbage truck, he had been sent to the Department's Employee Assistance Program, which had run him through an upstate rehabilitation program. Several years ago the P.B.A. had negotiated an agreement that prohibited firing an officer who agreed to treatment. But the guarantee of continued employment didn't include working the streets with a loaded weapon. That had to wait until the affected individual proved himself again. Most of the Department called those on temporary office duty members of the "Rubber Gun Squad."

Gil sympathized with Terranova. It must be difficult, he was sure, to be publicly labeled and to all extents and purposes demoted to a clerk's duties. He remembered when he first lost Diane, he had hit the bottle hard. So hard, a couple of people had started hinting that if he kept it up, it wouldn't be because of his loss, but because he had found a new love in the booze itself. He recognized the truth of what they said and backed off on the drinking. But the addiction he feared more than alcoholism was to raw feelings, like anger. The few times he had given in to the emotional tide, it had washed him away just as if he had been shot full of potent drugs. The adrenalin rush of his feelings had taken him through a loss of control like he might have expected to see in a drunk or an addict. Since he had begun a personal stair-climbing routine, things had improved and Gil had managed to keep the lid on. But under the "lid" he worried a monster might be whuffling and snorting, waiting for a lapse of attention, an unguarded moment.

As for the booze, he decided to test himself. He stayed completely away from the stuff for over a year. Now he indulged rarely, mostly on special occasions. When he saw someone like Frank, Gil was glad that he wasn't the one sitting there, trying to regain his job, while others who may have been borderline problem drinkers themselves, sniggered and traded snide remarks in the locker room.

"No problem, Frank. What's the message?"

"Just that 'Boom Boom' wants to see you."

"Boom Boom" was Sergeant Robert Mabry, the squad commander. A summons to the Sergeant's office usually meant an assignment, a gift of information, or a request for help in understanding something. Mabry got his nickname because he went around most of the time bellowing like an elephant. Yet he was basically "good people" and a good cop. Street smart, respectful of the men, short on bullshit, long on tolerance, slow to anger, quick to praise, he couldn't have been a much better squad commander. But that didn't mean he was the kind to take any shit, so Gil felt a certain subtle nervousness as he came into the Sergeant's office. He knocked on the Commander's door, and on hearing the characteristic, glass rattling "YO," stepped into the office.

Mabry glanced up, massive frame almost dwarfing the scarred desk. A ruddy complexion, the product of Irish genetics, made him look perpetually angry. The red face and loud voice often intimidated those who didn't know him for the careful man he was.

Whadja do?" The deep baritone reverberated in the small office, "Sleep in a cement mixer?"

Gil did a double take, on hearing the same phrase the Desk Sergeant had yelled earlier.

What, you and Wilson got the same gag writer?" Gil laughed. Their shared experience as classmates at the Academy entitled Gil to an informality with the Commander others would not be granted. Only in private, of course.

Mabry chuckled.

"No, I was just behind you coming in and thought such heights of humor ought to get at least a second shot. Or Wilson ought to get shot. I'm not sure which I would prefer.

"Well, since Wilson is sure to use the line at least twenty more times, I would go for the second option."

Beach and Mabry enjoyed each other's company as much as possible, considering they were separated by rank, education, neighborhood, ethnic heritage, and normal cop caution.

Mabry stood and turned away toward the wall. There was no window in the office, despite his rank—a lack of perks that helped endear him to the men. The sergeant stood facing a poor reproduction of a Van Gogh still life, as if staring off above the Manhattan roof tops.

Gil knew that whatever Mabry was about to say made the big man uncomfortable. Usually, if he didn't meet your eyes, it meant politics.

"Make this a priority, Gabby. It won't take long for this one to attract the Pulitzer Putzes," Mabry's term for reporters that would go overboard trying to make a shocking sensation out of any crime. "We don't need the headlines this month."

Gil could have acted like he was offended, but the Commander's stance told the story. He hated saying these things. He couldn't look a real cop in the face and speak the words. Somebody had told him to say them. If Gil wanted to grimace, pout, or sneer, Mabry would choose to look the other way. So why not give the guy a break.

It was late, the lab wouldn't have anything until tomorrow at the earliest, and Gil had accumulated enough feelings for one shift. He mumbled an acknowledgment to his superior and headed for the door.

As he exited, Terranova was leaning against a wall nearby. He looked up, and Gil shrugged. The other man smiled as he turned to walk out with him.

"It wasn't Boom Boom's idea," he confirmed. "It's the Lieutenant."

"Yeah, I figured."

"I hear a lot, hanging, around holdin' my putz while they decide what to do with me."

"I guess it's a drag."

"It sucks." Then, as if he had second thoughts about being too negative with the Detective, he added,

"But I guess I should be happy to still have a job.

"What are you, Frank, the poor man's Norman Vincent Peale?" Gil laughed.

Terranova broke into a smile, and nodded, Yeah, the power of positive stinking."

As Gil started down the stairs, Frank gave a wave and turned off toward the other offices.

"Take care," he said, and Gil had the feeling that this time it wasn't just a cliché.

"Take care."

Like it wasn't all that safe out there. Which pretty much matched how Gil was feeling. Now that he thought about it, he was feeling a lot. When he felt a lot, it was time for home... and for the stairs. That usually took care of excess feelings. He hurried to his car.

CHAPTER

8

Monday, 5:32 p.m.

The Detective drove back to his home borough of Staten Island in something of a trance, blocking all thought with a tape of Beethoven's Ninth Symphony at top volume on the car stereo. In an exception to his pattern of riding public transportation, today Beach had driven to work, so he had to fight traffic across the two-mile span of the Verrazano, once the world's longest suspension bridge, through the greedy tollbooths, then along the Staten Island Expressway to his exit.

Staten Island, or the Borough of Richmond as it was officially titled, was something of a stepchild to the other city boroughs, for years threatening to secede from New York State altogether. Once the retreat of the Vanderbilts and other wealthy knickerbockers, in recent times the island had become the place for upwardly mobile New Yorkers to escape some of the worst consequences of urban living. For cops, it was a way to meet the New York City residency requirements, while still keeping the worst of the city at a significant distance. Unfortunately, since the Verrazano Narrows Bridge was built in 1964, the mass migration had been so overwhelming that the island was fast taking on all the less pleasant aspects of the city while retaining many drawbacks that had been previously accepted as the price of isolation, like minimal public transportation, lack of city sewers in places, and the worst air quality in the Northeast.

It was a breezy day. The combined smog of New Jersey refineries, local simmering landfills, and industrial fumes had been dispersed enough to pretend it was the rural retreat it once had been.

Ancient geologic forces had humped a section of granite-like schist into a section of hills eons ago, with a fold or gap in the heights the settlers had named the "Clove." It was Clove Road that Gil followed through the pass, up to where Howard Avenue lifted the traveler to a vantage point prized for its view of New York Harbor and the surrounding environs.

Gil wasn't looking at the view. He was lost in a world of physical sensation, driven by pounding exertion. He had arrived at the stadium as usual and completed his customary ritual of warm-up exercises, before beginning. Now he was well into a familiar routine.

It was on the third trip up the multiple levels of steps that he glanced into the stands. That was itself remarkable, since he usually kept such a level of concentration on the way up, he might notice a gum wrapper at his feet, while missing a hippopotamus ten yards away. This was no hippo. To say the very least.

She looked to be in her early thirties, with that graceful maturity that made a person look comfortable in their skin. The light wind drew her dark hair like a fan across delicate features, dark eyes, skin the color of light chamois. Her limbs folded easily into natural positions, with one hand to her chin, a finger crossing her lips in an expression of studious attention. Stylish clothes found a balance between clean, professional lines and a subtle hint of the sensuous. At another level, Gil's thoughts were quicker, less analytic. He thought she was a knockout.

He became acutely uncomfortable. There was a sense of violation, as he realized he had been under observation. His intense discipline hadn't seemed abnormal until he found himself being watched. He wondered, disconcertedly, if she had been there long and seen him doing something embarrassing because he thought he was alone; the scratching of a scrotum, a hawk-and-spit over the ledge, or the occasional pause to pummel away at his tightening thighs and calves with fists and curses. What if she had seen him when he revealed his scarred torso, changing shirts?

As uneasy as he was, he didn't turn away, so his glance locked with hers. He saw eyes like polished obsidian, dark, deep as wells. If either of them had dropped their gaze then, it might have been over. But the connection lasted, and for a heartbeat, a crystal-pulse of time, Gil forgot that he was lonely. He pushed away the unfamiliar thoughts and feelings to concentrate on the woman sitting there.

He slowed his punishing pace, finally stopping two rows of seats from her. He searched for a clever opening line, but whatever was going on in his gut seemed to get in the way of clear thinking. The words that came out of his mouth were not exactly eloquent.

He said, "Hi."

Stupid, stupid, stupid! Another piece of evidence was added to Gil's lifelong courtroom drama in which he had long ago pleaded *nolo contendre* to the charge of terminal stupidity. But before he could run away, or say something worse, her reply intervened. She responded in kind:

"Hi.".

Ready to continue this awkward level of conversation, Gil just barely managed something better than 'Do you come here often?' Instead he said,

"I don't usually have an audience."

"Oh, well, I hope I haven't spoiled your training for whatever it is you're training for." A slight tilt of her head, a raised eyebrow, inviting more.

"Uh, no, not at all. I just do this alone so often; I forget that there are other people in the world for a while."

"And have I brought you back to a less pleasant reality?"

Inwardly, he bridled. The comment seemed critical. His natural inclination was to lash out with words that would push her away, but it was also the last thing in the world he wanted to do at that moment.

"You are hardly an unpleasant reality," he heard himself say. He was sure he sounded like a sophomore laying a line on a freshman co-ed, yet he was puzzled that a part of him meant the words completely. He wondered if he was being oversensitive to her reactions, but he was sure he saw a slight shadow of feeling cross her face. There was a brief narrowing in her eyes, a tightening around her mouth, a momentary furrow between her dark eyebrows. Only a fraction of a moment, a microsecond of a look, but to Gil it seemed a rejection.

Stupid, dumb, moron. Why can't I avoid acting like an idiot just long enough to keep her guessing about whether I'm a creep or not? But no, I start out like a nerd and go down from there.

In a burst of frankness, he said, "I guess that sounds contrived, doesn't it?"

Instead of answering, she gave a little laugh.

There was a moment of silence. Her expression shifted from amusement to mild puzzlement.

"You don't really enjoy this, do you? The running, the stairs?"

The question caught him off guard.

"Enjoy?" he repeated, like she was speaking a foreign language. "What does that have to do with it?"

"I didn't think so," she nodded.

Gil expected more, but she didn't continue. After a moment, there seemed a resolute move of her head. She stood and smiled. It was a striking smile. Maybe even dazzling.

"Sorry to impose." She turned toward the exit tunnel.

The Detective wanted to shout, 'No, don't go. Please stay and let me hear that voice, see that face, drown in those eyes.'

What he managed, was to softly mumble, "You didn't."

It wasn't even true. She had imposed. Not just on his exercise, but on his safe isolation, his carefully preserved, walled-off life. What he meant, though, was that it was okay. Whatever she had brought into his world was intriguing enough to be worth it.

She paused, half turned back, while giving another little grin. Just a pursing of lips, but a mysterious look that made the Mona Lisa's seem obvious in comparison. And then she was gone.

Gil stared for several long moments. He felt a rush of disappointment. He probably felt other things as well, but they only could speak to him through the tension in his shoulders, and a wave of excess energy.

He shook himself, took two deep breaths, and started up another set of steps.

CHAPTER 9

Tuesday, 6:15 a.m.

The water overhead swirled with refracting light. Gil could feel himself glide through the water effortlessly, more like a bird in flight than a skin diver. He amazed himself with the time he could remain under the surface without air, spiraling deeper and deeper into a hazy aquamarine vortex. It was a few moments before he realized that his movement had stopped. As he looked down, he saw that his feet were held by a giant clam or oyster of some sort. The gigantic bivalve then started to swallow him, opening its shell halves for a fraction of a second only to lurch forward and grab another inch of his legs, wolfing him down like a lizard gobbling a large insect. He felt himself being drawn downward into the soft tissues, deadened with an awful lethargy that kept him from fighting free.

Gil came out of the dream gasping and thrashing, as he always did. His heart was whumping a kettle drum solo in his chest. Perspiration wet his forehead and rode in the creases of his neck. The bedclothes were wrapped around his body in a mummy effect, that must have contributed to the feelings of being trapped, though the dream varied little, regardless of his surroundings. The suffocating sense of being bound was always there, as well as the helpless feeling when the teeth sank into him. Always, there was the pain.

He shook free of the covers, padding barefoot to the bathroom, where he threw off his dank nightclothes to step into a steaming shower. As the hot water stung his skin, he scrubbed with a loofa pad until the tingling sensation started to replace the tightness and crushing weight of unlabeled emotion. He kept the distraction going as he vigorously toweled off, viciously pulling a stiff brush through his hair.

A baby like yowl and pressure against his leg, alerted him to the cat's presence.

"It's gotta be another terrible Tuesday, Pepperkins."

Tuesday mornings, as far as Gil Beach was concerned, were worse than Mondays. Monday you had a little sense of renewed energy from the weekend—if you had gotten time off. Clearly by Tuesday, the amount of energy you still had was probably not going to last out the week. Monday held some mystery, but Tuesday was old familiar territory. Even if he had worked six days in a row, a common situation lately, his emotions told him that Monday still started the week, Friday ended it, and Tuesday sucked.

The Ninth Precinct station house was located on East Fifth Street between First and Second Avenues, a weathered sign noting it as number 321. It took Gil over an hour to reach the fortress-like building via ferry and subway. In a habitual gesture he touched his fingers to a plaque on the outside sandstone facade. The plaque commemorated two officers, Rocco Laurie and Gregory Foster, who had been killed on duty, February 27,1972. Years later, but on the same day, February 27th, he had joined the force. He had become superstitious about it, seldom failing to make contact on his way into the station house, as if by connecting to the two slain men's memorial he was protected from a similar fate. He mounted the two slab steps, stepping through the huge dark-paneled vestibule doors.

Dozens of uniformed men and women milled about the large muster room, forming blue-black clumps of officers scattered about the area. There was the creak of stiff leather, the jingle of metal hanging from belts, the rumbling whir of a huge floor fan that ran even in the winter to keep the smoky air moving. It was change of shift time. Half the precinct seemed gathered, waiting for the call to muster. He waved at a face or two, acknowledged greetings and wisecracks, then climbed to the second floor office where he flopped in his creaking antique desk chair, trying not to look at all the forms, reports and papers piled there, with blank spaces waiting to be filled or entered into the computer databases.

Telephones were easier than paperwork on a Tuesday. He started to tap in the Forensics number, when Frank Terranova approached.

"Another day, another thirty-seven cents, eh?" He offered.

Gil used the man's arrival as a way to put off the paperwork a little longer.

"Only if they double my salary!"

"I got something, might interest you. Don't know if there's any connection, but a uniform found something today, may have to do with the Bowery case."

Gil glanced at the report.

"Brain tissue? Could be. The girl was missing some. The vic's tissue should be in the lab by now."

"Anything else new on the case?" Terranova asked.

"Not yet. I was just going to call Forensics. Not that I'm gonna get the information I want. Most of the time I can't get past the secretary."

"Oh, you mean old tight-ass herself. Just tell her you're from the World Health Organization. She'll pass that to the Director quick."

"Right," Gil chuckled.

"No, I'm serious. Do it!"

"I don't think I could pull that off, without laughing."

"Want me to try it?" Frank asked, bobbing his head enthusiastically.

Gil found himself getting into the idea.

"Okay, wise guy. Go ahead. Show me how."

Terranova pulled himself up, assumed a mock serious expression and tapped a number into the telephone. He spoke in a clipped, impatient tone, tinged with a pseudo-european accent. It reminded Gil of his old nemesis, Dr. Brenkowski.

"This is Dr. Weisbrotten, calling from the World Health Organization, Office of Epidemiology. Please, to give me the Laboratory Director, yah?"

There was a pause as the person on the other end of the line reacted.

"Yes, dat is right," he snapped.

"WHO ... not WHAT!" Frank shouted into the phone. Gil was having trouble holding back his laughter, as the conversation sounded like an old Abbott and Costello routine.

"Not WHAT.... W.H.O.—da Vorld Healt Organization. Und iff you don't have the Laboratory Director on the phone in sixty seconds, you are liable to be in for YOU KNOW WHAT!"

By now, Gil thought, the girl must surely know she was being jerked around, but apparently not, because Frank nodded in affirmation, and handed Gil the receiver, a smirk on his face. On the other end of the line, Gil heard a spluttering sound, like a whooping crane with a salmon stuck in its throat. Then silence, and a moment later the voice of Jim Nedrow, the Lab Director.

"What is this?" he asked, impatience coloring his words.

"Dis is not a WHAT, dis is a WHO!" the Detective announced, in his best attempt at imitating Terranova's fake accent, gasping at the effort to keep from laughing.

"Oh Jesus, it's you, Beach. Kameesha here thought it was either someone with the wrong number or a lunatic. I see she was right on both counts."

"You meant this isn't the Chinese take-out place? Just when I had my heart set on Won Ton and a coupla' egg rolls."

"If the guys who think you are the silent type could only hear you now." Nedrow's voice changed to a more serious tone. "You obviously terrorized my clerk so you could get me on the phone. What are you after that I shouldn't tell you?"

"C'mon Jimmy, gimme a break. If I wait for written reports to get here on everything you find, I could clear about one case a decade. All I want to know is whether the brain tissue Boom Boom sent down is from the missing cranium of my Miss Granger."

"How should I know?" the Lab Director asked, in a tone that represented a verbal shrug of his shoulders. "Nobody asked for any comparisons."

"Crap!" Gil spat. "So we have two samples of brain tissue found within twenty-four hours of each other, and nobody thinks to compare them!"

"I didn't say that," the technician archly announced, "I asked how I should know, given the lack of any direction or guidance from any other unit of this screwed up rust bucket of a law enforcement agency'?"

Gil caught on.

"Nobody told you to make a comparison."

"You got it, Sherlock."

"Ahh, but knowing you, as I do, I also know that the laboratory is such a finely attuned organization, and you are such a crackerjack Director, that you probably thought of it, despite the fumbling ignorance demonstrated by the incompetent flatfoots who submitted the samples. Am I right?"

"Couldn't have put it better myself," came the laughing reply.

"So? In your infinite wisdom, oh Oracle, did you match the samples?"

"I compared 'em. But there was no match."

"No match?"

"'fraid not. Not even the same blood type."

"Crap."

"You're repeating yourself."

"So what have you got on the other one?"

"Well, I can bore you with tissue types and blood types and features of the cerebral fissures. But the only thing that might interest you at this point, is that it comes from a child. I'd estimate the age to be between four and six. I don't suppose that is good news, eh? Looks like you got more than one nut out there."

Gil didn't voice his actual reaction. The bad news was worse than having two killers. The worse news was that this was possibly a series. Brain tissue removed from a skull was unusual enough to suggest a pattern.

"Yeah, bad news."

If, in fact this meant a serial killer, there was other bad news too. Most murders were solved because the perpetrator was known by the victim. Most people were killed by someone they knew, and that meant connections—relationships, motives. Serial murders had motives too, Gil reflected, but they were all inside the killer's head. The victims could have been selected for no other reason than a certain resemblance to someone else, or due to some pattern of behavior or assumed pattern, seen that way only in the crazy emotional system of the murderer.

Gil also knew that there were often victims that never got found. Then there are also victims other than the corpses – the families and loved ones who had to deal with the horrific aftermath. He knew that if it was that kind of case, he himself would be victimized. He wouldn't compare his suffering with that of a relative, but still, he knew he would die a hundred little deaths. Like mini-strokes, the little burst capillaries that struck some aging folks, the pursuit of such a monster would result in tiny sacrifices of illusion and hope.

Novels often romanticized the tale of the hunter and the hunted, Good in pursuit of Evil. He knew the reality to be much less pure, much less satisfying. He had been the hunter before. It always ended with something being taken from him that he could not replace. As he considered the possibility of another such hunt, he wondered if there was enough of him left.

"The search team collected quite a pile of junk out of that crime site, you know. If you want to look, it will be here until sometime tomorrow afternoon."

"Right," Gil answered, "I was off Sunday and missed eyeballing the scene. I'll try to stop by later. Anything look interesting?"

"Can't say yet. We're still screening the stuff."

"Okay, catch you later."

The Detective dropped the call and looked at what he was scribbling on the paper in front of him. On the left side of the sheet there was a series of squares, with words in them. "Ritual" was written in one, and "pattern" in another, both with question marks. On the other side of the paper, he had listed, "short knife, wood object, barbed wire?" He decided to make his list more complete. He added other words to the left side, enclosing each with a border, like the squares above.

"Amount of time" was next, followed by, "missing head." Sometimes Gil found that it was better to let thoughts just flow, without censoring them, rather than be too logical. The logic would come, but intuition would provide the raw material for logic to organize. Now he let his imagination go and filled the page with words and phrases. "Labor of love, labor of lust. Mutilation. Axed and poleaxed. Opened from the back. Got into the head. Spilled the brain. Spilled other brains. How do you open a coconut? Angry, angry. Power over the weak is needed only by the weaker. Child woman, woman child."

The Detective knew that he would have to investigate the woman's acquaintances, job, school, and more, in case some evidence of the killer might turn up. As if it might be a boyfriend, a coworker, a relative who treated this human being like a cheap piece of meat. But already he was thinking otherwise. It was the other tissue that did it. The brain of a child-woman and the brain of a child. There were connections to be made here, but they were not going to be the kind you could see in the victim's lives. The connections were going to be symbolic ones, off- kilter visions of an insane intelligence who made sense of the world only through distorted lenses.

At the bottom of the sheet, he wrote the last piece of bad news. It put into words the speculation that had been rambling around in his thoughts for some time. The small brain found yesterday, confirmed his intuitive response to Meredith Granger's corpse. If there was a serial killer on the loose, then this murderer, this destroyer, this mutilator ... was after the young.

In block letters, he slowly printed "CHILD KILLER."

Chapter 10

An hour later the Detective was waiting in a side room of the Forensics Department, part of the complex in lower Manhattan at One Police Plaza, "The Big One." A white enameled ceiling fan revolved slowly, moving the air around the bare anteroom, having little effect on the stark and sterile atmosphere of the laboratory. Gil never felt comfortable here, or in hospitals, or the morgue.

He looked at a row of plastic bags lined up on the evidence table. The small transparent envelopes contained bits and pieces of debris garnered from the vacant lot where Meredith Granger's body had been found. In any piece of outdoor urban terrain, even a few square yards, there is an amazing variety of objects, the discards of the mass of humanity that passes any given spot in the city over time. He knew that various motives lay behind the deposit of this jetsam. Some items are tossed away on purpose, some are thoughtlessly dropped. Looking at the accumulation, he was glad that it was the job of the Forensics team to sift through the mounds of material. Still, he had the ultimate responsibility of determining what might be of importance to the crime which had occurred upon this well-traveled ground. Among the dozens of cigarette butts, was there one that might have hung from the lip of the killer as he waited for his victim? Mixed with the pop-top can tabs, the cellophane wrappers, used face masks, beer cans, tissues, toothpicks, and used disposable lighters, was there anything that might carry his spoor?

Earlier, the Lab Director had explained the forensics procedures that Nedrow had developed. These involved organizing the material according to several criteria. The first was "chronicity," which meant, as nearly as it could be determined, how close in time to the commission of the crime had this particular object been deposited. Gil translated this in his mind to how "fresh" a piece of evidence was. This allowed the sorters to dispense with a lot. Of the dozens of cigarette filters, only a couple were fresh enough to have been left in connection with the crime. Since both had lipstick smears, Gil dismissed them. He was sure that this was not the work of a woman.

Most killers were men. Those women who did kill, tended to do it in passion and used different means than men. Poison was the favorite. Although a rare female might stab someone repeatedly, it was unlikely that a woman would hack corpses into pieces. Despite a few notables like Lizzie Borden, women were seldom the perpetrators of serial killings. Gil knew of a few modern-day exceptions. One female nursing home attendant had sent dozens of elderly patients off to a premature end and there had been a woman hitchhiker killer that preyed on male drivers, but this was not the rule. The exceptions in his career had not included a random child killer. In fact, as far as he could generalize, women seldom killed children other than their own. Then again, this was the "twenty-twenties" and anything was possible.

Thoughts of women trying to kill children led inevitably to memories of his personal history and Gil jerked as an emotional hook sunk into him. He strode over to a water cooler and drank, trying to push away thoughts of his mother. Over the years, he had become adept at that. There was an internal "switch" that he could flip almost at will, to cut power from the errant thought before it could light up dark corners he didn't want to see. Dealing with his private demons never kept him from looking at every aspect of a case. Still, you couldn't go all directions at once, so he had to make decisions during an investigation to follow one path and set aside others. Nevertheless, the detective never completely closed his mind to any possibility, including the chance that this crime was the work of a woman.

He pressed his thumb and forefinger against the bridge of his nose, rubbing, as if he could massage away the depressing thoughts the same way he worked out a muscle ache, or perhaps squash them, like a bug under the surface of his skin. He sighed and turned back to the table.

There were several sheets of crumpled facial tissue in the evidence bags, noted as having mucous secretions. Not unusual in the season of colds, flu and Covid. Not likely to have been left by the killer, and not likely to provide anything useful. The elaborate tests needed to identify the characteristics of the person who had blown their nose in the tissue, were far too expensive and time consuming to use routinely. In addition, it would be necessary to have a suspect to match samples, and the person would have to be a "secretor," one whose body fluids allowed typing. If a suspect was ever apprehended, Gil had a feeling that the case would not be made on minor items of indirect evidence. Whether by luck or deduction, the Detective was certain that the finding of the perp would bring the evidence with it, like wiggling sea smelt drawn into the net along with a great white shark.

Gil pushed aside bags containing recently emptied soda bottles, Styrofoam cups, and various other "fresh" items. He was waiting for something to jump out, impressing him as notable.

"You might have a better chance with the anomalies," a voice interjected from behind him.

It was Nedrow, white lab coat shiny with starch, shoes glistening from a recent spit polish. The man was always immaculate and perfectly groomed. His sense of humor saved him from a reputation as a tight ass. Well, it almost saved him.

"Anomalies?"

"Yeah, things that don't belong, like a gold shield in your pocket."

"Thanks for the ego boost. Now what about the 'anomalies'?"

"That's our second screening criterion. If an object is normally expected to occur at such a site, like an empty soda bottle in a vacant lot, it receives a lower anomalous rating than an object that is seldom found in such a place, like fish scale on a bed. Level One anomalies are notable, Level Two are rarities, and Level Three is reserved for cases where it was hard to even imagine how they could have arrived at this particular spot of earth. These are rarities…ya know, like finding you at the P.B.A. annual dinner dance."

"Or like me getting any information out of you without a struggle and a wisecrack, right?"

"Hey, all I give you is information. Sometimes a little intrigue. Look at this Level Three item."

Gil picked up the plastic zip-lock bag. It was a glass eye. Not a children's toy, or a cheap plastic halloween version, this was an honest-to-goodness ocular prosthesis. What it was doing in the vacant lot, and how it journeyed there were questions that would fuel many fantasies, but Gil doubted it would have anything to do with Meredith Granger's murder. Still, he stored the information away in his mental file.

"I figure that it's from the other guy working the case."

"The other guy working the case?" Gil asked, narrowing his eyes.

"Yeah," Nedrow winked, to let the Detective know he was being kidded. "You know, the PRIVATE EYE!"

Gil groaned.

Having served up his pun, the Lab Director moved over to the table.

"Not much stuff, considering how long it took to sort. Anything look interesting?"

"Well, I was beginning to wonder if the eye found me interesting," Gil snorted. "I haven't looked at the Level One's yet."

There were no Level Two anomalies. Another bag contained the few objects the techs had thought to be out of their natural habitat at the crime scene.

There was a piece of jewelry—a scrimshaw oval with a picture of a whale expertly etched on its surface. The size and backing suggested a lost earring. Two miniature plastic tubes weren't terribly unusual items in the cityscape but were still remarkable enough to claim Level One status—they were empty crack vials. A curved piece of cardboard about an inch and a half long, with a jagged outer edge and a metal inner rim, caught Gil's eye.

"What's this?"

"Oh, you've probably seen one and just never registered it. It's one of those rip-offs from the vending machine in bus terminals. It's a gadget that's supposed to allow you to throw your voice. 'Be a ventriloquist! Amaze your friends! Special device to throw your voice—only fifty cents'. "

"Yeah? Does it work?" the Detective asked, frowning.

"About as good as those "X-ray glasses' they offer at the same places. I know, because I used to send away for all that stuff when I was a kid. Once I saved up five cereal box tops and got a cheap magic kit. It had a couple of Chinese linking puzzles, a disappearing coin gag, a card trick with three fake cards, and the ventriloquist gadget. I could only get one puzzle apart, the coin trick broke the second time I used it, the three cards weren't very good without a matching deck, which I never found, and I cut my tongue with the gadget. The only sound I could make with it was a sort of humming noise, which still sounded like it was coming from me, and I nearly swallowed the damn thing. I never knew anybody who made one work, but as far as I know they are still selling 'em to suckers along with magic worms and whoopee cushions."

The detective nodded, continuing to examine the remaining contents of the bag. A rusting pipe tool, the earbud from an ipod or mp3 player, a guitar pick, a plastic bookmark, the cracked disc of a music CD, "Endless Summer" by the Beach Boys, and a shoe tap.

"That tap is not the dollar store variety," Nedrow noted. "It's the kind tap dancers use. The guitar pick is a custom-made promotional item, advertising a music store in Newark: Bob's Musicland. And the CD is obviously from some perverted freak. Who else listens to the Beach Boys?"

"Right." Gil dutifully responded, "Anything on those wood fibers from the body?"

"That was used to penetrate her? Nothing exciting. It's just average run-of-the- mill pine. Probably a dowel of some sort. It was old, impregnated with body oils, perspiration, and so forth, so maybe it was used as a walking stick for a while, or a favorite club. No way to get more specific than that."

Gil shrugged. His expression was noncommittal, but his thoughts were dark. With what they had at this point, the chances were that little progress would be made until something else turned up. Like another victim.

CHAPTER

11

Tuesday, 5:50 p.m.

It takes about twenty-five minutes for the Staten Island Ferry to cross from Battery Park to St. George, except in unusual weather conditions. On a foggy day, it can take as much as thirty-five. Thousands of bodies are crowded onto the three decks, though more might fit aboard if every seat was filled. Many urban travelers have learned ploys to keep a seat or two vacant between them and the next passenger—artfully placed briefcases and shopping bags, picnic meals, or carefully planned postures that leave little choice but to grant a seat-width of insulation, and that was enough for most people.

It wasn't enough for Gil Beach. He required more space.

He had managed a better location on the boat, by taking advantage of some old contacts in the Port Authority. This had resulted in Gil getting a pass that allowed access to crew areas on the famous orange commuter boats pushing through New York Harbor.

Now he stood on the top deck, partially sheltered from a penetrating wind by the bulk of the wheelhouse, and from the press of human hordes by the "Off-Limits" signs guarding the upper stairways. After several years of riding the same few boats, he seldom needed to flash the special pass. Most crew members knew him by sight. They left him alone.

The condensed half-hour of salt air and sea gulls worked like a micro vacation for him. He let go of the day-to-day pressures and concerns, felt a sense of release and distance from the city. Most times he walked with a lighter step after the small excursion.

As the boat neared the northeastern shore of Staten Island, and moved into the Number Two ferry slip, he felt a change in the engine vibration, then an eerie calm, as the vessel drifted into its proper place. There was a great creaking noise, as the pilings and planks gave ground to the large boat. An invisible force shoved back, and passengers grabbed for handholds, or stumbled to maintain their balance. A deep rumble, and the water erupted in a foaming hump when the engines were reversed. Then silence again, drifting, until there was a return of shaking vibrations as the screws shoved them forward again, and a final whumping collision with the pier. The metal ramps dropped with a hum and crash, as people surged forward to find their cars, catch buses, or begin their next ride on the S.I.R.T., the Staten Island Rapid Transit or "Rancid Transit" as the locals wryly liked to call it.

Gil waited until most of the crush had eased, then walked down three flights to the vehicle transport level. He left the ferry by way of a car ramp, walking a block or so through the dark pillared parking garage to his Malibu. Traffic was heavy at this time of day, but he had moved quickly enough to swing out of the lot and up one of the long curving ramps without any significant delay. Normally it took only five or ten minutes to drive the mile-and-a-half to his apartment. Often, he walked the short distance to the ferry, but sometimes he drove—just because he felt like it. Who was to know or question him? The only one waiting was Pepper.

There was always a gym bag, packed with his workout clothes, in the car trunk, so he didn't need to stop at the apartment. He passed the steep driveway to his place, continuing up the hill along Howard Avenue to the college. Fifteen minutes after leaving the ferry he was at the stadium and changed. It wasn't until he was tying the frayed laces of his running shoes, that he realized it was the wrong day.

He had done the stairs Monday, and today was only Tuesday. Normally, he didn't do this work out on two successive days.

Sometimes he even waited till the third day after his last session. Between the severity of his workouts and the age of his body, he had found he needed at least a full day for his muscles to recuperate from the demands he placed on them. He might get in a good walk or something less strenuous, but didn't want to overdo the intense exercise. So why was he here?

As he scanned the rows of seats, he realized what he was looking for. He was looking for the woman who had been there Monday, and he was too impatient to wait another day to see her.

Of course, there was no one there:

"Stupid fantasy. Once in a blue moon coincidence. She wasn't here to see you," he mumbled to the wind. "Women like that aren't interested in guys like you. It's wishful thinking."

Gil felt the old frustration and anger building, the adrenaline rush beginning. He started jogging around the track, then headed for the stairs. Up flight after flight to the stadium rim, across and down the other aisle, he returned to the track and started the next circle. As he came around the first turn, thudding along, in his usual methodic, determined manner, he found himself thinking, *"How could this be confused with fun?"* If it had ended there, the thought would have been forgotten, but it pushed up another. *"What would it be like to enjoy this?"*

His head raised a little, and he noticed a tree with autumn flame-colored leaves overlapping another with bright yellow foliage. He knew this would fit the category of "beauty," but his first reaction was surprise, that these trees had been there for so long without his noticing them. The low sun was casting ornate shadows across the median. Cloud banks trundled up against each other in cuddled lines. There was a scent of burning leaves and sharp-edged pine in the air. He traveled three-quarters around the cinder oval, feeling light and disoriented. He noticed the bunching of his calf muscles and the eagerness in his thighs. It was a strong, free feeling. The stairway entrance came up on his right side. He had always seen it as a challenge, a dropped gauntlet. He was usually unable to back off from that summons to fight the enemy he would meet on the next set of stairs.

On an uncharacteristic impulse, he passed by the entrance this time and completed the oval, went past the opposite stairs as well, and started a second revolution of the track. His gait was an easy lope, noticeably different from his usual pounding drive. The confusion increased; he was strangely disoriented. Even though it was just a small instance, in this one moment he had chosen not to push himself harder. He had chosen the easier way. That was not his style. What he was doing now was not a struggle, this pace was not punishing. He almost turned around and ran back to redo the oval, but completed the track circuit before hitting the stairs. The next time he descended, he compensated for taking it easy on the last round, by sprinting across the bottom walkway to the opposite stairs and immediately going back up, determined to atone for his lapse.

He almost tripped, as he lifted his head and looked up at the higher levels, with the still-empty seats where he had been before. He cursed himself out.

Stupid- Stupid. Stupid. Don't be an idiot, don't be a moron, don't be a DUMMY!"

He did not notice the small figure, watching from shadow of a tunnel exit.

Chapter 12

Tuesday, 9:46 p.m.

The newer ventriloquist figures could never match this one. This was an original McElroy, made in 1933 by the brothers themselves. The Performer gazed lovingly at the childlike puppet sitting on his naked leg. He had needed to replace the wig, which had begun shedding, and repaint the facial colors with durable acrylics, but other than that, the figure was all original.

Not that he thought of it as a figure. This was Melvin, his sidekick, his partner, his friend. As the Performer slipped his hand into the back of the body, Melvin came alive.

"Yikes! If you're gonna stick your hand up my clothes, you could at least warm it up, first!" the smart-alecky voice cried out. The eyebrows shot straight up, and the eyes wiggled rapidly from side to side. "For a teacher, you sure ain't got no class!"

It was the start of one of their favorite routines, the ones he titled "School Daze," but the naked man didn't deliver the next line of the script. Instead, he dropped the stage voice and exaggerated mannerisms that he adopted in front of an audience.

"I have a confession to make, my little friend."

The figure turned toward him, leaned back a little, and answered in less jovial tone.

"Do you really think there's anything you do that I don't know about? What a stupid schmuck."

"So you know about Sally?"

"Gimme a break, numbskull. 'Sally?' You call that a name? That's about on a par with Jane, or Sue. I call her a disaster. That's two in one week, scumbag. That's what you get for trying to replace me."

"Oh, no, no. I wasn't trying to replace you, Melvin. I just have to show that I am the best, and I can't do that, unless I demonstrate my scope with a variety of characters. I have to prove how good I am."

The Performer gazed at the impassive mechanical creation on his lap with a pleading expression, as if the small figure he was manipulating could grant or deny him approval or absolution.

The figure stared back silently.

"Please understand, Melvin. I have to get another one."

"You know you're crazy, don't you?" the figure smoothly interjected.

"Crazy?"

"What, is there an echo in here? Yeah, crazy— bananas, nuts, bazoobers, cracked, not playing with a full deck. Capice?"

"I'm not crazy. Don't say that."

"I say whatever I want, asshole. I'm the only one who knows, remember? Don't give me a hard time, or one of these days in front of a big audience, I'll just tell them about all the dirty things you do, complete with fascinating details. I'll tell them what a nasty boy you really are. And don't think you 're ever going to get rid of me, because you aren't. We know who the DUMMY is, don't we?"

The Performer felt a shiver knife through his body. But before he could think of what to say, he heard another voice, small and distant, calling.

"Daarling, where arrre yooou? What are you dooooing?" It was the voice of a woman, coming from the next room. "Stop playing, and get dressed right awaaay. Or Mommy will have to tell Daddy, and he will punish yooou." He jumped up, carried the vent figure to the small trunk where it was stored, and lowered Melvin into the container. The leprechaun-like face turned to spit out a final warning.

"That trick won't work forever. Mommy's voice? Remember, I know everything. But for now, I'll keep your dirty little secret. Because I understand." The face turned away, as the man removed his hand from the inner workings. Now, there was no sound from the small figure.

The Performer closed the trunk lid, a waft of musty air escaping with the aroma of old paint and papier-mâché. He grabbed his robe from a hook by the door, slipped it on, and pulled open the door into the room from which his mother's voice had come. The room was dark and silent. He flipped the switch so light revealed the room. It was empty. Which wasn't surprising, considering that his mother had died five years before. As a matter of fact, he had killed her himself, though in his mind he thought of it as 'release' rather than murder.

It had not been an impulsive act, though there was impulse in the final moves. Mother, or "Dame Beatrice," as she had liked being called in her lucid moments years before, had reached the point of sloppy vegetating dependency when he released her from her body. The dementia had not seemed such a change in its earlier stages, as she had been certifiably insane for most of her adult life and often lapsed into long periods of catatonic immobility, either from her emotional deficiencies or the massive doses of psychotropic medications used to stabilize her. The boy's primary memory of his mother during his childhood was seeing her in the old Bentwood rocker, facing the bow window in the aptly named 'sitting' room. For days at a time, she would sit there with a dreamy smile on her face, looking up and out of the window at the trees, or sky, or most accurately, some secret vista projected solely within her mind.

Since he had taken over her care, there was no home health care aide or nurse to tend to her appearance, so she had grown disgustingly unkempt. Greasy scalp showed through tangled wisps of ratty hair, dried bits of foodstuff were embedded in facial folds, stray hairs sprouted from nasal passages and double chins. Sprawled in the old high back wooden wheelchair, she dribbled saliva out of one corner of her mouth. Despite all the degeneration, the vacant smile remained.

He had always resented that smile. She had no right to inhabit a pleasant world at his expense. It enraged him to know that is what she had always done. When he needed her to protect him from father, when he needed her to save him from Miss Carmen, when he needed her to just BE there, she was instead off in that private land of beautiful dreams and lovely visions that he could not share. Ultimately, therefore, he had dispatched her to her land of fantasy; releasing the earthly bonds that held her back.

It was the very first time he had used the knife for that purpose, which turned out to be quite satisfying. After he had removed her head, he had expected to feel something bad; remorse perhaps, or guilt. But instead, he had felt a wonderful wave of calm flood through him. For days, he had ridden that blessed wave of stillness. Only when he had to dispose of the corpse, had he lost the cool sense of control and relief. Putting her under the basement floor, and covering the area with fresh concrete, he felt the uncomfortableness begin to build again. It helped that he kept her head. It was his first special figure. For the first time, he was able to control what she said and did.

She had given up the right to control. As his mother, she should have kept him safe. But because she preferred her private world, he had been left to the whims of Miss Carmen whenever father was away on one of his many absences.

He had been seven or eight when the live-in nurse had started the games. Of course, there had been the baths before that—the baths where she insisted on making sure that his bottom was clean, by washing it repeatedly, and the other places too, until he was pink and throbbing. But the games were a new thing.

The first time, he remembered with a shiver, Miss Carmen had asked him if he wanted to play "dress-up." They went up to the attic, where there were trunks of old clothes and theatrical gear from father's career. At first it seemed fun. She found some silly clothes about his size from Melvin's wardrobe and told him to take off the ones he was wearing. But Melvin's clothes didn't fit, so she found a girl's dress and slipped it over his head. Wearing nothing underneath, he felt exposed.

"What a lovely little lady you are!" she effused, staring at him with a penetrating gaze, "and now we girls can play without worrying if the boys are watching."

The child didn't know what to make of this situation, so stood in embarrassed silence, the frozen stance he had already learned to assume in the presence of his father's cold rages.

"Now I think I should dress-up, also," Miss Carmen announced and began slipping off her dress. In his eight-year-old eyes, nakedness was a shocking, yet exciting concept. He was transfixed as this woman to whom he felt so close and dependent began to reveal things he had only imagined. He also noticed that she was very attentive to him, while at the same time seeming strangely upset. Her cheeks were reddened and she was breathing heavily, as strange undergarments fell to the floor. She seemed to ignore his slack mouth stare and walked about the attic, apparently looking for just the right costume. He was entranced. Her exposed breasts were large and pendulous, with dark, cone-shaped nipples. Various parts of her body seemed to sway and undulate as she walked. There was a dark mystery between her legs.

Then she spun around, as if catching him spying, and began the emotional blackmail.

"Oh ho, so you are a bad little boy, who thinks nasty thoughts, I see," moving toward him in a seductive glide. "You aren't as dumb as you pretend, are you?

"I should tell your papa, but he would be very angry and might hurt you. So I will keep your dirty little secret. You want me to keep this secret, don't you?"

The boy was shaking with confusion and fear, as the woman knelt in front of him. She lifted his hand and placed it on the velvet pillow of one breast, with a sharp intake of breath and a momentary closing of her eyes.

"I understand, my little fellow, that you are only curious. Your father would not understand, so we must not tell him. But I understand. You don't want me to tell him, do you?" As she spoke, she slowly moved his small hand over her breast, down her stomach, and nestled it in the bushy warmth at her crotch. There was wetness and a slippery feel as she moved his hand back and forth between her legs.

Now close to panic, the boy shook his head in a vigorous negative. Tears were welling in his eyes, his breath coming in short, labored gasps.

"Ah, you are too shy now, I see," the woman said, an eerie light in her eyes, which now fluttered, half-closed. "But you must not be afraid of your desires. Your father doesn't need to know. Just let Carmen take care of you."

The nurse gave a final press to his hand, pushing it firmly into her and shuddering for a moment, then released him and stood. She sighed, as she picked up a lace dress and slipped it over her head. "Now we will read a nice story."

The boy drooped in relief, as the woman selected a storybook from a stack on the floor. But as she held him and read of magical kingdoms and fairy princesses, he was conscious of her dark nipples pushing against the lace dress, a thick musky smell, and the warmth of her body pressing against his.

That night, he heard groaning in the next room where she slept. The door separating the rooms had been left slightly ajar. He tiptoed to the gap. In the glow of a candle over her bed, he saw her naked again, this time with her own hand moving purposefully between her legs, as she arched and writhed. He stood frozen, wondering if she was ill or having nightmares, until she shuddered like she had before and slowly relaxed. He thought he saw blood on her fingers and smears of it on her thighs, but she stretched languorously, like the cat often did after a long nap in the sun, then turned and stared straight at him, a smile slowly forming. He pulled away from the door and ran to his bed. There was no further sound from the neighboring room, but the door remained ajar, so he slept fitfully, wondering what she would do.

She didn't do anything for several weeks. He had begun to relax and enjoy the routine of meals, learning, and playing, when she announced that it was time to play dress-up again. This time she didn't ask, she just told him it was time, pulling him upstairs by the hand. The games again involved placing him in a dress, as she walked about naked. Soon, it became a regular routine. About once a month, she would display herself to him, while reinforcing the message that he could indulge his curiosity as much as he liked, and she would not betray him to his father as long as he was obedient. Sometimes she made him touch her, sometimes he was allowed to just watch as she displayed herself in a variety of ways. Often she would leave her bedroom door ajar that same evening to put on the second show of that day's double-feature.

The child was trapped. His curiosity was less than she implied, yet there was a sick fascination she could engender in him, so that he felt impelled to act as she said he wanted to, even when the desires seemed hers rather than his. With his father either absent or angry and his mother in her special private world, the only warmth and attention he got came from Miss Carmen. He dared to neither lose her nor face his father's wrath. So he did what she wanted him to do.

Eventually, she took him to bed with her. When he came to her door at the sound of her groaning this time, she claimed to be lonely. He could spend the night with her, if he first put on a frilly nightdress. She told him he could be a girl for the night. His father might not like it, if he found out that such a handsome boy was spending the night in her bed, she explained, so by this masquerade, the nurse could protect the boy and deny that he had slept there.

"You can call me Carmen, when we are together like this, for we are girlfriends."

The child did not know how to counter this strange idea, and still tried to believe the woman was protecting him.

From then on, he would sleep with her every night that his father was away, and even on occasion when the man was safely snoring away two floors above. For many weeks this resulted in little more than many hugs and a warm body pressed against his. But little by little, the intimacy increased. Carmen would smother him in warm kisses, murmuring her love for him, eyes closed, nightgown hiked to her waist, or opened entirely. She would touch him in special ways, then pull him over between her legs. He didn't want to enjoy it, but his pee-pee got hard anyway, and she liked that. He felt possessed by her, which was like being both loved and smothered, as she wrapped herself around him. Strange combinations of attraction and disgust, fear and exhilaration would fill him, leaving him weak and helpless in the face of powerful feelings he little understood. He didn't want this, but he didn't want to be alone. This adult kind of touching frightened him, but he was also afraid of losing the one person that seemed to care for him and promise to protect him. He felt helpless to control the spasms of his body that she elicited. He hated it, yet he loved the feeling too…the climax, a moment of release and relief.

He also feared that his father would literally kill him if Miss Carmen became angry and exposed his shame. Sometimes after she fell asleep, he lay motionless and silent to avoid waking her, with tears coursing down his cheeks, as conflicting emotions fought within him. He wondered a lot about what love was, and if he was being loved or used.

Then, one of the rare times his father was home, the boy heard the moaning in the next room. Usually that was how she let him know she was lonely and father was safely out of the way, so he slipped on the girl's nightie and went to the door. It was closed, but the knob turned easily, so he swung it open. There was violent movement on the bed. It took a moment, before the boy grasped what he was seeing. He felt waves of nausea break over him, as he realized that the naked, sweaty figure he was looking at was his father straddling the nurse, all hairy limbs and thick torso. In shock, the boy was unable to move before the man's eye caught the movement of the door and turned to face his son. Automatically dropping his head in shame, the boy's eyes were drawn to the father's exposed genitals. The man's organ jutted out like a huge snake, ready to strike, and dripping venom. To the boy, it appeared immense and threatening.

Frozen forever in the boy's mind would be that tableaux, of the massively potent figure of his father, in complete possession of the lovely Carmen, the woman physically pinned beneath him, as he visually pinned the boy in a look of conquering achievement, and power and scorn. When he realized that the boy was wearing a dress, Father s expression changed to rage. The child knew a beating would follow. He found that a beating was not to be the worst.

The boy ran desperately from the room, but his father soon followed, displaying his nakedness like a battle flag.

"So you are not only a dummy, but a little queer, you sorry excuse for a son. And you are a peeping-tom as well. Well, I'll show you a thing or two. First I'll show you my belt, and then I'll show you what it means to be a man!"

After he had the dress torn from his body, and his backside bloodied by dozens of vicious lashes with the belt, the boy was tied to a straight-back chair positioned where he had to watch the bed, as his father did a variety of unspeakable acts to the woman. Horror of horrors, it soon became obvious that she was accepting the assault with pleasure. She wanted the man to be on her, and in her. She was even doing things to his father that the boy had thought were special, private things only for him. The child had been sure that his heart would burst with an explosion of blood and pain and despair.

Only one thing saved him.

Through the opposing doorway, he sighted the ventriloquist figure Melvin, sitting silently in a chair. The eyes were staring straight at him, through the door, past the heaving bed, as if it did not exist. The child realized that Melvin was telling him something. He was silently communicating the way to survive. All the boy had to do was adopt Melvin's attitude. Humans were, after all, somewhat strange and impossible to deal with. All one needed to make it easier, was to become like Melvin. He too could sit impassively, unruffled by the horror of the primal scene before him, untouched by the pain of the welts on his back, unmoved by the insults, detached from needs for a mother or father or loving nurse ... detached from any needs whatsoever. He could appear dumb, yet know everything, seem a dummy, yet rise above them all. He would be the King of the Dummies, the Puppet Master, the Grand Performer.

And so it had happened. A transformation occurred, and saved him. The Performer nodded in self-congratulation. He had become the Grand Master. There was a voice that he had to listen to, but not this one.

The voice of his mother intruding today, had only been memory, nothing that could affect him now. His only hesitation was not true fear, but a sense of caution about the dangers of overconfidence. Ultimately nothing could defeat him but himself, so it was important to move only in the proper order and time. He reached out and flicked the light switch off again, casting the room into purples and blacks. The color of bruises.

Chapter

13

Wednesday, 11:43 a.m.

Through the dirt encrusted window of the P.D.U., Gil could see the sparkle of millions of slivers of broken glass on the pavement. So many bottles, headlights and windshields had been pulverized over the surface of this territory, the fragments had worked themselves into the very fabric of the street. It was like other parts of the city, yet it was different, and Gil felt a strange loyalty to this piece.

The Ninth Precinct is less than one square mile in area, but it contains almost seventy thousand permanent residents. On any given day there also fifty thousand or more additional small business staff, clerks, social workers and grifters. Not to mention visitors stopping for a drug buy, a quick trick with one of the hookers on Third Avenue between Twelfth and Fourteenth streets, or a bargain at one of the discount stores that dot the area. And there were politicians, cops and clergy, laborers, mechanics, students at one of several business and vocational schools, cab drivers, hairdressers, elevator operators, street cleaners, delivery boys, trades-people, street vendors, and a great variety of others that go home to someplace else at night. This piece of ugly real estate was Gil Beach's work, his hobby, his obsession.

"It's really some piece of work, isn't it?" a voice spoke behind him. It was Frank Terranova.

"What's that?" Gil asked, wondering what he was referring to. But it was almost like the other man had been reading his mind.

"You know. The Ninth. When I first came to the Precinct, I asked the other guys about the area. They told me that it's the most diversified mile in the city, whatever that means."

"They were right," Gil agreed. "It's got everything. And I think it might be unique in the whole country, maybe even the world."

Only fourteen blocks long, the Precinct includes an amazing array of peoples, languages, and ethnic businesses. A slight majority of the residents claim Hispanic origin, though divided into a dozen dialects and national backgrounds. Since another ten thousand blacks call the precinct home, the whites are outnumbered by persons of color, two to one. They are not unitary either, coming from the South, Africa, Haiti, Cuba and many other black communities. Recently there had been an increasing flow from Asia, along with many new arrivals from Arab cultures.

Among those to whom the Ninth Precinct was home were also the ironically labeled 'Homeless.' Some lived on the streets, others in empty building shells. There are many abandoned buildings and vacant lots, especially in what the police call Alphabet City, the eastern portion of the precinct that includes Avenues A, B, C, and D. That was where Gil was heading.

"Well, I guess I can't put it off any longer," he said with a grimace.

"It's better than sitting around here all day, every day," countered Frank.

Terranova eyed him with poorly concealed envy, as Gil slipped an automatic pistol into a holster at the small of his back. It was a Steyr GB nine millimeter parabellum. Weighing over three pounds and measuring almost eight-and-a-half inches in length, it was too bulky for a shoulder holster. It had a couple of important advantages over the lighter Sile-Benelli B76 he had carried earlier in his career. Neither gun was regulation, but that had never seemed a problem, as long as he didn't parade his weapon around in front of a commissioner, or one of the "suits" on their way up.

"Nice piece," Frank commented.

"Well, it works better than standard issue," Gil affirmed. In June of 1995, Beach had been involved in a stomach turning, pants wetting, lengthy gun battle, after responding to a code Ten-Thirteen, "Officer needs assistance" call. It was one of those unpredictable situations that kill more cops than any planned operation. Two P.O.'s accidentally walked in on a liquor store holdup being conducted by three hopped-up skinheads with automatic weapons and nervous trigger fingers. One tall gunner impulsively let loose on the officers, who were both wounded, but managed to return fire and call-in the Ten-Thirteen.

When Gil arrived in a screech of rubber and heart pounding desperation, the addicts were working their way down an alley, firing periodic bursts as they went, in a maneuver that reminded him of armed services training school. Gil ran ahead to cut them off but when he pulled at his gun, the exposed hammer of the Sile-Bennelli caught in the cloth of his coat. By the time he managed to wrench it free, a big muscular boy with a do-rag tightly fastened around his head was coming toward him. The boy was carrying what looked like an automatic rifle. Gil, close to panic, finally pulled his weapon loose and let off at least a half dozen shots before he remembered that the Italian gun only carried eight rounds.

The shooter fired, and a terrible numbness invaded Gil's whole body, as bullets whanged off pavement and wood splintered inches from his face. The I.P.S.C. street simulations had not prepared him for this. His limbs moved with the inertia of lunar gravity. He fired again, missing the oncoming gunman with one of his last rounds, damning himself for not having spent more time on target practice. He heard a little voice in the back of his head whispering, *"This is it. This is all she wrote. I'm going to die right here and now."*

Fortunately, the skinhead didn't know any of this, and with his eyes on the detective's smoking gun barrel decided at that point that he had enough, finally dropping his weapon. Gil was so strung out, that he just sat in stony immobility, until other officers ran up and made the collar. When he checked, the magazine of his Sile-Benelli was empty. He threw it in the trunk of his car.

Gil had always known that there was a brisk trade in extra sidearms among the members of service, the N.Y.P.D. Some cops are gun collectors, and are always interested in new or unusual firearms. Some officers want an extra weapon for unforeseen circumstances, as a non-regulation substitute, or a drop-gun to exhibit as justification for questionable shootings. He knew that some of these guns are purchased in the normal manner, others are taken from petty criminals, while still others are gleaned from large weapons cache confiscations. The difference between twenty-two or twenty-three weapons in a box of confiscated arms they carried off after a raid hardly matters, especially when the firearms are no longer needed for evidence and are on their way to be destroyed.

Gil acquired the Steyr GB from an undercover narcotics cop who charged him fifty bucks, about a tenth of what it would cost new, and less than half the used market cost. He didn't ask where it came from. It didn't have an exposed hammer to catch on clothes, and it had an eighteen-round magazine.

Having settled the weapon in the small of his back, Gil slipped on his coat and headed out of the squad room. Frank gave him a half-hearted wave and popped a jellybean in his mouth. Treadwell was busy at the coffee pot.

Gil was on his way to interview Meredith's boyfriend, over on Avenue C. Department procedure encouraged using two detectives on any interview, but recent cost-cutting and efficiency pressures had made superiors more sympathetic to any measures that maximized personnel utilization. Or at least that is how the suits would have put it. Gil just called them cheap. Besides, the only detective available was Treadwell. He wouldn't be much help.

The Ninth P.D.U. at this time consisted of nine men and one woman—one Lieutenant, one Sergeant, and eight Detectives. The eight were divided into two groups, one responsible for robbery, the other for homicide. That meant unless there was good reason to reassign a detective to the other team, Homicide operated with four men. The one female detective, Gina Esperoza, a good-humored and thick-waisted mother of three who was the third generation of cops in the family, worked most with the robbery team. In homicide, Dwight White (who was not white, but black) and James "Jimbo" West tended to pair off, rather than get saddled with Treadwell or try to penetrate the defenses of Beach. That meant Gil usually had to operate singly, which was fine with him, because he would just as soon work alone as play the games necessary if he took Treadwell along. The man just couldn't do the job anymore, but everyone tried to ignore the embarrassing reality and allow this hollow shell of a man to hold out until retirement.

Somehow, Treadwell got listed on reports as participating in investigative interviews he never attended, was included in conversations and conferences as part of the "we" who were pursuing leads. He even records occasionally as the arresting officer in cases where he had only been present in an auto outside the building at the time of arrest. Among themselves, they pretended it was easier than putting up with the shaky Treadwell on a real operation. The truth was, each detective knew that it could easily be himself burned out and demeaned. The job could fry anyone. So the P.D.U. staff covered—as much for themselves as for the tragic figure by the coffee pot.

For a moment, Gil considered inviting Frank Terranova along, but didn't act on it. He liked the man, who seemed to have a natural savvy and good sense of humor, but Department procedures required Terranova to stay put. Gil signed out an old tank-like car that served as one of the vehicles for the unit. This was a nine-year-old Oldsmobile with plastic seats that had developed splits along the seams, and a putrid odor of cigarette smoke, greasy fast food, sweat, and hair grease. He opened the window, ignoring the chill wind and traded the smell of the car for the neighborhood's fragrance of gutter, garbage, and gas engine exhaust.

Second Avenue was a one-way downtown street, so the Detective made a loop over to First Avenue, then up to Eighth, where he could cut over to Avenue C and the apartment of Greg Davis, the friend of Meredith Granger. "Boyfriend" seemed inappropriate for a thirty-year-old man, Gil thought. Yet what do you call him? Paramour? Lover? Companion?

Many of the buildings in this area were vacant, often sealed with cement and cinderblock which never seemed adequate to keep out the more determined of the homeless hoard that lived like a separate race in and around the more obvious city residents. Here and there a huge mural in primary colors bravely attempted to brighten the blight. Vacant lots were scattered throughout the area, providing places for rats, drug dealers, and other vermin to live, procreate and die.

As Gil sat waiting for a traffic light to change, there was a screech of brakes and the characteristic dull whump of an automobile colliding with something solid. The Detective jerked around in his seat and saw the accident behind him. A late model Cadillac was up on the sidewalk at the southeast corner. A crumpled old Chevy was resting at an odd angle on its side, partially wrapped around a light standard. He pulled over to the side of the street, jumped out of the car and jogged back to the scene. Shards of glass littered the street and sidewalk, some of which would add to the permanent glitter he had seen from the P.D.U. window. Liquid spread from the Chevrolet in a widening puddle. Steam hissed, there were muffled sobs from a cluster of people in a storefront doorway. The smell of steam and rust and gasoline, mixed with the street odor to form an overlying aroma that whispered of destruction and death.

Beach ran to the wrecked car, hunkering down to get a better view inside. The driver was a woman, or had been. Now she was a corpse, with half her face gone and her neck bent at an unnatural angle. Gil was about to move away, when he heard a soft whimpering sound. Sticking his head in the partially collapsed window, he saw a child pinned in the back seat. The eyes looked at him with a mixture of abject fear and entreaty. It appeared to be a girl, but the blood and dirt made it difficult to tell her age. She looked somewhere between two and five. She was flopping about in her panic.

"Take it easy, kid," he said. "We'll get you out in a jiffy." He slid farther into the window until his upper torso was through the opening, stretching to reach for the child. A few tugs told him she was not going to move. She read the frustration in his face, and her eyes flicked to the outside, as some idiot began to yell, "Watch out, its GAS! It's going to explode!"

Gil could see the despair clutch at the girl and panic flood into her eyes. The fear was like a virus, and he could imagine the infection beginning in his chest, a hard knot of pressure that took away his breath. Yet even as the fear clutched at him, he couldn't pull away. The child made him think of his niece, his brother's daughter, a shy first-grader with the face of an angel and a slight lisp that was so endearing, he dreaded the day she would speak without it. Though he was the girl's uncle, the relationship seemed much closer because of her father's death, which had led Gil to a more active role.

Now, there was no real decision, he just crawled forward into the car, scraping skin and clothing as he maneuvered through the small opening.

"You know what this reminds me of?" he started, desperate to say something that would divert her panic. She didn't answer, but her eyes stared holes in his, and the panic seemed delayed for a moment as she tried to make sense of what he was saying.

"It reminds me of when my daughter Jennifer and I went to Disneyland." Gil didn't have a daughter. It was the name of his niece. Jennifer was a brilliant child that attended a school for gifted children in the precinct, a circumstance that allowed Gil to be a very active and involved uncle to her. In small ways, he hoped to make up a little for his brother's death. He often picked her up from school or took her on trips. He had not actually taken her to the famous theme park but visited there himself and had taken her to other parks. He figured that the desperate situation called for a little creative remembering. Somehow it sounded better to say that it was his kid, like he was a father. He hoped that she thought fathers could be trusted.

It seemed to work. The girl stopped flopping around for the moment and a thoughtful look crossed her face. Was she picturing Disneyland, or wondering if he was a safe person? Gil figured it didn't matter. Her mind seemed to be off the little legs pinned under the crushed metal.

He fought to quell his own potential panic, as he smelled fuel, and realized that the moisture seeping up his pants legs was highly volatile. His breathing became labored, as gas fumes flavored the air.

His mind almost slipped into a daytime version of the old terrifying dream, immobilizing him with terror. With an effort of will, he shoved the fear into a back room of his mind. He found his voice again, enough to choke out a few more words.

"Yeah, there was this ride there, called 'Twenty Thousand Leagues Under the Sea.' Did you ever see it?" He raised his eyebrows, waiting. The girl stared for a moment, then slowly shook her head.

"Oh it's great. You get in this kind of upside-down submarine car, kind of like this one, and you go down under the water where there are all sorts of exciting things. First, you see these huge clams, and then ..."

The Detective kept up a running verbal tour for what seemed like hours, but was probably five minutes, expecting any moment for the gas to ignite and turn them into cinders. As he talked on and on, the girl's brow smoothed, her eyes drooped little by little. By the time the team arrived with the "Jaws of Life" to free her from the wreckage, she had dozed off with her head against his arm. When the fire-retardant foam was laid down, she woke up, clutching his arm like a life preserver. During the rest of the extrication process, she clung to him tightly, still not having spoken a word, but clearly depending on him to protect her. And he did. Twice, he had to stop the workers and have them reposition the tools to avoid injuring, or further injuring, the child.

When, finally, the girl had been taken in an ambulance to the nearest hospital, he started to move off, drained and stiff, stinking of gasoline. In the confusion, the uniforms didn't realize that the Detective was the same man that had been reaching into the wreck with the child. Richard Donovan, a second-year man that Gil knew slightly, was looking around like he had lost something.

"Did you see him?" he asked the Detective.

"See who?"

"The guy that stayed with the little girl."

"I didn't see anybody but the kid," Gil replied.

"No, there was a guy. Had a lot of guts. Stayed with the girl when the gas could have gone up any minute."

"Well, if I see him, I'll let you know," Gil mumbled, and walked back to his car. The meeting with Greg Davis would have to wait. He would have to change clothes before he interviewed anybody. He started to climb into the Olds. His arms were stiff from the cramped position he had held for such a long time in the wreck.

"God, I'm in such lousy shape," he mumbled, "No upper body strength at all. I'll probably be sore tomorrow." He wondered if he could find a way to expand his workouts to include some calisthenics. He thought about his discipline, and how it only focused on certain muscle groups. He mentally kicked himself. *"You never really go all the way, do you?"* he criticized himself. *"When am I going to get my act together, anyway?"*

He started the engine and moved the car forward, being careful to signal before pulling out into traffic.

Chapter 14

Wednesday, 1:13 p.m.

Twenty miles away, in a relatively undeveloped section of Staten Island, Pilar (she pronounced her first name "pee-lar") Murphy walked distractedly along an overgrown path, a shortcut through a wooded tract near the college. A few leaves, still tinged green, detached themselves from the trees and fluttered to earth. She sensed in the leaves a metaphor. Impatient to complete their life cycle, they rushed ahead of their compatriots, preferring the immediate gratification of resolution to the hope of glory that might come from holding on and changing. Metaphor or not, she was struggling with hopes and fears of her own. She sauntered, kicking the fallen leaves. She was troubled. Not seriously troubled, just uncomfortable with the reactions she was having to the man in the stadium. She had trained as a Psychologist. After years of therapy, group encounters, and studies of human motivation, she was quite aware that she was feeling a strong attraction for him. What bothered her, was that she was attracted for very questionable reasons. Thus far, she didn't know him well enough to feel this strongly.

He was intriguing, in a pitiful sort of way. The little boy combination of intensity of purpose and tongue-tied shyness was part of the appeal, she was sure. On the other hand, when she saw the bunching muscles of those well-developed legs, it was not thoughts of little boys that entered her head. Surely, she was past the point where she had to rescue every poor soul she saw in need. Yet she could not deny a strong urge to bring this withdrawn-looking man out of his shell. His eyes spoke volumes. They were intelligent eyes, with the look of one who missed little. They were uneasy eyes, like one who had been hurt. Nevertheless, they were warm eyes, reflecting a person who could be loving and kind.

Pilar stopped herself. "Am I using my counseling skills now, or am I reading into this man the kind of character I want him to be?" She was too honest with herself to believe that she was completely safe from wishful thinking.

Thus far, Pilar realized, she was acting more like a lovestruck teenager than a thirty-four-year-old Associate Professor of Psychology. For instance, there was her visit to the stadium on Tuesday. She seldom went there at all, except an occasional appearance at a ball game to show support for the team. Monday, though, she had been looking for a place to get away from people for a few minutes. After the grades were posted from the first tests of the fall semester, the students were practically breaking down her door to argue, question, plead, and ask for class drop slips. The stadium was only a block away from the Student Union, the site of her second-floor office. She had a master key given to her for opening classrooms and offices, which also fit a variety of other locks, including those of the gymnasium, the side entrance to Harborview Hall student residence, and by chance, the stadium media entrance door. Pilar had intended merely to sit quietly in the large empty structure so she could pull her thoughts together, before beginning the weekly lecture for Psychology 301, Learning Theory. A little quiet time away from people.

Initially, she had climbed to the upper tier without noticing the figure busy on the track below. She was just standing at the opening of an entrance tunnel, enjoying the fresh air and cloud formations, when she saw him driving himself up the stairs. She felt almost invisible, standing back in the shadows as he passed, thick-muscled legs pushing like pistons, breath blowing small clouds of vapor in the cool fall temperature. Her mind recalled a research study described in Psychology Today, in which instruments had been attached to people's heads that could record the track of where they directed their eyes at another person. Apparently, both males and females showed a high interest in the buttocks of the opposite sex. Despite efforts to do otherwise, people seem very taken with a nicely formed rear end. As she watched the vigorous athleticism of the man in the stadium, she realized that her eyes were directed there too. And it was very nice, thank you.

She was impressed further, when she saw the man complete his circle and begin again. She watched for some time before she stepped out of hiding and sat on the cold metal seat of the stadium chair. By then, she had already begun to form some impressions.

Her training had equipped her to notice more than the average person would see. In this man she noted there was an intensity and furrowed brow, an essentially narrowed focus, the look of determination. It was largely curiosity that made her step out and place herself where he would pass by on his laborious route. In all honesty, there was a physical attraction as well—not merely to his strong legs and well-rounded butt, as nice as they were, but also to the power and energy that his training demonstrated. Or was it training? It certainly was intense, and he was deeply involved in it.

Did this indicate anything about an ability to be deeply involved in a relationship. She dismissed that as a silly thought. Not that she had extensive personal experience in deep relationships. She had more theory than practice.

Pilar had not married, despite the pressures to do so from parents and peers. She had been very close to giving in and wedding a fellow student in her masters-degree program at Columbia, but she couldn't ignore the competitiveness that became apparent in their relationship. When she pursued the subject, it eventually became clear, that if he had his way, Doug's career would have to take precedence over hers. Ultimately, it appeared that he would have his way, or no way at all. They didn't break up immediately, but they stopped talking about a wedding. After several tearful split-ups and reunions, she found out that he was spending Friday nights in the bed of a buxom secretary to the Dean of Students, instead of the weekly card-party he had claimed to be attending. Accustomed to honesty and a model of faithfulness from her parents, Pilar swore off men for the better part of two years. Eventually, she began dating again, but with some significant hesitancy. She found that most men her age were unwilling to spend time developing a relationship before hopping into bed. Pilar was hardly a prude but had enough self-esteem to believe that she deserved more than most men were willing to offer her. She had not entirely given up on marriage but was also willing to entertain the possibility of a single life without panic.

A friendship with Peter Dewitt, a biology instructor at the college, had developed into a relationship of convenience. With no illusions of starry-eyed infatuation, they were available to each other for social occasions requiring an escort, and an infrequent session of sex, which she resisted calling lovemaking, due to the absence of romance involved. Their times in bed together were more in the nature of stress reduction than love.

It wasn't as though there weren't other men interested in her. As attractive as she was, she not only had to fend off various lovesick students, but also the attentions of numerous mature men, many of whom were married, including the President of a college where she had taught prior to joining the faculty of Wagner. In fact, she had left that institution largely because she had not been able to handle what she now knew had been sexual harassment. Unfortunately, she came to that realization only after succumbing to the pressure to leave. In retrospect, she now believed that she had been more vulnerable to abuse, because she had so many unmet needs.

So, as it happened, she and Peter had found each other. It wasn't love. It wasn't romance. In fact, as a behavioral expert, Pilar knew it wasn't even truly intimacy. In that respect, it wasn't all that different from some marriages she had seen. Many married pairs were no closer than Peter and Pilar. Some couples would have given anything for the placid absence of conflict that characterized this arrangement. As for Pilar she felt like a little part of her was dying. It wasn't a big part. No even a part that most people would notice in her, for she was a very capable and accomplished person. Still, there was something deep inside, a part of her since she was very young, that was crying out—the sound of a needy child.

It was that child who went back to the stadium Tuesday, to stand silently in a darkened entranceway watching a powerful man struggling with himself. She observed his desire and determination. She noticed little things, such as when he briefly changed his pattern. She read his indecision at that moment, and saw it for what it was, the battle between hope and resignation. She saw his choice for the positive. Her crying child recognized one of its own kind.

CHAPTER 15

Wednesday, 2:06 p.m.

Sister Mary Gertrude had been hearing the cries of children for her entire career. At the moment, the many small voices were muted behind classroom doors. She slowly worked her way down the worn marble stairs toward the main exit of St. Mary's Help of Christians School. Her arthritis was acting up something awful, which she blamed on the changing weather. At age 76, she could have retired from teaching, taking the opportunity to rest her weary bones at the Sister's abbey up in Garrison, New York. There was a place for her, she knew. The religious order was not yet in such financial collapse that she had any concern about being provided for—not that she considered it proper to worry about material needs anyhow. The Lord would provide, she was confident. But as for retiring to a community of elderly nuns, some who had drifted off into a limbo created by their deteriorated bodies and minds, ... well, that was another story. Sister Mary Gertrude, or just "Sister Gertrude," as she was usually called, could not imagine being separated from the children. For fifty-four years she had been teaching, guiding, chastening, nurturing - kept vital by the children of St. Mary's.

The school was located on East Eleventh Street, and Sister Gertrude had seen many changes in the neighborhood. The children had changed too, so she was glad that Spanish had been an important part of her training, including a two-year assignment as a missionary in Argentina. But children were still children. Without them, she was sure that she would just wither and die. For this reason she hid many of her physical ailments, fearful that the Mother Superior would demand she retire.

She had found a few shortcuts to reduce the wear and tear. For instance, she was cheating a little right now. The final bell ending classes for the day would ring at 2:25. Some of St. Mary's teachers had once been Sister Gertrude's students, yet for as many years as anyone could remember, they knew that the first thing they would see as they entered each morning, and the last thing they would see as they exited each afternoon, would be Sister Gertrude's beaming face. She was as aware of this as they were. She knew that her failure to appear would be the signal of the end…her end. Unfortunately, her arthritis and other assorted infirmities had so slowed her that she was physically unable to descend the front stairway in less than five minutes. In the past, she had easily been able to get to the front entrance between the time the bell rang, and the students managed to grab their books, negotiate the hallway, and race down the stairs like a tide of happy lemmings to the door. Now she fudged a bit, leaving her classroom five minutes early, on the pretext of sounding the dismissal bell itself. Actually, the bell was automatically rung, but her third-graders didn't know that, so sat properly in their seats waiting for her to ring the bell, while she was really working her way painfully down the staircase, one excruciating step at a time. God would surely understand her little misrepresentation.

She reached the atrium and had a moment to catch her breath before the harsh clanging sound echoed down the hallway, followed by a rush of sound reminiscent of a flood being loosed from monstrous sluice valves. She cocked an eyebrow at the first couple of students down the stairs, on the assumption that in any group of children, the law of averages would indicate that a couple were wild and unruly, and the second assumption that those wild and impetuous ones would be the first to reach the exit. Sure enough, there was a skid and guilty look, as the first to arrive at the door saw her raised brow. But coupled as it was with her trademark beaming countenance, they only paused a moment, then banged into the crash bars as they dutifully shouted, "Good afternoon, Sister."

There was a chill to the air, but the sun cascaded through the open doorway, so that the streams of children mixed with sunlight to merge into an explosive burst of color, noise, and movement. The old nun felt an inner smile swell and flow through her, deeper and more elemental than the fixed one perpetually on her face. Better than Motrin, better even than cortisone, this sight made her forget all the complaints of her aging body.

She followed the stream of lively youth with her gaze, as it poured out onto the playground, toward the buses lined up along the curb. Her practiced eye scanned the area for danger to, or among, her charges.

A bag lady was huddled in the doorway of a brownstone across the street. Sister Gertrude felt sadness and compassion for this example of what urban living had created. She watched to make sure none of the rowdier boys harassed the tragic figure. Two workmen huddled around a telephone switching station on the street corner. Probably legitimate and safe, but she kept her eye on them, just the same. Out of the corner of her eye, she saw a man in army fatigues and those heavy black boots worn by some veterans and imitated by certain fringe groups. She couldn't tell his race or age, due to his long-sleeved jacket and a jungle hat pulled down over his head. But he didn't linger, striding slowly away, his hands jammed into his pockets. As others passed the schoolyard, and parents mixed with bus drivers, teachers, and others, the image of the man slipped from Sister Gertrude's memory, like a drop of blood in water.

The Performer saw the old nun raking the area with her eyes like radar. He was surprised to see anyone still wearing the old-fashioned full nun's habit, which he thought had disappeared years ago. He had even stopped using a nun puppet in his shows, because the humor about "bad habits" and such seemed so trite and dated.

He turned and walked leisurely away. There was no hurry. Eventually an opportunity would come, when no one was watching, and the right figure was in reach. There were too many small ones for the big ones to watch every single moment. He could be patient.

He could wait. That had been one of Melvin's lessons. When necessary, he could sit or stand motionless, expressionless, for hours at a time. He could wait until it was the right time. It wasn't the right time at the place he called the 'Little Lamb place'.

Only a short walk south from the 'Little Lamb place' was the 'Dragon place'. Later he would go to the 'Place of Gifts', and the 'Rainbow place'. In fact, on the way to the Dragon place, he could even see the 'Mad Hatters place'. They were all special places. He had made them special, by giving them his attention and his special names. Also, in each special place, there were special figures which he had given names as well.

As he drew near the Mad Hatters place, he felt a tingling in his hands and feet, a dull thudding in his ears. He knew they were trying to stop him. The ones who thought he was stupid, ugly, and wrong. He wasn't sure how they were hunting him. An article in the POST had told about the increasing danger of radon. He was certain that radon was just part of the effort to poison him, along with the wood fiber they were putting in bread and other edible things. He marveled at the extent of the efforts his adversaries would go to kill him, efforts that would cost thousands of lives just from misdirected lethal substances.

But they would have a hard time getting to him that way, for he was no dummy. NOT A DUMMY! He ate sparingly, choosing only naturally grown grains and seeds, with unprocessed milk and fruit juices. He bought the things he could not make himself from a different store each time. Sometimes this meant traveling long distances, but it prevented them from planting a special poisoned batch of food in a store they knew he would habitually visit.

The fact that he could feel them directing some kind of beams at him, made him sure that he was close to something important. So the tingling actually worked in his favor, making him feel dangerous and special. He floated toward the Mad Hatters place in a nimbus of power.

This building was labeled with strange hieroglyphics, squares and upside-down letters, dots, and squiggles. The Performer couldn't choose a name based on that, as he had with some other zones of influence. He almost called it the Star place for the big six-pointed star, or the Candle place, because of the huge candlestick engraved on one wall. But a better name came to him as soon as he had seen the figures. There were larger figures and smaller ones, but they all wore hats. Some wore little beanie caps, while others sported large, brimmed hats, which reminded the Performer of the tea party from Alice in Wonderland, except the hats in the movie were colorful, while these were black.

"Alice" had been a favorite movie of his. After seeing it first when he was ten, the Performer had bought a hamster at the local pet store. He wanted to pretend that it was the dormouse at the party, who was regularly stuffed into a pot of tea. He enjoyed seeing the little thing scrabbling and clawing to escape drowning. Then he poured boiling water on top of it, pretending that he was the animal's father and needed to punish it. After that he tried some experiments with cats. He tried to remember if the Cheshire cat had been at the tea party but couldn't be sure. All he could remember was that in the movie, the cat's smile remained long after the body of the cat was gone. This created some problems, when his father came into his room one night and saw a detached bloody jawbone with teeth still in place.

That was long ago. Now he was at a new tea party. Everyone at this place had a hat on, and they were crazy. They wore funny clothes, with tassels hanging down from their belts. They were all males but wore their hair so that long curly locks hung down in front of their ears. To him, this became the 'Mad Hatters place'.

The occupants left this place about the same time of day as the ones who departed the Little Lamb place. They also rode buses. But the boarding process that had just begun on East Eleventh, by the time he had walked the intervening distance, was almost completed a few blocks away. The bigger people, who now figured their monitoring job was finished, disappeared into the low, mosque-like building. A few of the small figures waited inside the cyclone fence for a late bus or parent car-pool. The Performer didn't recognize any of the group. He was just beginning the process of naming a few of the Mad Hatters, and the small ones he had labeled seemed to have left on earlier buses. So, today he did not see Four Eyes, or Flatnose, or Wiggledy Piggledy. But a stranger is just a friend you haven't met, the Performer had been told. So this was a group of special figures he just hadn't yet named.

One small body detached itself from the group and left the schoolyard in a trotting gait that spoke of anticipation and excitement. Something was waiting at home, that the little one didn't want to miss. Unknown to him, something else was waiting much closer.

Chapter 16

Wednesday, 7:22 p.m.

Gil had finally arrived at the residence of Greg Davis, the vic's boyfriend, which was located on Avenue C. The interview was going about as he had expected, or maybe worse. The guy Beach questioned was so full of booze, he was falling all over himself. He was the kind of guy Gil sometimes thought of as a 'plastic person.' A perfectly formed imitation of the real thing. Like a fake plant, it was hard to tell what made him appear phony, but something made the young man look too perfect to be real. Perfect teeth, perfect hairstyle, perfect wardrobe, it was perfectly nauseating as far as Gil was concerned.

It soon became apparent that the boy knew nothing, could imagine nothing, and was pretty much worth nothing in relation to the investigation. As Gil was making notes in his pad, the designer imitation antique phone on the end table warbled an electronic tone. The young man picked up the receiver with clumsy paws.

"Who?" he asked, looking puzzled. "I think you ... uh, have the wrong num'er." But he didn't return the old-fashioned receiver to its cradle, continuing to staring at it with a wrinkled forehead, as someone on the line evidently refused to let the matter drop. "Wha? Oh, the detec'ive? Yeah, he's here. Jus' a minute."

Gil had already risen from his seat to reach for the phone. The young man fumbled the receiver as he handed it over, but Gil caught the instrument just before it shattered a glass coffee table.

"This is Beach. What's up?"

The voice nearly broke his eardrum. It was 'Boom Boom' Mabry.

"Yo, Gabby. You getting anything good?"

"Not really," Gil said, waiting for whatever the Sergeant had really called about. Mabry didn't make him wait.

"We could use you on something else. What say you take a little ride over by the Yeshiva on Thirteenth? There's a garage about a hundred yards west of the school. I'll meet you there."

"What is it, Sarge?" Gil asked, fearing the answer.

"I'm not sure, Gabby."

"Another kid?" the Detective whispered.

There was a pause, and in a rare quiet tone, the Sergeant answered, "Well, there's one missing, and they found something that may relate. I want you to take a look."

"Right Sarge, Ten-Seventeen," Beach responded, using the code that indicated he was on the way to the location.

He hung up the receiver, finished a note in his pad, then turned to the wobbly owner of the apartment.

"I want to thank you for your help, Mr. Davis. We may have to ask you some more questions later, but this will be all for today. I'm going to leave you my card, so you can call if anything else comes to mind that might be important. Okay?"

Davis mumbled something that sounded like understanding as he directed his puzzled look at the printed rectangle. It was just a plain business card, with "New York Police Department" in boldface type, the precinct designation and telephone number below. There was no fancy logo or police star—that had been eliminated when the earlier form of cards with their official-looking badge logo and embossed lettering had been misused by some enterprising recipients for other purposes. Put in a wallet or I.D. case, with perhaps a small photo pasted in the corner, the cards looked impressive enough to have gotten the bearers free admittance to ball games, theaters, and other events, discounts at gullible retailers, and assorted privileges offered under the mistaken impression that the holder was connected to the Department. It wasn't worth the trouble to prosecute every case as an instance of impersonating an officer of the law, so the design was changed. Gil slipped out one of the simple cards and wrote his name and telephone extension on a blank line at the bottom, since everyone in the P.D.U. used the same generic card.

"This isn't… uh, I mean, you know, like you're really a detec'ive, right?" the boy stammered, doubt clouding his alcohol-reddened features. Gil felt like making a snide retort, like *'No, I'm really a brain surgeon, but I like to spend my spare time interrogating obnoxious drunks about recent murders.'* Maybe some cop in a movie might do that, but not in real life. You would have a complaint registered before you could get back to the unit, an angry Lieutenant to answer to, plus a record of the complaint in your personnel folder to haunt you the rest of your career.

"Yes, Mr. Davis, I'm a detective with the Ninth Precinct. That was my squad commander on the phone. Would you like to call the Precinct and verify my identification? The number is there on the card, or you can call information."

"No, no… I didn't mean that, uhh, I just never saw a … I mean, I expected that… well, ya know, like a couple guys. Ya know, uhh… like par'ners, ya know. An…, well… never mind."

"More like on T.V., you mean?"

"Well, I know it's not exactly like that, but, well, ya know."

Gil hated the lazy habit, used by so many, of inserting the words, "you know" every time an explanation of something was required. It was as if the speaker insisted that the listener do half his work for him. Sometimes he was tempted to answer back to each "Ya know?" with a "No, actually I don't know what the fuck you are saying." Gil wasn't in the business of teaching communication. And he wasn't there to teach a drunk about the difference between television and reality, either. So he just swallowed his reactions, gave a friendly nod, and said goodbye.

When the Detective left the building, he observed three young punks eyeing his car. When he appeared and started for the vehicle, they feigned nonchalance as they sauntered off. Gil felt a brief moment of anger yet was a little surprised at himself. The situation was so commonplace, that he shouldn't react. Yet, for a moment he had a flare of outrage that the city was always so primitive and hostile. The veneer of civilization was very thin. Little separated these groups of humans from marauding packs of animals. Only a slight hesitancy prevented them from running amok. Without police, he believed, that hesitation would not exist. And as close as he could put it, that was why he remained in the Job. It wasn't like St. George slaying the dragon. No heroics about it. Just a sense that somebody had to keep piling sandbags on the bank, or the swollen river of evil would wash everyone away.

When he reached the garage, yellow tape already marked off the scene, announcing "Police Search Area, Do Not Enter."

Garages were not common in the borough. Manhattan was one of the few areas in the United States where a high percentage of the populace managed to exist without owning an automobile. For years the city had been discouraging private vehicles by reducing street parking, establishing exorbitant parking lot fees, and providing a massive system of public transportation. Real estate was so valuable, that a one or two car garage was usually a poor use of space. Yet, some still existed. In this block, there was a row of them, worked into the first floor of a four-story factory building. Mabry was standing outside the last in the row, wearing his usual street expression—the hardnose cop who doesn't want to be bothered by anything less than a major catastrophe, and won't be surprised by anything that could possibly come to pass in this world, or most likely the next.

Gil expected some verbal heat about how long it took him to arrive, but the Sergeant merely raised his head in a silent greeting, then led the way to a judas door set in a large garage entrance.

A crowd of dark-clothed men milled nearby, bearded and grim. The men were ultra-orthodox Hasidim from the nearby Yeshiva Lomza Petach Tikva Israel. Their faces had an intensity which spoke of fear, anxiety, hope, and desperation. Gil had seen that expression before. It was the look of those waiting outside a Welsh coal mine after an explosion, or that of a man seeking his child who had been on the San Francisco overpass when it was leveled by an earthquake ... of a mother whose child was trapped at the bottom of a deep well, a young man waiting for the list of victims from the airline officials after a plane carrying his wife had crashed. It was like glass waiting to be broken.

The two policemen moved into the shadowed interior, past a uniformed officer guarding the entrance. Gil was surprised to see Frank Terranova there, too. Apparently, he was no longer completely confined to the Precinct station, though he seemed to be keeping a low profile. Everyone was relatively quiet. Into the stillness "Boom Boom" Mabry's voice exploded like a cannon.

"So it seems this kid ..." Mabry looked questioningly over to Terranova, who consulted a clip board.

"Chaim Hemlich," he whispered.

"Yeah, Hemlich," Mabry continued, "was anxious to get home from the Schule ... didn't wait for the van. Nothing he hadn't done before. But this time, he never arrives home. The friends and relatives get rousted out to look for him about an hour later, and they cover the route with a fine-tooth comb. The guy over there, Abram something, ... Kastlewitz, Koselwitz, ..."

"Kostlavitz," Terranova interjected.

"Whatever. Anyway he pokes his head in here, and sees something weird. Fortunately for us, he didn't touch anything."

Gil looked in the corner. He hadn't noticed anyone there before. A bearded man sat on a crate, rocking slightly back and forth, his dark clothing and hair melding with the shadows. His expression was more hostile than those outside, probably a reaction to the waiting, and uncertainty, but still with the intensity and desperation hardly hidden. Gil looked to the other side of the dark room to see the reason.

A length of board lay across an old-fashioned nail keg, forming the shape of arms on a torso. In scarecrow fashion, a black garment was draped on these, with the sleeves slid over the board and a stuffed paper bag imitating a head, topped by a yarmulke, the typical head covering of the young Hasidic students.

"The boy's coat?" Gil asked, though the garment was hardly a coat anymore. It had been slashed and ripped to tatters.

"Yeah," Mabry answered, "the Yah-ma-kah too. It's pretty distinctive."

Gil was glad that Mabry was showing some restraint in his references. In the privacy of his office, the Sergeant called the skullcaps "beanies" and used racial epithets like "Yid" and "Hebe" even in the presence of Jewish cops. If you knew Mabry, you knew that this was a playful kind of affectation. He used all the prejudicial words for every conceivable ethnic group. He meant it as a kind of comic overstatement. It was as if such things could only be a joke, to his way of thinking. His generosity and openhearted ways belied the words, but you had to get used to his style to know what was going on. Rookies often had to be calmed down, until they got the idea. Gil was always afraid that Mabry would one day forget where he was and deliver a few "winners" in the presence of some ethnic standard bearer, who would then make life miserable for the Sergeant and the Precinct.

Mabry gave a sign to have the man in the corner ushered out. He turned to Gil.

"What do you think?"

"Not much to go on, at least 'till forensics takes a look."

"I'm not looking for a locked-up conclusion, Beach, just an impression."

Gil walked over to the arrangement of clothes and wood. He looked at it from several angles, then bent over to examine something more closely. His hand came up to his eyes, two fingers rubbing the bridge of his nose, like he wanted to push away some pain. His shoulders sagged, and he turned to Mabry.

"Did you know, when you called me?"

"Know what?" the Sergeant asked, thick eyebrows arched.

"That it's the same guy."

"Same guy as who?" Mabry replied, looking curious.

"Same guy that did the Granger girl."

"You know who did the Granger girl?"

"No, but I know it's the same guy that did this," the Detective replied, slowly nodding his head in certainty.

"What, you've got a hunch?" Mabry pressed.

"No, a lot more than a hunch. I know it's the same guy, and I know he is beginning to play with us. This was left here for us to find. He wants us to know he's out there. He wants us to know it's the same person."

"You got something solid?" Mabry asked.

"Yeah, this." Gil replied, pointing at where the head-like paper bag joined the nail-keg trunk of the scarecrow. There was a small, doubled piece of cardboard with serrated edges and a metallic band, wedged between the bag and the cask, where the neck might normally be.

"What is it?" Mabry barked at his characteristic high volume.

"It's his mark, I think."

"Mark?"

"His sign, his calling card."

"You mean like when a unit over in Nam left a playing card on a V.C. corpse?" Frank suggested.

"To warn the enemy," the Sergeant remarked, more statement than question.

"Yeah, that, and to announce their presence, sort of like a wolf marks its territory," Frank explained.

"To show off their power, too," Gil added.

"But doesn't that kind of work the opposite way? Wouldn't it make their unit a priority target for the enemy?"

"Yes, and that's part of it. It's like throwing down the gauntlet. It's a challenge."

"You're telling me that there is somebody out there that's taunting us?" Mabry asked, his lips tightly drawn.

Beach nodded slowly, eyes fixed on some remote point beyond this place or moment. He was remembering a case he had closed three years earlier. That time the killer had sent them human fingers in little boxes.

It was the boxes that had led them to him. They had been the type of container that was used to hold expensive tobacco pipes. Gil had plotted the geographical locations of the packages' postmarks, until he saw that they formed a rough half-moon shape on the map. Assuming the guy was trying to avoid detection, Gil projected lines from the ends of the crescent to form a pie-shape, and outlined a search area centering at where the pie wedge came to a point, twenty miles from the actual mail stations. His team had canvassed tobacco stores in this area without apparent success, until Gil noticed a name reappear on several interrogation reports. It wasn't the name of a person, but a supplier. Eventually, this led to the arrest of a travelling sales representative for the supplier, who turned out to have a finger collection at home mounted on the clips of pipe display boards. The bodies were in a swamp behind his house.

Mabry's basso profunda startled him out of his thoughts.

"So, what have we got on this guy, Beach?"

"Well, I have to put some of it together, Sarge. But it looks like he has some interest in magic, or novelties, or ventriloquism."

"Magic? Ventriloquism? You mean, like David Copperfield and Jeff Dunham?" Frank asked. "I love Achmed, the dead terrorist," he whispered, not allowing himself to smile, given the setting.

"I don't know, but this thing here is sold as a ventriloquist gadget. There was one just like it by the Granger kid's body."

"There's no body this time, Gil." The Squad Commander's jaw muscles clenched as he spoke.

"I know," the Detective replied softly, not looking directly at the frowning Sergeant. The implications of the missing boy and the defiant display were all too apparent. The corpse might not be here, but the human form that had once filled these clothes was not likely to be somewhere safe and well. Or alive.

The weather looked threatening, so Gil offered Frank a ride back to the station. They didn't say much on the way back. Frank offered Gil a jellybean and popped one in his own mouth. Beach found a spot on Fifth street a block away from the Precinct from where they slowly walked back to the PDU, past the storefronts and rental buildings, stepping around piles of debris and garbage cans with lids chained to prevent loss. Gil was appreciating a window box that had a few hardy flowers still managing to retain a bloom in October, when he realized that the sidewalk was crowded by large numbers of Hasidic Jews, converging on the stationhouse entrance.

Most of them didn't seem concerned about letting the cops get through to the entrance. Some were downright obstructive. It took quite a while to work their way to the building. Long ago, Gil had learned the technique of not trying to force his way through a crowd, but slipping and sliding through "soft spots" in the crush of bodies, penetrating little by little through the human log jam. The technique was less confrontational but effective.

Eventually, they got to the front where they were let in by the uniforms standing guard. Gil glanced at the plaques behind the long front desk, commemorating the members of the "Fighting Ninth" who had been killed in the line of duty. On other occasions he had wondered about the "Fighting" designation, and whether it was a good group image for "peace officers." But today, he wondered if anyone included in the line of memorial plaques had been killed by a superior officer driven off the deep end by the pressures of a crazy community. Wilson was at the desk, making entries in the ever-hungry ledger. He refrained from the usual wisecrack, but formed a grin like a cat that just ate a canary, as he announced, "Lou wants to see you."

"Lou" was not a name, but a rank designation. A holdover from the armed services, where many cops had once served, "Lou" was attached to any Lieutenant rank officer. In this case, the officer was Lieutenant Randolph M. Lincoln, who was inevitably saddled with the nickname of "Abe," though unlike the former president in countenance, build, personality, or race.

In contrast to Mabry, the earthy, street-smart veteran who got his wisdom from experience more than books, Lincoln was a "suit," i.e., a college educated, upward bound, politically responsive wunderkind. The Ninth P.D.U. was just a brief visit for Lincoln, who had to touch various bases on his way to home plate, which was One Police Plaza. Recruited out of college by an affirmative action program, the Lieutenant had many talents, including the ability not only to claim credit for anything anyone else did, but also to get away with it. Gil grudgingly admitted that the Lieutenant also had that necessary skill of any future administrator, which was to be able to describe a complete fowl-up in such artful language as to make it seem a success. He was less successful in gaining the trust of his command. Most cops, Gil believed, are suspicious of intellectuals. They are willing to tolerate academic degrees, if accompanied by demonstrated courage, toughness, and dependability. But the Lieutenant hadn't been anyplace long enough to prove himself in the trenches. He was too much of a star on the rise.

Usually, a civilian employee sat at the small desk outside Lincoln's office, but lately Frank had been stationed there.

"What do you think, Frank? Trouble?"

Terranova answered with a shrug accompanied by a wry expression.

"I can't tell you anything, but don't be surprised if there is a scoop of shit being tossed in the general direction of the nearest fan."

Frank grabbed a handful of the jellybeans he seemed to always have handy, popping them into his mouth like pills. Gil nodded, giving a little wave of his hand as he pushed open the door to the Lieutenant's office.

The room was immaculate. Bookshelves were filled with volumes neatly arranged according to size and subject, with little plastic labels on the shelf edges, noting the topic covered in the books. Unlike Gil's haphazard accumulation of papers, piled in untidy stacks, Lincoln's was carefully filed in cabinets, or in speckled boxes, labeled and aligned like legal books on top of a vertical file. Lincoln was studying law at Columbia part-time. It seemed to Gil that his office looked more like an attorney's workplace than a cop's.

The Lieutenant was holding a single departmental memo above an otherwise clear desk, covered only by a new blotter in a tooled leather holder, matching notepad, and pen set. On the wall behind the desk, were three walnut-framed photographs, showing Lincoln receiving an award from the Police Commissioner, shaking hands with the mayor, and another, dressed in casual summer clothes, between a well-known opera tenor and financier Winthrop Chalmers. If these were indications of Lincoln's true associations, rather than dime-a-dozen publicity shots, then it was hard to tell which affiliation was more useful, or how high he could aim. But it certainly looked like he was well connected.

"Well, hello Gil," the slim black man effused, "Glad you got here so quickly. How's the family?"

"What family is that, sir?"

"Uh, you have some family, don't you?"

Gil was just being difficult, calling the Lieutenant's bluff of pretending he cared about Beach's family, but decided not to press it.

"Yes, Sir. Thanks for asking. Everyone's fine."

"Good, good. Care for some coffee?"

"No thank you, Sir."

"Oh come on, Gil. No need for the 'Sir' stuff. After all, we are going to be working closely together on this Jewish thing. First names are fine."

"Jewish thing?"

"Yes, the missing boy. It's probably an anti-Semitic thing, don't you think?"

"Well no sir, I was thinking along other lines. The Granger girl wasn't Jewish, as far as I know."

"Ahh, yes, the Granger woman," the Lieutenant put the tips of his fingers together, tapping thumbs against each other, as he squinted and looked off at some distant focal point, "Now I think we must be very careful about jumping to conclusions there, Gil. What is to say that the cases are connected?"

"We've got at least three dead or missing children, similarity of M.O., and a repeated calling card. To think in terms of a common perp isn't much of a jump."

"Let's be more accurate, shall we, Gil. We have one missing boy, a dead woman, and some unidentified tissue. That doesn't necessarily add up to a pattern."

"But..." the Detective began, hardly getting the word out of his mouth before he was interrupted.

"... As for the weapon or weapons, all we know is that in two cases, there were sharp instruments involved. That hardly means the same blade or M.O."

Gil felt his blood rising, and an image flashed in his mind of a cartoon character with steam spurting out of its collar, a hat blown into the air inches above the head.

He knew that some of his annoyance was because the Lieutenant was right. Once convinced of the pattern, he may have been sloppy in adding up the evidence. If you took the pieces apart, they looked a lot less convincing than if you saw them in one piece. And the truth was, his belief was based primarily on intuition and one definitive piece of evidence. He threw it out like a trump card.

"But what about the 'calling card,' the ventriloquist gadgets? That's important. It's like a signature."

"We're not so sure of that," Lincoln replied, condescendingly. Gil wondered who he meant by the "we?"

"In one of your three instances, there was no 'gadget' at all. In the case of the missing child, there was some kind of object similar to what you describe. Since it is the kind of gimmick expressly sold to children, we are taking quite a leap of imagination to conclude that it came from the kidnapper, or Jew- hater, that took the child. Naturally, we won't absolutely rule out such a possibility, but a more probable explanation is that the object belonged to the child and fell from a pocket."

Gil felt his heart sinking, as he experienced a dawning realization about where this was going. But he gave it another futile try.

"But there was one with the girl, too!"

"Woman, Gil, woman," the Lieutenant corrected, not missing a beat, "I think you realize Gil, that IF the article found in the lot is the same type of item—a fact that is still open to some dispute— then the laws of probability come into play here. A search of an artifact-rich environment, like a city lot, is necessarily going to yield such an immense number of items, that the likelihood of a single similar object appearing in another search area is quite high."

Gil knew that the Lieutenant's arguments sounded logical and conservatively factual. He also knew they were bullshit. If he thought the superior officer was stupid, he could pretend that this was a case of ignorant or inept command. But this guy was not dumb. The depressing truth was that Lincoln or someone above him in rank didn't want this case treated as a serial murder. It didn't take a genius to know that some of the reasons they didn't want it were crowding up against the front of the precinct stationhouse, murmuring in guttural tones and glowering from under brimmed black hats.

"Then what do we tell our neighbors?" he finally snapped, resisting capitulation. The Lieutenant, catching the combative tone, drew himself up, and answered in a voice slightly colder than liquid hydrogen.

"You don't tell them anything, Detective. Sergeant Epstein will be issuing a statement momentarily, that acknowledges the concerns of the affected citizens and describes our intense efforts to apprehend the culprits."

"These intense efforts include...?"

"A special task force. Additional manpower. A special hotline. I will be heading the task force myself."

Gil could see it all now. The token Jewish sergeant Epstein placating the crowd, manufacturing misleading statements to avoid accusations that they had let a serial killer keep on killing until he took one of their precious children. They wanted to hide the truth about a child-killer to avoid public outcry and panic. At the same time someone, probably the Precinct Commander, would be keeping a direct and open channel into the investigation through Lincoln.

"All this for a missing boy? Don't you think somebody is going to wonder about that?"

"You can leave the manpower strategy to command officers, don't you think, Detective Beach?"

So much for the first-name basis.

As he left the office, Frank looked at him and nodded a world-weary nod of understanding. Terranova gave Gil a thumbs-up sign, as the Detective slumped away.

Chapter 17

Thursday, 11:56 a.m.

Gil glumly descended the iron-railed staircase from the P.D.U. offices to the first floor. He walked outside, hunched-up in his topcoat, using the upturned collars as blinders. The air was damp and chill. After years of smelling them, he hardly noticed the exhaust mixing with other odors. There was a stifling effect in the stationhouse that made the outside atmosphere seem almost like sea breeze or mountain air. He breathed deeply as he threw back his shoulders.

It was a short walk to Second Avenue where a dilapidated newsstand hunkered, run by a blind guy. Gil was not sure whether the man was really blind. There was no doubt that the old character could see some movement. Nobody managed to swipe a paper off the stack without paying. Gil gave him the benefit of the doubt, figuring that blindness did not have to be total to be a handicap. If he was playing at it, it was a hell of a good act. The Detective thought the man's name was Quint or Quenton, but everybody called him "Squint."

"Hello Squint, how ya doing today?"

"Thas' gotta be Officer Butler, ain't I right?"

"Not this time, Squint. It's Beach. But with this damn cold, my own mother couldn't tell my voice," Gil lied.

"Right, right. Shoulda caught that, though. Won't miss next time, you wait and see, Sergeant. I got that part right, didn't I?"

"Yeah, sure," Gil agreed, not wanting to hand the man two failures in a row. "You carry Variety, Squint?"

"Ya better believe it, Sergeant. Don't sell many, but usually somebody from the performin' arts school, or Cooper Union will ask for a copy or two. Nobody so far today, though. So you got first dibs."

He fished around under the plank counter, pulled out a copy with a crumpled front page, and slapped it down. Gil dug in his pocket to get the exact change, then realized that the stubble-faced old man always seemed to take pride in making the right change despite his apparent handicap. Gil didn't think this included the ability to tell different bills apart, so he spoke as he pulled one out of his wallet.

"All I got today is a fiver, Squint."

"No problem, Officer. Change coming up."

The fumbling which followed, seemed always to leave the news dealer curiously unable to locate the last twenty-five cents. The customer, embarrassed by the blind clumsiness and delay, usually told him to keep the rest. Gil thought it was probably a gimmick to get an extra quarter out of each sale but wasn't particularly offended at the thought. It must be an awful feeling, to be even partially blind. He remembered times he had felt powerless and cut off from the world, but didn't want to go there, so pushed down the memories and brought himself back to the dumpy little newsstand, where the grizzled old man stared through dark glasses taped at the temple, tobacco stains permanently fixed in the wrinkles of his chin. Beach told him to keep the change as he headed back down the street.

He walked into the Sportspage Bar, on the corner of Second and Fifth. There was a booth in the rear, out of sight of the large display T.V. where formula-one racing cars were growling away on the screen. After ordering an O'Douls, N.A., Gil spread the issue of Variety on the table and scanned the advertising section. It seemed a good place to find someone that knew about ventriloquism.

He saw several advertisements. One was for "Barstow's Magic Company" that claimed specialties in "Large Stage Illusions, Animal Effects, and Ventriloquist Supplies." There was a place in Chelsea, "Great Theatre Support Services," promising "Equipment, supplies, and support services for every specialty—from Stunts to Ventriloquism." An outfit in Brooklyn offered more general "Technical assistance to performers" followed by a list that included "Magicians and Vents." And finally, one that seemed more of a booking agent, "T. 'n T., Inc.: Home of Dynamite Talent" that proclaimed they were "Now Featuring the Talents of Internationally Acclaimed Ventriloquist, Tom Tyler and Gopher," although a line at the bottom of the ad mentioned that the T. and T. outfit was "Supplier of Vent Figures to Three Generations of Stars."

Rather than go back to the Precinct, Gil moved to the rear of the bar, where a rare pay phone stood its post, waiting for secret lovers who couldn't call from home, salesmen and marketing representatives trying to become friends with people who didn't want to deal with them, alcoholics calling their spouses to claim delays so they could keep on drinking, and cops that didn't want their conversations heard by critical superiors. The phone had a device to take credit cards, so it no longer could be classed as a coin operated device, but still fit under the old term 'pay-phone'.

The first call was to the Chelsea company, "Great Theatre Support Services." After a few rings, a computerized recording informed him that the number was no longer in service. Habitually frustrated by automated information services, he didn't waste time trying to get a new number from information. The next call was to Barstow's in midtown.

"B.M.C.," the voice of a carnival huckster announced, "How's tricks?"

"Barstow's Magic Company?"

"What do ya think B.M.C. stands for?" the nasal tone responded. "Didn't ya get the joke? Ya know, 'How's Tricks' coming from a magic shop, and all? Get it?"

"Right. So, who can I speak to about... ventriloquism stuff?"

"You're speakin' to 'im. Billy Barstow, at yer service, but what ya see ain't half of what you get. We can send you our catalogue, or you can come on in and check us out. We got soft figures, hard figures, marionettes, and wire puppets, plus a great line of animated objects."

"Well, Mr. Barstow, what I really need is information. Would you, or someone on your staff be able to fill me in on the ventriloquist scene—who does it, what kind of person has the ability? Are there many of them, and is there a listing of ... uh practitioners, or whatever you call them. Things like that."

"Three sessions, three hunnert."

"Three sessions? Three hundred? Three hundred what? Ventriloquists?"

"Gimme a break. Three hunnert bucks, o'course. Three lessons, a hunnert bucks apiece. An' I don't do less than three."

"What lessons?"

"Vent lessons, o'course. Ain't that what you was talkin' about? Lessons are half an hour each. You can't come three times? I'll do the whole thing in one ninety-minute push. I'll even take off ten percent, since I don't gotta tie up three days."

"Oh no, I don't think you understand," Gil protested, realizing he hadn't introduced himself or the reason for his call. I'm not interested in learning to be a ventriloquist; I just need information. I'm Detective Beach with the Ninth Precinct, N.Y.P.D. It has to do with a homicide investigation."

"I don't care if it has to do with the assassination of the President. Vent stuff is a magic effect. You want to know about it, you gotta be in the trade, or pay the price to get in."

Gil felt himself bristle. Without really thinking it through, he retreated to the cop's next resort, authority. It was a poor choice.

"Look, Mr. Barstow. This is a police investigation. You are required by law to cooperate or face serious consequences."

"Yeah? Well, push it as much as you want, Mr. Lawman, and see what consequences it has on my memory. By the way, the price o' legal testimony is five hunnert an hour. You want some expert consultation, I'll be glad to charge the Department."

This was getting nowhere. Gil made a couple of mumbled warnings about subpoenas and such, then got off the phone quickly. Only in cheap films did everyone respond willingly to the police out of their fear or helpfulness. In reality, you got a lot of lies, exaggerations, half-truths, secrecy, resentment, phony cooperation, and active obstruction. Solid information was harder to get. Half the time, you could learn more from what wasn't said, than what was, and more from behavior than from words. In truth, sometimes detectives were about as skillful at eliciting information as a monkey. Like the conversation he had just had with one Billy Barstow. That was a source that would be useless from now on. Gil didn't think the guy would have a lot to offer, but still kicked himself mentally. Barstow already had a bad attitude, and there was a big difference between a potentially hostile witness or suspect and voluntary resource person.

He felt like packing it in for the day but decided to finish his short list of calls. When the third number was answered by a machine that told him to leave a message, he almost hung up but thought better of it, so left his name and the precinct number. Only one more agency on his list. The address of T. 'n T. was in Greenwich Village a dozen blocks west of the Ninth Precinct, in an area of little theaters, cafes, and avant-garde shops. The woman who answered the call had a deep throaty voice that made Gil blink.

"T. 'n T., this is Annie. I ho-o-ope I can help you!"

"Uh, yes. Uh, this is Detective Gil Beach, N.Y.P.D. We are conducting an investigation, and I would appreciate some information."

"Now if this was a friendly little call, I guess I could call you 'Gil,' and ask what you'd like to know. But if I'm accused of something terrible, like tearing the tag off my mattress, it might have to be 'Detective Beach,' and I'd have to call my lawyer. Truth is, honey, I'd much rather talk to you. The only lawyer I know tried to screw me every way you can imagine, including a grab at my ass when I made the mistake of letting him meet me at my apartment."

Gil found himself smiling. "Sorry about that, Annie. I'm not after you."

"Oooh. My loss."

"Well, not professionally, anyway. You can call me Gil anytime." He was tempted to say, "You can call me anytime, period," but realized this was just a voice. He shouldn't treat a business call like a social encounter. His thoughts shifted for a moment to a persistent memory of the enigmatic and beautiful woman who had watched him work out in the stadium on Staten Island, but dismissed the irrelevant reflections and continued the conversation.

"Oh, sorry. No, you aren't under investigation, of course. I would have informed you if that was going on. It's just that there is a special element to the case we are working, and someone who knows about ventriloquism or ventriloquists might shed light on the matter."

"Well, I'm an expert on dummies, having married a couple and gone out with a whole passle of 'em. But I guess that's not what you had in mind."

"No, not really Annie. But thanks anyway."

"Well, Honey, I guess you should talk to Tommy. He knows the business from the inside out."

"Tommy?"

"Tom Tyler, sweetheart. One of the top ten Vents working today. His grandad built figures for Valentine Vox."

"I suppose I should know the name."

"Before your time, Honey. Unless you're a lot older than that sexy voice of yours sounds. He was a great one though, him and Cecil Wigglenose. That wasn't a Tyler figure, it was a McElroy, but some of Vox's earlier figures were Tylers."

"Figures?"

"Oh yeah. Despite my lame humor a coupla minutes ago, we generally never, call them 'Dummies. I guess it's sort of like people who are deaf and speech-impaired not liking to be called 'deaf and dumb.' The word 'dumb' means silent, but most people think it means stupid. When a good vent is at work, his figure isn't silent or stupid."

Gil noticed how the woman had dropped most or her vamp routine when she got into a discussion of business. She sounded as if she had a decent I.Q. in addition to that sexy voice.

"I suppose Mr. Tyler's father was in the business, too?"

"Oh, you mean the ad: 'Three generations' and all that? Well, three generations of stars got supplied, but only Tommy and his granddad did the supplying. Tom's pop was about as talented as a rock. Only thing he created was plenty of debt. Grandpa Tyler took Tom under his wing and taught him the trade. Performing brings in the bucks, but figure creation is Tommy's first love. If he could afford it, he'd do nothing else."

"Any chance I could speak with him?"

"No problem, sweetheart," she reverted into her femme fatale role again. "Trouble is, he isn't here right now. But if you have some time tomorrow, he'll be in the shop all day. Why don't you drop around and say hello? I'm sure he'd be glad to talk with you. He loves to B.S. with anybody interested in the trade. And I know that I would like to meet you, honey."

As much as he knew it was just a game she must play to flirt with anyone who called, Gil found himself very interested in a personal visit to T. 'n T., Incorporated.

"Tomorrow morning is fine for me," he replied, "Maybe around ten, ten-thirty?"

"Well, if you want to talk to Tommy, ten is a little early. He's usually in by then, but he and Gopher have a two-show gig tonight in Soho, and he might be a little late tomorrow. Eleven would be safe. But then, if you want to talk to me, I'll be here by nine ... all alone. So, if you want to come at nine ..."

"Well, maybe I'd better stick with ten or ten-thirty. That way I can talk to you for a while and then Mr. Tyler when he comes in."

Gil had no intention of showing up at ten, despite the temptation to pursue the deep-voiced charmer on the other end of the line. He was competent in a telephone dialogue, and could play the verbal game a bit, but face-to-face encounters with attractive women were often less successful. At a distance, he could fantasize with the best of them, but up-close, he tended to stumble over his tongue. For a moment, his thoughts again turned to the woman at the stadium, who he would likely never see again. After all, she was gone. He felt a tiny tug at his heart with this thought but ignored it. He was not in the habit of wasting time on hopeless matters.

The conversation concluded with small talk, and the enticing voice was gone. Gil flipped the receiver back on the hook, walked back to the booth and slid into the seat. The bartender glanced up at movement in the empty tavern. Gil ordered a double shot of Dewars. It went down like battery acid, which was fine with him. The next one was easier.

CHAPTER 18

Thursday, 4:48 p.m.

You couldn't exactly call it a hangover. Hangovers are usually the morning after a drunken night. It wasn't morning and he hadn't even gotten drunk. But his second double shot had been followed by a beer, and despite the corned beef sandwich that had accompanied it, or maybe because of it, Gil had been ready to fall asleep at his desk when he returned to the Precinct. After a few telephone calls and a halfhearted attempt to catch up on paperwork/data entry, he had called it quits and made his way to the ferry. Instead of his usual high perch on the boat, he had slumped in a first-deck seat and promptly dozed off. A cleaning woman woke him almost forty-five minutes later, long after the other passengers had disembarked.

There was a half full carton of orange juice in his refrigerator at the apartment. After a quick stop to finish off the O.J., he headed for the stadium. A good workout, followed by a long hot shower would sweat out what was left of the demon rum.

He was at the point of his exercise when he knew the body would not take much more. Suddenly there she was, standing casually near the place he had first seen her. He felt a surge of something powerful course through his body. Where a moment before, he had been at the point of complete exhaustion, he now felt a reserve of energy ready to carry him forward. If adrenalin is what Anton called the "fight or flight" hormone, it must have been something else, because he wasn't interested in fighting and the last thing in the world that he was about to do was run away. He was determined to make sure that she didn't either.

Her face was bright as she smiled a conspiratorial grin. He grinned in return.

"I came back looking for you," he admitted, "on Tuesday."

"I know. I was here."

"I didn't see you."

"I wasn't sure I wanted you to see me," she murmured, looking down at her shoes.

"But you do now," he spoke tentatively, yet it was a statement, not a question.

"Yes," voiced softly, eyes raising to meet his. It was as simple as that. Another line had been crossed.

"Do you think we're at the point of names?" he asked, taking the initiative.

"It would make things easier, wouldn't it?"

"Mine's Gil. Gil Beach."

"I'm Pilar."

"Pee-lar?" he repeated, imitating her pronunciation.

"Yes, but it's spelled P-i-l-a-r."

"Last name or first?"

"First."

Gil waited, wondering if she would choose to remain a mystery woman, or say more.

"The last name is Murphy. I got kidded so much as a child, that I still have a little insecurity about that, I guess."

"What's wrong with Murphy? Some of my best friends are Murphy's," he teased.

"No, I mean the combination. Pilar is Hispanic and Murphy so obviously Irish. They used to call me the "Mick Spick.""

"And it hurt, but you laughed?"

"Very perceptive, Officer Beach."

"Officer Beach?"

"Cops aren't the only ones that are trained to notice things ... like the police insignia on your sweatshirt."

Gil glanced down at his plain black top, then remembered.

"Oh, you mean Tuesday."

She nodded, smiling.

"So what else did you notice?" Doubt creeping into his voice.

"Are you sure you want to hear?"

"That bad?" he stammered, remembering that she had seen him when he wasn't aware of being observed.

"Oh no, not at all. I'm just in the habit of making sure a person wants my opinions before offering them. One of the rules for feedback is that it should only be given where it is requested."

"Sounds like encounter group stuff. What are you, a shrink?" His eyes narrowed.

She didn't answer directly. Her gaze bore into him, penetrating beyond the words he spoke to the feelings under them.

"You don't like mental health professionals much, do you?"

"Well, I had a bad experience with one."

"Many people do, Gil. There is very little quality control over the profession, and the training is all cognitive. A lot of crazy people are smart, and some of them seek out a career in mental health more because of the help they need than the help they can give."

"Yeah, there are some cops who are more problems than the criminals, too. But if you aren't a shrink, how do you know all this?"

"Well, I do some 'head shrinking' occasionally. But I'm a clinical psychologist. I had to do a lot of hands-on training, was required to go through personal psychotherapy, and have hundreds of hours of clinical supervision. I don't give out pills and don't make nearly as much money as a psychiatrist. I spend more time teaching than doing therapy, but I have a private practice so I can afford to teach."

"So if I want to know what you see, I'll get psychoanalyzed?"

"I don't do psychoanalysis, per se, and I don't read minds, either. But I have good observation and analytic skills."

"So what do you observe?" he asked, jaws tight.

She thought for a moment before answering. Putting her hand to her chin in the classic thinking pose, she pursed her mouth and formed a mock frown. Imitating the stereotypical germanic accent, she played a female Sigmund Freud.

"Vell, Mr. Betch, I see that you are a stair-climber, which means you vill get up in da vorld."

Her stillness, and laughter, made him realize how tense he was. He loosened, adding his chuckle to hers.

"I guess you don't have to be a psychologist to know I'm a little insecure," Gil admitted.

"Well, maybe more than 'a little.' But the truth is, a bit of insecurity is nice. As much as I try to help people gain self-esteem, too much self-affection can be damaging to the humble glands. I find a healthy amount of humility rather charming."

"You are very tactful. Was it my humility that brought you back here?"

"It didn't hurt. Neither did your obvious strength, discipline, or friendly manner. You have intelligent eyes, a nice way of speaking, and a cute tush."

Gil was surprised by her frankness and felt himself reddening. Yet he was also attracted by her honesty. He surprised himself with his matching frankness.

"Well I thought you were a knock-out the first time I saw you, Pilar. But I'm glad it's not just the package that's attractive. Am I going to get to know you better?"

"Oh yes, Gil. You certainly are."

Surprisingly, they started with reptiles. The Staten Island Zoo contends that it has one of the largest collections of reptiles on the east coast. Fortunately, reptiles don't take up much space, because other than that claim to fame, it was a small budget neighborhood facility, unknown to most people other than local residents. Pilar had suggested they visit the facility, and Gil was appreciating the choice. They could walk and talk comfortably as they could not have done in a more formal setting.

Soon they were standing outside a large wire cage, in which a large bird sat unmoving on a high perch. The sign said that it was a Golden Eagle.

"He looks a little bedraggled," Gil commented. "Somehow I can never get used to the idea of these big birds caged up."

"How do you know it's a HE?" Pilar countered.

It caught Gil by surprise. He hadn't really thought about it, just assuming that the big powerful bird of prey was male. He checked the printed sign again. The eagle was, in fact, a male, but when he looked back at Pilar, the grin on her face suggested that she had known that before her question.

"What, was I being sexist or something?" he asked with a nervous laugh. In recent years, words like "sexist" and "sexual harassment" had become familiar around the Precinct. Gil still wasn't sure about this woman. Was she a rabid women's libber who beat men over the head every time they used the wrong word? He had no problem with empowering women, but felt like sometimes the effort to be politically correct got unnecessarily aggressive.

"Actually, I think you're more sexy than sexist," she laughed. "You just looked so serious, I wanted to give you a hard time."

Gil found himself grinning. He had been kind of somber.

"Yeah, I guess I was kinda serious, wasn't I?"

"Let me guess. You were probably thinking that sometimes you feel like that caged eagle. Close?"

"I don't know if I like the way you can read me like a book," he laughed, though part of him meant it seriously. He still wasn't sure how much a psychologist could see into his thoughts.

"You're a nice book, mister. I like what I read inside. I just hope it has a happy ending."

"Maybe you should stick around and find out."

As soon as he said the words, he wondered why he had said them. The comment seemed kind of hokey. Besides, it was too soon in this relationship to start making noises about the future. Yet she didn't seem to recoil. In fact, she didn't say anything. She slid her arm into his and gave a little squeeze, as she led him away from the exhibit.

They were quiet as they walked, yet there was no uncomfortableness in the silence. As they moved past the cages, his hand dropped down, so that hers met it. Fingers found each other, intertwined. Gil felt a warmth spread up his arm from where her hand was linked to his. Something seemed to swell in his chest, and he couldn't get a silly grin off his face.

He felt like twenty, rather than forty years old. They bought crackers to feed the llama and popcorn to feed each other. At one point they raced each other to a water fountain; she beat him before he realized he couldn't outrun her unless he went all out, and maybe not then. She hadn't hesitated to give it her best. He liked that.

They exaggerated their negative reactions to the smell in the monkey house, made growling noises at the big cats, and made jokes about the huge tortoise. They stuffed themselves on junk food and were the last ones out when the gates closed for the night.

As Gil drove her back to where her car was parked at the college, he had fantasies of inviting her to his apartment, but did not act on them. He didn't want to spoil the day by rushing things. If he was entirely honest, he would have had to also admit that he was a little frightened by the intensity of his feelings. It all was a little too fast.

Her car was a four-year-old Volvo, parked near the end of the faculty lot, under a roof of solar panels. His police habits made him notice how deserted and dark the area was. His romantic impulses made him realize that it was also rather private. When he helped her out of his car, he felt an urge to kiss her. Yet in the end, it turned into a simple embrace. Or could a touch like that be called "simple?" She made the first move, stepping close to put her arms around him. He was conscious of her smell, the brush of her hair against his neck, the touch of her cheek to his. But it wasn't exactly a chaste hug, either. There was passion in it, and a hint that there was more to come.

He waited until she started her car and backed out of the spot, then followed to the parking lot exit. When she turned left on Howard Avenue, he found it hard to turn the other way. He drove the mile or so to his place and pulled slowly into the driveway. He didn't get out of the car right away, but sat there for a time, looking at the stars and twisting the wedding ring he still wore, from a relationship long ended.

Chapter 19

Friday, 10:25 a.m.

T.'n T., Inc. was located in a loft above an old paper factory. There was an ancient freight elevator, but Gil preferred the stairs. He climbed the four flights with little effort, his breathing normal a few seconds after reaching the big metal door of the office. The T.'n T. logo was a stylized picture of an explosion, with the agency name in the center of the blast, and "Home of Dynamite Talent" printed along the bottom. The logo was enlarged to cover the door and ten feet of wall. The door was the 'D' in Dynamite.

Gil rang the bell. A moment later a buzzer sounded, which released the lock. He pulled back on the handle and walked into a small combination receptionist office/ waiting room. One wall was covered with star photographs, posed and airbrushed to make aging performers look young, the homely ones attractive, and most likely, the bitchy ones friendly. A large desk was situated by the opposite wall, neat as a pin. As he looked around, a woman who could only be the "Annie" of yesterday's phone call came floating through a side door. A swirl of color and sheer fabric, she was swathed in scarves and blousy silken folds.

'Annie' was tall, standing only a few inches short of Gil's own six feet. Her jet black hair was precisely coiffured into a contemporary style that reminded him of a Roman centurion's helmet. Strong features with high cheekbones made her look the part of a fashion model, though she obviously carried more weight on her body than those emaciated types. The drape of the silks suggested a high and prominent bustline, narrowing to slim boyish hips. She wore a little more make-up than Gil liked to see on a woman, but the vivid red lips and cheek blush against a pale, almost-white base was striking. With dark ebony hair she had a stark look that gave the impression of a Kabuki theater actress, or Geisha. A characteristic head tilt as she spoke, made Gil wonder if she was purposely imitating some of that Asian tradition. Only the voice didn't match the image, as a sensual throaty resonance sounded echoes of wild days and wilder nights, whiskey-roughened songs and long forgotten innocence.

"Ahh, this must be the reticent Detective Beach. I had a pitcher of Bloody Marys mixed at eight forty-five." She mimed a little pout. Gil couldn't tell if she was joking or serious. He decided it was an act. After all, this was a theatrical agency, wasn't it?

"Well, that's your fault, Annie. After you mentioned the tag on your mattress, I mentioned it to the Lieutenant, and he had me up all night checking for people who tore theirs off."

"You didn't check on my mattress last night. But if you'd like to come around tonight, I'm sure something could be arranged," looking at him with hooded eyes, the lids iridescent with metallic eyeshadow, she blinked twice.

Gil was searching for a reply, when an inner door popped open near the side of the desk. A cherubic-looking man, perhaps in his forties, stepped through, dressed in painter's coveralls; squinting through eyeglasses grimy with dust. Medium height, with curly brown hair thinning on top and a quick energetic manner, the man was carrying what appeared to be a human head. The Detective started for a moment before he realized he was looking at the head portion of a ventriloquist dummy. Gil reminded himself he should use the term "figure" that he had picked up from his previous conversation with Annie. The man pulled off his glasses, and blinked, as if he had just come out into the light.

"Say, have you seen ... oh, hello. I'm Tom Tyler. You must be the detective Annie mentioned."

"Yes, the name is Beach, Gil Beach. Is this a good time for you?"

He was looking to escape the lure of the secretary as quickly as possible. It wasn't just his usual problem with women. After last night, the only woman he could think about was an intriguing psychologist on Staten Island. They had spent hours together, and in some portion of his mind he was still with her.

Today he had been up at the crack of dawn, bouncing around the apartment with an energy he had thought he would never again experience. He had a pretty good idea what was happening but drew back from the words to label it.

"No, this is fine," the answer to his question startled Gil out of his reverie. "Annie told me you were coming. Care for some coffee? It's decaf, if that's important to you."

"Fine, fine," the Detective answered, though he actually hated the de-natured stuff. If he ever had to give up caffeine, it would be the end of his career, he was sure. Real coffee was the life fluid of stakeouts, long interrogations, and late-night meetings. If you cut the artery of an average precinct detective, dark roast was likely to flow out rather than blood.

"I take it black, thanks."

"How about a couple cups, Annie?" Tyler waved the disembodied head on a stick at his secretary.

"Coming up," came a cheery reply.

The energetic craftsman gestured at Gil to come into the larger portion of the loft, darting ahead enthusiastically. The space was wide open, with no partitions or dividers, yet there were obviously different work areas suggested by furniture, cabinets or color schemes. Against one wall was a three-sided canvas enclosure coated with multiple swaths and specks of color, that must have been a spray-paint cage. Another wall held a dozen inanimate heads in varying stages of completion. A third was set up like a small theater, complete with microphone and lights. In front of it stood several large mirrors, facing toward the raised platform. The last side looked like a carpenter shop, with bandsaw, drill press, and grinding wheels standing in front of a huge pegboard panel where numerous hooks and holders were festooned with tools, coils of wire, rolls of different color tapes and other mysterious objects and supplies. Through the center of the vast loft were sewing machines, mounds of fabric, and racks holding a variety of what looked like children's clothing, much of it garish and gaudy. There were stacks of cardboard boxes, labeled with intriguing titles like, "hair" or "eyes," and barrels full of cotton-like fluff. Tyler moved two chairs together near the stage, pulling over a box to prop up his feet like a hassock.

"Welcome to the funhouse, as Kurt Vonnegut might say. Annie tells me you want to know something about vents."

"Yes, I do. And I appreciate your time. I'm kind of out of my element here, Mr. Tyler, so I'll apologize in advance if I use the wrong terminology, or step on any sacred cows of your profession."

"Step away. You can call me Tom, or T.T., and I don't offend easily. What do you want to know?"

"Well, I can't reveal some aspects of the investigation, but we think the person we're after has an interest in ventriloquism. Sometimes, in cases like this, the person uses an object or picture that is a central symbol to them, and this guy leaves a ventriloquism gadget at the scene of each crime."

"A vent gadget? Like what?"

Gil reached into his pocket and pulled out a baggie, with one of the little devices inside. Tyler looked at it briefly, and then smiled, and shook his head.

"Oh one of those silly things. Vents don't really use those. They're a con. It's a play on people's ignorance. You don't use tricks, gimmicks, or gadgets to be a vent. It's skill and talent."

"Very few people seem to manage doing it," Gil offered.

"Well, it's a complex skill, or actually 'skills', plural. A vent really is mastering four different things simultaneously. First, there is the technical aspect, the voice and mouth part- rapid back and forth speech without lip movement. Second, is the script writing, editing, and memorization of two parts. Third, this has to be delivered with decent vocal and acting skills. Then, finally, there is the puppet part, manipulating the figure to support the illusion."

"Illusion?"

"Yes, and that is why ventriloquism often gets tied in with magic. It's one specialized illusion, that consists of making people think a voice is coming from someplace it isn't."

"But don't uhh ... vents, throw their voice?"

"Of course not. Voices come from vibrating vocal cords. The only place a voice can come from is the person working as a vent. The rest is illusion, trying to get you to think it's not coming from there."

"I won't ask how that works."

"That's okay. It's no big secret."

The secretary oozed through the partially open workshop door, balancing a tray with two cups of steaming liquid, milk, sugar and a plate of cookies. As Gil grabbed a mug and a handful of Keeblers, the ventriloquist hardly paused in his lesson.

"Actually, the Gestalt psychologists explained it generations ago. But maybe you aren't interested in the theory."

"No, no, go ahead. I'm not sure if I'll understand, but let me try. What's psychology have to do with it?

"Well, it depends on a mental operation we all do without realizing it. The behavioral scientists call it 'completion.' If you see a series of dots in a circular pattern, your mind doesn't see a lot of unrelated dots, it completes the picture. So you see the pattern of a circle. The picture is mostly empty space, and separate dots, but the mechanism of 'completion' in your brain, links the dots into one figure you experience as a circle. The same thing works with sound and image. If you see an image and sounds that seem like they ought to go together, your brain unifies them."

"If you say so."

"Well, if you want an everyday example, consider television. What part of a T.V. set does the sound come from?"

"Speakers?"

"Yes. And often they are little tinny ones on the side of the set. The sound is never coming directly from the spot where the picture shows moving lips, or explosions, or whatever. But when the person in the picture moves their mouth, where does it seem like the sound is coming from?"

"I see what you mean."

"People flatter themselves that they can locate the source of a sound, but our abilities in that area are very limited. If I'm up on a stage fifty feet from you, there is no way you can distinguish whether the sound source is in one spot or another spot two feet adjacent. So my job as an illusionist is to make it more logical to your other senses to believe that the sound is coming from the figure I am holding, rather than from me."

"For instance?"

"For instance, the voice tone and character. I am a man, my figure is a little kid. If the voice sounds like a little kid's voice, your mind is more ready to expect it from the figure than from me. And then if his lips move, and mine don't..."

"My mind completes the picture, by connecting the voice to the dum... Oops, I mean 'figure'. "Gil answered, like an eager student.

"Right. And don't worry about the terminology. Although most of us prefer the word 'figure,' we use 'dummy' a lot of the time, too."

"But Annie said ..."

"Yeah, well…," Tom glanced around. The secretary had left the main area of the loft, but the office door was still ajar. He dropped his voice to a whisper.

"Annie can get a little opinionated at times. She has amazing knowledge of the field, but she can be a bit rigid about rules, traditions and all that."

Gil noticed that Tom had settled back, like he was enjoying his role of answer man. The Detective didn't mind priming the pump with a few questions. He wasn't entirely sure what he was searching for anyway. Perhaps something would reveal itself, as they discussed different parts of the subject.

"Are there many suppliers of figures?"

"Well, I don't know how many little amateur operations there are, but if you are talking about classic hard figures, I have about four main competitors. There are a lot of others that do soft figures, and a fair number of vents attempt their own constructions."

"Is that pretty complicated?"

"Definitely, though it depends on the type. Do you remember Paul Winchell?"

"A bit before my time, but my folks were fans Oh sure, he had a television show, didn't he? Paul Winchell and ... and ..."

"Jerry Mahoney. Winchell was one of the greatest, and he made his own figures. He started with figure construction and became so creative that he ended up leaving the business and becoming a medical inventor."

"You're kidding."

"No, really. He developed an artificial heart valve, among other things. Probably got the idea from some of his lever and spring machines for the figures. Want to see one?"

"Sure," the detective answered, though not sure if the ventriloquist was referring to a spring mechanism or a dummy. It turned out that he meant both.

Tom walked over to the row of puppets under construction. Each head was fastened at the neck to a wooden dowel. It reminded Gil of some awful scene out of history where a villain had impaled enemies' severed heads on poles. Tom selected one male head that looked complete, a kind of goofy country bumpkin with freckles and a turned-up nose. Tom swung it around, reaching under the hairline to expose a small clasp. He undid the hook, which allowed him to swing a portion of the scalp back on a hinge. It reminded Gil of the autopsy procedure, where the examiner opened the skull to examine the corpse' brain. But instead of the folds and bulges of a living being, Tom exposed a jumble of wires, springs, swivels and couplings.

Gil suddenly felt a wave of weakness flow over him, and was glad he was sitting down. There was no longer any doubt in his mind about the killer's intent. Seeing the artificial skull opened like a cookie jar was enough to make the connection. Now Gil knew. The monster they were seeking was making grotesque parodies of a ventriloquist dummy. And he was making them out of humans.

"Are you alright?" Tom asked, noticing the pallor of his visitor's face.

"Yeah, I'm okay," Gil shrugged off the concern, "But I'm sure now, that the guy we're after has some experience in all this. Some of this is too familiar to be a coincidence. You say that you know your main competitors?"

"Not personally. But I know who they are."

"Like Billy Barstow?" Gil asked, trying to show that he had done his homework. Tyler gave a guffaw.

"Hah! Barstow? That's like saying the guy selling watches off a blanket in Times Square is a major timepiece producer. Barstow doesn't even create figures; he just sells cheap mass-produced dolls.

No, there isn't anybody in New York. Three of the four are in California. One is in Texas. I'm not counting the McElroys, who are retired. The best right now are probably Bill Nelson and Chuck Jackson."

"Present company excepted, I suppose," Gil added good-naturedly.

"Yeah, well, I do try to make the best product possible. No short-cuts, no cheap materials. I almost hate to see them sold, I put so much time into each one. Most builders are the same. It's hard to believe that craftsmen would get involved in criminal activity. If the crime was in New York, I guess I would have to be a prime suspect, since the others aren't local."

Gil began to see that tracing the killer this way was not likely to get very far, but he decided to keep fishing.

"Not to worry. Where would I learn more about all this?"

"Well, I'll be glad to tell you anything you want to know. As for figures and the history of the field, you'd probably have to go to Kentucky."

"Kentucky?"

"Yes, there's a museum there, called the Vent Haven Museum, in Fort Mitchell, Kentucky, right near Cincinnati, Ohio. It started as a personal collection of a guy named William Shakespeare Berger, but now it's open to the public. The last I heard, there are around six hundred figures on display, many of them very rare or famous. There are also books, pictures, carving tools, films, and all kinds of other stuff."

"Did you say carving tools? To carve the heads?" Gil thought of a hacked and sliced corpse lying on a stainless-steel gurney in the morgue.

"Well, yes, that was the old way. We don't use real wood anymore, except for the handle. Some have used plaster, and some of the new ones are made of plastic. It's just a matter of time until 3D printers start making them, but it will be a while before the traditionalists go that route. I'm sort of a middle-of-the-roader, since I use plastic wood and wood fiber strips."

"So a contemporary builder wouldn't be likely to use carving knives?" the Detective pursued his thought.

"No, that's historical stuff. Nobody has actually carved a figure for a long time. If you go back to the time of Harry "The Great" Lester, there were some wood figures. He was inspired by Arthur Prince, an English vent who helped popularize the specialty before the turn of the century. Lester gave lessons to Edgar Bergen and Charles "Master" Bradley. If I remember correctly, a guy named Bill Wallace carved the first Charlie McCarthy for Bergen in 1945, and Bradley did his own woodcarving for the first Melvin, when "The Master and Melvin" made their debut in 'forty-eight'."

"Doesn't sound like much you don't know about this, Tom. What about your family? I understand you go back a-ways in this field."

"I guess we do. Grampa Tyler got into it by accident. He was a toymaker by trade. In 1896 another English vent, Fred Russell, was touring the States, and met my grandfather over a glass of ale in a Philadelphia pub catering to English nationals. Grampa Tyler had just come over from Surrey. He was only twenty-two years old but was talented at making toys and getting laughs with his storytelling. He probably would have made a good salesman, too. It only took him a few minutes to convince Russell that he could carve him a figure better than the one the performer was currently using. The vent took him up on the challenge. A month later, my Granddad had a new sideline. As eager young vents turned to Russell for inspiration, he directed them to Grandpa for quality figures. Gramps was more a father to me than my own dad, and he taught me the trade. He died a few years ago, but up until the last he was still active, even at ninety-two."

An insistent beeping noise caught Gil's attention. It was his own phone, reminding that it was noon. He had to get back to the Precinct for a mandatory training session and then pick up his niece Jennifer at her school. As it was, lunch would have to be a hot dog from Nedicks. He grinned an apologetic smile and shrugged his shoulders.

"I guess that will have to be it. I appreciate your time, Tom. You've been very helpful."

"Well, I don't know what help I've been, but if I can provide any assistance, please call me, or stop by. Come to think of it, if you want to how it looks on stage, you can catch my act this weekend at the Lonestar Cafe. I work between the big-name country western acts. Gopher and I do our "Pardners" routine. Annie can give you a pass for free admission—just ask her on your way out."

The Detective nodded, then started to walk toward the exit, but stopped and turned.

"Okay Tom, but I wonder if you could satisfy my morbid curiosity. Do ventriloquists really talk to their dummies when no one else is around?"

T.T. laughed. "The old weird stuff, eh? Somehow ventriloquism has always seemed creepy to people. Maybe it's the connection to magic, maybe it's the similarity of figures to dead people, or maybe even some of the ways ventriloquism has been used in the past to fool or manipulate people. I don't know, but vents are mostly folks just like everybody else. Probably a good twenty-five percent of active vents today are evangelists and other religious types using their skills in kids' services or revivals. There are good guys and bad guys, crazy and sane, just like any other profession. Do vents talk to their figures? Sure, some do. Just like little girls talk to their dolls, or boys to their action figures. Most of us aren't schizos, but we spend much of our professional life doing everything we can to make it seem like that figure has a personality and life of its own. After a while, it's easy to treat him like he's real. Sometimes it's just for fun."

"As for me," Tom continued, but with a more subdued tone. "There were times I had nobody around and I needed someone to talk to. Even as a kid I was doing vent routines professionally. My first figure was named Checkers. Plenty of times, I would pull

Checkers out of his trunk and tell him what was bothering me. He was a pretty good listener."

Moisture started forming in the man's eyes, but he gave a sniff, picked up the disembodied head, and started tinkering with the workings.

"Thanks." Gil said simply. It could have been for the two hours of information, but he meant it as much for letting Gil get to know the real Tom Tyler.

As he left, Annie was nowhere in sight, so he didn't have to ask her for a "pass" and get the expected flirtatious response. He let himself out of the door, his head spinning with thoughts of talking mannequins and dead children.

Chapter 20

Friday, 12:10 p.m.

"You can't be serious! You are seeing a COP? What is it, some kind of macho obsession or something?"

Pilar's friend, Rosemary Ginzberg stopped shoveling spoons-full of ice cream and gooey toppings into her mouth long enough to drop her jaw in mock horror. She was on a 'slip' from her diet program and making the most of it. Roe was a psychiatric social worker at an outpatient clinic near the college, one of the few persons who related to Pilar without contrivance. She was as flamboyant and individualistic as she was intelligent. Whatever Roe thought, Roe said. Sometimes that could be embarrassing, but it was a breath of fresh air compared to the controlled style of academics and psychiatric prima donnas Pilar often had to deal with. Rosemary was anything but dull.

"Look, honey, if you like guns, I know a Freudian analyst that would love to get you on his couch. Actually, he got me on his couch a couple times and showed me his big gun! Ha-Ha. But, honey, a cop? You know…"

"Yes, I know, I know," Pilar cut her off, which was about the only way to have a conversation with the energetic eccentric, who would talk nonstop for hours if allowed. "And frankly, I'm still not totally sure what the original attraction was, but he is really a special person, once you get past the surface."

"Oh sure, every bum has a heart of gold."

"No, that's not what I mean. Actually, his surface is pretty nice, too." They exchanged glances, Rosemary raising her eyebrows in a lecherous expression, while Pilar grinned. "I mean, he is very sweet and shy, and intelligent. But he's obviously had a lot of pain, and he has to work hard to let down the defenses."

"This isn't one of those 'savior woman finds troubled man to change,' is it?" Pilar's friend asked.

"Well, I know I can't be very objective, but I don't think so, Roe. I don't think he needs all that much changing. In fact, I think the main thing he needs to do is realize that."

"Love is in the air ...," Rosemary began the chorus of an old tune.

"Okay, okay, give me a break," Pilar protested, then added in a serious tone, "you know it's been a long time since I met someone that made me feel anything exciting. Don't be too quick to categorize him. I am, you know, a pretty good judge of character."

Rosemary knew when to be serious. "I agree it's been too long, Pilar, dear. And even if I'm a pain in the ass, I am really happy for you. I'm just a little behind you in getting to know this guy. Maybe a little protective, too. You feel like you know that much about him?"

"We talked last night for over three hours, during a trip to the zoo."

"Nothing like overwhelming the girl with extravagance."

"It was my idea. I wanted to talk, not be pampered. The zoo was just right. Look, Roe, I can do a complete psych evaluation of a client after a forty-five-minute interview. This was four times that much time."

"Something tells me he was doing some interviewing, too."

"Of course. But I think I know what I'm getting into here. I like him, Roe, I really do."

"You plan on mentioning this to Peter?"

Pilar's eyes rounded, her shoulders slumped. "Oh shit."

"Me and my big mouth, eh?" Rosemary said, wincing.

Pilar straightened. "Well, I'll cross that bridge when I come to it." Her thoughts, however, were not so easily marshaled. Scenarios kept forming in her mind, of Peter angry, Peter devastated, or perhaps worse, Peter completely unconcerned. Conversely, she imagined telling Gil Beach about her current arrangement with the fellow faculty member, or his finding out, and various possible reactions that might follow. Then she thought about losing both relationships. But her habit of self-honesty came to her rescue. There was no relationship with Peter, she decided, or at least no relationship sufficient to meet her real needs as a woman, as a human being, and as a person of value. She had been selling herself short for a long time, but it took a taste of the real thing to realize she had been eating a non-nutritive substitute for love.

Last night had ended with a hug. Not a kiss, not a sexual encounter. Yet she had never felt closer to a man, even when physically joined in the sex act. In a matter of hours, they had developed a relationship. Still tentative? Yes, but there was also a true sense of intimacy. Pilar had a suspicion that physical union would eventually follow. The chemistry between them was potent. But there was no hurry. When that part came, it would only add spice to the recipe, the main ingredients were already there.

Pilar was glad that Gil was not one who bolstered his self-esteem by sexual conquests. She gathered that he had been faithful to his wife, even during her long illness, and appeared to have had limited emotional entanglements in the years following her death. Although he spoke lovingly of that first marriage, he did not appear to be obsessed with it, either. There was some unfinished business for him in his relation to women, but she couldn't quite peg what that was, yet. Every now and then, he seemed almost frightened. Trust was clearly an issue, but so far, he had been able to overcome his hesitancy, or at least set it aside enough to disclose himself. Eventually, she would have to get a better picture of his family of origin. From the conversation of last night, she had learned that his parents were dead so he had been raised by grandparents, but nothing of the quality of that environment, or how his parents had died.

She suddenly became aware of Rosemary's amused face, across from her.

"You've really got it bad, Pilar. Do you think you can come back from dreamland long enough to split the check?"

"Oh, sorry Roe," she reached for her shoulder bag.

"I guess I'm not very good company today."

"No sweat, hon. Actually, it's nice to see a crack in that totally capable, wonder-woman facade once in a while."

They split the check, agreeing to get together later in the week at a continuing education workshop. Roe extracted the promise of a telephone call, if anything new developed in Pilar's romantic relationship.

The Friday faculty meeting had been in session for almost half-an-hour when Pilar eased in the side door. Wallace "Wally" Washburn, the Dean of Fine Arts was nearing the end of a presentation on the need to support the local community theater group. He must have been his usual long-winded self, as this was the first item on the printed agenda. Pilar slid into a seat next to Margaret Jameson, a new instructor in the chemistry department, and opened a loose-leaf notebook. Notes of important items of business were recorded on one side of the book, but on the other side she started a letter to her mother. Seventy-five per cent of the meeting content was usually useless or irrelevant to the Psychology faculty, so Pilar saw little sense in wasting all that time. Tapping away at a laptop would have been obviously rude, but during the less vital agenda items, she kept up on her correspondence with paper and pen. She felt something had been lost in the current reliance on email instead of actual written letters. She tried to write to her mother, Maria, at least every other week, calling on the phone the alternating weeks.

Maria Velez Murphy was a tiny woman with a big heart. She was Puerto Rican by birth. A tough little fighter, she had overcome a difficult childhood of poverty and struggle. She had been raised by her mother, after her father had decided family was not his main priority. Maria tried to find security by marrying Willie Brady, a car-parts retailer who treated her like one of his carburetors. She was very religious, so was dismayed to find herself falling in love with a dynamic priest, Father Ian Murphy. Certain that her feelings were the epitome of sin, she told no one and carried it in her heart for years. As fortune would have it, Willie was killed in an auto accident, along with a nameless woman, about a hundred miles from where he was supposed to be at a training session. The priest spent a great deal of time comforting Maria. Over time, to her amazement, the long suppressed affection found an answering response.

Pilar never found out if Ian decided to leave the priesthood first, and then began a romance with her mom, or vice versa. But if there was such a thing as a match made in heaven, this was it. You couldn't imagine a more devoted couple. They always referred to each other as "my fit," and Pilar never had the trouble most children had in picturing their parents as sexual beings. The romance of the relationship was apparent in every look and touch.

Pilar was actually the child of Maria's first husband but thought of Ian as her true father. She had legally taken his name. She had a good experience upon which to build her image of men, and a great model for patterning a love relationship. That was part of the reason her emotional hunger was so intense. She knew what a meaningful union was like. She also knew that she didn't want to live with something less.

The faculty meeting seemed to go on forever, but finally it concluded with a great scraping of chairs and tension-relieving laughter. Pilar headed toward the Hawks Nest coffee shop with a sense of foreboding. She would meet Peter as usual but did not look forward to the ritual. After an evening enjoying uncomplicated conversation with a down-to-earth yet more exciting man, the word games she expected from Peter would contrived and childishly indirect. He was waiting in a booth near the video game room, two coffees already sitting on the table.

"Ah Pilar, how nice to see you. The coffee is hot, just poured."

"Thanks, Peter." She threw her coat over a hook and sat down. She found it hard to meet his eyes.

"Nada, my dear, nada. Thank God it's Friday, eh wat?" he bubbled in an odd mixture of a Spanish term with his usual vaguely-English-accented affectation. "Looking forward to a nice weekend. Probably just stay around the old chalet, you know, but not a spot of work if I can help it. How about you? Got plans?"

'Got plans?' was code for an invitation to end up in bed. He had skipped the usual preliminaries. Pilar recognized the invitation to spend the weekend at his place. Instead of answering in code, she just replied spontaneously.

"I don't know what I'm doing this weekend, Peter."

He looked puzzled. This wasn't how the conversations on Friday usually went. His hands fluttered in his lap. Had he always had such effeminate mannerisms, Pilar wondered or was she contrasting him to the powerful male presence of Gil Beach? Peter tried again.

"Ah yes, I see. Well, as I said, I'm up for a weekend at home. Actually, my dear, I could really use some friendly relaxation."

Pilar recognized the invitation to sex. She sighed. It all seemed so phony, so invented. The thought of uninspired sex with Peter seemed about as appealing as fornication with a department store clothes mannequin. How had she gotten mired into this pattern anyway? It wasn't like her to be false and obtuse. Then and there, she decided to stop.

"Peter, there's no one anywhere near us. If you want me to come over to your place and have sex, why don't you say so?"

After he stopped choking on his coffee, Peter blustered and fretted for several minutes, without saying anything worth hearing. It mostly consisted of wondering why she was being "difficult."

"I don't know what's gotten into you, my Dear."

"Nothing's gotten into me, Peter. Nothing's gotten into me in a long time. Nothing fresh, nothing new, nothing nurturing, nothing exciting."

Surprising herself with the level of anger she was expressing, she found herself rising to an even greater level of venom.

"You may have fucked me, but you didn't really get into me. You didn't put anything in me that counted." She could hardly believe the passion of her outburst. It was obvious that she had been saving up feelings for a long time. Truthfully, Peter didn't deserve the intense lambasting. A lot of the anger she was channeling was directed at herself. She had let herself get into the situation. She knew that she was an adult and generally took responsibility for her own choices. But before she had a chance to apologize, Peter had already flounced off, mortally offended. Direct expression of feelings was not his cup of tea. Pilar wasn't sure if she was disappointed or relieved.

An hour later she was on the phone with Gil. They talked of music, finding they had similar tastes; both enjoying a wide variety of jazz, popular music, classics, folk music... even some country and western. They discussed books, discovering they were entirely different in their favorites—she loved Geraldine Brooks and Margaret Atwood, he liked C.J. Box and William Kent Kreuger. They were closer in their movie preferences, although he was more into action films and she enjoyed more romantic themes.

She suggested getting together after classes but was disappointed that he had other plans. When she learned it was a long-standing commitment to his little niece, her disappointment was mixed with warm feelings for this man who kept his promises to a child.

Chapter 21

Friday, 3:13 p.m.

The Stuyvesant School for Bright and Gifted Children was located in a large brownstone on East Sixteenth. Gil pushed through the glass doors, etched with the torch symbol of enlightenment, poking his head in the first-floor office. He often picked Jennifer up on Fridays when her mother got home late from work as a cosmetologist. The school was only blocks from the boundaries of the Ninth Precinct, and Gil loved the role of favorite uncle. The child could take a bus to her uptown condo home, where a neighbor would babysit until her mother got home. But if Gil wasn't tied up in work too much to get her, he enjoyed the time with Jennifer. Today he was fulfilling a promise to take her shopping for a new dollhouse. It was near her birthday. For weeks she had been looking forward to buying the miniature dwelling he had offered as his present. She knew exactly the kind she wanted.

It probably wouldn't have mattered what they were buying. They usually had fun together. Sometimes the two of them just went to a nearby ice cream shop where they goofed around for an hour or so until Sheila could be expected home, waiting. Occasionally, they even set off on a discovery trip to a museum or other attraction. The secretary at the school knew Gil, so he was caught off-guard when he found a different person sitting behind the desk.

"Can I help you, Sir?" a middle-aged woman with elaborately styled silver hair and jeweled eyeglasses hanging from an ornate neck-cord challenged, a subtle note of aggression in her tone.

"I'm here to pick up Jennifer—Jennifer Beccarelli. I'm her uncle."

The woman's attitude did not relax.

"We don't allow anyone to pick up a child, except the parent or guardian."

"I pick Jennifer up at least twice a week."

"I don't make the rules, I just enforce them."

"You sound like a cop."

"Sir, if you are going to be rude, I will have to ask you to leave."

Gil felt himself begin to grow angry but tried to keep control. He read the woman's name from an identification tag on her blouse.

"Ms. McCallister, I don't know where Kathy, the regular secretary is today, but most of the staff here know me by sight. I realize you are trying to do your job and protect the children, but you're going a little overboard."

The woman stiffened. *Wrong choice of words.*

"Whether I know you or not has nothing to do with it. Unless you have a written authorization to show me, you had better leave, or I will be forced to call the police."

It was a perfect verbal set-up. Some officers waited for moments like this. The hot ones could yell, "I AM a cop, asshole, so do the fuck what I tell you to do!" The cool ones preferred to stare an icy glare, and casually flip out their badge to the chagrin of the threatening citizen.

Gil was not cool, and, unfortunately, he couldn't always predict his own thermostat. He never knew if he would stop at "hot," or keep going until an emotional explosion happened. He didn't know how well he could control his anger, so he usually tried to keep a lid on it.

In this situation Gil was already past the point of calm reasoning. He could have shown his badge. He could have forced the stubborn woman to check her records or the written authorization which was on file. He could have insisted on seeing the headmistress, Ms. Armbruster. But right now, he couldn't think of anything but taking the woman's head off. Before he completely lost his cool, he turned, seething, and walked out of the building.

Regina Bradford McCallister watched him exit, heaving a sigh of relief. Though refusing to show it, she had been frightened. He was a big man, angry, like the man who had once tried to assault her. Regina had a hard time trusting men anymore. Underneath even the most placid exterior, she knew, might lie the heart of a rapist.

She had heard very little of what the big man had said. When he walked right in, unannounced, it was too upsetting for her to maintain her composure. She suspected that he was potentially dangerous. In any case the brute shouldn't have the right to walk in anywhere he wanted. The idea of letting him take one of the little girls was more than alarming. To her he seemed a shady character, or he would not have left the minute she mentioned the police. She had a mind to call them, just the same, to report the strange visitor. She could also tell them about the other one—the man in camouflage army clothing and big boots who had been sitting on the stoop across the street for almost an hour. That one pretended to read a paper, but she knew he was watching. She was afraid he was watching her through the office window and might be waiting for her to leave for the day.

Regina decided to call her driver to bring the limousine early. She was only helping out at the school while the secretary was ill. She was a volunteer, after all. As a benefactress of the institution, she liked to see how things were done now and then, but that didn't include taking personal risks. She really ought to call the police, but that was sure to result in a lot of bother. Perhaps they would laugh at her, like ignorant men often did. Kathy, the usual secretary would be back tomorrow, so if any problems continued, the regular worker could handle them. She would be much better prepared, since she worked there daily. Regina picked up the telephone which she used to call Juanita, her driver.

As an afterthought, the woman glanced out the window, just as the man who tried to get Jennifer emerged from the front entrance, exiting through the etched glass portal. From the bow window of the office she could observe him without herself being seen. She huffed, as she saw him climb into a car parked in an illegal zone. As he pulled out from the curb, with a squeal of burning rubber, she thought "Good riddance," and turned away from the window, just as the man in camouflage clothing stepped out of concealment behind a parked van. The man's hidden eyes narrowed under the bush hat, and the hands clenched until his knuckles showed white.

CHAPTER 22

Friday, 3:20 p.m.

It was like being violated, seeing the loathsome policeman enter one of the zones of influence. The Performer stood rigid, trembling with emotions this triggered in him, this trespass. The interloper had entered the 'Place of Gifts', where there should be no power in competition with his own. He, himself, had not even entered the zone physically. It was not yet time. Each place had a precise chronological position in the grand cosmic pattern that was being revealed. The Performer had to be very patient.

He had spent an hour at the Dragon Place this afternoon, staring at the entrance sign. They called the nondescript building on Sixth Street, "St. George's Catholic School," but the observer in his army fatigues and jungle hat knew that they were wrong. The picture on the sign showed a crusader thrusting at a serpent with his spear, and the ignorant might think the lance-wielder was victorious. The Performer knew better. It was the dragon that carried the power—the dragon with his armored scales, as impenetrable as the defenses of the Master himself. No attack could overcome such a shield.

He recalled a game his father liked to play with admirers. Proud of his ability to wear a role, a mask, the evil man had bragged that he could keep his face expressionless, no matter how someone acted or tried to get him to smile. Sure enough, true to his boast, no matter how they mugged or joked or acted outrageously, the man's face never broke into even a trace of a smile. In show business this expressionless pose was called "deadpan." Now deadpan was a skill that the Performer had mastered even beyond his father's level. He could live within a shell impenetrable to the outside world, under complete control. No one could approach his ability to deadpan. The word was ironic, as a matter of fact—"DEAD pan." Because it was the mask he favored when he chose to release someone—to set his chosen ones free from the burdens and tragedy of life. It was not killing, in the mind of the Performer, it was a bestowal of freedom. It was release, a benefaction.

The Performer realized that he had almost forgotten his latest acquisition. He had not released the little one yet. There hadn't been enough time since the last one. He hadn't even buried the left-over parts under the basement floor, with the others. He was still in a state of grace—a pocket of calm in the chaos of life. There had not yet developed the other less comfortable state of need in his gut which signaled the right spiritual plane. This more agitated state developed slowly. The first time he released a soul had been followed by several months of peace. After the second, it was a month. For quite a while, four to six weeks was enough, but then it had gotten to be less. Lately, he felt the urge more and more often. Even a week seemed long, now. But still, there had to be a waiting time, a ripening. Up until this afternoon the Performer had not been ready. But having seen the policeman violate the Place of Gifts with his unholy presence, made the inner psychic door swing open. Inside was the molten fire of rage, to match the glacial chill of the Deadpan.

It took only a few minutes to reach home and ascend to the museum. The cage was stored in a large closet near the rear of the display area. With the closet doors closed, you could hardly hear the moans and whimpers of the new figure.

The Performer carefully removed the fatigues he was wearing, completed the necessary ritual, then slipped into his carving clothes.

Chapter 23

Friday, 4:22 p.m.

Detective Colin Treadwell was tired. Lately, it seemed he was always tired. Last night had been like so many others. He probably hadn't slept three hours, total. Throughout the workday, it seemed like an immense effort to do anything. He arranged files, did some of Dwight White's paperwork, carried a couple of files down to Record Retention, busying himself with any unimportant task he could find, drank dozens of cups of coffee, and checked the mailroom half a dozen times. He always carried a couple of inter-office envelopes with him on his trips, to make it look like he had a purpose. The envelopes were as empty as his spirit.

He sat in on a training session about new developments in computerized record-keeping which used up most of the afternoon. Normally, Colin would have left work by now, but he preferred to avoid the crowd that filled the muster room at change of shifts. He was supposed to attend, but seldom did so anymore. No one seemed to notice.

Checking the mailroom once more would take the necessary last few minutes until the assembly area cleared out. Colin walked downstairs, where he slipped into the gloomy closet that served as a mail and communication transfer point. In the cubbyhole marked "P.D.U." with fading label tape, he found an inter-office envelope addressed to "Mabry," and a small package for Gil Beach. The good news was that this gave Colin a valid reason for his last trip to the mailroom that day. The bad news was that he had to go back upstairs to deliver the contents. He made a note on his ever-handy pad, then worked his way up the iron staircase and down the dimly lit hall to the glass door of the unit offices. He dropped Mabry's envelope into the Sergeant's "In" tray, then flipped the package onto Beach's desk.

Finally, he felt it was late enough to leave. Slowly, with effort, Treadwell slipped a coat over his slumping shoulders and made his way out to the old Chevy that he drove to work. There was a new Pontiac at home, but he knew better than to bring it into the city. Easing out of the parking lot where he got a special discount rate, the wilted detective turned uptown. Although not an official vehicle, the car was equipped with a police radio. Treadwell usually turned it off as soon as he left the Precinct. Over the years, he had managed to arrange his work so that he seldom had to be out in the street, and never in a direct-action responsibility. At some point it had just gotten too much. Just coming in to work each day was like climbing a mountain.

It hadn't always been that way. It was only a couple of years ago that he had stopped believing he could accomplish anything as a cop, or as a person. His personal life had convinced him that the evil was stronger than anything the law could throw against it. So he stopped believing in such a thing as safety and security. That was when he started entertaining a constant companion called fear. He stopped believing in possibility and in the future, which taught him dread. He stopped believing in the Job, which took away his sense of purpose, and he stopped believing in himself, which took away his spirit.

The radio buzzed, crackled, and squawked with the dispatchers' voices. A robbery was in progress at the Roosevelt projects, and a marauding gang of vandals were reported over by Jacob Riis Homes. Housing Authority Police were supposed to respond in the projects, but there were so few of them, that they seldom were anywhere near the location they were needed. As far as Treadwell and many other members of the N.Y.P.D. were concerned, this was probably not a big loss. To most civilians, a cop was a cop. And when it came to certain subjects, law-enforcement officers presented a united front. But there are many different species of cops. In Treadwell's less than objective opinion, Housing Authority cops were just a step above

Police Auxiliary, the poorly trained and monitored civilian force that supplemented the real force at major public events and such. But he knew that no cop thought less of anybody, than one of their own that wouldn't be available to back up a fellow officer.

As long as he was able to remain in the stationhouse, Treadwell never had to face the inner conflict that a code Ten-Thirteen would create. Normally, if an "Officer Needs Assistance" call came into the Precinct, he wouldn't even hear about it until responding officers had already taken care of the incident. In his car, however, it was another story. As long as he was physically on the territory of the Precinct, Treadwell forced himself to pretend that he was available for an emergency. But in truth, other than a Ten-Thirteen, there wasn't much that could cause the burned-out man to even consider responding. So it became a little game he played. He kept the radio on, waiting for the call that would force him to choose. He always made a note of the time when he switched off. Twice that he knew of, an emergency call had gone out within ten minutes of when he left the net. One day he would be too slow. An inescapable emergency would happen while he was still on-line. As he crossed Fourteenth, Treadwell reached over and turned off the receiver, marking the time on his pad.

Back in the Precinct office, blue shades cut off most of the light to the area. For the moment, except for Lieutenant Lincoln, who was closed in his private room, Gil was the only person in the shuttered PDU. He stood, staring at a fraying wall map, trying to cool down before calling Sheila and explaining why he didn't pick up her daughter from school.

He glanced over at his desk, saw a package lying there, walked over and picked it up. There was no return address. He tore open the paper to reveal a slim box, similar to the type that held wallets or coin purses.

At first, when he opened the container, he didn't understand what he was seeing. When the nauseating reality dawned, he almost threw the box down. Instead, he carefully lowered it to the desk in a slow-motion descent, before collapsing in the chair. For a moment his thoughts were of war. Gil's brother had died in the war. Despite his step-parent's objections, Beach had signed up, too. He found it was different than he had expected. Not the training. That might surprise some pale weak-kneed nerds, but Gil soon found he was able to handle both the physical and mental demands. Being deployed for real was something else.

For one thing there were some crazy yahoos in the 'Sandbox' that took to killing like flies to horseshit. Some of them turned into little more than sub-humans. Others took the opportunity of that insane war to live openly as the animals they had always been. It was not unusual to see a soldier with a cluster of little shriveled pieces of flesh tied to his belt or helmet. But that was war. Another time, another place. This was Gil's town. This was not supposed to be a slaughter house. Yet, what was in the box was a child's ear, with a curling strand of hair that could not be anything other than the ritual ear locks worn by Hasidic Jews.

"Damn, Damn, Damn," the Detective repeated, slamming his fist onto the desk surface. Wetness blurred his vision. Then a chill ran through him, as he grabbed for the wrapping paper, looking for an address. There it was, just as he had expected. "Detective Gil Beach, Ninth Precinct, N.Y.P.D., 321 Fifth Street, New York, N.Y." There was no zip code, and no postage. The implications were shaking. It meant that the killer not only knew he was on the case but had managed to have the package hand-delivered to him.

Gil felt a wash of emotion flow over him. There was no going back now. First there had been the taunting set-up in the drafty garage, inviting someone to play. Now the opponents had been chosen. Forget public relations handouts and theoretical task forces. Now it was hunter and hunted. And like a mongoose and rattler locked in a dance of deadly attraction, once engaged, neither could back-off until there was a winner and a loser. He dreaded the siege to come, yet welcomed it too. At least some of the uncertainty was past.

He sat in frowning concentration for almost ten minutes, then reached for a battered worn file box, pulled out a card and picked up the phone. The number he entered was for the F.B.I.'s National Center for the Analysis of Violent Crime (NCAVC) in Quantico, Virginia. There were cops who would avoid any contact with the F.B.I. that they possibly could, but Gil was not one of them. In some cases, the feds' reputation for ignorant arrogance was justified, but they had access to technology no local force could match, such as the use of artificial intelligence technology in crime analysis and criminal personality profiling. Several computer systems are involved in the FBI's Violent Criminal Apprehension Program (VICAP). The VICAP computers, themselves, are located at F.B.I. headquarters in Washington D.C., but a secure telecommunications network links them with those of the NCAVC in Quantico. Through what they call "template pattern matching," any crime can be compared with an immense data bank of violent crimes, producing the top ten "matches," i.e., crimes similar to the one reported. The system was also able to produce a criminal profile, describing the motivation and behavioral characteristics of the perpetrator. The analyses aren't flawless, but often very accurate in describing the kind of person to look for. AI was making it even better.

That was the treasure. Unfortunately, you had to go through an elaborate maze of bureaucracy and red tape to get to the gold. Each of the forty-nine FBI field offices has a "Criminal Profile Coordinator," to whom any case must first be submitted for review and administrative handling. If the Coordinator is convinced that it is worthwhile to submit a request to the Behavioral Science Unit, only then is the process initiated. A "Crime Analyst" is assigned to the case at VICAP, to whom the computer reports are returned, after predictable delays. The Analyst determines what data to send back to the Field Office Coordinator, who then decides what data to give to the requesting agency. Gil didn't intend to go through all that. Instead, he called a friend.

It's amazing how much police work depends on what you have going outside the system or at least outside the regular channels. A detective's own network of contacts, friends, and people who owe him favors can make the difference between an effective investigator, and one who gets nowhere.

Gil had attended the police academy with Archie Eastwood. Among other favors, Gil helped him get through the two-mile run when it seemed he was doomed to failure. Archie moved to the State Patrol as soon as he could manage it. Then, after five years in "New York's Elite," as they liked to style themselves, he applied to the Bureau and was accepted as an Agent-In-Training. Eastwood already had a bachelor's degree in applied psychology, laboriously completed through years of night school, so he quickly moved into the Behavioral Science Unit. His normal duties were devoted to the 'proactive' investigation strategies, which was the jargon for preventative or anti-crime police work, as opposed to 'reactive' strategies, which were the PDU's bailiwick. But when Gil needed entry into the NCAVC information system, he had a marker with Eastwood that he could call in. The conversation was brief.

"Yes, who's this?"

"Gil Beach, up in New York."

"Oh, hello, Gabby. What can I do for you?"

I need a favor, Harry." Gil used the nickname they had given Archie at the academy, derived from linking the name Eastwood to the actor, Clint Eastwood, and then applying the name of that star's famous role, "Dirty Harry."

I didn't think you called to wish me happy Thanksgiving. I haven't heard from you in ages. But I owe you one, Gabby, so if I got it, it's yours."

Gil outlined the situation including an overview of the killer's M.O. Archie told him what information he needed, and gave Gil the office fax-number, so he could transmit any documents necessary. If Gil could get the data together before Saturday, the F.B.I. employee promised at least a "rough draft" profile by Monday. It would mean extra work, but the information could make a difference to the case, so Gil prepared to plunge into the research.

First, however, he called Sheila, to explain why he hadn't picked up Jennifer from school. He disconnected when her machine answered again.

Since he couldn't reach Sheila and wasn't meeting Jennifer, he remembered turning down a date with Pilar for that errand. He decided to give it another shot. He got her on the first try. He explained that he needed another hour for his paperwork but wondered if she was available after that since his plans had changed. She was thrilled, when he suggested meeting later for a hike across the Brooklyn Bridge.

By seven-thirty, they were walking, hand in hand, along the elevated walkway of the New York landmark. Up close, the bridge wasn't the filigreed net it appeared from far away, but instead a forest of ugly woven cables and peeling grey paint. But between the view of the East River and each other to look at, Gil and Pilar hardly noticed.

CHAPTER 24

Friday, 9:44 p.m.

The audience was excellent tonight. No obnoxious drunks trying to be funnier than Melvin, no buzz of side conversations. Out in the hostile environment of New York's entertainment world, the Performer was at the peak of his skills. It wasn't the same as his private theater, it was a different challenge. But he was equal to it. He could feel every pulse of the crowd, manipulating the crowd, like they were all puppets and he had control of the strings. He and Melvin were in the middle of the routine they called, "Ghostbusters." He was telling Melvin how to get to the graveyard, though of course, he was not using Melvin's real name tonight.

"... so you come to a fork in the road," was the Performer's straight line.

"Will there be knife and a spoon there, too?" the figure wise-cracked. Tonight, he was playing "Freckles," which only required a few dots of make-up with an eyebrow pencil, a different colored wig, and a slight alternation of the basic voice-quality Melvin normally used.

"Of course not, Freckles. That means a place where the road goes in two different directions."

"Oh, well, why didn't you say so?"

"I did."

"Well, I guess your tongue must a been over your eyeteeth, 'cause you couldn't see what you were saying! Har har!"

"Oh, Freckles. You are being obstreperous," the ventriloquist said with mock exasperation.

"I'm being what?"

"Obstreperous, obstreperous!"

"Gesundheit. You'd better take care of that cold!" As expected, the audience of drunken salesmen, reprobates, and their painted women screeched in dull appreciation of the sophomoric humor.

"No, Freckles," he lectured the figure. "Obstreperous means "unruly," or "boisterous.""

"Well, I ain't goin' to be GIRL-sterous! Ha!" The figure leaned out toward the seats, obviously playing to the crowd at the expense of the apparently inhibited human holding him. A fat man in a checkered sports coat yelled at a waitress not to block his view of the stage. She had gotten interested in the performance and stopped to watch.

"C'mon now, Freckles, settle down. I was trying to tell you how to get to the graveyard."

"Okay, so what comes after the spoon in the road?"

"It's a fork in the road. And when you get there, you bear to the left."

Melvin, in his disguise as Freckles, began shaking violently, and pulled back from his master.

"I ain't goin' where there's any BEARS!"

"No, no," the Performer chuckled, "there aren't any bears, stupid."

"You said there's BEARS to the left."

"No Freckles. Don't be stupid. 'Bear' to the left means you TURN to the left."

Melvin fixed him with a round-eyed stare. His eyebrows slowly elevated, to the giggles of the audience. They were waiting for a punch line. Instead the voice became chilling.

"Who do you think you are calling stupid?"

The Performer gasped. Melvin was not sticking to the script. That line was not part of the routine. Desperately, he tried to cover the variation from the usual lines.

"Now don't go getting a chip on your shoulder, Freckles. You have enough wood on you already!"

The ad-lib wasn't perfect, but it made it appear like the previous interjection was part of the routine. Unfortunately, Melvin wasn't through yet.

"You should never call me stupid, dickhead."

The audience, conditioned to laugh at the figure's wisecracks, was caught off-guard by the new element of profanity, and interpreted it instantaneously as merely a more outrageous comeback. They roared in laughter. The Performer shivered in abject fear. Melvin had warned of breaking loose in public. Now it seemed, he was doing so. The voice was rising in volume and timbre.

"Do you know what this dummy standing here, holding me, really does, when you can't see him?" Melvin howled to the audience.

"Yes, the secret is out, I do magic!" the ventriloquist shouted, near panic, trying to head off what sounded like immanent horrid self-disclosure. He had to stop the uncontrolled figure from shouting out horrible secrets.

"If you will all take your napkins, and wave them up and down, like this...," he quickly instructed, "you can do a magic trick, too!" He desperately mimicked a waving motion. Enough of the audience began flapping their napkins, that he was able to plow on before Melvin could continue.

"That's right, and the trick makes Francois and Freckles disappear for tonight. Bye, bye! Thanks for being a great audience!"

He moved quickly off-stage, waving his hand in an exaggerated goodbye. There was a smattering of applause, a few laughs, but not the ovation to be expected. The performance had been poorly concluded, and significantly shorter than usual.

When he reached the wings, out of the audience view, he felt wetness, realizing that he had urinated involuntarily, soaking the front of his trousers. Melvin glared at him, silent now, and pernicious. The Performer shoved his glowering companion into the large suitcase used to transport the figure. A last verbal barb shot out, as the lid closed.

"You can shut me in, but you can't shut me up!"

The ventriloquist slammed the lid down and snapped the two latches shut.

But it wasn't enough.

In addition to working with a figure, many ventriloquists develop a technique known as "the distant voice." A slightly altered version of their usual vent voice, it requires a combination of volume reduction, muffling, and drawing out of the words, tike Helllooo," instead of "Hello." When the audience is properly set-up to expect it, as when the person on stage suddenly turns, and says, "Did you hear that?" his quieter, muffled voice with a hint of echo, gives the impression that the vent is truly "throwing his voice! In a slight variation, the Performer and Melvin had once done a whole routine, in and out of a trunk situated at center stage. There would be a threat of dismissing the "dummy," with loud protests from the figure. As he was lowered into the truck, the voice tone would change, growing muffled as the lid was closed. After a comical series of exchanges with the now hidden voice, the performer would appear to have a change of heart and open the trunk again, with a perfectly timed return of volume and clipped tones. When they were in good form, it was a sure-fire routine. The audience loved the demonstration of technical competence along with the humor.

Now the routine came back to haunt, because closing the lid of the suitcase did not stop Melvin's voice. The dampened sound continued.

"You can't shut me up. You can't shut me up."

The Performer threw on his coat to cover the wet pants. He walked quickly to the stage door, smiling as the voice continued to attracted attention. People turned, puzzled at the small voice repeating itself, like a broken record.

"You can't shut me up, you can't shut me up, you ..."

He grinned as best he could and mugged on his way out, as if he were staying in character and giving a free demonstration to the backstage crew and other acts.

It was drizzling outside, but the Performer paid little notice, as he walked faster and faster, soon breaking into a trot, water splashing and soaking his clothing as he ran. The voice did not vary.

"You can't shut me up. You can't shut me up. You can't..." He dashed down an alley, panting and gasping, his mouth a rictus of panic, eyes wide and desperate.

Then he sighted the dumpster. A great green monster, its top was gaping open, a huge mouth looking to be fed. In a single motion, hardly slowing, he ran to the opening and swung the case up and in. His body slammed into the metal side of the container, as his momentum carried him forward, and bounced back from the force of the collision. The suitcase sailed into the dumpster. For a moment there was silence.

Standing there with the rain dripping down his face, the impact still numbing him, he felt a moment of stillness and calm. Then the voice began again, only in a quieter, more subdued tone.

"I thought I taught you the deadpan. No feelings, no fear, no panic."

"But, but... you ...," the ventriloquist stammered.

"I was only testing you, my pitiful friend," the voice echoed from the gaping maw of the dumpster. "And reminding you that we are a team. You can't control me, my friend. But you can't get along without me, either. So take the suitcase and come along now. You are a mess."

The soggy Performer stood, trembling for several minutes, the rain mixing with his stage make-up to run in colored rivulets down his face and drip onto his coat. Finally, he moved forward, leaned deeply into the garbage receptacle to retrieve the suitcase. The rain and liquefied make-up hid the tears that welled from his red-rimmed eyes.

In his bedraggled state, the first two taxis passed him, despite his waved signal. Finally, a gypsy cab slowed and stopped.

"Where to?" the East Indian driver queried in a thick accent, swinging the car door open from the inside. The Performer gave an address two blocks from his own, and got in. It was a fifteen-minute ride. By the time the cab pulled up to the curb, it was a 'deadpan' that stepped out, paid the driver, then strode to the rear entrance of an old building. A dark staircase led to the upper floor where he lived. The museum was a level above that.

Once in the living area, the Performer stripped off his wet clothing. He showered and toweled off vigorously, until his skin was raw from the friction. Still naked, he moved to a cabinet marked "Maquillage," his father's make-up kit. Sticks of camouflage coloring were mixed with the greasepaint, powder, and spirit gum. He took these and slowly painted his body in shades of black and green. All except his groin area, which he coated with bright red lipstick.

The museum was up another narrow staircase, which he quickly climbed. The room was murky and still. The slap of his bare feet echoed through the attic. He moved to the stage area, turned on the multi-colored footlights and several overhead spots. The focused beams bathed him like sunlight. His posture straightened. Here he was in charge. Here he was the Master. The rows of silent figures beyond the footlights were only waiting for him to begin, so they would come to life again. He could give life, and he could take it. He was the Master.

To the side, behind the right 'wing' curtain, a chair was positioned. In it, waited a small, slumped shape. The ear had been a problem, but the Master was quite capable with needle and thread. A piece of leather had been cut to shape, then attached to the new figure. It was the policeman's fault, of course. "Beach," - he name was anathema. This was the interloper who had entered one of the zones and polluted it. This was the one they had selected to find the Master. What he didn't know, was that the Master had selected him as well.

The Performer reached down to plug in a power cord. As he turned to a control panel and flicked several switches, a video camera was activated. The garishly painted apparition reached for the figure on the chair. On top of the artfully constructed doll body was the head of a human child, a boy, with a curling ear lock of hair hanging from one temple. On the other side where an ear should have been, there was just a bloody patch with a piece of leather tacked in place. Despite being impaled on a dowel, the head lolled and wobbled in a sickening parody of puppet movement. The Performer propped his foot up on a stool, after which he set the figure up on his raised knee. He turned to the camera, a diabolical smile spreading across his features, and began.

"Detective Gil Beach. This performance is for you !"

Chapter 25

Saturday, 7:47 a.m.

Stained Styrofoam coffee cups joined crumpled napkins and gnawed pizza crusts in the litter of Gil Beach's desk. A gap in the blue window shades allowed a beam of light to stab through the foul air, illuminating myriads of dust motes, turning them into a cascade of silver specks. The shaft of light reached a hand, twitching in sleep. The Detective lay with his head on his arms, hunched over a desk, slumbering restlessly in the chair. A telephone rang. He jerked. One hand reflexively clutched at his chest as pain lanced through his breast, again and again. After a few deep breaths, he began to relax. Years ago he had worried that the pain was due to a heart problem, arteries clogged like the Brooklyn Queens expressway at rush hour. But eventually his required annual physical had included an electrocardiogram and nuclear stress test, which showed no problems. Eventually, he realized that the pain was just part of the old dream, reliving childhood horror.

As he fought his way out of sleep, the phone rang again. One hand pushed back through his hair, fingers spread like a clumsy comb, as the other reached for the device.

"Ninth Precinct, Detective Harrigan," he answered groggily.

"Oh, I was looking for Detective Beach," the feminine voice responded. The sound was familiar.

"Pilar?"

"Yes.... Gil?"

"Yeah, it's me."

"What's with the 'Harrigan' business?"

"Oh, that's our phantom detective. Sometimes it's not good to be too available, or quotable. If a reporter or somebody calls and talks to Harrigan, later we can always say there's no such guy."

"Clever," she observed, before changing subjects. "You're at work bright and early. I tried your apartment first. You must have gotten up at the crack of dawn."

Was that a questioning tone? For a moment Gil hesitated, wondering if Pilar was checking up on him. In the past he had quickly dropped a woman who became too possessive, or didn't give him enough breathing space. In Pilar's case, he realized, he felt something deeper than he had in a long time. Interestingly, he didn't want to hide as much, either.

"Never got home. Been here all night. After our walk on the bridge, I came back to work. I had to follow up on some stuff for a case I'm on," he mumbled.

"The ventriloquism murder? You told me a little about it, last night. It sounds fascinating, but a little creepy," Pilar offered.

"More than a little, I'm afraid."

"Well, maybe you can tell me more about it at lunch. We still have a date, don't we?"

"Oh yeah, definitely," he assured her. "Twelve-thirty at Sal Anthony's."

"On Irving, west of Third Avenue, right? But that's why I was trying to reach you, Gil. I'm running a little late this morning. Could we make it one, or one-thirty, instead?"

"No problem. I could use the time, too."

"Are you sure you're up to it? With no sleep and all?" Pilar inquired, hesitantly. After all, she had been using up a lot of his time.

She guessed that the reason for his late night was the time he had spent with her.

"Well, I didn't go home, but I grabbed a few Z's on the cot in the holding room. And I dozed off again for a while, just before you called. I'll grab a shower and be like new. I'm looking forward to seeing you."

"The feeling is mutual, I assure you. So shall we make it one-thirty?"

"Fine. See you then," he agreed.

"Can't wait," she bubbled. "Bye for now."

Gil added a goodbye, then disconnected.

He smiled, thinking of their time together, and their first kiss. Actually, it hadn't been a big deal, just a nice little kiss good night. Yet, an intense chemistry was just below the surface. They both sensed where this was heading, but for their own reasons, neither one wanted to jump too far or too quickly.

The evening had been wonderful. They found that their differences, far from separating them, just added to the interest they had for each other.

The only problem was that Gil didn't really have enough time for serious dating. He ended up coming into work after saying good night to Pilar. Now he felt like a dishrag. But he also felt a sense of responsibility. The longer he took to solve this case, the greater the chance that someone else, perhaps another child, would die. Some cops had found that their spouses got tired of the long hours and compelling work. It wasn't unusual for someone to leave, with words like," You aren't married to me, you're married to the Job."

He tried not to think of that. So far, he had been able to keep up his fledging relationship with the psychologist, and he wasn't going to curse it now with fears about the future.

Picking up the phone, Gil entered the number for T. 'n T., Inc. The secretary answered on the second ring.

"T. 'n T., I hoo-ope I can help youuu!"

"You got away with syllables, Annie."

"Now, if I remember those macho tones, I'd say that this has got to be that tough Detective."

"Very good, Annie. Is Tom around on Saturdays?"

"Absolutely. But don't try to find him on Monday. You want to speak to him, handsome?"

"Well, I'm having lunch near there, and wondered if I could stop by for a few minutes. I have a few more questions I think he could help with."

"Hold on, sweety," she told him, and he heard recorded music in the background for a minute or two. "Tommy says it would have to be before one- thirty, if that's okay?"

"Fine, that's when I have to be at Sal Anthony's. Let's say I drop by at twelve-thirty, quarter to one?"

The Detective could hear the secretary passing along the information to her boss in a stage whisper. After a distant voice mumbled an unintelligible response, she confirmed the appointment. He made the necessary flirtatious goodbye and ended the call.

A murmur of conversation drifted from the area of Lincoln's office. The Lieutenant's 'task force' had been formed and put into motion on Friday. Gil thought of Shakespeare's line, "Full of sound and fury, but signifying nothing." It was a fair description of the task force. The additional manpower never materialized. Instead, a personnel roster was made up listing Lincoln as Commander, Detectives Beach, and Esperoza from the usual P.D.U. complement, plus Sgt. Epstein, the P.R. officer, Frank Terranova, Lincoln's clerk, and a civilian secretary from the typing pool. Without a single change of the precinct's normal personnel, Captain Occhiogrosso, the

Precinct Commander, had managed to release a bulletin to the newspaper, which stated:

> *In a bold response to the unfortunate disappearance of a community youth, Captain Anthony E. Occhiogrosso today announced the formation of a Detective Task Force, which will be assigned exclusively to the case. The diverse unit includes experts in cases of racial and religious harassment. Commander of the task force will be Lieutenant Randolph M. Lincoln, recently liaison to the Governor's Commission on Crimes of Bias, and his assistant will be Sergeant Solomon Epstein. Male and female officers conversant in several languages have been recruited, as well as support staff. No effort is being spared in the efforts to locate the missing youth, who disappeared after leaving school unaccompanied, on Wednesday.*

Besides counting everyone twice, and making singulars sound like plurals, the release even cast a slight shadow on the Schule, implying that they hadn't supervised properly. No effort spared? More like no effort made. Fortunately, most news writers would edit the release to a simpler statement. Anyone who knew how things work, understood that not much effort was being expended.

Gil made an appearance at the first planning meeting, which predictably was long on talk and short on action. When he received the grisly package the night before, Gil had immediately reported it to Lincoln, listening passively to the Lieutenant's lecture on this being a standard tactic of kidnappers. Instead of focusing on the psycho's identification and targeting of Beach, the "Task Force Commander" bawled Gil out for handling the wrapping which might yield fingerprints, accused him of trying to be a "Lone Ranger." The comments were close enough to the truth to make Gil hesitate. He had no desire to be a hero but did prefer to work alone. And although he knew there was no way he could have known the package's awful contents before opening it, he had indeed torn and handled the paper. At least Lincoln had sent the box to the lab, where Jim Nedrow could work his magic.

There wouldn't be any news from there yet, but Gil reached for the phone to touch base with the technician anyway, hoping to provide more background. The Lieutenant had only written, "Check for prints and other evidence of handler's identity." That didn't give the lab much direction.

Most non-scientists were mystified by laboratory analysis, expecting it to work in a vacuum. Television didn't help, Gil knew, the way it created charismatic detectives or M.E.s, who merely asked lab personnel for results, after which they were handed conveniently dramatic hidden clues. In real police work, the more information you gave a lab, the better chance it had of finding something. For instance, a piece of steak, accompanied by note about possible poisoning as a cause of death, would lead to toxicological tests that would never be performed if the request for analysis just asked where the steak came from, or how old it was.

Before he could call, however, the ring tone sounded for an incoming call.

"Ninth Precinct, Detective Harrigan," he answered, still not anxious to take calls.

"I don't know if I should talk to you, or Detective Beach. This is Norman Popowick of 'Showtech' in Bay Ridge. He left a message on our answering machine."

"Yes, Mr. Popowick," Gil replied, adding a little more nasal quality to his voice, "I'll transfer you to Detective Beach." He pushed the hold button and waited a few seconds, before coming back on the line, making sure his voice was as full and deep as he could make it.

"Hello, this is Detective Beach. How can I help you?"

"Uh, well, yes. But, actually, uhh, I'm just returning your call, so I don't know what this is about. I'm Nathan Popowick from Showtech."

"Oh yes, Mr. Popowick. The reason I called was that we are looking for some technical information about ventriloquism to assist in an investigation."

"Oh, I see. What is it, one of those 'stole my act' things?"

"Do you guys always answer strangers with wisecracks?"

"Oh ... I see. You think I was making a joke, but I was serious. You see, a vent routine is very creative, and besides the patter, uhh ... 'Patter' means the ... uh, dialogue. Every comedian tries to protect his jokes, of course, but each vent has a figure with certain style, look, personality. And of course there are the specials."

"Which are?"

"Oh, well, like tricks. A standard one is drinking water while the dummy sings, but some vents have special effects that are all their own, and occasionally they try to copyright or otherwise protect them from being used by others. Ron Lucas does this thing with a sound coming out of his hand that is amazing. I don't know if he has tried to protect it, but if he hasn't, he ought to. The effect isn't that difficult technically, so lots of people could imitate it, but the ingenuity and vision to come up with it, were his."

"I think I understand, now, Mr. Popowick, but I don't investigate copyright infringements. You sound like you really know the field."

"Oh yes, officer. I, myself, do ventriloquism. In addition to my work with Showtech, I am a minister of the Four Square Gospel Church, and I have done hundreds of shows for our "Y.E.S. project. a stands for "Youth Encounter the Savior.

"I see," the Detective said, noncommittally, then perhaps you could tell me if there are any distinguishing marks of a person in this field. Something that would point to him being a…uhh, practitioner? I mean, could you recognize another ventriloquist in any way, just by observing him?"

"Ummm. Well no, I don't think I could do that. Of course there are both male and female vents. Sometimes, if they used a traditional figure mechanical mechanism you might see a callous on certain fingers, but that would vary according to the particular style mechanism, and they aren't always that obvious anyway. A lot of vents don't use that mechanical type anyway. Some figures are just elaborate hand puppets. I'd have an easier time recognizing another Christian, I think. Are you Born Again, officer?"

"Pardon me?"

"Are you Born Again? Baptized in the Spirit?"

"This is official police business, Mr. Popowick. Perhaps we can discuss personal matters another time. Right now, I need to ask you if you know of any list of practicing ventriloquists in the Metropolitan New York area."

"Uhh, well, I guess I have my answer, anyway," the caller stated, now in a cooler tone. "I don't actually know of a list, but uhh, well there is a periodical called Newsyvents published by Maher Ventriloquist Studios. You could contact the editor, Clinton Detweiler, and see if he could give you the mailing list for this area. A lot of vents subscribe."

Popowick didn't have a telephone number for the periodical but was able to give the Detective an office address from one of the recent issues.

"Thank you, Mr. Popowick, you've been very helpful. I may need to speak with you again."

"Well, I'm going to be in Manhattan this afternoon at an Evangelical prayer luncheon. Perhaps you would like to meet me there?"

"No, I'm afraid not. About that time, I hope I'll be enjoying the pasta primavera at Sal Anthony's. But thanks anyway. I will give you a call, if we need your help."

"Well there's more help available than you realize, officer, but you have to be open to it. Beach was the name, wasn't it?"

"Right," Gil admitted, wishing he had stuck with "Detective Harrigan." He almost laughed, as he pictured swarms of religious fanatics swooping down on the precinct, lugging stacks of bibles, crosses, and other paraphernalia, intent on saving his poor lost soul. He thanked the man again before disconnecting. He also breathed a sigh of relief.

Gil looked at his watch, seeing that it was almost ten o'clock. The growling of his stomach alerted him to the fact that he hadn't had any breakfast, so he decided to go out to the coffee shop around the corner. Part of Lt. Lincoln's exercise of power was his instruction that all members of the new "Task Force," keep him informed of their whereabouts at all times. Gil shuffled toward the Lieutenant's office, feeling a heaviness that came from a combination of no decent food, little sleep, lack of exercise, along with the emotional weight of losing a child to the killer.

Now there were two desks outside Lincoln's office. Frank Terranova was sorting papers at one of them.

"Morning, Frank. What's your new helper like? Good-looking?"

The other man made a grimace and only responded with a sound.

"Woof-woof."

"But I'm sure she has a great personality," Gil kidded.

"Maybe, if you like girls who think Taylor Swift ought to be president and a major life decision is what color nail polish to wear."

"So, is there anything for you to do?" Gil asked, more seriously.

"Well, I've been promoted to 'Research,' whatever that means. I think it may give me a chance to get out in the street more. No gun yet, but it might keep me from going stir crazy."

"You never were one to sit around on your tail," Gil agreed, remembering the other officer admitting he had been something of a "cowboy."

"Yeah, this is the first time I kept a set of teeth for so long. I got busted-up so often, I even kept a dental mold at home, so they could just make-up a new set of dentures from them."

Gil knew the man was exaggerating but chuckled along with him.

"When can you go back on the street?"

"Well, the psychologist at Riverside House said I was ready for full duty, but this old guy Dr. Eagleston that works for the Department has been around since Day One, does pretty much what he pleases. He'll let me out when he's good and ready."

"Sounds frustrating."

"It is, but I'm learning to turn-it-over."

"Pardon?"

"Oh, sorry. That's a phrase we use around A.A. Basically, it means to relax and let my higher power take care of things."

Gil nodded but must have given a facial signal that betrayed his inner reaction, because the other cop hurried to qualify his statement.

"Don't get me wrong. I'm not very religious at all. In A.A. they're pretty flexible. You can have any kind of God you want. They call it your 'higher power.' Mine is pretty vague ... kind of a 'Power of Good' or something like that."

Gil didn't know what prompted Frank to tell him all this, but it was done in a fairly low-key manner that didn't have the same feeling as the 'born-again' ventriloquist he had fended off earlier. Frank didn't sound like he was recruiting. Gil was glad because he was beginning to like the guy, and that would have been an obstacle. But the conversation set off a disconcerting train of thought.

Gil wasn't sure what he believed, anymore. After his wife, Diane, had been taken, he was mad at whatever or whoever took her. She had claimed that it was God, but Gil didn't want anything to do with such a God. Yet the idea of a "Power of Good" intrigued him. He knew that he believed strongly in a power of Evil. It was the flood that he was always trying to hold back. If he was doing that, and others were doing it too, then perhaps they were part of something bigger ... something positive, something constructive, fighting the other negative thing. Maybe that was a positive, good power. He had never thought in quite those terms before.

Gil thought of Pilar, and the destitute basket-case type clients she often counseled at the Hope Center. It was only after a bit of probing that he learned she did that work for free. He liked the idea of the two of them being on the same side in this great positive- negative struggle. He had brief fantasies of standing behind a defensive rampart, Pilar reloading his musket, as he drove back hordes of evil-looking creatures, dressed in human clothing. He caught himself, realizing he was day-dreaming. He had been doing a lot of that lately.

"Sounds interesting," he allowed. "Look, Frank. I'm going out. I'm going to drop in on the head of the Yeshiva this morning, and a woman in the same neighborhood who claims she saw a suspicious vehicle the day of the abduction. I'm probably going to fit in one more interview before I meet someone for lunch."

"Since you don't identify the last stop, I assume you would prefer that 'Lou' doesn't know," Frank suggested. "You still pursuing the ventriloquist murder idea?"

"It's more than an idea, Frank. You know that. You were in the task force meeting. Even Lincoln knows it is, I think he just has to play games for political reasons."

"Look, Gil, let's be straight, okay? Don't worry about me. Just because I was assigned to be the lieutenant's gofer doesn't mean he's my "rabbi." If what you say is true, he would be at least giving you a wink or two, to let you know he supported you. I think the guy's got a hard-on for you, and he's going to oppose any idea you offer."

"What did I ever do to him?" Gil objected, raising his hands in a questioning gesture.

"I don't think he likes too much competence."

Gil shifted uncomfortably at the implied praise. It was not common for cops to complement one another directly. Friendly insults and ribbing were more the rule. Terranova seemed to sense the discomfort and changed the subject.

"So you got a hot date for lunch?"

"Yeah, I guess you could say that," Gil admitted, "I'm meeting her at Sal Anthony's at about one-thirty, so I should be back by three-thirty or so."

"I'll put you down for a five o'clock return."

Gil smiled. "Okay, okay, give me a break. By the way, if you are the 'Research' department, how about doing some for me?"

"What have you got in mind?"

"See if you can contact this Maher Ventriloquist Studios, who put out a newsletter." Gil copied out the name and address from his notebook. "The Editor is named Detweiler. Find out if we can get a copy of their mailing list."

"Shouldn't be too tough," Terranova offered. "I could probably get it today. And I don't see any reason why I need to mention it to Lou."

"Thanks, Frank."

Gil started to turn away, but a hand reached out and caught him by the sleeve. Terranova's confident manner faltered, as he continued in a more hesitant tone.

"Look, Gil. When Lincoln put me in the task force, he said I should make myself visible, run errands out in the community, even accompany one of the other staff on information-gathering trips, or whatever. Look, I know I don't have much of a track record at this point, and I know you usually like to work alone. But I thought maybe if you were ever going somewhere and wanted a little back-up … I mean, not like today, or anything. Just sometime when it wasn't all that important, and I wouldn't get in the way. In fact, I'd understand if you just said, 'forget it.' But I thought maybe you could think about it for a while, and if you didn't feel like ..."

Gil interrupted the apologetic monologue, placing a hand on the other man's shoulder.

"Frank, why don't you shut up and get your coat?"

"You mean ...? Oh yeah, sure. Gee thanks, Gil." He almost kicked over a chair in his haste. "Uh, I'll leave a note for Beverly about where we'll be. The Schule first, right?"

"Right. And look, Frank, you can put down where I'll be for lunch, but you aren't included in my time with the lady."

Terranova laughed, enjoying himself, "Not even if I pay?"

"Not even then. And I'm going straight there from my last interview, so I'll drop you back here about noon. But if you're so interested in buying me food, it just so happens I haven't had any breakfast yet."

"You're on!" was the cheerful reply.

The two men moved down the hallway and stairs toward the street. One walked with a heavy tread, while the other seemed to bounce along on an invisible trampoline.

Chapter 26

Saturday, 11:10 a.m.

"Very smart!" Gil grumbled to himself. "It's not like I'd have to be a genius to remember which day of the week it is! Sometimes I'm so stupid."

Frank Terranova, walking beside him, put on a face of mock-seriousness.

"Ah yes ... I, too, made an error once. Well, actually, I just thought I made an error. I was wrong."

Gil turned, a scowl beginning to form. But the facial expression of his companion was so comical, that the frown melted into a grin and a shrug. They laughed.

Their visit to the Schule hadn't been so humorous. They arrived at the Yeshiva, only to have an offended Hasid slam the door in their embarrassed faces, as he reminded them in less than gentle terms that it was the Shabbat, which only unthinking heathens would think of defiling with goyim concerns. A severe chain-link fence topped with concertina wire separated the property from the world outside. Gil leaned against the barrier, a snippet of Robert Frost poetry that he had learned in high school tickling his mind.

"...be careful what you are walling out, and what you are walling in."

The Yeshiva was located at the far northwestern corner of the Precinct on Thirteenth street. The youngster's family lived on St.

Mark's Place, only about ten blocks away. Van transportation was provided by the Schule, not so much due to the distance, as to the harassment or danger a Hasidic child might encounter on the journey. Eight-year-old boys, however, have their own ideas about what is dangerous, and how long a wait can be endured.

The garage where the boy's shredded coat had been displayed, was only a few hundred feet from the western edge of the school property. The two police officers decided to walk over to the scene.

"I don't get it," Terranova ruminated. "If the kid was heading home, why did he go west?"

"Good point. He could have just been taking the round-about way, but maybe he was heading someplace else."

"You know, another possibility," Frank added, "is that he was taken to the garage from some other spot. But wouldn't somebody have seen him go back past the school?"

"Not if he was in a vehicle."

"Guess we better pay Mrs. Schottingham a visit." The two men headed back toward their car.

"You've been around the P.D.U. too long, Frank, you're starting to think like a detective."

They climbed into the car and sat in preoccupied silence for a few moments, Terranova at the wheel, while his companion scribbled in his notebook. In the quiet, the driver finally spoke softly, not making eye contact.

"You know, Gil, I really appreciate this. I was dyin' - shut up in there."

"It's your life. Don't let anybody else live it for you," was all Gil could think to say.

"How would you like to live your life, Gil?" The question caught Beach by surprise.

"I like what I do. I'm good at it."

"And that's it? You wouldn't change anything?"

"Not anything? I wouldn't say that," Gil admitted.

"I hope you don't think I'm out of line, but you seem different lately. From old Mr. Workaholic, married-to-the-Job Detective, you've recently become a man with a social life. Is it somebody special?"

"Her name is Pilar. I think she's pretty special. I don't know what she sees in an old fart like me, but I'm not complaining."

"Amen, Amen, Mr. Detective, Sir."

"I'm not going to stay a detective much longer, if we don't get some work done."

As they moved out, Frank asked if Gil had heard the latest joke about the Mayor. After he told that joke, Gil had one too. By the time they pulled up to the brownstone where Roberta Schottingham lived, they had been laughing so hard, they were reduced to gasps and wheezes. They had to sit in the car a few moments before they could get themselves back together and climb the steps to the entrance.

The faded label on the bell read "Nigel Schottingham." It was several minutes before the door opened a crack, a wizened face peering out at the waiting men.

"Police," Gil explained, showing his identification. "We are looking for Roberta Schottingham."

"I'm Missus Schottingham," the face replied, pronouncing the name "Shot-en-um," in an accent that echoed off the White Cliffs of Dover.

"May we speak with you for a few minutes, Ma'am?" Gil asked, not attempting to imitate her pronunciation of the surname.

The woman nodded and swung open the door. They were ushered into a dark showcase of doilies, trinkets, plants, and collectibles.

Glass-fronted cabinets displayed Hummel figures and ornate teacups. Shelves and brackets held spoons, thimbles, darning eggs, and commemorative plates. A large sideboard was jammed with an assortment of music boxes, while trailing branches of Wandering Jews, Swedish Ivy, Philodendrons, and Spider plants intertwined with figurines and glassware on various shelves, window ledges and end tables.

She offered seats on a settee draped, as were most other pieces of furniture, in elaborate Afghans, probably handmade. She fumbled with a switch, turning on a Tiffany-style lamp as she situated herself in a Queen Anne chair, cushioned with a crocheted pillow. Dressed in a modified cotton pinafore with a tiny flower print and lace collar, the elderly woman looked like an aging maidservant in a BBC production. She folded her hands in her lap, assuming a businesslike demeanor.

"It's a bit too much, isn't it?" she began.

"What's that, Ma'am?" Gil asked.

"The junk."

"The junk?"

"Quite. All this hugger-mugger." She extended her arm in a sweeping motion that included the jumble of objects and greenery. "It's really a bit of a bother, all this mishmash. I don't really care for it myself, but I can't bear to disappoint the wee ones."

"Children?" Frank interpreted.

"Quite," the tiny lady nodded, "I taught the wee ones for over 'af a century, and they were always lookin' to give me a bit of something at the end of the year, or my birthday, or the odd holiday, right? Early on, one little lad brought me a lovely teacup. I suppose it made sense to give an old limey something for tea. I told 'im it was perfect, and would fit right into my teacup collection. Not that I really collected them, but it was all I could think to say to the lad. Before I knew it, all the wee darlin's were bringing me teacups. After they filled two cabinets, I told a lass that I had more cups than spoons. So the lovely girl brought me a souvenir spoon from her vacation trip to Wales. Next thing I knew. I was getting spoons by the dozens. Then it was darning eggs, and later it was something else. Since the boys and girls were always comin' around for a bit of help with the hard subject, I didn't dare put away all their dear gifts. So here I am in a hodgepodge. Times, I'm tempted to pick up and move into some nice clean flat, without any clutter. The dusting alone is a bloody bother, let me tell you, not to mention watering all these plants. After all, I'm near ninety now. But a lot of the wee ones like to drop by. Sometimes they bring their children and grandchildren. I just couldn't disappoint them, now could I?"

"No ma'am, I guess you couldn't," Gil agreed. Before he had a chance to redirect the conversation, the little woman saved him the effort.

"But you didn't come to hear about my silly little troubles. And I know you have your hands full with all the drug dealers and addicts and all. So, I thought, maybe I can help. You see, I keep an eye out from my front window." She gestured toward a lace-curtained bow window, facing the street.

"Wednesday, I was sitting here watching for the postal carrier, when I noticed this strange bloke climbing in and out of a small bus."

"A bus?" the detective asked.

"Oh, what do they call them, these days. A lorrie, no, something of a panel truck, or…"

"Maybe a van?" Frank couldn't resist suggesting

"Yes, that's it, a … van," she confirmed. "This bloke was in and out of the thing a dozen times. From where I was, I could see something that looked like a knife in his 'and. I figured he was some kind of scurvy bloke, even though he was in that official looking truck."

"What do you mean, official-looking?" Gil asked The woman waved her hand, as if clearing the air of cobwebs, "Oh you know, all business-like, with printing on the side and such."

"Did you happen to notice what the printing said?"

"Why, I don't know exactly. It was something about magic, as I recall. 'Barndoor Magic,' 'Wheelbarrow Magic,' or something like that."

Gil had a flash of memory. "Could it have been 'Barstow's Magic Company?'" he ventured.

"Why, now that you say it, I do think that could have been it," she agreed, bobbing her head like a small bird.

Connections began clicking in Gil's mind. He didn't believe in coincidence, and the presence of Barstow's van in the same area as a crazed ventriloquist's crime was not within the limits of normal chance. He would have to pay the difficult supplier a visit.

"Yes, Ma'am," Gil nodded. "Could you tell us what the man looked like?"

"Well, he wasn't large. Though it's hard to say for sure. It was from a distance, you know. He seemed a bit chunky and had a shiny pate.

"He was bald?"

"Yes, well mostly. You know, wi' a wee bit of hair on the sides."

"Could you tell if he was black, white or another color?"

"Didn't look colored to me. More Italian, I would say. Maybe one of those Mafia types. Looked shifty to me. And he was playing with some kind of knife."

The two policemen exchanged glances. Gil pursued the subject.

"What kind of knife?"

"Don't know much about knives, Officer. My eyes are good for my age, but they're still ninety- year-old eyes. I just saw something shiny and sharp-lookin'."

"How about the van. Could you tell us anything more about it, like it's make or color?"

"I'm afraid I wouldn't know one brand from another. Seems like it was sort of blue. It looked pretty new."

Gil and Frank kept up the questions for almost half an hour, but the most significant piece of information came out when Gil asked the woman what made her think the man should be reported.

"What caused your suspicion—was it the knife, the way he was waiting, or what?"

"Oh no," she waved the suggestions aside with a flip of her hand. "It wasn't that. It was the boy."

"What boy was that?" Gil asked, straightening up from his slouch.

"Well, this boy came along, and it looked like he must have gotten some of those drugs."

"I'm not sure I understand," Gil said, trying to get more.

"Well, the boy started talking to the man in the ... uhh, van, and then the lad got into the thing, and they closed the door. The man took a real careful look around, and I didn't want him to see me, so I closed the drapes for a minute. When I took another peek, they was gone. I was a bit shy, you know. The bloke looked pretty tough. He was one of those army chaps, you know."

"What made you think he was in the army?"

"Well, he was wearing a uniform. You know, those uniforms with big spots all over 'em."

"Cammos."

"Pardon?"

"Oh, sorry. That's a nickname for camouflage clothing. It's worn by a lot of people who aren't in the service, ma'am," Gil explained.

A few more questions made it clear that the boy was likely to be the missing child. His clothing matched the Hasidic pattern. But who was the man in the cammos? Was it Barstow, or someone using his van?

Mrs. Schottingham talked a lot over the next twenty minutes, but didn't provide much additional information. Lonely lady. Gil left his card and returned with Frank to the car. They traded a few jokes about old widows and English film characters, as they moved through midday traffic. It was still early, so the two men decided to pay a surprise visit to Barstow's Magic Company.

Gil drove up First Avenue north to the thirties, then without explanation pulled over into a no-parking zone. He reached in the back seat, to grab a lumpy package.

"Watch the car, will you, Frank? Gotta run a little errand. Or grab a cup of coffee, if you want. I might be a few minutes."

"Yeah, sure, Gil, no problem," the other man agreed, noting a furry plush limb poking out of the bag. As Beach left the car and moved down the street toward an entrance, Terranova noticed they were parked at New York University Medical Center.

Gil mounted the steps, stopping at the information desk. "Ann Marie Romanti," he told the clerk, who tapped the named into a computer terminal before directing him to the elevator. He found the floor and the right room. There were three children, one sleeping in the corner of a metal crib, one seated near a window, and another watching the television.

Ann Marie was by the window, a tiny figure in a body cast, extending from under her arms to her toes. Stainless steel pins jutted out of her ankles, attached to ropes that looped over pulleys and were tied to weights. She lay motionless, looking up at the ceiling.

"Hi, Ann Marie."

She turned her head, considering him quietly-

"I don't know if you remember me, hon. I helped you get out of that car wreck."

No response. Large eyes staring.

"I brought you someone, to keep you company," he continued, pulling a large stuffed teddy bear out of his bag. She didn't react at first, but when he handed the plush animal to her, she took it, and nestled it at her side, as if it belonged there.

"I was in the hospital once," he explained. "It was no fun being alone."

The girl didn't say anything, but tears slowly welled in her eyes and trickled down each cheek. Gil was afraid he was upsetting her but didn't know what to say. Her silence tore at his heart. He impulsively reached out and took her tiny hand in his. She stared up at him for another moment, then wrapped her other arm around his, leaned her head against it, and closed her eyes. Quietly, she sobbed for a while. When it became quiet, he saw that she was asleep.

A few minutes later, Gil returned to the car. Frank was standing there, leaning against the fender.

"Sorry I took so long," Gil apologized.

"Someone you know in the hospital?" Frank ventured.

"Sort of. A kid who was in an accident down in the Ninth a couple days ago."

Frank waited for more, but the Detective just started the car and joined First Avenue traffic, turning at 34th Street. He gave it another try.

"You know the parents?"

"Dead."

"Oh."

Frank thought a moment about Gil's nickname, then turned and started fiddling with the radio.

Barstow's was located in an office building on Thirty-eighth. In the lobby there was a weedy little man of indeterminate age wearing a threadbare all-purpose uniform, which apparently allowed him to play elevator conductor, security guard, maintenance man, information clerk, and doorman, all-in-one. On the wall, a scratched and clouded plastic cover plate almost obscured the building directory listings. Barstow's was on the eighth floor, along with L.G. Bornkamm, Attorney at Law, and Whizz Cleaning Services. The cramped elevator stopped six inches below the floor level, forcing the two men to step up out of the car, as it wobbled and creaked. Frank gave a sigh of relief as they reached solid flooring.

At the end of the hall, a metal fire door with a small wire-reinforced window was labeled with Barstow's name. The door was locked, and there was no bell, so Gil pounded on it a few times. Eventually, a voice responded.

"Ya, whoizzit?"

"Police. Please open the door."

Gil held his badge up to the small window. There was a moment of silence.

"Just a minute," a muffled voice called. The minute lengthened into two, and the Detective was beginning to suspect the occupant had found a rear exit, when there was the sound of a lock being turned, a chain unhooked. A heavy-set fellow pulled the door open. The man's height was on the short side of medium, so Gil's eyes went quickly toward his head, to see if he was also balding. The match to Mrs. Schottingham's description ended there, as he sported a full head of sandy-brown hair.

"Mr. Barstow?" Gil asked.

"At your service, Officer. What can I do for you?" The voice was a rich baritone, with precisely enunciated syllables, totally unlike the voice Gil had encountered on the telephone.

"Are you Billy Barstow?" Gil asked, a little puzzled.

"Yes, sir, I am. But I don't believe I have had the pleasure," the man spoke regally, accompanied by a slight arch of the eyebrow.

"Oh, sorry," Gil offered, "I'm Gil Beach of the NYPD Detective Unit. This is my partner, Frank Terranova."

Frank's head jerked around at the word 'partner' but as Barstow turned, to acknowledge his colleague, Gil winked. Frank couldn't help grinning. Gil kept speaking.

"I don't quite understand, Mr. Barstow. Thursday, I called your number and spoke with someone who identified himself as Billy. I assume that wasn't you?"

"You assume correctly, Detective. I wasn't in on Thursday. The only person you could have spoken to was Arnold, one of our staff. I wouldn't find it incongruous to imagine that he attempted to pass himself off as someone other than his own disreputable persona."

"Could you describe Arnold for us?"

"I could, but perhaps first, you might let me know the nature of your inquiry."

"Yes, of course. We are trying to gather information for an ongoing investigation concerning a missing person. Our sources say that one of your employees may have seen something relating to the investigation. We are not free to reveal the details, but I can reassure you that no one is being charged with a crime at this time. We are just looking for information. This employee of yours may be able to help. Could you describe him, and tell us where he might have been on Wednesday afternoon?"

"I see. Excuse me, if my paranoia suggests that you are only telling me part of the story. Nevertheless, I am always happy to cooperate with the police. Let's see, now. Krentz is about my size, but a little shorter, thinning on top, and tends to have a stubble beard most days. His nose is on the prominent side and looks like he enjoys a bit too much of the refined spirits. I'm afraid I can't help you with his whereabouts on Wednesday, as he called in sick that day"

"Do you use a van in your business, Mr. Barstow?"

"When it's running. It's been in the shop for two weeks. I've been making do with a U-Haul lately. Can't understand why a muffler should take so long, but what can I say?"

"You're sure the van hasn't been used this week?"

"Well, I assume that is the case. Arnold was supposed to pick it up Monday, but he said the garage hadn't gotten to it, yet. Do you have reason to believe he would be lying?"

"What color is your van?" Gil asked, not answering the man directly.

"Sort of an off-color. I call it azure, but the manufacturer used some term like lazulite."

"Kind of blue?"

"Well, yes. I suppose that would cover it, if you wanted to simplify the matter."

Gil caught a motion out of the corner of his vision. Frank was making signals with his eyebrows. He was also trying to stand where only Gil could observe him, tapping his head with a finger. Unfortunately, Gil couldn't read him. Was Frank trying to say "think, think?" Was he suggesting that Barstow was crazy, ... or what? Since Barstow was looking right at him, he couldn't ask for clarification.

"When could we speak with Mr. Krentz?" Gil continued, checking his notes for the last name.

"I really couldn't say," Barstow replied, archly, "Arnold doesn't work here anymore. Thursday was the only day he came in all week.

That's why I have to be here on a Saturday. When he called in again on Friday, I told him he needn't return."

"I see," Gil responded. "Can you give us an address and telephone number?"

"Yes, I suppose I have one somewhere, but I wonder if I could get back to you a little later? I'm in a bit of a crisis situation here, with an immense order that has to be delivered today, and my employee records are not easily accessible. I might be able to call you later today after I get this order completed. Will you be in your office?"

"Not until four or five," Gil said, glancing at his watch. It was nearing noon.

"I'll be available," Frank interjected. Then leaning toward Gil, he confided, "You can call me from Sal Anthony's, if you want to check in." He handed Gil a slip of paper. "Okay if I meet you at the car? I have to make a pit stop."

"Yeah, sure," Gil agreed, sensing some hidden motive. The slip of paper had the word "RUG!" scratched on it. Gil's eyes automatically dropped to the floor, where there was nothing but linoleum tile. Then he realized the meaning of the cryptic message, as well as Terranova's earlier head-tapping. Frank was trying to tell him that Barstow was wearing a wig. This was not new information. Gil had sighted the hairpiece early in the interview, but he was glad Terranova was keeping his eyes open. He nodded at Frank and finished up the usual loose ends of an interview—exchange of phone numbers, available times, assurance of confidentiality, cautions, and such. A few minutes later he was sitting in the car when Frank re-appeared, looking smug.

"You look like the cat that just ate the robin," Gil observed. "If it's about the wig, I agree. He was definitely wearing a 'rug.' Did you see the lifts on his shoes?"

Frank's grin faded for a moment, as he added this bit of obviously new information, but it quickly returned.

"Yeah, that fits. Subtract a couple inches, change the hair, and I'll bet we've got Arnold, himself. But just to make sure, I checked with the guy in the lobby. He calls himself the 'building supervisor.' According to him, there is only one occupant of that office—just Barstow, no staff at all."

"Not bad for a Researcher," Gil chuckled.

Terranova started to turn pink, as a blush crept up his face. "Gee, I hope I didn't step outta line or anything, I …." Gil interrupted.

"Look, Frank, give it a rest. You're not a rookie, so let's drop the puppy dog bullshit, okay? If you get out of line, I'll be glad to tell you, but that cuts both ways, so you may have to pull me up, too. In the meantime, anything you can add is okay by me."

Frank's face seemed to struggle through a list of possible expressions, trying to decide which to adopt, but then he straightened, and with a snort threw the car into gear and started it forward.

"You got it. Let's go see a ventriloquist."

Chapter 27

Saturday, 12:38 p.m.

Tom Tyler didn't believe in maturity. Or at least he didn't believe in what usually passes for it. He suspected that most people are afraid to grow up, but don't want to admit it, instead they try to hide that hesitancy by pretending they accepted the inevitable. They think they can make peace with it. Perhaps they believe they will somehow be spared the pain of lost childhood. Tom knew better.

As far as he was concerned, childhood can last as long as you keep it alive. But once lost, it can never be regained. So, much of his life he devoted to keeping alive the child in everyone. As for himself, he privately admitted that he had found a vocation that allowed him to spend his life playing with dolls, creating make-believe, and poking fun at authority through his small companions. Most of his time was devoted to model-making, and the pursuit of laughter—basically, the same priorities he had followed when he was seven years old.

The big Regulator clock on the far wall tolled the half-hour. Soon the Detective would be here. Tom slipped his ring finger through one of the wire loops on the vent figure he was completing. A tug of the wire pulled a lever behind the ears of the figure so they flapped forward. Most of the heads didn't include this feature, because adding too many functions created such complexity that smooth, lifelike action was impossible. For the most part, Tom limited puppet action to the mouth, eyes, and eyebrows. On selected models, he included closing eyelids, flapping ears, and even a device that made a section of hair stand up straight, to simulate great fright, surprise, or other extreme emotion. Some of the figures were constructed with hollow-sleeve arms, that allowed a second puppeteer to supplement the facial expressions with arm and hand motion.

For the most part, however, Tyler was a traditionalist manufacturer. He felt that figures with all sorts of complex functions tended to substitute for the real art and skill of a professional vent. It was like a kid with an electric guitar that had dozens of special effects, built-in electronics and cheaters, but only mediocre skills. He would rather listen to a classical guitarist playing the lacquer off a six-string acoustic. The point was not what devices could do. The point was what the performer could do.

His own career as a vent had only begun as a sideline. He dropped out of school, after several years of trying to earn a living and do the schoolwork too. His job at a local cabinet shop allowed him to refine the skills his grandfather had taught him. The day he left school, he opened the back room that Gramps had used as a workshop and began his first vent figure. In time, his work was compared favorably with that of his mentor and other craftsmen.

Eventually, he prepared a brief act of his own, mostly to test out the figures, sort of like typing "The quick brown fox ..." when you wanted to check out a keyboard. He was surprised at how well the act went over. He could easily have devoted himself to performing full time. But after all was said and done, he found the stage was a lonely, isolating place. When Tom appeared before audiences, he was famous, and rewarded, but he was alone. Up on the stage, in front of all those distant faces, observing and evaluating, he felt like a freak of nature, an aberration. It was like audiences would pay to see just because he was different, like a cow with two heads, or a bearded woman. The applause was like a drug— it got you high, but it didn't last. When he went into the workshop and picked up the old, sweat-darkened tools, he could feel Gramps hand guiding his along the wood, like he did when Tom was six or eight. In that feeling was a certain strength and security.

Consequently, Tom turned down most offers to perform, limiting himself to those that did not require extensive travel or exhausting commitments of time. He enjoyed doing occasional club dates and benefit gigs on weekends, using the extra income to keep the main business relatively worry-free.

When the doorbell rang, he laid the model head in its holder and walked to the entrance, surprised to see the detective accompanied by another man.

"Nice to see you, Gil. Who's your friend?"

"This is Frank Terranova, Tom. I was going to drop him off at the station, but when I described your place here, it was hard not to bring him along for a look. Besides, I thought he could distract Annie."

"She can be a little aggressive, can't she," Tom laughed, "but I don't really need her full-time, so she only works mornings. You missed her this time. Glad to meet you, Frank."

The men shook hands and moved to the chairs by the stage. Tom offered coffee, which was refused when they saw the muddy brew left in the bottom of the pot. He started a new pot.

"How is the investigation going, Gil?" Tyler asked.

"Like most of them, slow and frustrating," Gil laughed, "but maybe you can help us shed some more light."

"What would you like to know?"

"Well, with a case as strange as this one, it's hard to know what to ask," Beach explained, "but the ventriloquist connection seems to make sense. What I'd really like to do, is bring you in on the case. I mean, I've asked you questions before, but only what I knew I needed to ask. Maybe if you hear the whole story, you might have some ideas that wouldn't even occur to me."

Terranova joined the conversation at this point.

"The important thing is that if we fill you in on the entire case, it would mean you'd have to keep it completely confidential. You'd be receiving official police information. We'd have to pledge you to secrecy."

"I don't know what we can offer you in the way of money," Beach warned, "the brass aren't being real helpful on this one, but I can usually come up with something ..."

Tom waved aside the offer.

"Forget that. I don't need any money. I mean, don't get me wrong, I'm not wealthy. But I have a comfortable income, and anytime it isn't enough, I can always do some extra entertaining. To be honest, the idea sounds fascinating, though I have no idea whether I can help or not. I have no problem with the confidentiality. I'd be glad to help any way that I can."

"Before you agree so quickly, there is one more thing," Gil warned. "There is the slight possibility of some personal danger. In a similar case several years ago, the suspect made an attempt on the investigating officer's life, and several innocent civilians were injured. I'm not saying anything like that is probably going to happen, but just to make sure you know the whole deal."

"I see," Tom nodded, "and what happened to that criminal, Officer Beach?"

The Detective looked at the ventriloquist intently for a moment.

"He died."

There was a moment of quiet. Tom stood and walked over to the workbench. He picked up a small file, the old wooden handle dark with grime and perspiration of over fifty years. He weighed it in his hand for a moment. After returning it to a holder hanging from the pegboard, he came back to the circle of chairs, sat down facing Gil and spoke in a soft voice.

"I guess you had better fill me in."

Chapter 28

Saturday, 1:26 p.m.

Vito, the head waiter at Sal Anthony's, was staring through the front window of the restaurant, wondering if it would rain. A car pulled up to the loading zone in front of the entrance. He was tempted to go out and tell the driver to move his automobile, but then recognized the car as a police vehicle. Sure enough, one of two guys that emerged was a detective that often dropped into the restaurant for meals. He remembered the name was Beach. Remembering and using names with customers was one of Vito's talents and a sure way to increase tips. The two men outside were obviously waiting for someone. When they turned in unison, he saw an attractive woman striding toward them from down the street. She wasn't a Kardashian, he thought, but she wasn't bad either.

At first, he didn't understand why puffs of dust appeared to be moving in and around the men. When one of the two dived for the woman, he realized that the dust was from bullets, chipping up chunks of concrete from the pavement. He saw the cop that he knew as Beach give a jerk, like he had been grasped by an invisible hand, then lurch to the ground, clawing at his back. As he hit the pavement, however, the movement stopped. The Detective lay still.

A large pane of glass in the door turned opaque as it crystallized and shattered, points of light spewing inward. That was when Vito first realized that he might be in danger. By then it was too late. Bullets pulverized a decorative light globe, splintered oak booths and shredded a hanging plant. One slug slammed into the waiter's upper left chest, twirling him around so that the next bullet entered his head from the rear, carrying globs of gray matter and blood with it, when it blew a huge exit hole at the eye socket. His pirouette spun him another half turn, to throw his body against the cashier's booth where an enlarged picture of the menu was displayed on the wall. His lifeless corpse slowly slid to the floor, trailing a gooey red smear from the appetizer section ...to the side-dishes.

Across the street, a figure scurried down an alley and slipped out of sight.

The Master was pleased, but not totally satisfied, as he glanced back and saw the inert forms scattered about the street. He hid the automatic weapon under his coat, pulling himself away from the scene of carnage with difficulty. There was an incompleteness to doing things this way. Guns were not his preferred means. Although sometimes necessary to protect his zones of influence, the guns were distant killers, not allowing him to either be a true part of the release or to take heads back to the museum. When he used blades, he felt the warmth and throbbing of the chosen one's spirit in his hands. He felt it gush out with their blood. He felt a luminous glow leave when they finally terminated. As their life spurted out, thankfully so did his dark burdens and evil fluids, leaving him light and clean and powerful.

Explosives or bullets weren't the same. The life force was wasted, dispelled into the atmosphere instead of incorporated into his own being, as was preferable. He sighed, recognizing the need to maintain his distance and safety for the time being, yet regretting the loss of peace and calm that came with a more personal act. That peace came too infrequently. Soon he would need to release someone else ... more intimately.

Chapter 29

Saturday, 3:07 p.m.

Colin Treadwell was cutting out of work early. No one was in the office to see him leave. As always, he had a cover story to explain his early exit, should anyone ask. Despite the coolness of the weather, he had not worn a coat into work. Therefore, his clothing gave no hint that he was leaving for the day—he could have been emptying some garbage, grabbing a newspaper, or just stepping outside for a breath of fresh air. At least that was what he reasoned.

He walked easily, in no apparent hurry, nothing to make anyone notice. He made his way to the car, then headed for the precinct boundaries. As he neared Fourteenth, he was reaching for the knob to turn off the police radio, to sever his link and responsibility when his worst fear became reality. The voice of the dispatcher announced one of the dreaded emergency codes in the same monotone that she might use to say that a cat was up in a tree, or a back-up car was needed at a water main break.

"Code Ten-thirteen, Forty-seven Irving Place, at the restaurant, shots fired. Use extreme caution, officers down."

To Treadwell, it was like hearing a summons to hell.

For any cop, code Ten-Thirteen, "Officer Needs Assistance," is an absolute priority. If you can't count on immediate support from your fellow officers in an emergency, you can't go out and face the realities of police work in the city. The trouble was, Colin couldn't face them in any case.

Initially, instinct and training were stronger than fear, so Treadwell's foot slammed down on the accelerator as he switched on the flasher mounted to the grille and dashboard. Yet, even as he swung the car around and headed for the address, a civil war was going on within him.

Self-preservation told him to stay out of it. Every nerve seemed to be shouting for him to disappear. Half his brain kept inventing ways to avoid responding. He could pull into a gas station, later saying he was out of gas. He could simply turn off the radio and pretend he hadn't heard the code at all. The other half of his mind kept shouting a silent message, saying "What if it was you?" Maybe this was the final line between self-respect and self-loathing. Did he dare cross it?

The fear almost won out. Maybe the deciding factor was that earlier he had seen a note describing Gil Beach's itinerary for the day. The information included the address just now mentioned by the dispatcher. Treadwell suspected, therefore, that one of the "officers down" might be Beach, the closest thing he had to a partner...the closest thing he had to a friend. It was enough to keep him moving in the direction of Sal Anthony's, ... and whatever waited.

He wasn't the first to arrive, but he got there— heart whumping in furious protest, muscles knotted in tension. He grabbed for his sidearm, as he threw open the car door and scanned the street, already feeling the searing pain of imaginary bullets slicing through his body. There was an awful white noise filling his head, that made it difficult for him to understand the situation for a few moments. Then it dawned on him that since uniformed officers and others were standing casually in full view, it could only mean that there was no fusillade to dodge, no battle in progress, no immediate threat to life. Two stretchers were already filled. Through a broken front window, he could see a crumpled bloody figure. Someone had died.

Colin stood, confused and motionless, his gun hanging from his hand, when a voice startled him. It was Lieutenant Lincoln who had just arrived on the scene.

"Good response, Treadwell. We came from the station, but you obviously made better time. Is that the first officer over there?"

The "First Officer" was the earliest uniformed cop to arrive on a crime scene and according to standard police protocol, consequently became the person responsible for a number of recording and communication duties.

Colin looked in the direction Lincoln was pointing, saw a uniform with a pad in his hand, so he vaguely nodded. The Lieutenant hurried on. The mutilated body in the restaurant beckoned to Treadwell like a siren. He didn't want it to be anyone he knew. He especially didn't want it to be Gil Beach, yet he had to see. He moved forward slowly, not sure that he wanted to see what was under the bloody cloth.

Chapter 30

Sunday, 9:28 a.m.

Gil didn't know where he was. The soil was sandy and sunbaked around the post where he was tied. Bloodstains colored the parched earth. A few yards away a group of men in nondescript cammo uniforms stood in the slouched postures universal to waiting soldiers, cigarettes dangling from lips, hands moving unconsciously over oiled rifle stocks. Occasionally, there would be a wry expression accompanied by a comment in some guttural language, followed by scattered laughter. Despite the blazing sun, he could feel a chill working at his innards.

From a bleached wooden building on the opposite side of the courtyard, a man appeared in the uniform of an officer. It was difficult to make out the face from a distance, but he was black, thin, and walked with a stiff authority in his step. The officer, who wore the silver bars of a lieutenant and a shoulder patch with the picture of a stylized clam shell on it, veered away so that his face remained hidden, moving toward the group of waiting men. When they caught sight of the Lieutenant there was a change in their stance. Drooping men straightened into postures approximating attention, though tinged with a resistance born of too many pointless deaths and senseless commands. Another series of orders prompted the men to shuffle into a ragged semi-circle and raise their weapons.

He felt his stomach knot, as he realized that the final moment had arrived. They were going to shoot him now. There was no way out. He wondered that they had neglected the traditional blindfold but knew that he preferred to see the faces of those who were killing him, anyway. They were hard faces, worn and wrinkled, with leathery skin cured in the desert sun. Or was it a desert? There was a faint smell of the sea.

There was something familiar about the officer, whose uniform seemed to be fashioned out of some sort of terrycloth. As he turned, the facial features were revealed. Gil recognized Randolph Lincoln, shouting the orders for his execution.

Gil tried desperately to free himself from the ropes holding him, as the metallic sound of rifles being cocked, bolts snicking home, echoed. He looked up, just as the command to fire was given, but was amazed to see projectiles issuing from the rifle barrels in exaggerated slow motion. Instead of lead slugs, however, the missiles were sharp-pointed objects resembling small knives, moving in streams of razor-edged death toward him. All the while, Lincoln was shouting at him.

"You are a loner! You are only out for yourself! There are children dead because of you!"

Gil fought the ropes and the words, sensing that this situation was not only unbearable, but impossible. As he thrashed, his head slammed into the post to which he was tethered, sending waves of dull pain radiating down his neck into his shoulders. One of the knives thudded into his chest. Blood sprayed out, like from a punctured water balloon. But instead of the hard-edged metallic odor of blood, the liquid that spurted from his chest was a clear nectar that reeked of rotten shellfish. Another blade slapped into his body, then a third. Piercing agony shot through his chest and arms. Hands were clutching at him now. Lincoln's voice grew softer.

"... alone ... by yourself... not alone. I'm here, Darling."

The voice was not Lincoln, not a man at all. Gil exerted a massive effort, managing to get his eyelids partially open. A woman was bending over him, something in her hand. He yelled as one nightmare merged with another, pain lancing him as he felt the certainty of his doom, his life ready to be sucked out, like water down a drain.

But as he thrashed, the hurt became less intense, and the woman's words began to make sense.

"It's all right, Gil. You're okay. No one is hurting you. You're dreaming. You are safe, Darling."

The voice was familiar. It was Pilar, the woman he loved. His eyes opened fully, and in clearing vision he saw her sculpted face, eyes glistening with tears. What he had imagined to be a knife in her hand was a rolled cloth, which she now used to wipe his perspiring forehead. Slowly, his tensed muscles loosened, so he was able to settle back on the bed, head still throbbing. The surroundings began to come into focus, and he recognized the place as Pilar's apartment. It was all coming back now.

Frank and he had been hitting it off well. So, after he met with Tom Tyler to bring the ventriloquist onto the team working the case, Gil decided that if he had Terranova drop him off at the restaurant, Frank and Pilar could meet at the same time. His colleague could take the car. Gil could either ride back with Pilar or take a cab.

The whole sequence of events started to come back to him. He remembered now. As Pilar approached, Gil had seen, rather than heard, the first gunshots, immediately recognizing them for what they were. The Detective didn't need sound to know that the puffs of dust and concrete chips were deadly. Fortunately, Frank also understood the situation quickly, and since he was closer to Pilar, made a dive to get her out of the line of fire. A slug caught the loose part of Gil's coat, which was enough to jerk his body forcefully, knocking him off balance. The same high-powered round shattered the restaurant window.

Gil instinctively reached for the Styr GB at his back, but between the tug of the bullet, the sudden move for his gun, and a cascade of glass hitting his feet, he lost stability and went down. The 'good news' was that he was not actually wounded by the bullet, which passed harmlessly through his coat. The bad news was that, as he fell, he struck his head against the building's foundation, dazing him. He lay there for a moment, stunned, unable to return fire. Also fortunate for

Gil, his sudden drop to the ground either spoiled the shooter's aim or convinced the gunman that he had eliminated his target. There was no doubt in the Detective's mind about who the target had been. He also knew that the gunman had to be the killer he was pursuing. The only question was how the would-be assassin had located him.

As he looked at Pilar, Beach saw the concern on her face. He realized that he was still gasping for breath and wet with perspiration—surfacing from the dream, like a skin-diver who has over-stayed his lung capacity.

"Do you want to tell me about it?" she asked.

Gil had never told anyone. Not even Diane. Of course, his deceased wife had known that he had the dreams—for years he had awakened in the throes of them. She had assumed it was a case of post-traumatic flashbacks, from some police gun battle or his combat experience. She had read that it was not wise to press someone about these. Whatever she read, it made enough sense to her that she didn't press him. Gil had been glad to avoid the whole matter, so had not corrected her. Now he had to answer Pilar's question. He had always been honest with her, and figured he couldn't stop now.

For the first time, Gil began telling about the dreams, the terror, the pain. He didn't even make a conscious decision to share, he just found himself letting it all out. At first, he was worried about her reactions, watching for signs of ridicule or scorn, but little by little he relaxed. She seemed to understand. After almost an hour of talking, interrupted only by an occasional question from Pilar, the pounding of his bruised head made him stop to ask for aspirin. She brought him the container and a glass of water, sat down opposite him, taking his hands in hers.

"You realize, of course, where this is coming from, don't you Darling?"

Gil noted the "Darling," but didn't know how to respond.

"I don't want to make you a client, Gil, but you must know that these kinds of recurring dreams are always the result of some unresolved conflicts of the past."

"Yeah, my wife thought it was P.T.S.D., or something, a stress thing. But I don't think so. It's not war I dream about."

"Well, she may have been closer to the truth than you think. There are many kinds of traumatic stress besides war, and dealing with it is pretty much the same, no matter what the origins. I have clients who were the victims of incest that showed similar symptoms."

Gil gave a huff. "Well, nobody sexually abused me!"

"I hear you. Now just tell me, if I am intruding where you don't want me to, Darling, but the way you say that sets off little red flags in my psychologist's mind. Was there another kind of abuse?"

Gil felt himself getting light-headed. An icicle of something like anxiety darted down his back. Between the stresses of the last week, the crack on the head, and the effects of the dream, his barriers were not up as high as usual. His shoulders slumped and he sighed.

"When you passed out on the bed, I tried to loosen some of your clothes to make you more comfortable," Pilar said softly, "and your shirt came open. Those scars on. your neck and chest—they aren't from the Job, or the war, are they?"

He answered with a shake of his head. Moisture began welling up in his eyes. Pilar nodded and waited. He sat for a long moment, then began to speak in short, labored phrases.

"My mother... Sick woman... She tried to... to...," He choked out, unable to get out the horrid words, *'**she tried to kill me.**'* "...I was four. Don't remember much."

"Perhaps your dreams are fragments of that memory," Pilar suggested. "You said there were recurring images and sensations?"

"Yeah..., there is always terrycloth somewhere ...with the blades."

"Terrycloth, like a towel, or washcloth?"

"Yeah, or a robe. One of those towel fabric robes. I think my mother practically lived in one of those."

"What else?" she prompted.

"Well, then…uhh… pointed things—teeth, knives, blades, whatever … get me in the chest."

"And you feel a somatic memory, that reproduces pain you experienced as a child."

"A somatic memory?"

"Yes. We don't only retain memories of thoughts and ideas. We also store sensations which are often linked with the memories, like feelings of pain and anxiety, or even tastes and smells."

"Maybe that's why my dreams always have the taste, smell of seafood, or the sea."

"What do you associate with those words?"

Gil tried to come up with a memory, but all he could think of was clams, which he hated, and a clam knife. At this point he blocked. The feelings slipped away. He felt spaced-out and confused.

"Well, don't worry about it," Pilar reassured him. You'll remember it when you are ready.

She lifted his hand in hers, bringing it to her lips. "And never forget that I am here now."

Her lips were soft against his fingers. He reached with his other hand to touch her lustrous hair. A waft of some delicate scent was released—not an artificial perfume smell, but clean and natural. As she looked up into his eyes, he felt his heart doing flip-flops. He exerted a slight pressure on her neck, pulling her up to his face. As she slid forward, her body came to rest against his, their limbs easily intertwining.

With a finger, Gil traced...cheek, her mouth. When their lips met, there was a delicacy at first, then a more intense hunger took over. His tongue explored her mouth, and she responded in kind. Startled by the intensity, he could feel himself being swept away. He pulled back. She did too.

"Wow," he murmured.

"Yeah," she agreed.

"I've got a feeling that I know where this is leading," Gil grinned.

"You may be right," she laughed, "but not right now. I'm already late for a last-minute review session. If it wasn't the only possible opportunity to meet my students before the test, I might be convinced to stay. But how about a rain check?"

He made a goofy face and shrugged.

"Hell, I'd even sit through the class, if it kept me close to you. But tonight, no excuses will do. We'll have dinner at El Bandido, and find something... special, for dessert."

Chapter 31

Sunday, 2:14 p.m.

The Master Performer lay still as a corpse. He was attuned to the messages of his body at a level that transcended normal abilities. He thought of the electronic sensors in complex spacecraft, which telegraphed data about heat build-up, malfunction, and other internal operations. His heightened sensitivity was as superior to that feedback system, as a mainframe computer was to a hand-held calculator. He began an inventory.

The hairs in his scalp were growing back after shaving his head for the impersonation. He could feel each follicle manufacturing proteins and pushing its shaft through an oily pore. He recalled that it was a divine attribute to be able to number the hairs on one's head. Along his back, he felt the sheet of foil on which he lay. It had been difficult to obtain the old-fashioned alloy, instead of the aluminum which had now taken its place on supermarket shelves. There were no current manufacturers, as far as he had been able to determine. So he began a lengthy search of stores specializing in memorabilia, antiques, and collectibles which had finally taken him to a junky little shop in Connecticut. The place was stocked with shelves of old products. Many had original contents or packages—and outrageous prices. Antique metal boxes nearly obscured the three original, unopened containers of tinfoil, but his powers had been swollen with the energy of the latest release, so the Performer had spied them out. He was able to purchase all three, bringing them home to use as a shield against the rays. Aluminum didn't stop the beams, thus he knew part of the great conspiracy was the elimination of real tinfoil from retail stores.

Now he was protected. He could feel the same sort of electro-chemical reaction between his bare skin and the foil, that occurred when someone bit down on metal with a silver filling. It was this chemical reaction that created the barrier, a shimmering zone of energy which deflected radon and other lethal particles aimed at him.

His thigh muscles quivered from the exertion he had just completed. While holding his stance with a foot on a chair, to perform with Melvin, he had developed the additional trick of lifting the raised foot a bare fraction of an inch off the chair. Then he held that one-legged position while delivering a routine. There was a sense of mastery and superiority that came with this hidden maneuver. While audiences were concentrating on the 'patter' and 'business' between him and Melvin, he was performing a feat of power and strength of which they were not even aware. There were so many things of which he was the only one aware. The Performer knew he existed on a different plane than normal humans, a plane he shared only with Melvin and 'The Master.' Each of them was able to perceive things beyond sensibilities of the common hoard yet exhibit absolute control over their reactions.

That was the exercise in which he was now engaged. Naked on the floor of the stage, with the heat turned off to help preserve the new figures from spoiling further, he recorded and stored the sensations, without allowing himself any reaction, any movement, any relief. His face was frozen in a perfect deadpan, while lying still as a corpse. He merely controlled his inner being, separating it from the external environment. In this self-determined space, all was possible.

For the moment, he willed himself to be warm. To accomplish this, all he had to do was detach himself from this place and time. In a moment, he was eleven years old again, and back at the Bethlehem Home, as it burned to the ground. Waves of heat swirled around him again, as he observed the results of the device he used to start the fire. An old electrical cord had not been frayed until he made it that way, but he was confident that the inspectors would think it was the cause of the fire and cite the home's owners for allowing such faulty electrical equipment to be near oily rags in the basement.

On the museum stage, the Master Performer shivered with excitement and sensation, as he relived his early exhibit of power and control but continued to lay perfectly still. Surrounding him was a collection of objects, arranged in a circle, so that he was part of a mystic rosette. At his head was the Ingram M-10 rifle he had used against the policemen, at his feet packets of PETN explosive. By each hand was a grenade, and at each remaining point of the clock, blades he had previously used to release one of the chosen. The arrangement was a mystical transmitter, a talisman which called out the dark presences that guided him.

It was growing dark in the museum, when he finally heard the voices. Barely discernible at first, they spoke in whispers of disturbed air and the creak of floorboards contracting in the cold. They spoke to him of his mission and uniqueness, dispelling self-doubt and reassuring him of his ultimate success. The voices were not always easy to hear, for they merged at times with other voices—of Melvin, of his mother, of the first Master, his father, of psychiatrists and guardians, social workers and agents, audiences, and victims—all howling at him for attention, trying to break his resolve, deflect his calling, control his will. Now, however, the voices reinforced his determination and soothed him.

He recalled being emotionally shaken, when he returned to the place that he had sprayed with gunfire, only to see that the Detective had managed to escape death. He was worried that the enemy had some undetectable force field which would protect him against any retribution. Burdened as he was by his failure to kill the Detective, it was soothing to know that the voice acquitted him of his transgression, helping him see that there were other ways to penetrate the interloper's zones of influence. The policeman had found what was sacred to the Performer and polluted it. This was a travesty against his special zones, which hurt the Performer more than if the pain had been inflicted on his physical corpus. The voice helped him see that it was time to do the same to the enemy. The difference was in vulnerability. Safe within his deadpan, the Performer was self-contained and self-sufficient. This lent to his invulnerability. The Detective, on the other hand, had people he cared about. That was his weakness. Now the Performer cared about them too.

Chapter 32

Monday, 6:46 a.m.

There was no reason he should be feeling this good, especially considering what he had been through in the last forty-eight hours. Usually the stair routine left Gil in a dulled state, despite the vigorous exercise. Although athletes and amateur sportsmen spoke of a heightened energy level, or even "high" associated with their workouts, Gil usually had a different experience. His exercise normally depleted him, leaving a sense of dissatisfaction.

But today had been different. He had cut short the usual regimen. There was a point in his exertions that he always reached. He thought of it as a challenge point. This was a predictable plateau, when the body rebelled, and the mind had to make a decision to ignore the signals of depletion ... to push on through the pain and exhaustion. Gil had always felt that to stop at this point was unacceptable—it would make him a quitter, a failure. At a barely conscious level, he feared something inside that had to be controlled. The evil that had led him to almost kill that criminal punk long ago, remained within him, ready to spring free. So, in a way, just as he saw law enforcement as the discipline which held off the chaos ready to overflow in society, he felt a need to force discipline upon himself to hold off the chaos inside.

But today, as he made his circuits of the track and steps, he found himself smiling. Thoughts of Pilar kept intruding on his concentration. When the level of fatigue became significant, he eased back a bit, to continue his pleasant meditations. The alarm on his sports watch began chirping. It was a reminder that he had to get changed and down to the ferry. Gil was surprised to find that he had not reached the point of exhaustion and mind/body conflict which usually hit him. He felt vaguely guilty about that, yet this was eclipsed by a delicious feeling of well-being.

Gil's body glowed. His mind did too. He felt a reserve of energy that usually was not available to him. His thoughts of Pilar added an electric charge to it all. He wasn't sure why he was feeling this way. He wasn't sure that it was right for him to feel so good, but he knew that he liked it.

Back at the apartment on Howard Avenue, Gil showered and shaved. When he went to the closet, he eyed the anti-ballistic vest hanging there. He almost put it on, hesitating for several moments with it in his hand, but finally folded the bulky garment, shoving it into a large plastic shopping bag he could carry to work. He wasn't scared enough to wear it yet.

After he was dressed, he went to the bureau, fishing in the back of the top drawer. The gun that he pulled out was a Browning 7.65 mm pocket pistol. He flipped the stripping lever on the left side ahead of the trigger guard, removing the slide and barrel, to reassure himself that the stubby little pistol was cleaned and oiled. About five and a half inches long, weighing less than a pound, the Hungarian-manufactured gun was similar to a Walther PPK which made it a handy extra weapon that could be carried in a pocket, purse, or other hidden place. Gil strapped an ankle holster on his leg, and slid the small, but lethal piece of hardware into it.

During the ferry ride to Battery Park, he began making a list of everyone that could have known in advance about his plan to have lunch at Sal Anthony's on Saturday. Tickles of fear crept through his belly every now and then, telegraphed through his nervous system every time his brain considered the fact that someone was trying to kill him. This was very personal. The killer wanted him, had made specific plans designed to eliminate him and had carried those plans out. Though unsuccessful this time, there was no reason to think he would not try again.

Beach worked on the list to keep his mind busy and to develop a base line of information. He had no illusions that the killer would be revealed immediately. In time, he knew, other lists would be generated, or were already being made. Given enough lists, perhaps a name or two would eventually match.

The inventory began with himself, Pilar, and Frank Terranova. This was not a list of suspects, rather a flow chart of how the information could travel.

Frank had left a description of their plans with the Task Force secretary. More accurately, he had left it on her desk, which meant anyone in the unit could have had access to it. Considering the earlier arrival of a gory package directly into the Precinct, without the benefit of postage, security there seemed an issue. Nevertheless, he listed Beverly, putting Lincoln's name and "other P.D.'s" with a question mark beside them. Tom Tyler knew where the Detective was heading after their meeting, so his name went on the list, and Gil thought that perhaps he had let the information slip during his conversation with Nathan Popowick. He had no idea if Pilar had told anyone, but he hoped the killer didn't even know of her existence or would be in a position to gain information from her.

He couldn't recall telling anybody else, but reviewing the events of Saturday, he placed two more names on the list. In his enthusiasm and lack of training, Frank had made a mistake Saturday. During one of the interviews, he had unwittingly mentioned Gil's destination in front of a civilian, by telling Gil that he could make a call from there. At the moment, the Detective couldn't remember whether the slip had occurred during the interview with Mrs. Schottingham, or the one with William Barstow. For now, he listed both names, but underlined the name of the latter, with no particular justification other than his suspicion of the man's attempt to disguise his appearance. He added question marks to both, until he could confirm the matter with Terranova.

Wilson was on the front desk when Beach arrived at the Precinct. The desk officer didn't remember receiving a package or have any suggestions as to who might have left it. A wire basket sat on the huge bar-like counter, where mail and other items often were placed. Wilson suggested that anyone could have left a package by that means. Gil surveyed the room, noting that constant confusion was normal here. A continually changing mix of cops, perps, and civilians entered the station for any one of a hundred reasons. He realized how easy it would be for a person to move to the desk and drop a package into the basket unnoticed.

As Gil entered the PDU office, Frank was already at work. When reminded, he remembered revealing Gil's lunch plans when they were at Barstow's. Realizing that he had made a mistake in judgment, Terranova began apologizing. Gil stopped him with a glare.

"Okay," he responded to Gil's look, "let's just say that it won't happen again."

Frank handed the Detective a pile of paper and mail. One envelope was from Quantico, the home of the National Center for Violent Crime Analysis (NCVCA). Archie Eastwood had come through, as promised. Another packet contained several sheets of names and addresses.

"What are these?" he asked Terranova.

"That's the New York area mailing list you wanted for that magazine—Newsyvents."

"Good. Have Gwen open a file in the computer for this case. Enter that list, and we can add anything else when we get it. Eventually, we'll be able to some cross-checking."

"What shall I tell her to label the file?"

Gil thought for a moment. The case had finally been entered in the Green Book, the big ledger that listed every reported homicide case in the precinct. Lincoln still had reservations but had eventually agreed to treat the case internally as a homicide, despite public relations efforts to the contrary. The decision, like so many others by the police brass, was not based so much on logic as politics. A widely publicized kidnapping almost required the involvement of the F.B.I. When Deputy Inspector Madigan pointed that out, Lincoln decided that Gil's theory of murder made more sense than it had before.

The large clothbound volume listed the case as a "missing person, possible homicide" and assigned it the case number H-25-053. Though this information was all in computer files as well, tradition kept the physical book a part of the process. H classified it as a homicide case, the second set of numbers specified the current calendar year, and the third set indicated that it was the fifty-third reported homicide in that twelve-month cycle. The numbering system allowed for any amount from one to a thousand. The total was almost always under one hundred. Sometimes, when there was a particularly large number of homicides in a given period, you might hear P.D.U. detectives speak of their worry that it might become a "three-digit" year.

There had not been fifty-three murders in the Ninth Precinct, but between reports that proved to be wrong, suspicious deaths that eventually were determined to be natural or suicide, and cases shared with neighboring precincts, the total was inflated. The actual number was more like two dozen by this time of year, with half as many cleared. Last year the P.D.U. had worked on thirty-one bona-fide homicides, clearing twenty-six, although half a dozen of those were what Gil called BCTS cases—" better cleared than solved," where administrative decisions allowed the cases to be closed for the sake of improved statistics. Front line detectives knew that sometimes the investigation was still unfinished and certainly not 'solved.'

Gwen Curry, who handled most data-processing for the Precinct, had an information-handling program that was able to cross-check items on various lists. In the past, Gil had been forced to rely on memory and dogged determination, when comparing records and rosters. Since the data gathered during an investigation was often chaotic, immense amounts of time could be spent merely organizing it in a way that would allow the matching of information from many sources. The computer saved a lot of time. Just as importantly, the electronic device never missed a name, never forgot an item, never failed to compare one piece of data with the others, and never had blurry eyes or groggy thinking from lack of sleep, days of junk food, and other bad human habits. There was no way that a computer could even approach the intuitive skills of a good detective. But it had become an important weapon in Gil's investigatory arsenal, and he believed in using everything that could possibly help.

Gwen always asked for a case name, when opening a new file. At first, she had been willing to assign titles herself but got such teasing about some of her choices that she refused to do it anymore. She was still living down the one she called, "Stud-4."

Gil thought of possible abbreviations that would match his image of the killer. The man was a ventriloquist, or lover of ventriloquism, who killed children. He mutilated his victims. He was bold enough to try killing the detective hunting him. He was not satisfied to be the hunted, making it clear that he would try to reverse the relationship to become the hunter.

Gil realized that he had not yet opened the envelope from NCVCA, which might add to his mental picture, so he told Frank to wait a few minutes as he sat down at the desk. Using his finger as a letter-opener, he tore open the envelope to remove the contents. A small note was attached from Archie Eastwood, which said he didn't really need to call in a favor in order to contact a former friend. Gil felt the intended twinge of guilt, making a promise to himself to send a response. Maybe they could get together during his next long weekend. He knew he had been getting isolated. The experience of closeness with Pilar, together with a developing friendship with Terranova had given him a taste for more.

There were several pages of computer generated print-outs, each headed by standard cautions. They also cautioned against release of the information except when interpreted by an official. Eastwood had made a slash over these statements with a yellow marking pen, and added in pencil, "You didn't get these from me, pal. Kapish?"

The profile was in narrative form. Gil planned to take the content with a grain of salt, recognizing that much of the information was based on averages, statistics, and suppositions that might not hold true for a particular case. The average American family might have 2.2 children, but not a single real family had exactly that many, and any given family might have ten children or none. He settled back and read.

The perpetrator is likely to be a white male, between the ages of 30 and 40. He is of average appearance, stands between 5'8" and 5'10", weighing 150-175 lbs. He has served in the military and hunts as recreation. He has limited relationships, which include few friends and distanced relatives. He lives alone, in hotel or apartment in Manhattan or neighboring communities.

He is unemployed or works nights.

Gil knew where that came from. He had described to Eastwood the hours when the crimes had happened, already guessing it was likely that killer had to be available during the daytime, though he also kept open the possibility of someone with a flexible work schedule or self-employed. He read on.

The man is intelligent, and is capable of skilled work, though he prefers to be in a position of dominance, or works alone. He has great resentment of authority, which leads him to challenge law enforcement.

"To say the very least!" Gil thought, "Challenge, as in shoot to kill!"

The subject is likely to feel superior to others. He will have little sense of guilt or remorse. He will tend to taunt investigatory agencies by leaving evidence he wants them to find. He does not expect to be caught, and sometime engages in high-risk behavior, supposing himself to be invincible.

The perpetrator falls within the category of an "Organized" pattern of the sexual homicide type, as opposed to the "Disorganized" pattern. This means he will tend to be socially competent, able to perform sexually, and maintains a controlled mood during the commission of his crimes. He is mobile, using a vehicle in the crimes, and follows the news of them in the media.

As a child, he was of high birth order status, and his father's work was stable, though childhood discipline was inconsistent, possibly abusive and one or more parents may have been absent. He probably has a history of juvenile delinquency, including violence and possibly arson or animal torture.

He is likely to be compulsive in his habits and will demonstrate a consistent pattern and modus operandi. Victims will tend to be targeted strangers, with elaborate planning preceding the crime. The victims will be personalized and killed at a different location than where they are taken. Trophies or souvenirs will likely be taken from the victim, and the body will be transported before disposal.

This concluded the profile. There was a note that the template program had identified several persons whose profiles had a match of seventy percent or more of the traits listed. None of them were in New York, and none of them seemed to fit the hunches Gil was developing about this case. He let the NCVCA information merge with his own impressions. A picture began to form of an intelligent, but deranged adversary—a psychotic that needed to prove superiority. Unfortunately, this madman seemed to have selected Gil as his foil. Although he tried not to let that get to him, it made Gil nervous.

The rest of the mail included a letter from the P.B.A., a notice of upcoming promotional exams, an advertising circular from a uniform store, and a small envelope addressed to "Master Detective Gil Beach" in hand-printed block letters.

He checked the postmark, which was smeared but appeared to be local. Holding the envelope up to a light, he could see that it contained only a small sheet of paper. Still smarting from the Lieutenant's previous reprimand, Gil opened the letter carefully, touching only edges, while using his handkerchief and pocketknife to avoid smearing any possible prints. As he suspected, the note inside was from the killer. In the childish printing, the words read:

DEAR GIL

I FEEL wE ALREDY KNOW EACH OTHR, DON'T YOU AGRee? WE ARE BOth MASTERS. BUT WHICH MASTER will MASTER the MASTER? SOON YOU WILL BE RECEIVING SOMETHING I MADE JUST FOR YOU. I Hope YOU LIKD

THE LAST gIFT. SO FAR YOU HAVE NOT BEEN VRY SMART. YOU WILL HAVE TO Do BETTER, OR I WIL MAKE YOU LOOK LIKE A DUMMY.

Gil was surprised to see a name at the bottom of the note. It was signed, "MEL."

His adversary wanted to be known by name: "MEL."

It was unlikely that the name was his real identity, but the detective found himself attaching it to his mental image of the killer. The mistakes and oddly mixed upper and lower-case letters could have been evidence of ignorance, but Gil didn't think so. He figured they were more likely signs the guy was falling apart.

There was something unpleasant going on in Gil's stomach. Maybe it was caused by his disgust at the arrogance of this "MEL." Maybe it went along with personalizing the killer. It could be fear. Whatever it was, it made him want to respond. At this point, the killer was too much in control of communication, offering only what he wanted Gil to have, and yet somehow getting any information he wanted.

Gil's mind kept coming back to the way the man was able to know what was happening in the police investigation, or more specifically, Gil's own conduct of the case. The man might or might not have access to department information, but Gil wanted to make a point, even if it was only a symbolic one. He called Frank over to his desk.

"Frank, that file I want Gwen to open ..."

"Yeah, did you decide what you want to label it?"

"Yes. Just call it 'DUMMY.'"

CHAPTER 33

Monday, 7:41 p.m.

Gil was relieved to get away from the PDU that evening. The small Mexican restaurant they found was squeezed into a row of shops on St. Mark's Place. Unless you had heard about it, you would never expect it to be as fine as it was. Gil feasted on tostadas, enchiladas, and fried plantains, while Pilar downed an immense taco salad and went through two orders of nachos, dripping in spicy cheese and jalapeno sauce. They topped the meal off with the restaurant's special flan, covered with a delicate sweet sauce. Even the guitar player was good. Mercifully, nobody requested 'Guantanamera.'

After the meal, there was a moment of uncomfortableness, as they decided where to go next. Finally, Pilar insisted that he come to her place for a cup of her special gourmet coffee. They both knew that the stage was being set for an intimate evening, but they skirted around the subject. Nevertheless, there was an exciting extra tension between them as they drove to her apartment.

They didn't get to the coffee for a while. When they arrived at her place, Gil started to help Pilar with her coat. As he took it, she turned and melted into his arms. Their lips came together, while hands hungrily searched and touched each other. She gave a moan and pressed her body closer.

"I want you," he said.

"Yes," she replied breathlessly.

His fingers fumbled at her clothing. She was wearing a silky blouse that slipped from her shoulders with a whisper. Gil heard her gasp in pleasure when his hands touched her bare skin. She was pulling at his shirt, even as he released the clasp on her brassiere. A hunch of her shoulders, and the bra slid off, exposing her breasts to his exploring hands and mouth. When she, in turn, slid down to his chest, Gil felt a clutch of insecurity, realizing that his scars were exposed, but she covered them with kisses. Soon he forgot his hesitations.

They moved to the bedroom, where bedding was thrown aside, and hands fumbled to remove garments, as they let themselves be swept away by the urgency of union. She moaned in eagerness, as he eased her onto her back and moved between her legs. She was moist and ready when he entered, both of them expelling sounds of uninhibited pleasure at the joining.

The lovemaking might not have been exceptional in its technique or variety, but neither Gil nor Pilar had ever been so caught up in a sexual experience before. They shared a wild and crashing ride on the rapids of an emotional river, bursting through peaks of feeling, disappearing in troughs of passion, calling out to each other and whatever gods might be nearby, with pleasure and abandon.

Chapter 34

Tuesday, 10:25 a.m.

It wasn't easy for Gil to leave his memories of the previous night, to concentrate on the Lieutenant's monotone. The Task Force was using one corner of the large room as a conference area. Lincoln was doing most of the talking, while Epstein scribbled notes on the chalkboard. The group was bigger now. Several uniforms were doing the door-to-door interviews, a thankless task, but necessary. Their only reward was to sit in on a conference like this occasionally. A detective from the Tenth Precinct, Jim Washbyrne, had been temporarily assigned, and another clerk typist was taking notes. Captain Occhiogrosso stood by the door, observing. Sergeant Mabry lounged in a chair, clipping his nails.

"A city-wide memorandum has developed additional leads, including a possible related homicide," Lincoln intoned, avoiding Gil Beach's eyes. "A decapitated child's body has been sitting in the morgue of Mt. Sinai for several months. God knows what it has been doing there all this time. Some royal snafu. Heads will roll for that one."

A giggle from Gina Esperoza made Lincoln look up and dart his eyes around trying to identify the source of the laughter. He was obviously unaware of his own poor choice of words. When no one ventured to explain, he pursed his mouth and continued.

"Detective Beach has received a letter, apparently from the perpetrator. It is being analyzed in the lab. This may indicate that the killer has targeted some of our personnel."

At this point, Frank Terranova jumped in.

"It seems pretty obvious that Gil is the target. Or what do you make of the shooting?"

"There are a lot of possibilities to consider," the Lieutenant waffled, "including a rather questionable lifestyle of the waiter who was killed. He may well have been the target."

Gina guffawed. "INSIDE the restaurant? Shooting through a group of people outside?"

At this, even Captain Occhiogrosso who up to that point had made a point of not reacting, showed a ghost of a smile. Lincoln looked flustered, and changed the subject.

"At Detective Beach's suggestion, we did a stake-out on Barstow and caught him making a run for it. Stopped him at the Port Authority with a Greyhound ticket to Canada in his pocket. Unfortunately, he seems more worried that we will reveal his finances to the I.R.S. than about the crimes we are investigating. He has a righteous alibi for Wednesday."

"But he matches a witness's description, if you take off his wig and lifts," Frank protested.

"Yeah, well, pick a day and you'll get a different description of this bug," Gina responded, "but I checked out his story and he has a doctor and two nurses at the Chelsea clinic who swear he was being examined at the time. Would you believe hemorrhoids?"

"The guy IS a hemorrhoid," Frank commented.

Lt. Lincoln frowned at the general laughter. He turned to Gil, who had been silent through the meeting.

"Any suggestions, Beach?"

"We still need an explanation for Barstow's van being involved. With the description of the driver matching his physical appearance, something ain't kosher, and it isn't the Hasidic kid."

There was more laughter. Occhiogrosso used the pause to step forward, asking for the attention. He introduced Deputy Inspector Madigan, one of eighty-five deputy inspectors in the New York Police Department, who gave what he probably thought was a pep talk. It was more like a sleeping potion. When he finished, bodies stretched, chairs scraped, conversation began, and the meeting broke up. Lincoln had prepared assignment sheets for each person. He placed himself where no one could get out of the room without receiving one. Gil glanced at his list. As soon as Lincoln was out of sight, he crumpled it, then made two points with a hook shot into the nearest waste basket.

Gil had more important things to think about, like the hunted who was trying to become the hunter. He imagined the cold rage inside the madman, shivering at how vivid it seemed. Moving to his desk, the Detective grabbed the telephone and punched out a number for the lab. He was lucky, after only a few seconds wait he got through to the Director himself. "Hi, Jim," Gil began when Nedrow came on the line, "this is Gil Beach."

"Ahh, Detective Beach is it? But it's so quiet. I thought you were always surrounded by the sound of gunfire.

"Ok, okay. Give me a break, Jimbo. So, if you know about the shooting, can you tell me more about it? Anything recovered from the crime scene or whatever?"

"As a matter of fact, we were lucky, though your walk through a wall of bullets, unscathed, makes for a new standard of luck. The sonofabitch scattered cartridges all over the alley across from the restaurant, kindly leaving them for us to look at. With the firing location pretty exact, we were able to determine the range, velocity, and a few other choice pieces of data, not to mention being able to analyze the signature of the weapon from the shells."

Gil waited, knowing that any attempt to prevent the scientist from displaying his knowledge would be counterproductive.

"At first I thought it might be an Uzi," Nedrow continued, "but the signature was wrong, and the firing pattern was too wide. I can't say for sure, but I'd say you were looking at the wrong end of a Cobray Mll/9."

"Is that something new?"

"Not really. It's just the current market name for the old Ingram submachine gun."

"I didn't hear it firing."

"Right. The Ingrams are externally threaded at the muzzle to take the MAC suppressor."

"A silencer? Wouldn't that make it ineffective at that range?"

"Not really. That's the beauty of the MAC suppressor. Unlike the conventional silencer, the MAC allows the bullet to reach its full velocity, which is faster than sound. It suppresses the gas velocity of discharge, and thus dampens the sound without slowing the slug." -

"What's their availability?"

"Not my department," the Lab Director apologized, "but I know it's of U.S. manufacture. Somewhere in Georgia, I think. It's not widely used. I only saw a couple of the Ingram model 10's in a drug seizure a coupla years ago. Uzi's are more popular. But the Ingram is a handy little bastard, if you are looking for concealment. It's much smaller than the Uzi. With the butt folded, the M-10 measures only about 10.5 inches, compared to over 18 for the Uzi. I haven't seen the Mil, but the specs make it even shorter and lighter."

"Small enough to conceal inside a coat, or a lot of other places," Gil noted. That tickle of fear tried to work its way up his spine again, but he had his own type of suppressor at work. Instead of sound, it suppressed emotions. So he managed to push down the fear.

Gil asked about earlier lab work. He got confirmation that the ear had matched the Hasidic boy's blood type. The hair had also been a match. The other body which had turned up was being shipped from

Mt. Sinai to the city morgue - into the capable hands of Anton Krispnick.

The Detective inquired about Nedrow's family, said 'goodbye,' then ended the call. He felt his foot pushing against a plastic bag. Under his desk was the Kevlar vest he had brought from home. He tapped his shoe against it, then stood and walked to the window, thinking thoughts of fear and courage and death.

At another window, uptown, the regular secretary and receptionist at the Stuyvesant School for Bright and Gifted Children stood looking out. It was hard coming back after several days out sick. Kathy was already exhausted, and the day wasn't over yet. That old biddy, McCallister, had made a royal mess of the paperwork. She might be rich, but she wasn't much in the commonsense department.

The girl brushed a wisp of hair back from her eyes. She was hoping her boyfriend would show up early. Since their decision to share an apartment, he had seemed to be taking her more for granted. There was a comfortableness about that evolution of the relationship that she could understand, but part of her felt a sense of loss. She wasn't ready to give up romance yet. After all, they weren't even married. As she stood, looking out into the street, she thought about whether she ought to say something to him about this, or let it go.

Across the road she saw a man standing, looking toward the school. He was dressed in army fatigues, though he seemed rather disheveled for a military man. His shirt was half out of his belt, with a smear of brown across the front that even the camouflage could not obscure. Something about his stance bothered her—a tense, wound-up posture, with hands clenching at intervals. Kathy was tempted to call someone, before the children were dismissed for the day, maybe even that nice detective who sometimes came to pick up his niece. But then the man moved down the street and out of sight. She decided she was just being paranoid. After all, New York was full of weirdos.

Chapter 35

Tuesday, 12:40 p.m.

The coffee was so strong, it left mud in the bottom of the cups with a burned, bitter flavor that only an inveterate caffeine addict could tolerate. In spite of that, Gil and Tom Tyler were sipping the caustic liquid as they talked in the PDU office. At Beach's suggestion, Tom had stopped by the Precinct to discuss the case.

"I'd like you to look over the Newsyvents mailing list, to see if anything stands out. I don't know what might be there, but maybe a name or address will make you think of something."

"No problem," Tom replied, "I have time to do that today."

"We also have a name."

"A name? Then why are we still looking?"

"It's just a first name, or nickname, and might not even be real. Have you ever heard of someone named 'Mel' in the business?" Gil handed Tom a photocopy of the note he had received.

"Looks like a sicko," Tyler observed with a grimace, handing the page back to Gil like it was contagious. He scrunched up his face in concentration.

"Mel... Mel? Well, there was a famous act some years ago, by a guy called Bradley. I think I may have mentioned him to you before. He and Edger Bergen learned from Lester the Great. One of the best. Trouble was, this asshole knew it. He went by the name Bradley at first, then it was 'The Great Bradley' and eventually 'Master Bradley.'

His main character was named Melvin, so he billed himself as "The Master and Melvin" at the top of his career."

"Where is he now?"

"In the great vent museum in the sky. He died twenty years ago."

"Doesn't sound like much of a suspect."

"Not unless Melvin is working on his own. If you want to check, you could go talk to him. Last time I was there, he had an honored spot at the Vent Haven Museum."

"No thanks. If I want to talk to a dummy, I don't have to go to Kentucky. There's plenty right here in New York. We call them superior officers. Any other ideas?"

"Hmm, let me think," Tyler said, scratching his head, "Well, there is a pretty sad act called 'Mellon and Mellon' doing some of the cheap clubs in Manhattan. The guy's real name is Denker, Jesse Denker. He had some potential but got in some trouble a few years ago and has never lived up to expectations."

"Trouble? Like what?"

"The rumor is that he is into drugs. It would fit."

"You have any idea where he is working now?"

"Not off the top of my head, but let me call the office, and I can tell you."

Gil nodded and shoved the phone over to his visitor. Tom called his secretary.

"Hi, Annie? It's me. Look, would you check the current city entertainment guide on my desk. I want to find out where 'Mellon and Mellon' is working. I think it's some joint on the West Side, where he's the regular feature. I'll hold, while you check. Yes, I'm with the Detective ... Yes, ... yes, I will."

He turned to Gil, winking,

"Annie says to say 'Hi,'" then cradling the phone while he waited. "It's probably a dive, if they keep giving him the gig despite everything, but it makes it easy to locate him."

"Yeah, I'm still here," he spoke into the phone. "Have you got it? ...you're kidding," as he scribbled a name on the back of an empty envelope.

"What? Yes, Gil and I might drop by to see the act." Tom's face started getting red. "Oh yeah, sure, sure. Come on, Annie, get your mind out of the gutter."

He looked at Gil with an embarrassed shrug, and cupping the mouthpiece, whispered, "It's a topless bar." Then he spoke again into the receiver, asking the details about when the club was open and the act appearing on stage. He told his secretary his plans for the day, then hung up, shoving the envelope over to Gil.

"The Warm Pussy!?" Gil laughed, "Sounds like a real class joint. You want to come along for the investigation, or for the entertainment?"

"Now don't you start. I got enough of that from Annie. But if you expect to get anything from Denker, you'll have a better chance with me along. He isn't too keen on cops, but we've been running into each other for years. I made all his vent figures."

"Do we have to wait until the weekend?"

"No, the club is closed Mondays, but the rest of the week they run at least a minimal show. How about Thursday night?"

Though he would have preferred sooner, Gil agreed. They made plans to meet at the club. He walked Tyler to the door and watched him move down the street.

Coming in at the same time was Epstein, the Public Information officer and king of the gossips, playing task-force detective for now. The short, stout man stopped when he saw Gil.

"Just the guy I want to see. We really need a better bio on you, Gil. What I had was very complete, but not really up to date. Not enough current data."

"Enough for what?"

"Enough for release. You know, if we need to release information about you to someone."

"What in hell would you do that for? Are you telling me you release personal information about us to whoever wants it?"

"Oh, no, no," Epstein protested, "not to anyone. Only to proper sources. Like the Mayor's office. In fact, that's who asked for it this time."

"Why would the Mayor's office need personal information about me anyway? Who did you talk to?"

"Uh. It was a Mr. Magister of the Mayor's personal staff, Mel Magister."

"Oh damn," Gil moaned, leaning back against the nearest wall.

He could almost picture the cold smile of his adversary. Once again, the killer had been a step ahead. Again, he had gained information Gil didn't want him to have. This time the Detective knew how it had been obtained, but that wasn't as important as the nature of the information itself. Gil felt a sick sense of violation, like someone had just robbed his home, or stepped into his bedroom while he slept.

"What's the matter, do you think you're in trouble with the Mayor?"

"Worse, much worse."

"Worse?"

"Yeah, you just released my Bio to the guy who tried to kill me last week."

The other cop looked startled, then a little sick. "How do you know that?"

"His name is Mel."

"Couldn't it be another Mel?"

"Look, Epstein. The Mayor's office isn't interested in me. Besides, in school I had to study a book called "Magister Ludi" by Hesse. I remember the teacher told us ... 'Magister' in Latin, means 'Master.' That's what the perp has been calling himself in his letters."

The P.I. officer just stood there gaping, in a reasonably good imitation of an out of the water goldfish.

"So what did you tell him?" Gil pressed. "Just the standard stuff— year of graduation from the academy, time on the force, citations...?"

He stopped when he saw the distressed look on the other man's face.

"Well..., I had no way of knowing, Gil. He said all the right things, named all the right names... said they were looking for some personal interest stuff about you, real human side and all that..."

"Oh God, what did you tell him?" Gil's voice rose as he grabbed Epstein by the shirt front. "Listen, you'd better stop worrying about your sorry little ego, and fill me in. Stand up and face the fact that you blew it. Don't make it worse by leaving me in the dark!"

Epstein swallowed hard, and nodded.

"Okay. I'm sorry Gil, but I told him everything— where you live, what you do, who you know."

"Who I know?"

"You gotta understand, Gil, this guy was smooth, real smooth. He made it seem like I was doing you a favor ... like maybe they were going to do one of those 'This Is Your Life' kind of things and wanted to invite everybody you cared about. So, I told him. Who you worked with, who you grew up with, who you have a relationship with."

"Sheila and Jennifer?"

Epstein nodded, his eyes on his shoes.

"Pilar?"

Another small nod.

Gil felt like something was pushing at a trapdoor in his gut, trying to get out. It was a foaming, searing thing, like lava. He stopped speaking, turned and went back to the office, head pounding. As he mounted the stairway, his legs beckoned him to run, to push, to hurt... to retreat into the mindless discipline of the stairs. He stopped, realizing that this was the first time he had ever thought of his exercising as a 'retreat.' Yet that is what it had become. He knew that he wanted to lose himself in it, to exit from the real world to a simple existence of drive and purging and exhaustion.

His world was not simple anymore. Now there were others in it, others that he cared about. He was sure that someone else now cared about them, too. But it wasn't a pleasant thought. He was able to get enough of an idea of Mel's thinking now, to sense the rage there, and what it meant. It meant the man would strike at Gil's most vulnerable area, at those he loved. Up until this point, the Detective had not allowed himself to feel anything he might describe as fear. There were a lot of unpleasant sensations, but the danger was an inherent part of the Job. Now a new element had been added. A sense of dread invaded him, as he thought of putting those he loved at risk. This creature was capable of anything.

He called Pilar to tell her the general outline of the situation, suggesting some basic precautions. He didn't mention his sense of the man's dark compulsion or his need to strike out at precisely the ones Gil cared about the most.

"I don't want to frighten you, but this guy is not predictable. I don't want you targeted. I love you."

It was the first time he had spoken those words to her. It felt strange to say them out loud - scary and exciting and true.

After promising Pilar that he would stop by later, he tried to call Sheila who did not answer, so he left a message about taking precautions. He thought of calling Jennifer's school, but remembered the shrew, McCallister, who had obstructed him before. As much as he still resented that, he felt somewhat comforted that Jennifer was almost overprotected in this case, and decided to wait until Sheila had picked up her daughter. They were safer at home anyway. He could call again later. Right now, he needed to find something to eat and get out of the confines of the Precinct. Gil went to his desk, grabbed the plastic bag underneath it, before heading to the locker room. He had only taken a few steps, when Lincoln appeared.

"How are you doing on your assignment list?" the Lieutenant asked.

"Fine, fine," Gil mumbled, trying to remember what had been on it. He attempted to keep moving, but the other man blocked his path. The ballistic vest was peeking out of the plastic bag. Gil felt annoyed that the Lieutenant had to come along just when it was obvious. Part of him saw no reason to hide the safety equipment, but another ancient vestige didn't want anyone to think he might be afraid.

"Then you're going back to the Yeshiva?"

"Yeah. Heading there now," the detective lied.

"Good. Take Treadwell with you."

"What?"

"Take Treadwell with you. Is that a problem?"

"Well, actually I've been using Frank a lot, and ..."

"Terranova has plenty of work to do right here. And until he gets his gun back, he isn't much back-up for someone under threat."

The Lieutenant may have been sincere, but the tone of his voice left Gil wondering if he was being sarcastic.

"Treadwell showed some real hustle the other day," the officer continued,"—one of the first to back you up. He beat me to the scene. Had his weapon out, ready for action. I don't think he is being properly utilized. Let Frank push paper until he's fully reactivated. I want you to take Treadwell with you."

"Well, sir, uhhhh ..."

"You can consider that an order."

Gil stood staring at the Lieutenant, wondering how much of Treadwell's story and status the officer really knew. He considered whether he should say anything more, but finally decided it wasn't worth pushing. So now he had to find Colin.

He knew where to start, and soon found Treadwell lurking outside the mailroom, holding the usual inter-office envelopes, along with his ever-present notebook. Beach described Lincoln's order to accompany him.

"What's going on, Gil?"

"I don't know Colin. I just know Lincoln wants you out in the street, so you better move. You know my car. I'll meet you outside in five minutes."

"Sure, Gil, sure. No problem. Where are we going? It's nothing hot, is it?"

Gil reassured him, watching as the worried man walked slowly away, occasionally putting out a hand against the wall, as if he wasn't sure of his equilibrium. He probably wasn't.

Gil saw that Treadwell had even left his faithful notebook lying on the desk, so picked it up to return to him. The man was off balance enough without losing his security blanket.

A brief stop at Gwen's computer confirmed that the "Dummy" file had been opened. Without cracking a smile, the technician drolly asked, "Does that mean the perp is a detective?"

They traded insults and flirts for a few minutes—a year earlier they had gotten into a brief romantic liaison. She was looking for something permanent, he wasn't. So the relationship went nowhere. Now they were just friendly, but the shared secret of their short involvement always gave a special flavor to their conversations. He blew her a mock kiss and headed for the exit. There was a stiffness in his walk, an unspoken tension. It isn't paranoia, he told himself, to be nervous when someone is really gunning for you.

Treadwell was leaning against the car, looking pale and confused. When he saw Gil, he moved around the fender to the passenger side, pulling open the door. Beach was still a hundred yards away.

There was a flash of light, and a split second of silence before the sound of the explosion reached Gil's ears. He felt a whump of concussive power. Suddenly, he found himself sitting on the sidewalk, a tinkling rain of glass shards, metal slivers and smoldering pieces of plastic showering him. His eyes burned from the flash, the dust, the airborne particles thrown into his face. Looking down at himself, through a blur he saw a spattering of red on his skin and clothing. It was Colin Treadwell's blood.

Gil carefully rose to his feet, brushing off bits of debris, while feeling around his body with trembling hands to see if anything was broken. He heard voices shouting, the hard-soled slap of shoes running toward him. He stiffly walked forward, slowly approaching the smoldering ruin that had been his car. Metal panels were bent back like a peeled banana. Some tattered lumps of smoldering cloth and blackened flesh were the only identifiable parts of the frightened little man who had not wanted to come out into this deadly world, a world to which he was ill-fitted. Now all that was left was the worn notebook Beach held in his hands, a possession he hadn't managed to return to Treadwell, a pitiful memorial.

Gil looked again at the burst vessel that had been an automobile only moments before. In a way, it reminded him of a cocoon, splayed out, empty after the butterfly had emerged. He tried, for a moment to imagine that Colin had shed his body like the butterfly, only to materialize in a new form and better place – maybe a place where daughters were not ensnared by drugs, and child-killers did not exist. Gil wasn't much of a believer, but he hoped so. As for himself, he intended to make sure that at least one less of these monsters existed in this world. He intended to do that very soon.

Chapter 36

Wednesday, 9:30 a.m.

Gil lay beside Pilar, winding a lock of her hair around his finger. Her hand absently stroked his arm, eyes closed, a dreamy smile on her face. Their lovemaking seemed to get better every time, as they learned to read each other's subtle signals of desire and pleasure. After Colin's violent death, they had felt a special urge to cling to each other.

Now after a long period of common urgency, building excitement and release, they lay cuddled together on the couch. Wrapped in satisfaction and security, they were taking their time easing back into the everyday world.

"You have a lot of energy, lately," she murmured, then gave a little giggle.

"I've been doing less stairs, and more of you."

"I like your choice of exercise."

"It's nice to have a choice," he said, more seriously.

"You could have had a woman any time you wanted one, Gil."

"That's not what I meant. The exercise—it was- more of a need than a choice. I needed it to keep, from ... from ..."

"From exploding?"

"No ... not exactly. More like being overwhelmed, washed away, or maybe just... lost. Sometimes I wonder what makes me different from somebody like Mel. Maybe nothing but fear. I've been afraid that the anger will just sweep me away, but right now, I'm more angry than afraid. I want to get the bastard who did that to Colin."

"Of course you do, darling. That doesn't make you like him. You are a special person. That's why I love you. Everyone has a part of them that is the dark side, the shadow. It's what makes us seek the light."

"I don't understand."

"It isn't so strange. Tell me. Why do you try to overcome anything?" Gil's eyebrows almost met as he scrunched up his forehead.

"You're losing me," he finally admitted.

"Okay, let me use some simple examples. Why do you brush your teeth?"

"So they won't rot and fall out of my head." "Right. And why do you clean up your house?" "Bad example," Gil laughed, "I don't... or at least not very often. But when I do, it's because I can't stand the mess anymore."

"Right again. Your fear of the decay, and your dislike of the chaos lead you to do positive things to counter them. Likewise, what makes you different from the monsters you hunt down, is that you see the darkness and you know that isn't what you want for yourself. The sick ones are the ones who see the dark side and want to embrace it."

"That's just what scares me. Sometimes I feel drawn to that... other side. When I get angry, I think I want to kill. Once I almost did. I could have."

"Do you think that's unusual? Listen, darling, anger is a very elemental emotion. Deep down, every rage is a killing rage. We are all murderers in the heart of our anger. But like you, most of us see that undiluted raw primitive killing urge and are repulsed. Sure, we toy with it. Sometimes, if conditions are right—our defenses battered, our resources depleted, our hope lost, we even act out that rage. But what happens next is very important. When you almost killed in a frenzy of anger, how did you feel afterwards?"

"Terrible. Unclean. Unfit to live. I would have jumped off a bridge, except I thought that was too easy ... a coward's way out."

"Is that when you started punishing yourself?"

"Punishing? I guess I hadn't thought of it in those terms, exactly. But yes, that's when I started doing my discipline."

"Gil, my darling. That is why you are so different from the sick ones. When they step over the line, acting out the violent and sick fantasies, it feels GOOD to them! And they want more."

"Sometimes I forget that you're a psychologist."

"I'm not your psychologist, darling. I'm your love. But if you want to use me as a professional resource, I am happy to oblige. I could tell you some things about your killer, I'll bet."

"Like what?"

"Well, if you aren't already aware of it, you can expect that the frequency of the killings will increase. There is a cooling-off period between incidents in this kind of pattern, but the periods tend to get shorter and shorter."

"Yes, I had an idea of that from an earlier case. And the FBI has created some generic profiles. What else?"

"Depends on what you want to know. I could wax eloquently on cognitive mapping and processing."

"In English, please."

"These types will often do a lot of visualization. In extreme cases, where they imagine their wishes to be fact it can even border on hallucination. Something in their feedback system filters out reality. Their fantasy themes center on domination, revenge, power, torture, all that good stuff. They draw a mental map that includes those themes and follow it like it was a real road."

"You used the phrase 'these types.' What type are you talking about?"

"Sadistic killers. Sexually motivated murderers."

"You think this guy is after sex?"

"No, not at all. Actually, I would expect that he's generally turned off by real sex. That's for healthy folks, like us." She gave a sly wink. "He might play around with kinky stuff, like maybe pornography, but he probably sees no connection to the murders. No, the sexual motivation is a deep, unconscious sort of thing. Some childhood trauma may have perverted his ability to develop along normal lines, so it comes out in the sadism. The fact that he chooses children suggests a terrible sense of inadequacy. The 'Master' stuff is another attempt to undo that feeling of not really being enough."

"Childhood trauma, inadequacy. I never put it in those terms, but I know what you're talking about." Gil concurred, "The scary part is that I can understand. It's different from me, but not all that different. This is kind of weird, I mean, I'm used to looking at myself a certain way. This is quite a different angle."

Pilar nodded. She realized that he was rethinking his whole self-perception. That meant new doorways were opening into seldom visited emotional places.

"But I'm still having trouble with the idea that if I have some of that stuff in me, I'm not really different."

"You aren't the same, darling. I couldn't love you if you were like him."

"Maybe that's what worries me."

"Do you really think you could hide so much from me?"

"I don't know. All this navel-gazing has me mixed-up. I guess I've been afraid I would find that I'm a monster inside, no different from Mel—just disguised better."

"There is no monster inside you, darling. You are such a kind, caring person. Oh, there are some monstrous feelings, we all have those. But they're feelings that you can own. They don't have to own you."

"Whew! I think I've had enough of this. I think I liked it better when it was just the bad guys versus the good guys."

"Well, darling, if it makes you feel any better, make no mistake. That sick killer is one of the bad guys. You? You are definitely one of the good guys."

With the last statement, she nuzzled his neck.

I can't believe we're lying here naked, discussing sadistic sexual killers," he finally said.

What would you like to discuss? Masochistic asexual nurturers?"

'I don't think I want to discuss anything, right now" he said with a leer, "but there are some very sexual things I would like to do."

He slipped down a few inches where he began running his tongue around one of her nipples.

"Ummm. Say no more!" she purred.

Almost an hour later, Gil lay beside the sleeping form of Pilar, a furrow between his eyes. As long as he was physically here, he felt some sense of control. But he knew he would eventually have to leave, and the farther he was from Pilar, the more room there was for someone else to appear ...the more room for the darkness of a killer to cast a shadow over this woman he loved. He realized that it was a cat-and-mouse game now. But who was the cat and who was the mouse? *Better to make the first move,* he thought.

237

Slowly he slipped from the bed, stood and padded across the floor to the phone, grabbing his bathrobe on the way. He sat down to call the Precinct, hoping to get an update from Frank Terranova. The place was hopping since Treadwell's death. The good news from Frank's briefing was that Lieutenant Lincoln was no longer able to operate on his own terms. Too many watching eyes. The bad news was that there was enough brass hanging around the Precinct to form a marching band. Madigan had stepped in, Inspector Colgan was on site, and everybody from the Mayor on down was getting into the act in some way.

As much as possible, Gil wanted to stay clear of that madhouse. Technically, Treadwell had been his partner at the end. In reality, the relationship was much less significant than that. However, when Captain Occhiogrosso, who knew little of Colin's real status, had told him to take a couple of days off as "compassionate leave," he jumped at the opportunity to stay away. That way he could avoid the conflicting orders, task duplications, and memo blizzard going on at the P.D.U. He had every intention of honoring Treadwell's death, but he would do it by hunting the dead detective's killer, and he would do it more efficiently by himself. All he needed from the Precinct was information—research developments, lab results, incoming data. Frank had agreed to help. As he punched numbers into the phone, Pilar blew him a kiss and turned back to her nap.

Frank had been busy. At Gil's suggestion, he had been contacting the Army Entertainment Corps, U.S.O., and allied organizations to see if there had been a ventriloquist doing service shows where there was the potential of acquiring weapons and explosives. The lab had quickly identified the type used on Gil's car. It was RDX (Cyclonite), set off by a booster charge of PETN, both military explosives. The PETN in turn, had been detonated by an L2A2 anti-personnel hand grenade, wired to the car door. Frank told how proudly Jim Nedrow from the lab had bragged of his ability to identify the precise grenade, a product of the U.K., by bits of the notched wire that became projectiles when the thing was detonated.

In the information from the U.S.O., it wasn't hard to find a specific stage act that had been contracted through the organization. There was the name of a ventriloquist named Bradley who had worked with various dummies, including Freckles, Vinnie, and one named none other than Melvin. They didn't know if Bradley was the first or last name and had no current records of his whereabouts. Frank was trying to get more from them now.

Lab analysis of the letter from Mel had turned up two partial prints in the glue strip. Gil told Terranova to see if he could get prints on Denker, a.k.a. "Mellon and Mellon," Billy Barstow, as well as that U.S.O. entertainer, for a match.

Gil checked his notes to see that his memory was correct. Tom Tyler had mentioned a Melvin figure which had been popular in entertainment circles a generation ago. It was too much of a coincidence that the act had linked a Mel-like name and the title "Master." Unsure of how there could be a connection, he still felt that they should find out more. The links between names and this entertainment specialty seemed worth checking out. Since he couldn't justify a trip to Kentucky, at this point, he used the telephone.

Through the operator he got the number for the Vent Haven Museum in Fort Mitchell. The phone was picked up on the third ring, and a well-modulated voice answered, using the name 'William.' Gil quickly identified himself, and his need for information.

"I'm just doing a little fishing at this point," he explained, "I wonder if you could tell me anything about the Melvin figure you have there that once was part of 'The Master and Melvin'? "

"Well, I'll be happy to tell you anything I can," the man assured the detective, "But unfortunately, we don't really have Melvin, only a simulacrum."

"A what?"

"A copy, a counterfeit. The original Melvin was stolen from the museum several years ago. A staff member disappeared at the same time, so we suspect he was responsible, but we haven't been able to trace either of them."

"What can you tell me about the staff person who disappeared?"

"Not a lot. He was a cleaning man. Came in at night to do maintenance. Name was Brad I think."

"As in Bradley?"

"Maybe. His family name was Smith, if you can believe that. Always seemed a bit conceited for a common service worker, it seemed to me. We were mostly glad to see him go, except for the missing figure. There were some reports of strange goings-on at night."

"Strange in what way?"

"Oh rather disgusting things, like finding dead animals there, or blood stains. A neighbor claimed to have seen someone through the window, that seemed to be cavorting naked in the middle of the night. We couldn't definitely pin it on the service worker, but there were too many odd things going on. Then when he and the figure disappeared, we figured the mystery was solved. The strange night action stopped. We considered filing a missing person report on Melvin, "he chuckled, "but we did file a stolen property report.

"Do you have any records on this maintenance man? Address, next of kin, references?"

"Possibly the cleaning service does. We let out a contract for that."

Gil asked a few more questions and was able to get the telephone number of the cleaning contractor in Cincinnati. Although it was in Ohio, Cincinnati is the closest sizeable city to Fort Mitchell, Kentucky. After asking William to send any brochures or other information on the museum, Gil placed the call. It took a while to get through the personnel staff's excessive concern about confidentiality, but he finally spoke to the person in charge, only to find that the records were pretty much useless. The references sounded fake, the address a hotel in Cincinnati. The man had disappeared four years ago.

Another dead-end. Gil had an uncomfortable feeling that time was running out. Soon something bad was going to happen.

CHAPTER 37

Wednesday, 1:40 p.m.

The air was filled with the buzzing sound of flies, accompanied by a tap-tap-tapping as they dashed themselves against the translucent glass windows. There had been a warming trend over the last few days, and the Performer's private museum was filled with a rank odor ... the smell of putrefaction. It would have turned the stomach of someone who had not already adapted to the ghastly fumes. Mel didn't think of his stomach. He hadn't eaten in several days. Not because of the smell or the flies, he was used to that. But he hadn't been able to bring himself to make the necessary roundabout journey for food to stores he felt were safe. He couldn't be too careful.

Hollows were showing in the man's cheeks, his clothing hung on him like on a wire display hanger. Not that he was wearing any clothes right now. The stained and crusty cammos were thrown in a corner, while nothing insulated him from drawing power out of the other life forms. The flies and roaches were small, but each carried a spark of energy, a tiny bit of life force. He held absolutely still as they settled on his body or toured its crevices. Minuscule pinpricks of pain accompanied their explorations and bites, but he did not falter. By his failure to react, he demonstrated his control over not only his feelings, his body, and his will, but also over all vulnerable creatures. So with every insect that touched him, he knew he was actually gaining power, sucking in another microscopic portion of vitality.

Mel felt a stirring between his legs, distressed that he was being betrayed by his body. Despite all his will, that ugly little part of him insisted on moving. The more he fought it, the more the offending organ jerked and came to life. He punched at his groin. Flies rose in a buzz of sound. He knew the demonstration was over.

He pulled on the same filthy clothing, oblivious to the stains and odor. He left his haven, driving the van out of the alley, moving it slowly through city streets and carefully on highways toward the Place of Gifts. Cautiously, as he didn't want to be stopped.

He parked two blocks away, then walked to the corner opposite the school, in order to resume the surveillance he had been conducting. It was becoming more and more difficult to be patient. His hands clenched and unclenched at his sides, as he waited for the children to be excused for the day. Things were not acting normally. He was distracted by the way the pavement refused to stay solid. One moment the concrete was hard, but the next he could feel it softening—probably from the radon. Light posts also bent minutely and contracted infinitesimally. His heightened perceptions were able to sense the vapors of departed spirits roaming the building across the street. A slight movement in a window alerted him to the fact that he was being watched. A woman was spying on him. He turned and slipped around a corner. But not far.

It had not taken long to identify the chosen one. She was blond and small, with a habit of wearing small bows at the base of her two braids. She reminded him of a character he had seen in a movie, the one named "Heidi." She exhibited all the necessary qualities. Of course, the extra thing this time was that she was related to the Detective. This child was important to his adversary. Even better. He made his selection. She was now Chosen.

As he reflected on this special circumstance and the object of his choice, his thoughts kept returning to her previous name, the one his adversary used for her. As he sounded it out, he was reminded of a popular song of many years earlier, sung by some English-accented rock star.

"Jennifer, Jennifer, da, da-da, da-da," he intoned, mocking the British pronunciation, almost spitting the words in hostile intensity,

"Jenni-FUH, Jenni- FUH!" Then he calmed, as he realized his complete control. He didn't have to worry. After all, he was the Master. Yes, she was part of the adversary's circle, part of the Detective's zone of influence. But soon she would belong to the Master. It was ordained. It was inevitable.

The Performer had gained another piece of information, when he called the police station, pretending to be a reporter. He had inquired about his case, only to find that he had been labelled the old indignity, "Dummy." It enraged yet exhilarated him. The contest was joined. For this, the Detective would pay. Soon he would learn the difference between a Dummy and The Master.

In a deep pocket, his soiled hand stroked the gore-encrusted blade of the curved woodcarver's knife.

Chapter 38

Thursday, 11:36 a.m.

The smell of sawdust and paint mixed with the aroma of coffee to create a unique atmosphere in the loft workshop. Combined with the display of vent figures, the small stage, and a wall plastered with show posters, the effect made Gil think of carnivals and circuses. He and Frank were lounging around the coffee pot in the production area of Tom Tyler's place. Tom was at the phone. Since his secretary had called in sick, he was trying to turn on his answering machine to take calls, hoping they wouldn't be interrupted. The machine was giving him such a hard time that he finally gave up and said he would field his own calls for a while.

"Well, the worst possibility is that we will get interrupted," he shrugged, "and maybe I just won't answer the phone for a change."

"It's really no problem, if you take calls," the Detective reassured him, "we're just kicking ideas around anyway."

"Well, the truth is," Tom explained, "I don't like talking on the telephone. I joke about it with friends, telling them I have an allergy to phones. That's one of the main reasons I hired Annie. It's also why I bought this machine for when she's not working. I'm really not much of a businessman, in the sense of talking money or shipping schedules or whatever. That's most of the calls. Unfortunately, I'm not very good with electronic gizmos either."

As he spoke, he fiddled with the answering machine, clearly unfamiliar with the various buttons and switches.

"Other calls are from weirdos, asking me to do kids' birthday parties at some ridiculous fee like twenty-five dollars a shot, or they want to talk to one of the figures I used at a performance they saw, as if they all live here in a back room or something. That kind of nutsy stuff. If this machine doesn't do its thing, I think I'll just let the phone ring."

Tom grinned and poured himself a cup of coffee. He settled into a nearby chair, clutching some papers in one hand.

The answering machine was still making hissing sounds, which were followed by a beep and clacking noise. Then a voice issued from the small speaker, a message from some earlier time. It was a quiet voice, but somehow all the more sinister for that.

"This message is for Detective Beach, who by now will be visiting with you ..."

"What the hell?" Frank blurted. Tom jumped, spilling coffee out of his cup onto the floor. Gil waved for them to be quiet.

"... You see, I always know where you are, Gil Beach. I know everything about you. I even know how you will die ..." the voice whispered from the machine.

"Give my love to ...," the voice paused, "... oh, on second thought, I'll see to that myself." There was a sound of breathing for a few seconds, then the recording changed to a hiss of electronic noise. The message was over.

The other men looked at Gil, who kept his head lowered, as it had been while he listened to the tape. He held a ballpoint pen in his hands and it slowly changed shape, the plastic bending and finally separating with a snap. The noise broke his trance. He looked up at the others, staring.

"He's true to form, isn't he?" Gil remarked quietly. "Save the audio, Tom. Maybe we can get a voice print from it. Let's keep a sharp eye out, when we leave. This guy may be tailing me. He knows too much, that's for sure."

For a moment Beach's eyes looked like hot coals, then they became more hooded. Those who knew him, would recognize his ability to turn anxiety and dread into purposeful action. The men gathered in the factory loft soon sensed his drive.

"Okay, if he knows so much, what do WE know?" Gil asked, all business now, voice direct and forceful.

"I've looked over this mailing list," Tom said, waving it in the air, "and picked out a few names that caught my attention. I don't know if they are significant, but you said I should just look for anything that stood out."

"What did you come up with?" Frank asked.

"Well, there's this Gene Goodrich in Brooklyn. 1 think that's the guy who was ripping people off last year."

"Ripping them off, how?" Gil probed.

"Several ways. If it's the guy I think it is, he booked gigs for a nonexistent act and insisted on advance payment. Same thing with some mail-order stuff. Advertised cheap figures, effects, and so forth, and never sent the merchandise. Prepayment required, of course."

"Did he sell those little ventriloquist reed gadgets?"

"I couldn't say, but I wouldn't be surprised. Basically, the guy would do anything to catch a sucker. But of course, he disappeared, with no forwarding address. So this mailing address is probably no good."

"Okay, who else?" Gil pressed.

"Well, this guy Francois is pretty legit, even though he isn't that great a vent technically. But I was surprised at the address."

"What about it?"

"Well, I'm pretty sure it's the old Regency Theater over in the West Village. I mean it isn't unusual for a performer to have mail sent to a theater address, but the Regency has been defunct for twenty years. It's a fifteen-story monstrosity, boarded up and falling down. This is a current mailing list, right?"

"Yeah, I just got it this week," Frank agreed. "It could have some entries like that other one, that are wrong because of recent changes, but not more than six months to a year. They told me that they keep it pretty much up to date. It's a small operation, so they watch mailing costs carefully."

"We'll need a phone number, or maybe we need to stop by and see if the place is occupied," Gil said. "Is there anyone else you pulled out of the list?"

"Yes. Three more. Denker is on the list—remember 'Mellon and Mellon?' So is Barstow, who you said might somehow be linked to the case. Actually, I'm on the list too, though I forgot that I subscribe. I hope I'm not a suspect. On the night of the crime, I have an alibi. I was mugging an old lady in Queens."

After a chuckle, he continued, "But there is also one more name that seemed odd. It's Charles Bradley. I suppose there could be more than one person by that name, but more than one ventriloquist? That's 'The Great Bradley.' He's been dead for a number of years."

"Could it be a 'Junior,'?" Gil suggested, "a son?"

"Well, the guy had a son alright, but the name wasn't Charles. It's a hard name to forget. Believe it or not, he was called... Dumme."

The other men looked at each other and at Tom in disbelief. "Oh come on," Frank protested, "you're putting us on!"

"No, I'm serious. It's true. I don't know if the name was on his birth certificate or not, but that's really what his father called him. Maybe the kid was retarded or something, I guess the term would be 'developmental disability', but I doubt it. I told you Bradley was no winner in the personality department. Everybody thought it was a joke at first, but then when they saw he meant it, they just tried to ignore the cruelty. It was a real messy situation, if I remember right, with Bradley's wife a real nut job, according to rumor, and the kid supposedly developmentally disabled. I only know all this, because it was a secret scandal when I was a kid learning the trade. Bradley was humping every chorus girl and cleaning lady he could impress with his name, while his old lady was vegetating and the boy was getting into serious trouble—too much trouble I think, to be as dumb as they said he was. Bradley came to my grandfather for some of his figures, so I overheard some of the talk. It kind of frightened me, so Gramps tried to explain it to me. When the mother disappeared, the boy was put in an institution, I think."

"Maybe he grew up and got himself a real name," Gil suggested, "... and why not his father's name, since the old man wouldn't give it to him?" Gil thought about his decision to choose "Dummy" as a computer file name, and whether by some strange coincidence it could be the actual name of the killer. Then again, he always said he didn't believe in coincidence.

"Well, I don't know about that," Tom shrugged, "but this guy has an address in Staten Island, where you live. Does Summer Street mean anything to you?"

"Umm. No, I don't think so. Unless it's that little street over in the Fort Wadsworth area where there's a Little League field."

"You follow the Little League?" Frank asked, grinning.

"Yeah, well, I do a little officiating, Gil mumbled, looking away.

"No kidding," Frank responded looking at Gil with new awareness. "You umpire for the kids? Most folks only get into that stuff because they have their own kids involved."

"Yeah, well, anyway," Gil said quickly, changing the subject, "What else do we have?" Terranova grinned at Tom Tyler and the other man smiled back, as Gil's neck got rosy, but they didn't press the Detective's embarrassment.

"Well, I'm waiting on some stuff at the Precinct," Frank answered, "including prints on the envelope, and more information on the USO performer. Captain O wants to see me later today. I don't know if it has anything to do with the case, or if I'm in more trouble. Lincoln has been on my back all week. He's got me doing scud work all the time. Yeah, and he's always taking cheap shots. Not too obvious, just little digs to keep me in my place. Like asking me if alcoholics can handle cleaning products.

"Yeah, I think of Lincoln sort of like that early version of Pinocchio," Gil said wryly, beginning to loosen a little from the tension the answering machine recording had sparked in him. "…tries to act like a human being, but doesn't have much success at it."

"But what do you mean by 'scud work'?" Tom asked.

"I guess that's something left over from the Iraqi war," Frank explained, "We used it to refer to something we could say was like a Scud missile. It keeps you busy, but in the end doesn't amount to shit."

This time, everyone laughed, then continued with small talk for a few more minutes. Finally, Gil and Frank got up to leave, agreeing to meet Tom that night at the club where the 'Mellon and Mellon' act was performing.

When the two policemen reached the car, Gil held Frank back with one hand, carefully approaching the vehicle alone. After a lengthy examination, including a look under the chassis, he gingerly inserted his key, and eased the door open. Some of the tension left his stance. He motioned Terranova to join him. Frank could see the pulse still pounding in Gil's neck, but said nothing- It slowed as they headed off through the snarled traffic.

Chapter 39

Thursday, 7:20 p.m.

In the evening, the 'brass' had vacated the Precinct, so Gil felt he could come into the office without getting hassled. He was too tied up in knots to want to deal with that B.S. now. He was sorting out his piled-up mail, thinking sadly of how Colin Treadwell's death had so little effect on normal operations. Nothing was any more screwed up than usual. There were various letters, circulars, and interoffice envelopes stacked on his desk. There was also another package.

Before he had decided how to deal with the package, Frank came walking up to him. It was a moment before Gil noticed that there was something different about the guy. At first he had trouble figuring out what it was, but there was definitely a change. The man walked straighter, moved more easily, even had a smirk on his face like a groom joining his buddies after the wedding night.

Gil figured something was up, so stopped what he was doing. At first, he said nothing, waiting, but Frank just busied himself with some papers and kept silent.

"Okay, okay," Gil finally relented, "what's going on?"

"Nothing. What do you mean?"

"C'mon Frank, you look like you just won the Heisman trophy, laid the entire Dallas cheerleading squad, and bought a winning lottery ticket."

Terranova stood fidgeting, obviously uncomfortable, yet grinning an embarrassed grin. Then Gil noticed a holster peeking from under the man's sport jacket, and the handle of a pistol.

"Well, son of a bitch!" he exclaimed, "You got your gun back!" Frank's face brightened even more, and he nodded.

"That's what Captain 'O' wanted. Gave me the gun ... and a promise."

"What kind of promise, Frank?"

"That I could be assigned to the P.D.U. on a regular basis, work with you as a replacement for Treadwell temporarily. If that went okay, there could be a gold shield in it for me. I mean, I have to pass the tests and all, but…."

The two men stood facing each other. The faces had gotten more serious. Nothing had to be said. They just looked straight at each other for a moment, and then Gil held out his hand. Frank grabbed it firmly, his other hand clasping Gil's also. Soon all four hands were in a knot of connection.

When emotion threatened to break through the tough male cop exterior, the men moved back, and with a nod went back to work.

Gil picked up the package he had been examining. Frank told him it was safe to open. He had run it through the scanner before bringing it up to the PDU. This one had come through the regular mail, but considering recent events, he figured it didn't hurt to take precautions. It turned out to be a video.

Before looking at the video, Gil leafed through the other mail. Most of it was junk, but there was an envelope from Vent Haven Museum, which included a brochure. The glossy folder showed scenes from the ventriloquist shrine. Charlie McCarthy and Mortimer Snerd appeared in one photo, sitting propped up at a table, as if they were talking over tea. Gil wondered how many folks today even remember the names of Edgar Bergen's figures. Another picture showed what appeared to be a large audience of children, but on closer examination was row after row of ventriloquist dummies, lined up like humans viewing a performance. There were male and female figures, blondes, brunettes, redheads, and mixtures. Perhaps fans of ventriloquism thought it was impressive, but it gave Gil the creeps. So did the video, even though he had not yet seen it. The note from Mel had warned him to expect a package. This must be the "gift" he had been promised. It made his stomach do a flip-flop just to think about it.

Gil closed the door before he opened the computer to play the recording. He held the thumb drive up to the light, at various angles, until he was sure its shiny surface held no fingerprints. He plugged the drive into a slot and waited. The screen went from snowy blankness to a dark indoor scene.

Like most cops, Gil had developed an unflappable exterior in most situations, even those typical civilians would find overwhelming. At the police academy they taught you that it was a necessary technique of police work to maintain the image of power and control, no matter what goes on inside the man or woman wearing the badge. But now the Detective had to swallow down some rising bile, as he viewed a bizarre scene, soon recognizing the grisly nature of what he was seeing. The video quality was poor, but the red smeared crotch highlighted the fact that this was a man who was on display. "Display" was probably the right word, since the ruby-painted genitals seemed to be stiff and prominent, as if being flaunted. But Gil's attention was drawn more to the puppet body sitting on the man's knee, and the appalling sight of a child's head lolling on its shoulders. There was no longer any doubt about what had happened to the Hasidic boy, Chaim.

Gil stopped for a moment, to calm himself. Then, he directed his attention on the screen, replaying the brief scene again and again, trying to see through the caked make-up and cheap wig, to the person underneath. It was a man of medium height, slim, with wiry muscles—especially in the legs. Between the poor video quality and the man's make-up, it was hard to tell more than that, but seeing the man in action gave Gil an uneasy feeling. Gradually, the Detective felt that he was getting to know Mel, inside as well as out. In fact, he kept feeling a kind of "deja vu." Something kept telling him that he knew this man already, that it was someone he had met. Gil knew this was unlikely. Probably it was just that intuitive part of him that tried to second guess the person he was hunting ... or the person who was hunting him.

On the fourth or fifth replay, Gil noticed the mouth movements of the man. It dawned on him that the killer was speaking at the camera. He moved to the monitor, to see that the sound had been turned off. It was probably better that he had viewed the video silently at first. It had allowed him to really concentrate on the visual part. But now he restarted the video, with the sound turned up. The next few minutes were a dark and sickening venture into a lunatic world, as the killer's voice spoke in tones almost like someone he knew:

"...Detective Gil Beach, this performance is for YOU!"

Chapter 40

Thursday, 9:32 p.m.

A garish neon sign flashed the name "Warm Pussy" from the front of the club. Gil and Frank waited outside in the car, sipping cardboard containers of coffee. The night had cooled, so the temperature felt more like early winter than fall. Steam rose from the coffee in clouds. Every few minutes, Frank would start the car in order to run the heater long enough to take off the chill. They had agreed to meet Tyler for the ten o'clock show but had arrived early.

"I'm having second thoughts about having Tom along," Gil remarked. "This guy Mel is farther out than the right field fence at Yankee stadium. He's already taken out Treadwell, and he tried for you and me at Anthony's. Thank God you were alert, or he might have gotten Pilar."

"Yeah, I know what you mean. But we weren't being as careful back then. We practically broadcast where you were going to be. This time, nobody but the three of us knows about this little visit. I didn't even leave word at the P.D.U. I made sure we weren't being tailed, either. The dummy would have to have a crystal ball to ..."

"Don't call him that!" Gil blurted out.

"What? Why not?" Frank responded, surprised. "Isn't that the file name?"

"Sorry, I didn't mean to overreact. Yeah, I used that term on the computer file, but it isn't right. He isn't a dummy. He's damn smart. And nobody has ever given him credit for it."

"You sound like you feel sorry for the bastard."

"No, not sorry. It's just that I think I understand what makes him tick. If we call him 'Dummy' we become part of what makes him what he is today. Too many people have made the mistake of underestimating him. He counts on that."

"You talk almost like you know the guy," Frank observed, looking closely at his partner.

"In a way, I do, Frank. In a way I do."

A man in overcoat and large furry hat walked quickly up the street toward them. It was Tom Tyler. He complained that he had to park five blocks away and pay almost twenty dollars, while the cops could get away with pulling into a loading zone. The men exchanged wisecracks about perks, then moved into the club.

The tables were postage-stamp size, arranged around a small stage with two brass poles rising to the ceiling. A dancer was winding herself around one of the poles, like it was her lover, in a graphic and exaggerated imitation of sex. From a distance you could almost pretend that she was pretty, but as they moved to a table halfway between the door and stage, her imperfections began to show. Heavy pancake make-up couldn't totally hide the sunken cheeks and bags under her eyes. Gil made her out as an addict. Her strip act never included removal of her shoulder- length gloves, which was a good way to hide needle track marks. Her backbone was like a string of beads, and her ribs stood out in relief. It was probably her breasts that got her work as a go-go dancer, because without them she would have been a skeleton. Her boobs jutted out with the unnatural thrust and firmness that spoke of silicon supplements. A microscopic G-string barely covered the woman's crotch, but provided a hook for several dollar bills, which were folded and hung over the string. The idea was that men near the stage would stick a bill there, to give her a tip and cop a little feel at the same time. Since most girls added the first few dollars to the waistband as a hint, it didn't look like this dancer was doing too well.

To catch the customers farther from the stage, another girl worked the tables in a flimsy black peignoir. Her large breasts showed whitely through the lace garment. Unfortunately, so did her ample belly and rolls of fat.

She moved in on the three men, asking for them to buy her a drink. Frank gave her some money and told her to go get one at the bar, flashing his badge. She took the hint and left quickly, in the direction of the manager's office.

The emaciated dancer finished her act with a simulated orgasm, done in rhythm to the loud beat of a monotonous R&B song. When she completed her last open-mouthed gasp, she abruptly stood up to saunter off the stage, with a bored looking expression. There was a smattering of applause from a couple of drunken sailors and a table of Japanese businessmen.

The M.C. returned, trying to be funny by throwing out a couple of disgusting remarks about the woman dancers. He called them "the girls," and made lewd gestures as he described their offstage specialties. No one laughed except one of the sailors, who was so drunk he thought everything was funny.

Denker was then introduced as the "fabulous 'Mellon and Mellon,' "straight from a command performance in Europe." Maybe the 'command' was to get out of the European country. He looked more like a refugee than a star.

Denker was a pear-shaped person, with a large nose and bad teeth. His clothes looked like they had come from a thrift shop. The vent figure was in better shape than the man, its thin-nosed gamin face making it the only figure on stage this evening that didn't look burned-out. But the dummy's movements were artificial and jerky, poorly coordinated with the dialogue, such as it was. The routine relied mostly on cheap jokes about homosexuality and bodily waste.

The performer stumbled through a few minutes of raunchy humor and mumbled lines, with the vent's mouth moving as much as the puppet's. Gil could only guess what hold the management had on the man, or what he had on them. There had to be something other than the quality of the work.

The three observers suffered through most of the act, then moved to the backstage area, the police showing a threatening bouncer their credentials. They saw several dancers, now fully clothed, who glared back at them with a combination of hostility and suspicion. Apparently, word of the cops' presence had preceded them.

They waited in a drafty dressing room that looked like it had been a storage closet. When Denker came in, he almost bolted, but when he saw Tyler he paused, looking puzzled. Tom explained and was able to convince him to talk to Gil and Frank. After a few minutes, Tyler excused himself. With a wink to Gil, he said he had to make a telephone call. He wanted to let them conduct the interview on their own.

It wasn't much of an interrogation. The man was used up. It took about five minutes to eliminate him as a suspect. He was probably a drug addict, a sleeze-ball, and a gutter dweller, but he wasn't the man they were after.

Tom was waiting at the bar, his eyes riveted on a huge woman dancing with a rubber boa constrictor.

"It wouldn't fit," Frank whispered in his ear.

Tom jumped, then grinned at being caught gawking. He playfully waved a finger as if to indicate something forbidden, and headed for the exit.

The cold air outside the club relentlessly bit through their clothing. Returning to the car, Gil found a piece of paper stuck on the windshield under a wiper. A chill deeper than the one caused by the wind knifed down his back. The note had several lines of block-printed lines, written in a shaky hand. The scrawl was uneven, punctuated by places where the pen had poked completely through the paper.

SRpRIZE, surpRZE, MaSTR DETECTIfVE.

YoU WoN'T FnD ME iN SUCH PLAZES.

YoU ARe MUCH ToO INTerested in FLTHY PLazES and FILTHY WIMIN. You WONT find ME THOZE Cesspools. You Do DIRTY THNGS , BUT I Am FREEEEing YoU FROM This. I have SOMETHING of yours that WILL surprise yo.

FOndLLy,

MEL

Gil stood, hunched over, staring at the note for a moment. What was the madman trying to do—scare him? He would have to do more than leave nasty little notes around. It was a little creepy that the man could follow his movements so well, but there would eventually be an explanation for that. If the crazed man thought Gil would be petrified about being followed, he had another think coming. That was no big deal to the Detective. He had been tracked before. In a way, it gave a certain exhilaration to the chase. Besides, Gil would much rather know where the killer was, than where he wasn't. As long as this Mel character was trailing him, Gil reassured himself, at least it was impossible for the madman to....

The Detective jerked his eyes back to the grotesque note. He focused on the last sentence of the letter, the one that spoke of freeing Gil from something. In a flash of recognition, Beach realized that the man was talking about someONE rather than something. He jerked his head up and yelled.

"Frank, get in the car! Tom, I have to leave.'

"What's up?"

"I think he's going after Pilar."

As soon as the two policemen jumped in the car, Gil grabbed the radio handset to call the dispatcher. When he was connected, he asked to be patched into a phone line, and connected with Pilar's number. There was no answer except from her machine, so he left a message to take extreme precautions, and call him right away. At her work number, the unanswered ring reminded him that it was late in the evening. He pounded the dashboard in frustration.

Chapter 41

Thursday, 10:37 p.m.

The Performer had purchased a Mannlicher carbine shortly after reading an old, dog-eared copy of the Warren Commission Report. While other students of this report may have focused on the identity of the Kennedy assassin, Mel noted the range and accuracy of the weapon used to shoot the President. There was something wonderful about owning the same rifle that had burst a President's head like a ripe melon. He added it to the arsenal he had collected.

Most of the ordinance had been picked up during his U.S.O. tour. He had conned a faggot sergeant in the Quartermaster Corp who had access to everything. The man's perversions were an easy way to gain power over him. After the Performer seduced him by pretending to be homo, it was easy to have the man indecently involved, it was easy to get whatever he wanted by using blackmail. Threatened with exposure, the soldier found it easier to let certain items go missing.

Few civilians realize how many times items disappear, or are unaccounted for in the vast stream of military supplies.

Later, Mel had to eliminate the Sergeant by staging an accident. That not only prevented his acquisitions from being discovered, but also meant that the filthy man could never tell about the things that Mel had let him do. Just because he allowed the man to touch his physical shell for a while, didn't mean that The Performer was a queer like the soldier, it was only a necessary and temporary role. But it was important that no one ever heard about it and got the wrong idea.

Whenever he thought about the way the man had stroked and then invaded him, The Master got angry and excited. He was forced to find release.

That word, "Release," is a magical word. It describes two mystical realities—the emptying out of a life, when he finally allows his chosen ones to depart, and the emptying out of his darkness, which gave him calmness and peace after it was done. Guns were not good enough for this, too impersonal. But so far, he had only used these remote methods on adults. They weren't as good anyway. The spirits of children are pure and undefiled, unlike those of adults who had dirtied theirs. Most adults were like Carmen, who was full of evil desires and would let anyone do filthy things to her.

He would have liked to have used the knife on this new woman, the one who reminded him of Carmen. She was called Peel-lar, the woman of his adversary. It was fitting that the names were both Latina. She had the spirit of Carmen in her, and he would have taken a long time with her, sharing the ritual; introducing her to the knife. However, he knew he had to kill her from a distance. It was better to stay far away. If he had gotten too close, she might have enticed him the way she did the Detective, seducing him and forcing him to fulfill her evil desires. Besides, his primary goal was this man Beach, not the woman. It seemed, for the time being, the detective was still too powerful. So far, he had been almost invulnerable. By taking the woman, however, the Performer was confident he could demonstrate mastery over the detective. It would surely reduce the adversary's power.

As soon as he learned that Beach had a woman who was important to him, the Performer began tracking her. The Detective himself had revealed her name, so it was relatively simple to locate her dwelling. Finding an unoccupied apartment across the street had taken longer.

First, Mel had donned his invisible disguise to approach the entrance of the building, where each apartment had a separate bell. He pressed one button after another, until he had found several that did not answer. Every few days later, he had returned to ring the same bells, each time narrowing the list of those that had not answered. After a week, he had the numbers of several apartments which were probably vacant, or the occupants were away. Two of them faced the way he needed. He checked the mailboxes and found one of them empty, the other filled with mail. Since there was no response from Apartment 307 for several days and it did not receive mail, it was probably vacant, the voices told him.

Next, he used a late night visit there to see the locks. Sometimes these places used old locks that could be bypassed with a shimmy card. The lock on 307 was better than that, but only consisted of a single bolt. When it came time to take the woman, he merely used a pry-bar to pop the door open and gain access. In his weakened condition, it took several tries. When he had reclosed the door, no one noticed the signs of forced entry, especially after he took a light bulb out of the hallway fixture, throwing the whole area into deep shadow.

The Master waited, loaded Mannlicher ready, watching the woman's windows across the street, until she appeared. Nothing existed for him but the small square of light and the voices in his head that told him what he must do. His deadpan face was frozen, immovable. His bloodshot eyes were lasers, knifing through space to find her and hold her. When she arrived, he gasped, because it seemed to be Carmen who walked through the room. At first, he could not imagine how his childhood seductress could be there. But then he realized that evil knew no bounds of mortal flesh. The wicked force that took the form of Carmen to pollute him, had lived on in different physical forms. Now it had assumed the image necessary to seduce the Detective. In public, she held that form, but now that she was alone, she reverted to her earlier likeness. Therefore, he did not hesitate, even when her image rippled and changed again to look like his mother. He knew that the evil female force remained the same, no matter how she tried to change her outward appearance.

The woman sat down in a chair, creating a stationary target. He was glad, because, in his depleted state, he was having trouble holding the heavy rifle steady.

Mel fired the first shot at her midsection, selecting center-mass, the most sure target. Although he had not originally intended this, it pleased him, not only because it made sure he blasted any babies in there, but also because it would prolong her life. Gut wounds took longer than head shots to kill the victim. He liked the idea that she would know what was happening, before being released. He wanted her to feel his own dark sense of despair and emptiness. The Detective would find her body, so he would feel those feelings too. Most times the Performer had buried the bodies of those he had released, but sometimes, like with 'Merrydeath,' he had wanted the remains to be found. Once he dropped brain tissue on a New York City sidewalk. The world needed to know' what it felt like to be wronged, as he had been wronged. He felt the satisfying snap of the bolt, as he chambered another shell. He put the next shot in her head.

"Pee-lar is Kaa-put," he whispered to himself.

He felt the wave of peace flow over him. The disabling tautness in his gut, uncoiled a millimeter. There was a small taste of the release that would ultimately be his. Yet, as gratifying as the act had been, it was not enough, not like when he was able to feel the warm blood run out and afterwards hold the head in his hands. The Master needed more power. He could feel himself weakening. His eyes kept blurring, and he felt stabs of pain in his middle. He sensed that the power could be obtained only with his blade, and only by getting another figure, by releasing another small one. But he was still leery of the Detective's apparent magic. He was worried until the voices told him what to do. He could reduce his adversary's power further, they told him. He could simultaneously obtain another figure in the same operation.

He began to sing his tuneless refrain, "Jennifuh, Jennifuh, da,da-da, da-da..."

Chapter 42

Thursday, 11:27 p.m.

Frank Terranova was humming an off-key version of a popular tune as he drove. It sounded vaguely like Viva la Vida. Beach was more intense, and silent, chewing a piece of gum like he was trying to kill it. They were just approaching the entrance to the Brooklyn-Battery tunnel when a call came through on the police channel. It told them to go to a telephone and call in. That indicated there was something that the brass didn't want to broadcast, even to other cops. "Use land lines," the dispatcher said.

Frank pulled over by the toll booths, where there was a row of pay-telephones. Gil jumped out, ran to the first phone where he punched in the number of the P.D.U. Beverly answered, but told him to wait for the Lieutenant. He didn't like the tone of her voice, which sounded hesitant, quiet, tense. As he waited, his left hand was white from its tight grip on the receiver, his other pounded against the metal side of the small enclosure. In a moment, Lincoln picked up the receiver.

"Hello, Gil?" he asked carefully. That was not a good sign. The Lieutenant didn't usually use first names, especially when speaking over the telephone. It was even rarer for him to speak hesitantly.

"Yes."

"Ahh, well, ... there's been a shooting, Gil. It's ... it's your lady."

"Pilar?" he asked, densely, a numbness invading his body. He had trouble asked the next question.

"Is ... Is she...?"

"No. She's not dead. But it doesn't look good. They took her to Bayley-Seton Hospital. I think you better get there as soon as possible."

Gil slumped against the phone. The slamming of his heart echoed in his ears, his legs felt like they would not hold him up, his stomach felt sick. Then, bit by bit, the hot waves of nausea and tingling numbness gave way to a cold rage. He felt it travel through his body like ice water. He straightened, jaw muscles hard as granite, ears set back like a leopard ready for a kill.

Frank put on the flashing lights and siren, careening through the tunnel, down the Gowanus Expressway, over the Verrazano Bridge to Staten Island. His hands were tight on the steering wheel, as they flew down Bay Street, a patched and potholed ramble of a road, once even driving half a block on the sidewalk to get around a knot of traffic caused by an unloading truck.

Bayley-Seton was the former Public Health Hospital, now privately owned and named after the first American saint of the Roman Catholic Church. It is a great sprawling red-brick facility located on a hill north of the ferry slips. If their mission were less urgent, the men might have smelled the scent of the sea and imagined the days of whalers and immigrant hoards arriving in New York, when Herman Melville visited his brother up the road at Sailor's Snug Harbor and the main residents of Staten Island were the Vanderbilts, and other wealthy knickerbockers. But this was not a night for history appreciation.

The car sped through the massive wrought iron gates, screeching into the emergency entrance. Both men bolted from the car, pushing through the electrically operated doors before the automatic mechanism could open for them. The wrathful look on Gil's face, combined with the aura of authority projected as they pursued their goal, made obstacles melt in their path. The badges they flashed didn't hurt either. In moments, he learned that Pilar had already left surgery and was now in the Intensive Care Unit. A ward clerk tried to tell Gil the rules regarding visitors, but he ignored her, vigorously walking into the room.

The I.C.U. was laid out in a rectangle, with cubicles around the four sides and a nursing station at the middle, like the hub of a square wheel. He quickly located Pilar in the corner, next to a fire exit.

Gauze bandages covered half her head. Her eyes were dark and bruised looking. A cardiac monitor gave a rhythmic beeping sound, as a pump muttered away by the side of the bed, a glass jar below, slowly filling with blood-tinged liquid. Machines s sucked, trilled, and whished as oxygen was pumped, fluids injected, and substances removed. She was spread out on the bed, a sheet draped loosely over her. A woman in a white lab coat was standing, looking intently at one of the monitors. When Gil entered the cubicle, she turned. He saw a name tag, "Sylvia Poole, M.D."

At first, no one spoke. Gil walked to the bed, gently taking Pilar's hand. For a moment, the cold rage took a back seat. He looked at the woman on the bed, then raised his eyes to meet those of the physician.

"Are you her doctor?"

"I'm a resident here at the hospital. Dr. Malcolm did the initial care, Dr. Edwards performed the surgery. If she has a personal physician you would like to call, we can do that. But for now, I will be following her case."

"What can you tell me?"

"I'm afraid it's touch and go, at this point. Are you her husband?"

"No," Gil began, then other words came unbidden to his lips, "... but I'm going to be."

"I see," the doctor said, sympathy in her voice. "Well, she was shot twice. All things considered, she was very lucky. Despite its appearance, the head wound is the least serious. The bullet just struck a glancing blow. She has a concussion and might have a permanent part in her hair, but there was no significant damage. The abdominal wound is another matter."

When she paused, Gil nodded for her to go on, spreading his hands in a questioning gesture.

"Well Dr. Edwards is great, or she might not be alive right now. He had to do a little quick damage control and repair to some of her G.I. tract. Actually, the tissue damage isn't much worse than a moderately serious abdominal operation, except there is a bigger concern about infection. Frankly, she got off surprisingly easy for someone shot twice with a large caliber gun. I've seen worse. The biggest problem was loss of blood. Between the wounds and the shock, her total volume was so low when we got her that there may have been loss of circulation to the brain sufficient to cause some nerve damage. We don't know yet. The bullet in her abdomen may also have chipped the spinal vertebrae on its way out. There could be trauma to the spinal cord. It depends on swelling, and some other things we can't assess fully yet. Her heart is doing well, but we're just going to have to wait to see on some of this."

"But you think she is going to live?"

"In my opinion, yes. Every hour that she holds on, increases that likelihood. Thanks to Drs. Malcolm and Edwards, most of the damage has been caught and treated. There are a lot of question marks right now. Some of it will depend on her determination to recover... to fight back. Some people have a tremendous will to live, and it helps them overcome conditions we never expected them to surmount. That's why smart physicians don't make dramatic statements, like 'you'll never walk again' or whatever. Far too often, people have proven that kind of prediction wrong."

"Is that a possibility? Not walking again?"

"I'm sorry, I didn't mean that," she cautioned, grimacing. "We don't have enough information to even get into that yet. I was just using it as an example. My point is that nobody can make hard and fast predictions."

"What can I do?" Gil asked, helplessly.

"Well, I suppose it's a cliche to say this, but if you have any kind of belief, I'd say you could do some praying."

Gil though about her advice and the question it implied. What did he believe? For a long time, he hadn't believed in much of anything. That was before Pilar was in his life. Maybe it was her unique character, maybe he was finally ready for real living, or perhaps a combination of the two, but whatever it was, he was alive again. Part of him wanted to run away from the pain of hoping, the work of believing ... to retreat into a protective cloak of cynicism and disbelief. But he could not run away from Pilar, or her belief in him. He needed to believe in something. He didn't know about much else, but he knew he had faith in her.

So Gil Beach, semi-atheist, general cynic, laid his head on the limp hand of this violated woman and prayed to a power he hardly knew, asking life and healing for the one he loved. It was the only way he could think to counter some of the other powers arrayed against them.

Chapter 43

Friday, 2:56 p.m.

It was finally the time. The waiting was over.

The Master moved toward the school entrance. He knew that except for days when the Detective picked her up, the child took the small van-type school bus. Sometimes the bus was waiting at the curb when classes were dismissed, but most days it didn't arrive right on time, so the children milled about in front of the place for a few minutes, waiting. Sometimes Jennifer was in the middle of a cluster of students, but it was a fluid group. Individual children would be at the center for a moment, then drift to the edges. Often, they would even separate themselves from the others for a dash to make a childish discovery, run from a teasing classmate, or just feel the energy of their growing bodies. It was only a matter of time until she detached herself from the others.

Mel took his position by a parked car, pretending to be examining the tires. Eventually, the right moment came. The child stepped away from the others to chase a rubber ball gone astray. He moved quickly forward swooped up beside the girl, and placed one hand over her mouth. He slipped his other arm around her waist, moving past the corner of the building out of sight before anyone noticed.

He had the van stationed fifty yards down the block, with the front nosing up to a hydrant. That way no one could park in front of him, and he wouldn't have to jockey back and forth to pull out of the spot. The engine was running with the door ajar, so he was able to step up into the vehicle, slip in the driver's seat and pull out into the street without pausing or letting go of the girl. Once he was several blocks away from the school, he pulled over to the curb long enough to tape her down, then slipped a nylon bag over her. It was the same bag he had used for the running girl, Merry-death, but on Jenni-fuh it fit all the way to her waist.

His safe place was not far away. He looked forward to seeing the museum and all his figures. It was difficult to drive, with the voices in his head and the way the sunlight kept flashing alternate colors, like a display of the Northern Lights. His brain hurt.

The girl was quiet, in shock. His brain was far from quiet. Multiple voices competed for his attention. He concentrated until one voice could be made out through the cacophony in his head. It was a familiar voice. The voice said it would be happy when he released the girl.

On the street behind them, an old blue rubber ball came to rest in the gutter.

CHAPTER 44

Saturday, 7:18 a.m.

A ramrod drill instructor of a nurse had finally shooed Gil out into the waiting area by the Intensive Care Unit, where he stood vigil through the night into the next day. When he fell asleep slumped in a chair they let him rest. He didn't wake up for almost three hours. He only woke when Dr. Poole tapped him on the shoulder. The surgeon then spent a long time explaining that unlike movies where comatose patients suddenly opened their eyes and spoke, the return from such a state was a predictably slow process that could be anticipated by watching for certain definite signs.

In other words, he didn't have to worry that Pilar would wake up without warning to find him absent. If he left for a few hours, he could be assured that they would continue to monitor her status and promptly inform him if there were any indications that she might be coming out of her deep sleep. The doctor explained that this would surely take many hours, perhaps days, so he should not plan to stay at the hospital without a break. The next time Frank showed up, Gil agreed to be taken home.

He was so exhausted that when he got to the apartment, Gil fell into a sleep not that different from Pilar's coma, except that a few hours later he revived. This time there were no dreams, but the tangled jumble of bedclothes told him he had not slept peacefully.

He realized he had missed most of Friday. Now it Was Saturday. He went immediately for the telephone. After some heated discussion, he managed speak to Dr. Poole, who told him there was no change in Pilar's condition. He struggled with the impulse to return to the hospital, to stay with her every moment, no matter what. Eventually, however, he made a different decision. He wanted to be with her when she began coming out of the coma. He counted on that outcome, refusing to accept the other possibilities. Still, the doctor had assured him that there would be advance notice of her waking up, and for a time she wouldn't be ready to communicate. So while she was not conscious he could better use the time to find her would-be killer. Finding the "Bad guy" was no longer a career objective, now it was a mission. Maybe it was an obsession.

Ninety minutes later, he was at the P.D.U office.

Frank wasn't in yet. Gil pulled a pad out of his drawer, threw it on the desk and began making a list of things to be done on a priority basis. As he was noting data to be researched, leads to follow and people to be interviewed, his desk blotter shifted a fraction, which caused a small figurine to topple over. It was a commercial toy called a "Care Bear," in pink with a heart printed on its tummy. A Christmas gift from his niece, it reminded him that he had never heard back from Sheila, Jennifer's mother.

He grabbed his phone to punch in Sheila's number at her job. She worked as a cosmetologist at Renaldo's, specializing in "Depilatory Science." Although currently not employed directly by the salon, she had an arrangement that allowed her to rent a chair there, next to the hairstylists. She used the business name of "Sheena" and managed a decent income out of women's desire to rid themselves of body and facial hair.

Sheila had one sign adapted from a radar-detection d device advertising slogan, that proclaimed her as 'Sheena, Fuzz-buster."

The woman who answered, told him that Sheila was "in session" at the moment, so he left a message for her to call him as soon as she got free. He was becoming less and less confident of anyone's safety. He had already seen the woman he loved, shot down like an animal. As he cradled the phone to his neck, Frank walked into the office.

Seeing Gil, he moved quickly over to the desk, his expression showing concern.

"Good to see you, Gil. How's Pilar?"

"No change yet. They say they will know when she starts to improve. In the meantime, I've got to keep busy. What have you got?"

"I think we're getting close. Gina, Woods and Tompkins are checking out a couple of leads, including the address of that Bradley guy Tom told us was supposed to be dead. I just got some more information from the U.S.O., and it looks like the ventriloquist that did a tour with them was the same guy we're looking at. He hit most of the Officer and N.C.O. clubs in the Southeast, ...went by the first name of Charles, and used a dummy named Melvin, among others. Some of the contact information was obviously faked, but it looks like the same man."

"Good. If you have the names he used in his act, we might be able to find out if he's working in this area. I can check with Tom."

Frank's face got solemn. He was fidgeting in a way Gil knew went along with having something difficult to say. He waited until Terranova found the words.

"Look, Gil, this might be off the wall, but... I mean... well, don't take this wrong or anything, but how much do you know about Tom?"

"What are you saying, Frank?"

"Well, look, Gil. I'm not jumping to any conclusions, or anything, but did you notice that Tom disappeared a few minutes before the note was put on your car? I mean, that isn't a big deal by itself, but then, this is a guy who's a ventriloquist, right? I'm no psychologist, but maybe he had a lousy childhood, no dad and all that."

"If that made somebody a suspect, we'd have half of New York on the list, including me."

"Yeah, I know. But there's more than that. Did you think about who knew we were going to the "Warm Pussy?" Nobody knew, except you, me, and Tom. He also knew that you were going to Sal Anthony's the day of the other shooting, and of course he knew when you would be at his place to hear a message on the machine. I mean, I like Tom. He seems like a real nice guy. But don't a lot of psychos seem normal most of the time? I'm not sure he likes women. Or at least there's no sign that he has a lady, and you could see that he doesn't even give his secretary a second glance, as foxy as she is. I don't know, but I just don't think we can afford to overlook anybody, Gil. There are a lot of pieces that fit."

Gil was more troubled by this idea than he wanted to admit. It wasn't that he refused to believe that Tyler could be a suspect, he always tried to keep an open mind about anyone being a suspect. But the Detective was upset with himself that it had taken Frank to point out the connections. He had let his personal attachments interfere with his objectivity in the case. That was not like Gil Beach. Even now, he could recognize a part of himself that did not want to pursue the idea of his new friend being the killer. That part of him responded to Frank.

"No way, Jose. I see your point, but the personality just doesn't fit. Psychos aren't like that. Tom is too decent. Besides, we wouldn't even be this close, if it weren't for the information he's been able to give us."

That is what he said out loud. In his private thoughts he was less confident. Then he thought of the video.

"Frank, get that video, if it's back from analysis. Was there enough to get a physical description from it?"

He knew that the experts in the Tech Department could analyze the video and by comparing the person with surroundings, measuring physical parts, and using various formulas, come up with an accurate description of the person, despite the make-up, wig, and other disguising stuff.

"I don't think they got around to it, yet. I'll give them a call and put a fire under their asses."

"Better let me do that. I've got a little more clout at this point," Gil said, but noticing the other man's crestfallen look, he added, "In the meantime I won't dismiss the possibility. See what you can find on Tom's background."

Frank left, looking placated. Gil started going through a pile of paper on his desk. The stack included a bunch of "fives," DD5 reports of door-to-door interviews around the school area, junk mail, and inter-office envelopes, all jumbled together. He had let the papers accumulate as he kept up to date with most of the digital data he was receiving, but tended to put off the more cumbersome old stuff. He noticed there was an autopsy report on the body from Mt. Sinai. It wasn't done by Anton, but Gil thought he recognized his friend's hand in the "conclusions" section. He picked up the phone and dialed Krispnick's number, punching the telephone's buttons like he was squashing bugs.

"Anton, how are you doing," he greeted the pathologist when he came on the line.

"As good as can be expected, considering I get so many stupid phone calls, I can never get anything done."

Gil ignored the crotchety tone Krispnick used. He knew it was all an act. He kept it light, firing back a dig.

"Work? Since when did you start earning your salary?"

"Since wise guy cops started coming to me to answer all their questions."

Having satisfied the need for verbal jousting, Anton asked in a more serious tone, "So what's up?"

Gil thought about all the things that had happened in the last few days, and didn't know where to begin. His rumbling stomach also reminded him that he hadn't eaten in a long time. Sometimes he ignored the signals of hunger when he was deeply involved in a difficult case, but he felt like he was going to need all of his strength this time. He could quiz his friend over lunch, as well as anywhere.

"Well, since you're so busy, I guess lunch would be out of the question."

"Depends on who's buying."

"Okay, tightwad, it's on me."

"Well, how about that. Now that I think about it, it is Saturday, isn't it? Why should I work the whole weekend, without a little break now and then? Where do you want to meet—Tavern on the Green?"

"Not if I'm buying. How about Cohen's?"

"Ahh ... best pastrami in New York!"

A few minutes later, the two men were seated in a back booth of the popular delicatessen.

"I just got the post on that John Doe from Mt. Sinai," Gil mentioned as he smeared spicy brown mustard across his rye bread. Anton waved a large dill pickle like a baton.

"Oh yeah. They didn't win any friends on that one."

"What do you mean?"

"Oh, they just stuck the kid in the freezer for a coupla months. Never bothered to do an exam. Not even a thorough external. I don't know if that is because it's a kid. I'm annoyed. Normal procedures were not followed. In the case of an unclaimed body, they have a standard operating procedure that should have taken place, but somehow the usual Jane Doe burial got delayed, and eventually everybody forgot why the cadaver was there. The postmortem never got done."

"So what happened? One of your guys do it?"

"Yeah, I had Shapiro take this one. I could've done it, but a case with an extended- delay post-mortem is a little different, and he can use the experience. Not that he's any slouch. He might not have a lot of years under his belt, but it took him about thirty seconds to find the artifact. It was inserted in the rectum."

"The report doesn't describe it in detail. Is it what I think?"

"I don't know. There was a one and a half inch curved piece of cardboard with a serrated metal edge?"

"Bingo."

"You know what it is?"

"Yeah. It's a ventriloquist gadget. The guy I'm after uses them as calling cards."

"Sounds like a sweetheart."

"Yeah, a real darling." At the words "sweetheart" and "darling" Gil's mind jumped to thoughts of Pilar. There was a clutch in his stomach, as he imagined her lying there on a morgue table. A rush of adrenalin surged through him when he thought of the madman who had shot her. What would be his next move? As if reading his thoughts, Anton asked about Pilar.

"Speaking of sweethearts, Gil. How's your lady doing?"

"I don't really know yet, Anton. She's still not conscious."

"Damn. Look, I'm really sorry, Gil. I hope you know that if there's anything I can do, you can just say the word."

"I don't think there's anything that isn't being done right now, except to catch the bastard that did this to her."

"I'm sure you've thought of it already, Gil, but there's gotta be an information leak somewhere. How the hell did he know about Pilar?"

"I've got Public Relations to thank for that! That idiot Epstein got conned into telling everything about me down to the size jockey shorts I wear. But I've got a hunch there is more going on than leaked data. I've got a feeling that this guy is close, too close."

"Not guilty!" Krispnick said, raising his hands in mock surrender.

"Don't worry, I know it couldn't be you. Not that you aren't a ghoul. But I know you wouldn't make any extra work for your department." He managed the flicker of a smile.

They finished their lunch and parted, Anton vowing to drag Gil to a Mets game sometime, if he could manage free tickets from another friend. Somehow the thought of baseball seemed like a slice out of a different world to Gil. Maybe there would be a day again when things like sports and movies would mean something to him, but right now he felt like someone on the front lines, face-to-face with the ghastly truth of war, knowing he was going back to stark life and death... the ugly and ultimate realities.

When Gil got back to the Precinct, the pile of mail and papers was still waiting. One of the inter-office envelopes contained a stack of glossy photographs. They were taken the day of the shooting at Sal Anthony's. As he spread them out on his desk, Gil felt waves of anger washing over him. This might have been when the killer identified Pilar, seeing her meet Gil at the restaurant. He could have followed her afterwards in order to learn where she lived, so he could try to slaughter the woman Gil loved.

For a moment, he thought of the first time he had shot a deer, sixteen years old and out with Dave Senne, the man who had volunteered to be his "Big Brother" through a charitable organization. He had never killed anything before, though he had dreamed of blowing up a few dorm counselors and social workers. It was his third unsuccessful hunting trip, he was getting used to the idea that he would never bag a trophy. He was dozing in a patch of brush, when he realized a deer was standing only fifty yards away in a grove of acacia trees. He raised the Marlin .22 caliber rifle Dave had loaned to him, in a dreamy fog, squeezing off two shots. To his amazement, the animal dropped on the spot. But when he went to see the results, he found himself looking into the big liquid eyes of a doe, still alive. He was shocked and disgusted at what he had done. Not only did he lack a doe permit, but he had never realized what it would be like to look into the eyes of a beautiful creature that knew you were killing it. Dave finished off the deer, and one of his friends who had a doe permit, claimed the kill to avoid problems. Still, the experience was shaking to the boy, so he didn't go hunting again, until he had been through a combat tour and years on the Job. By then he felt differently about hunting animals. It wasn't even in the same category as hunting humans.

Some of the photos showed the shattered front of the restaurant, others were of the waiter's corpse. Some of the pictures included Gil. He was thankful he was shown only after he had revived from his head-banging fall. There were also the usual crowd photos. These were taken as standard procedure, because often the perpetrator of a crime would be found among the onlookers, pretending to be an innocent bystander. By itself, it wasn't conclusive, but along with other evidence, a person's presence at the crime scene could be important. Gil leafed through the pictures, scanning faces. He was about to return the last of the shots to the envelope, when he had a flash of recognition. A woman in one of the photos looked familiar.

The face was partially hidden, but she was tall for a woman, and he could make out her dark hair and contrasting light skin. The flow of a billowy sleeve helped him make the connection. He wasn't sure, but he would bet it was Annie, Tom's secretary.

The Detective's mind raced. As much as he didn't want to believe that Tom was involved, he had always refused to believe in coincidences. To classify something as a coincidence was to dismiss it. A good detective dismissed nothing. The word "coincidence" just described the fact that two "incidents" happened together. Gil believed that there were always reasons for that co-happening. The reasons might prove quite innocent, but there were still reasons. And often, those reasons turned out to be significant.

Could Tyler be using his secretary to gather information that he couldn't get himself without risking discovery? Or could there be some sick relationship, where they were in league with each other? Gil thought of the shocking stories about day care centers where a family or staff cooperated in systematic patterns of child abuse. Then again, could there be another, completely innocent explanation for the secretary's presence at the crime scene? Could she have been a messenger sent by his friend to find out if Gil was okay, or someone driven by an obsessive desire to follow him, as police groupies had been known to do? There might be many other strange explanations. Unfortunately, Gil knew, Occam's Razor said the simplest explanations were often the ones that were true.

As Gil was sitting, considering this new development, the phone on his desk rang. It was Sheila.

"Hi Gil. What's up?"

"Well, Sheila, I was just concerned about you and Jennifer. Did you get my message?"

"Yup, I got all of them. You scared the heck out of me with the one about taking extreme precautions, but it was good to know you were picking her up from school."

"What do you mean, Sheila?"

"Huh? You know, the other message from your friend. You did pick her up, didn't you? Of course you did. She stayed over with you, right?"

"Sheila, I don't know what you're talking about."

"What? You don't know? You mean you didn't keep her? Then where is she?" Panic rose in the woman's voice. Gil's voice remained more in control, but his emotions were a tornado of disbelief, shock, fear, and anger.

"What makes you think I had her?" Even as he asked the question, he already suspected the awful answer.

"The other message. The one from your friend, Detective Melvin, that said you were picking Jennifer up from school and going to a circus, then keeping her for the night. If it wasn't you, who has her?"

"Oh, my God! He's got her."

Chapter 45

Saturday, 1:35 p.m.

The tone may have been middle C, but the Performer thought it was higher. The moaning of the child was monotonous in its regularity, sounding like a quiet violin tone, repeated again and again. The Performer tried to hum along at the same pitch, until finding it, he added words, "Jennifuh, Jennifuh, da, da-da, da-da." She was securely in the enclosure. Now he was waiting for the Voices to tell him that it was time.

Soon he would put on the clothes, but not too soon. It couldn't be rushed. All the forces had to be in convergence. The new figure had to be properly prepared, aged like cheese to the right consistency. The Performer had to be at the proper level of being, when the inner door was ready to be opened, the molten fire ready to come forth— a purifying plasma of fire. The voices would tell him when they were ready, with their knowledge of the universal powers and dark secrets. He knew there was a vast pattern that had to come together, and the pulse of the macrocosm could not be hurried. He took comfort in the thought that the Detective was being buffeted by the winds of fate now. He smiled as he thought of the man's fear and helplessness when he learned of the latest addition to the Master's collection. He would leave the extra parts somewhere for the Detective to find. It would help drain the man's puzzling energy, while saving the Performer the effort of digging up the basement floor again.

The Master was satisfied for now to wait. He sat naked on the foil. His bowels had emptied, forming a pool of putrid liquid under him, but he hardly noticed. He had risen above the mortal plane; was not subject to normal human needs or reactions. Wearing the ultimate deadpan expression, he could choose to either notice sensory input or ignore it. He reveled in the extent of control over himself, over the new figure, over the adversary. The waiting served another purpose, that of extending the Detective's period of ignorance, anxiety, and fear, implementing a slow torture that would help to siphon off more and more of his power. The Carmen-clone's release should have weakened the man significantly, as she was a source of great evil power. Yet the Performer knew that he and the Detective would have to meet, so he wanted to have control over the time, the place, and the circumstances. He wanted to make sure the adversary had as little power as possible for the coming confrontation when it arrived.

In a way Mel longed for that day, which he believed would allow him to find his own final release. He knew that when the two adversaries met, the Master would either be vanquished or draw such power from the release of the adversary that he could ascend to the final plane on his own. Either way, it would be over. But for now, he had to wait. Soon the whirl of sound and color would slow. The voices would break through again. Soon it would be time to begin the ritual for releasing. Soon he would put on his cutting clothes.

Chapter 46

Saturday, 2:10 p.m.

Gil's call was answered on the fifth ring. It was Tom, who spoke with the breathless voice of someone who had just finished a hundred-yard dash. When he heard who it was, he apologized for taking so long to answer.

"Sorry, I was in the production room. I'm really behind in my work and trying to do everything myself."

Despite his simmering sense of urgency, Gil engaged in small talk for a minute, before daring to ask the questions he had called to ask. He was having a hard time confronting Tom, but the anxiety about Jennifer was driving him crazy. He had to move as quickly as he could to get more information, so he swallowed and plunged ahead.

"You're there by yourself? Where's Annie?"

"Well, she isn't usually here on Saturday afternoon, but Gil, the truth is that I don't really know, and frankly, I'm worried. That's partly why I'm so far behind in my work. She hasn't been in for days, and I haven't heard from her."

"Do you know where she was the Saturday afternoon before last, around one-thirty?"

"Saturday? A week ago, right? Uh... wasn't that when someone tried to shoot you? You don't think..."

"Do you know where she was?"

"Well, no, not really. She only works half days, remember? She was here in the morning, but I don't know where she went later. Gil, you couldn't think that she was somehow involved in that, could you?"

Gil found himself torn between believing the innocent attitude, and not wanting to be conned by an act. Which of the two was he dealing with here, a simple guileless bystander, or an evil soul hiding behind a mask of respectability? He couldn't afford to make assumptions.

"Where were you that afternoon, Tom?"

There was dead silence on the other end of the line. After a few moments, Tom spoke again, but his voice was not as warm and friendly.

"Am I a suspect, Gil? What is it? You think all ventriloquists are a little weird? You think we are all a little schizoid, so it would be easy for us to go berserk, is that it?"

"Tom, cut it out. I have to ask these questions. Annie showed up at the scene of the shooting. We I.D.'d her in the photos. How did she know about it? Did you?"

"I knew where you were going that day. So did Annie. You told us. I didn't learn about the shooting until much later. I don't know if Annie knew. As for where I was, you can ask my wife."

"Your wife? I didn't know you were married."

"Did you ever ask?"

"You don't wear a ring."

"Not except on special occasions, because the paints and solvents might damage it. We've been together for seven years. We're waiting on an adoption application. That's where I was Saturday afternoon. Four years on the waiting list, and we thought we finally had a chance. We were down at the Catholic Charities office, talking with the child placement worker. It turned out to be another disappointment. You want the number, so you can verify that?"

I'm sorry, Tom ... for your disappointment, and for having to ask these questions. It's not me, it's the job."

"Are you sure that's all it is?"

"Look man," Beach hesitated, then continued. "This killer...he's taken my niece, Jennifer."

"On no! Oh crap. I'm sorry Gil."

"I have to track down every possible lead. I don't want to offend you, but some information is missing in all this, and I can't afford to skip over anything."

There was another moment of silence. Tom wearily shook his head, then replied, "Forget it. I guess you have to suspect everyone. It's just hard, when somebody is..., well, when you're a..."

Gil knew that at some point he had to either give up his suspicions of Tom or lose a relationship. He was just beginning to open up a little and find out what it is like to have some friends. He wasn't anxious to lose them now because of excess caution. The ventriloquist's tone and understanding attitude about Jennifer helped him make the decision to go with his feeling that Tom could not have been involved. Gil's instincts had served him well for a long time. He decided not to distrust them now. He completed Tom's unfinished sentence for him.

"...when you're a friend?"

"Yeah, I guess I'd like to think so."

"Sorry, Tom, you're right. You aren't really a suspect, it's just that I have to figure out what Annie was doing at the shooting scene. I need to call the Catholic Charities office to confirm your account, just so I have a record that I did all due diligence for my Job, but I never thought you were capable of being the killer. Still, I'm left with a question mark. What was Annie doing there?"

"You've got me, Gil. She's always been a little weird, but we put it down to eccentricity. She's smart as a whip and knows more about the history of this field than I do, but if you think I keep my life secret, compared to Annie I'm a publicity hound."

"Well, what DO you know about her?"

"Uh, well, let's see. I'd put her around forty years old, even though she claims to be thirty-five. She has a stocky figure but wears clothes that hide the fact. She has worked a lot of different jobs, including a tour of England in the army. She claims to have been married a couple of times, but the stories about her husbands keep changing, and don't always compute. I'm not sure she's ever really been hitched at all. I think the seductive routine is all a fake. Any time a guy has ever followed up on her flirting, she beats a hasty retreat. She's never come on to yours truly, which is fine with me. It's fine with Mary Anne, too."

"Your wife?"

"Right."

"What about her moods? Has she been acting strange lately?"

"Acting strange? That's like asking if Donald Trump ever acted arrogant. She always acts strange. For the most part, I don't care, as long as the work gets done. It sort of adds a little color to my operation, anyway."

"How did you find her?"

"I didn't. She found me. I was getting along with only a 'temp' worker, two days a week. Then she wrote me a note, offering to work five mornings for the same price. You want to see the letter? It was an email, but I'm sure I kept it. It's probably in the files."

"Yes. And I would like her address and telephone number, too, if you have them."

Tom asked him to wait a minute. Then he came back on the line, with a rustling of paper.

"Here it is, I printed it out, so I have a hard copy for the files:

Dear Mr. Tyler:

I am an excellent Girl-Friday and office manager, who loves ventriloquism, and would be willing to work at a rate lower than my usual salary in order to be close to the field. I sometimes work as a temp, and was offered a fill-in job to take your days, when your other girl was on vacation. I am aware of what you pay for a two-day position, and would be willing to work five mornings a week for the same amount. I'm sure that daily office hours would be much better for your business than occasional days. I am a master worker, with lots of experience and an interest in your work. I know a number of performers who have used figures manufactured by you and your grandfather, and I have a great appreciation for your performing career. You are a Master, and I would like to work with you. Please write to me at the address below, as my telephone is not working at present.'

Sincerely, Melanie Charles."

"What did you say the name was?" Gil asked in a rush of understanding.

"Charles, ... Melanie Charles. But, as you know, she prefers to shorten the name, and just goes by 'Annie.' "

"Oh hell, Tom. Don't you see? If you take the 'Annie' from 'Melanie' what are you left with?"

"... Mel? Oh, my God. You mean, Annie is really involved?"

"I don't know. What address do you have on her?"

"Let me see." Tom continued. "Here it is. It's on Staten Island. Number 10 Summer Street. Why does that sound familiar to me?"

"Because ... if I remember now, Tom it's the same address as the 'Charles Bradley' we saw on the Newsyvents mailing list."

"My God, is that right? You mean she lives with him, and never said anything?"

"No, Tom, I don't think so. I think Annie IS him!"

The killer was a man, and yet a woman too. Gil's mind struggled to wrap itself around this strange situation. For some reason, an image of his mother's face kept creeping in to distort his memory of Annie's appearance. Man, woman, mother, killer... his mind spun with the thoughts, and he felt slightly nauseous at their impact.

Chapter 47

Saturday, 2:38 p.m.

Finally, it was time.

The Performer gathered his strength. Gobbets of drool hung from the corners of his mouth. The floor kept changing into a spongy surface that threatened to swallow him into undulating folds of plasma, but he was confident that he would ride above it. He knew the coming ritual would purify and empower him. The voices had finally spoken through the pandemonium. His head throbbed with the clamor that threatened to drown out the voices, but he had heard them. The voices told him all was ready in the cosmos. He could begin the ritual.

First there was the 'showing.' He walked to the cage, displaying himself to the cowering creature inside. There was no response except a slight increase in the volume of the moaning. She had not eaten the food he had put into the cage, even though he had used a silver plate. She did not know that she was special. They never understood that they were the Chosen of the Master. They should be grateful and happy, but in their ignorance, they drew back from their destiny. He felt a tickle of hot feeling but shoved it down. There would be no anger. The releasing had to be done calmly and with precision... in deadpan. The steps had to be properly ... executed.

After the 'showing,' came the ritual bath. He ran a hose from the sink to a large metal tub that he filled to the brim with cold water. To purify, it had to be cold, because that prevented him from having an erection, which was very important. When the evil Carmen had bathed him, it was in warm water, and she had controlled him by making his organ do what she wanted it to. His father could see his helpless reaction and take revenge. The cold water ritual undid that.

The lace dress hung on the door, waiting. It was no longer white, caked as it was with blood. Yet, it was holy blood, and the dress was the holy garment. The dresses he wore to work were quite different. That was the invisible clothing. When he wore those garments, no one could see him. They did not see the Master, they did not see the Performer, they did not even see Mel. They only saw a woman named Annie and she did not really exist.

His real essence was invisible, when he wore the Annie clothes. That is why he had been able to walk into the Police Station and place the package on the main desk, without being seen. It was how he had been able to enter the apartment building across from the evil Carmen-clone's dwelling. It was how he was able to talk to his adversary, the Detective and learn his secrets without revealing his own. He was the master. His powers were great. He would need them all to destroy the tricky adversary.

But first the child.

Chapter 48

Saturday, 2:48 p.m.

They were working through the weekend again. That wasn't unusual—several other Detectives were in the office, too. But this time there was a terrible sense of immediacy, an urgent pressure to move before the madman did. Gil yelled for Frank. The other man came running.

"Did Gina check out that Staten Island address yet?"

"Yeah, Gil, she did. She took a couple of the guys with her. There was nobody home, but there was an awful smell, so they talked the building manager into letting them in. As soon as Gina took a look, she closed the door and called for a search order. Sharp lady. She didn't want any evidence thrown out because of improper search. The smell was dead cats."

"Is that all they found?"

"No, they found plenty, including some body parts that we think may be the Hasidic kid, minus head."

"Shit. Not that I expected him to be alive. Better let Occhiogrosso know. He has a political bomb to handle on that one."

"Right. They also found some other stuff. There were some posters advertising an act—a ventriloquist act, called 'Francois and Freckles.' There were some newspaper clippings about our current case in a scrapbook. There were also books that had references to several other cases that we didn't know about from other places and times. We're certain now. This is the guy."

"Yeah, it looks like Anton was right about a leak. It seems that this ... guy ... is also a gal. And she is Tom's secretary, the one named Annie."

"No shit!" Frank marvelled, "So we've got him ... or her."

"Well, then, where is he?" Gil shouted, "Mel, Annie, Melanie, whoever the hell he is ... he's got Jennifer." He pounded the desk in frustration.

"I guess that explains the note."

"What note?"

"Well, at the Staten Island scene there was something written on the mirror in lipstick—at least I think it was lipstick. I hate to think of the other possibilities. It was pretty vague... didn't see it at first. But when the hot water went on, you could see the letters on the mirror in the steam. Anyway, it said 'All my love to Jennifuh ...' it was spelled funny, ya know, 'Jenni- FUH' not 'JenniFER.'"

"Damn, damn, damn! He knew we'd get there eventually. I don't suppose there's anything that gives us an idea of where he might be now?"

"I don't know, Gil. We have a lot of stuff from the guy's apartment. If you want to look through it, you may see something we don't."

They went upstairs, Gil jumping two steps at a time, to look through the piles of papers and objects. Gil had to try hard not to paw through the material desperately in order to make the information come out quickly just by storming the stacks of paper. He knew that would be foolish. He might miss some vital clue in his haste. So, he examined each item carefully, often closing his eyes and trying to let the intuitive side of his brain take over.

Nothing.

He leafed through an address book, which contained mostly blank pages, with a few emergency numbers, and a lot of store listings, that sounded like health food outlets. There was a stack of magazines in the accumulation of things, old issues of Newsyvents with some articles cut out, leaving holes. The articles often reappeared, pasted into in a huge notebook of clippings. These included mentions of Bradley, the deceased star, as well as a brief reference to "Francois and Freckles." As the detective leafed back through the book, the clippings became more yellow and dated to the time of that long dead "Master and Melvin."

There were other scrapbooks, one of which was devoted to recent news items about this case. As Gil paged through it, he wasn't shocked or surprised by the clippings or the underlined sections, which were mostly phrases like "outwitting police" that had been gleaned from the less objective tabloids. Nothing seemed strange. It all appeared very understandable, oddly familiar.

Gil had reached that point where he could feel Mel's presence in the belongings that had been gathered. As he took a breath, at some subtle level, he could smell the man's scent, feel his body heat, sense his aura. There was an invisible cloud of menace surrounding the pile of personal effects. Gil knew he couldn't stay out of that dark cloud, if he ever expected to gain the upper hand. He closed his eyes and let his mind drift into the darkness, so he could view things from inside the mad world of the killer. He felt his chest tighten, as he entered the dark mind of the psychopath. Could you enter the bizarre world and still come back? He imagined Mel smiling a welcome, his heart thudding heavily at the thought. It was strangely similar to the way his chest felt when he awoke from one of the death dreams, born from his childhood terrors.

The words of Pilar came to mind, reassuring him.

"You are definitely one of the good guys," she had said. "You can own the feelings; they don't have to own you."

He laid aside the scrapbook, to pick up a stained wooden box filled with small cans and tubes that had been gathered by a well-meaning technician who thought they might have contained drugs. Gil knew that they were nothing but make-up containers. He opened a container and saw the greasepaint inside. Heavier than normal street cosmetics, he noted, the materials were more like stage makeup. He wondered if traces of DNA could be gleaned from the pasty stuff, bagging it for the lab, just in case.

Something was bothering Gil about what he was seeing but he couldn't figure out what. It had to do with the show-business feel to all this. "The smell of the greasepaint, the roar of the crowd" was a phrase that came to mind. He retrieved one of the containers, dipping a finger in the stuff. He was sure the lab didn't need all of them. He took a smear of the stuff, which he then smoothed over the back of his hand. It looked like Annie's skin tone. Maybe it was all in his mind, but it felt oily and dirty to him, like his skin would not be able to breathe. For a moment the tightness in his chest and the feel of the greasepaint combined into a terrible sense of need and deprivation, a hunger for air and relief. He didn't fully understand how, but he knew that for a brief moment he was feeling what it was like to be Mel. It was a desperate feeling of need and craving ... a dark weight of asphyxiation and hunger to breathe. There were no boundaries which such a need would not cross.

Gil shook himself and took several deep breaths. He scrubbed the make-up off his hand with a piece of tissue, rubbing vigorously, until it was almost raw. He went back to the first scrapbook, the one tracing a show business career. The clippings were often repetitive, probably written by hack reporters who just repeated standard press releases. What could be significant about them? His mind wanted to move on, but something more primitive told him he was missing an important clue. That moment in the dark shadow of Mel's mind had tickled a hunch. He leafed through them again, this time trying to read more carefully. Time after time, he saw the same information, with slight variations. The name of the act, the name of the theater, the date and time of each performance. What was it?

Finally, he gave up and went for a cup of coffee, hoping to let his mind slip into another gear, out of the neutral one it was caught in now. He took the coffee back to his old, cluttered desk on the second floor and flopped in the creaking chair. He glanced at the papers to see if there was anything new. One of Treadwell's notebooks lay there, a silent memorial. Gil thought about the man and his few belongings. He wondered how you can get so frightened that you stopped being what you needed to be. Treadwell had become an office manager instead of a cop.

Gil leafed through Colin's book, so different from his own. Instead of arrest records, investigative leads, interviews, it was filled with useless notations of shift changes, calls logged, mail deliveries. He turned to the last page, where he saw what amounted to an interoffice communication log. It ended days before Treadwell's death.

The intercom buzzer sounded. It was Wilson at the front desk.

"Somebody here to see you, Gabby."

"Yeah, who?"

"Says her name is Chrissy Treadwell."

Gil sat up straight. It was Colin's daughter. This was blowing the hell out of his theory about coincidences.

"I'll be right down."

The last time Gil had seen Treadwell's daughter, she had been strung out on coke, looking ten years older than her age. The girl at the desk seemed younger, prettier, and more poised.

"Chrissy?"

"Oh, hi Gil. Thanks for seeing me. Sorry about the last time you had to put up with me."

'I've heard cussing before, no big deal."

"Yeah, but I didn't have to kick you."

"Well, you weren't exactly yourself, back then, kid. But gee, you look great now."

"Yeah, thanks. I just wish Dad was around to see me," she said with a little sniffle, eyes aimed at the floor. "I just got out of Phoenix House, and I'm like a new person."

Her eyes rose again, sparkling. "Clean and mean living machine. I think I got the idea, this time. Before, I just wanted to give everybody a hard time, especially Dad. I don't need to do that anymore. I got clean for myself this time. But I still kinda wish he knew."

"I'm sure he would be proud of you, Chris."

"Thanks," she took the tissue he offered, to wipe her eyes and nose. "By the way, when they gave us his personal effects, they put in some stuff that probably belongs to the Department. Anyway, you might want it."

She offered a crumpled brown paper bag, which he took without looking inside.

"Do you think you'll find who did it?" she asked.

"Count on it, Chrissy. Count on it."

She stepped forward and gave the surprised Detective a hug, turned and ran out the front entrance.

Back at his desk, Beach opened the bag. There wasn't much. A few official reports that looked too old to be significant, a stack of unused arrest forms, one of Colin's trusty notebooks, some handcuffs, two boxes of thirty-eight ammunition, and a sturdy book - for the Sergeant's exam, yellowed and out of date.

Gil opened the notebook, wondering if it was Colin's last. Sure enough, the first page was a record of the last days before he died. Pink smears dotted the pages. It must have been picked up from the site of the bomb blast. The communication log format was continued from the previous book.

Gil sat up, when he noticed some of the entries.

"Pkg. to Beach, deliv. by woman—Annie." Gil could hardly believe his eyes. Treadwell's notes were not so useless after all. In fact, if he had taken them more seriously—if he hadn't dismissed the man and his help, he might have tumbled to the Annie connection sooner.

Now he pulled his desk light closer and scanned the notes Colin had so compulsively made each day. As he read, he leaned forward in increasing excitement. He flipped through several pages. There were lists of calls received, including hang-ups or apparent wrong numbers. There were two messages that jumped off the page. Both were from variations of the name "Mel". There were also notes indicating the reasons for the calls. It was clear that Mel had used false stories to cover himself. One of the notations referred to something about theater tickets. Theater tickets!

Gil blanched. He slapped the notebook shut and spoke his thoughts out loud.

"Colin, you sonofabitch, you had it all right here. You are gonna help catch the creep that killed you."

Beach ran to the stairs, where he shouted up, as he mounted the steps two at a time to the next floor.

"Frank! Get the car. I think I know where he is. I think I know where he has Jennifer."

"What? ... where?"

"Look, Frank. In these clippings," Gil ran over to the table and jabbed at the pages of the large scrapbook, "over and over you see this same theater, The Regency. There are lots of others, too, but this same one keeps showing up."

"Yeah, so he played a lot at the Regency theater. So what?"

"So that's the address Tom noticed on the Newsyvents mailing list. The Regency is closed. Nobody is supposed to live there. But the list suggests that somebody does."

"Look here!" he said, holding out the worn and stained pad.

"Treadwell's notebook lists calls from somebody that had to be Mel, and they refer to theater tickets. The Regency is the theater name printed on them.

"I can't exactly explain how I know this, but I think I am beginning to understand this guy's thinking a little, so I have a better idea of what he needs. I think he needs a STAGE. I think the Regency is his place. I think our man is there now. I'm going to find out." His voice tone fairly crackled with intensity.

"Just a sec, Gil," Terranova said, pulling a sheaf of papers from his pocket, "I've got the mailing list right here."

"C'mon, we might not have much time!"

Frank threw aside several sheets, as they ran out of the room, like a flower girl scattering rose petals at a wedding until he found the list. He scanned it quickly, then gave it a punch with his fist. "You're right Gil," he shouted at the retreating back of his partner, "and the name that goes with the address is Francois ... as in 'Francois and Freckles!'"

They headed down the stairs faster than high schoolers at the sound of the dismissal bell at school. But they didn't look like gleeful teenagers. They looked like avenging angels or the deadliest two of the Four Horsemen of the Apocalypse.

CHAPTER 49

Saturday, 3:30 p.m.

The lace dress slipped easily over his head and onto his freshly prepared body. The ritual bath had been challenging; his physical being rebelled against it. Even now, the muscles and tissues tried to betray him. The Master of so much, yet he could not completely subjugate this mortal vessel. His teeth chattered and knees shook from hypothermia, his breath coming in small gasps. His sex organ was shriveled to almost nothing, his scrotum drawn up into his groin. Goosebumps stood out all over his skin, like a pebbled Mat. Now he was in his cutting clothes. Mel had applied the make-up carefully. He knew that all would be well.

The soon-to-be new figure moaned in the cage, as he approached. He opened the gate and pulled her out.

"You don't need to be afraid," he reassured her, "I am a girl now. We girls are going to play together, and no one will mind that, not even Father."

He was just repeating words that the voices were whispering in his mind. They sounded like words he had heard before, but it was hard to remember, hard to concentrate. Great rushes of sound slammed back and forth through the air, echoing in his pain-saturated skull. Lights flashed and whirled in his vision, sometimes blinding him for seconds at a time. The air was filled with odors of birth and death and putrefaction. Strange things were happening to his body. He felt his chest ripple and change, his pectorals swelling and ballooning into large breasts under the lace, crowned by dark purple nipples that oozed blood. There was something alive inside his stomach, he was sure, wanting to be born. Between his legs, he could see it trying to get out, a fleshy finger wiggling and beckoning. He hit and clawed at the foreign projection, trying to force it back inside, or kill it altogether. He was rewarded with excruciating pain, but the thing retreated for the moment.

Melanie led the girl to the stage, then used barbed wire to bind each limb to a frame that caused the limp body to stand erect. The screams of the girl went unheard, so eventually the sound became hoarse, then whispery, and finally halted.

Melanie's voice was also hoarse, as it abstractedly recited long ago memorized words.

"Things fall apart; the center cannot hold;

Mere anarchy is loosed upon the world,

The blood dimmed tide is loosed, and everywhere

The ceremony of innocence is drowned."

The stage seemed to shift and slide under Melanie's feet, causing her to stumble and fall. The voices interrupted the recitation, telling her to get the knife.

Jennifer understood little of what was going on. Hours in a darkened cage had disoriented her, and her fear was paralyzing. The man kept doing dirty nasty things that her mother had told her were bad. When he put on the dirty dress, he looked like he was very sick, acting strangely. He pawed at his chest and beat at himself between the legs. His pee-pee was bigger than little Jimmy's who had once taken a bath with her, but now it had blood on it. The black wig that he wore had slipped to the side. She could see a little of his head, where there was short bristly hair. Sometimes he slipped, almost falling down. He smelled like doo-doo.

When he led her to the stage, she saw the awful scene of rotting heads and insects buzzing about. At first, she thought it was a display of dolls. Then the lights came on, showing her the awful reality. Her screams of terror were as much at that sight, as from the piercing jab of the barbed wire he wound around her wrists and ankles. She screamed until she couldn't make a sound any longer. Then she waited, sobbing, chest heaving, to see what would come next. The only thing in the world that she wanted at that moment was her mother. But instead, the horrible monster in bloody lace and clownish make-up went to a cabinet and began taking out knives.

Chapter 50

Saturday, 3:55 p.m.

The Regency was near Washington Square Park, sandwiched between high-rise apartment buildings. Its white brick exterior was peeling and patched with cinder-block plugs and plywood panels, whitewashed to a sickly gray color that fit with the decrepit air of the old playhouse. It was in the antique style of such urban theaters, with multiple floors above the auditorium section. Architectural step-downs of reduced width occurred at intervals of about ten floors, fashioned on the old "wedding cake" layer design. There was a fortress-like cornice at the top level.

Gil and Frank fishtailed around the corner, the Buick they had grabbed from the motor pool sliding heavily into an alley alongside the building. They jumped out of the car, quickly circling the structure on foot, looking for an entrance.

On the way to the theater, they had called Gina who was also working the weekend, asking her to roust a judge for a search order and bring it to them. As long as she eventually got there, even if it was a bit after the fact, they wouldn't worry too much about the rules of entry. Getting a warrant shouldn't be a problem.

In the rear of the alley they found a door with a relatively new lock. This entrance had been used recently. Somehow they had to break in. Gil hesitated, recalling that he had sprained a shoulder once, trying to bust open a door the way television detectives do. If there had been a place to put his back, he might have been able to kick the door open with his stair-hardened legs, but the alley was clear, the door was flush in a wood frame wall. He told Frank to stand back, hopped in the car, then shoved down on the gas pedal. With a splintering crash he backed the vehicle right through the door and wall.

His unorthodox choice saved both their lives, because no sooner had the bumper pushed the door in, than an explosive blast shoved the car back out again, flipping the trunk lid off like a pop-top can, and shattering the windows. The door had been booby-trapped.

They were expected.

Both men remained still for a moment, shaken by the blast. Then, drawing their weapons, they moved into the darkened recesses of the old theater building. It was like street-fighting in a war, one moving forward, while the other covered. Frank stepped through a side door, then called for Gil to come see what he had found.

It was not a room, but a garage, the doors facing the back lot. Inside was a blue van, the words "Barstow's Magic Company" block-printed on the side in sloppy letters. Gil walked over to the truck and scratched at the lettering with a fingernail. The paint scraped off easily.

"I guess Annie knew what she, ... or he, was doing. Made up a fake Barstow truck to throw us off."

"Yeah, look here," Frank agreed, peering into the rear of the truck, "looks like a hair clipper outfit. He probably shaved his head to look bald and wore padded clothes to look like Barstow. When you wear a wig and costume every day, what's another disguise?"

Gil led Frank through the next doorway, to a set of stairs leading up. He stared up into the darkness. A shiver went through him ... an intuition. The darkness was like something alive, hovering in this place like a malevolent being. He could smell it; he could feel it.

"He's here Frank. He's here, and he's got Jennifer." The Detective led the way up the stairs, wincing at the creak of old wood boards which must have telegraphed their movements. Perspiration stood out on his forehead. They reached the main floor without incident, spending long enough in the huge empty auditorium to satisfy themselves that the quarry lay higher up. The old stairway continued up to a level over the large hall, a strange odor hung on the air. It became stronger as they moved upward. Somewhere, Gil knew, the man would be waiting. He knew the psychotic mind too well now to believe that Mel would just run. The only question was where and when the meeting would take place. They put in a call to the precinct for back-up.

The next door was unlatched, but Gil checked it carefully before going through. His caution was rewarded by the discovery of a fine wire stretched at ankle height. After stepping over it, they found one end attached to the pin of a grenade. Frank gingerly disengaged the trip wire. They found themselves in an atrium, or entranceway to a larger attic room. The main area was dark, so Gil groped for a light switch on the nearest wall. He was almost overcome by a disgusting stench. As he moved his hand on the wall, a buzzing sound began, like a million flies.

The lights flickered on, white neon fixtures like work lights dangling from the ceiling. The grim scene was daunting. Frank looked for a moment, then leaned over a wastebasket to vomit. Gil managed to avoid upchucking, but still reeled at what he saw. Small heads, some darkened and dried, others wet and rotten sat on puppet bodies in row after row of nauseating display. Only a few seemed human. Many were animals—dogs, cats, even a pig. Some wore ratty wigs, while others still had their own hair, though often patchy and matted with blood. There was a scurrying sound, as various vermin ran to hide from the glare of light. The buzzing of flies ebbed and flowed, as clouds of the insects rose and settled.

Light-headed from the smell and shock of what he was seeing, Gil moved toward what appeared to be a stage. He knew it had to be the set for the video he had received. To reach it, he had to weave his way through the grotesque figures. Frank had stopped emptying his stomach. Gray-faced, he followed, waving his arms to keep the flies away.

"It's just like the museum in Kentucky," Gil whispered, "only the figures are flesh. I saw pictures in their brochure. Mel must have been the janitor that disappeared. He must have taken the original Melvin figure with him."

There was no sign of the killer, or of Jennifer. But a quick search of the area turned up a cage large enough to hold a child, and some short lengths of barbed wire hanging from a frame in a way that could have held someone in place. It looked like it had recently been occupied. There were signs of use, including blood stains. There was also, incongruously, an empty beer can attached to one of the wire strands. Gil glanced at it, looked away, then turned back slowly. He reached out and took the empty can in his hand. Muscles twitched in his jaw, and his eyes narrowed to slits.

"The bastard!" he growled.

"What? There's something important about a beer can?" Frank asked, puzzled at Gil's reaction.

"Not just any beer can, Frank, it's Genesee."

"Yeah, so? A lot of people drink it, especially upstate."

"Yes, and the ad campaigns always try to get you to order it using a nickname for the beer."

"Oh yeah, I remember, 'GIMME A JENNY!' Jenny? Oh shit, Gil, you mean Jennifer? You think he did that on purpose?"

"Oh yes, Frank I certainly do. Look at the thing on the bottom." He turned the can, showing what appeared to be a fuzzy coaster, made of animal skin, taped to the underside.

"What is it, a patch of hair, ... a piece of fur?"

"It's fur. Think about it. Together with the can, that makes 'JENNY' plus 'fur', doesn't it? *JENNIFER!*

"The sick bastard is making jokes—puns?"

"In a way, but not to be funny. He isn't really laughing. There's no humor in his soul. Just hate and sickness and evil. He wants to show his superiority, by ridiculing me and playing on the things and people that are most important to me."

Gil crumpled the container like paper. He wished it was the neck of the monster that had Jennifer. He threw the crushed can aside and rapidly moved on, steel in his glare. In addition to the cage and frame there was a lot of other strange paraphernalia, some using foil and wire, but Gil wasn't interested in analysis at this point, he was racing time for Jennifer's life.

Another staircase was located on the opposite side of the room, near an elevator. Gil heard a sound behind him, which caused him to jump nearly a foot in the air. He and Frank whipped out their weapons. They turned toward the sound, assuming firing stances. They leveled their aim at the elevator, from where the sound had come. When the automatic door suddenly opened, Gil almost pulled the trigger of his gun, but the car was empty.

Breathing heavily, he moved to the nearby stairway. As he reached out to open the door, two sharp reports sounded, ... gunshots, and a pair of large holes suddenly splintered the wood. He dropped to the floor, narrowly missing a pool of some dark fluid. There was a clatter of sound, as someone made a dive for stairs. Through the splintered door, there was a momentary glimpse of an apparition dressed in what may have been a red and white dress.

"Cover me," Gil shouted, pulling back the door. A few feet beyond, was another door, a fire door leading to the outside stairwell. He slowly pushed at the metal panic bar, easing it open. Despite their hurry, he knew that rushing through a door when you didn't know what was on the other side could be a quick ticket to a body bag. There was no movement or gunfire, so he went through to an alcove below the steel-reinforced concrete stairs. Frank stood a few feet back, his pistol at ready. Faintly, Gil heard the tap-tap of feet climbing further up, and a sound that could have been the whimper of a child being dragged along ... Jennifer?

Gil knew he had to stay close enough to know if they exited at any of the intervening floors, but far enough away to avoid a sudden shot in the head from above. He thought they were at least a full floor ahead of him, perhaps two or more. It was difficult to be exact, because the acoustics were so distorted in the passage. Sounds could echo down the concrete-walled stairwell for several levels. He didn't intend to lose them. He darted up the stairs, Frank close behind.

The killer had a better headstart than they had estimated. By the time Gil and Frank reached the fifth floor, they still had not caught sight of the man and child, though the sound of labored breathing and shoes slapping the concrete was still audible. Gil could also hear the heaving gasps of Frank Terranova, who called out before following to the sixth floor.

"Gil, ... Gil! ... sorry, but I can't keep up. I just don't have the legs for this."

Frank's shout rebounded loudly in the narrow space. Before Gil had a chance to respond, a series of reverberating blasts filled the stairwell, the sound of shots magnified and reflected. Chips of paint and concrete flew, as bullets whanged and zinged. There was no way that the killer could aim directly at them, but the ricocheting slugs could still find flesh on one of several bouncing paths. Gil ducked instinctively, though it was impossible to avoid the unpredictable route of a caroming bullet by hunkering down. He glanced at Terranova, and saw a surprised look on the man's face. Then a trickle of blood appeared from his temple. Gil froze, wondering if he was seeing another friend dying. There had been too much death already, and Gil had lost enough. But Frank spoke.

"Son of a bitch! That felt like I got whacked with a hammer," he ran a hand over the side of his head, "Jesus, I nearly lost an ear on that one. And I don't hear too good with two of 'em!"

His words were light, but his expression was pale ... battlefield bravado.

"I've got an idea, Frank," Gil suggested. "There's a working elevator inside. We nearly shot the hell out of it, a couple minutes ago. If you take it up, say three floors at a time, you can come over to the stairs, and back me up at intervals."

"No Gil. I can't leave you. I know I'm not in as good a shape as you are, but you can't go at him alone."

"I'm not going to, Frank. You can help this way, better than if you stay with me on the stairs. If he stops, you can come down on him from above. If he exits, you can be waiting, or come in at him from his opposite side. From here, I can move faster alone."

Terranova finally acknowledged the wisdom of this plan, and headed through an exit door toward the elevators, clutching a handkerchief to his head. Gil turned back to the stairwell. Mel must have been close a moment before, when he fired the shots, but now he had been given a chance to widen the lead again.

Gil moved quickly up the stairs, toward the sixth floor, his legs working like pistons, weapon out in front. When he reached the landing, he went on toward level seven, not pausing or slowing. It felt like his stadium climbing exercise ... the old way. In his regular exercise he wasn't working out the same inner turmoil anymore, yet in this situation rage had surfaced again. It felt like the return of an old lover that had betrayed him ... familiar, tempting, but not the same. He couldn't embrace this rage, but he used it to give himself added energy. He pushed himself up the risers, ignoring the protesting muscles.

Flight followed flight of stairs, as Gil settled into the pounding rhythm he had used so often at the stadium. He passed the seventh and eighth floors. He wondered, as he approached the ninth-floor landing, if Frank would suddenly appear, as planned. Perhaps it was his glance toward the door that distracted his attention, perhaps it was the habit of shutting out the world when he ran. Whatever it was, he was not prepared for the loop of barbed wire that dropped over his head from the staircase a few feet above. A reflex movement brought his hand up to his neck just in time to prevent the wire from garroting him completely, but he was jerked off his feet, as the wire bit deeply into his neck and hand, drawing blood. He pulled at the wire, but went down, his gun clattering on the concrete.

From the stairs above, a specter appeared. The figure was a mixture of man and woman, his crotch showing his maleness through the bloody lace of a woman's dress. His face was painted with exaggerated make-up smears, and garish patches of red were daubed on a brassiere worn over the gown. A tangled wig hung over one ear, giving a half-and-half look to the face, with one side showing short, cropped hair still bristly where it had been shaved earlier. The eyes were sunken points of fire. Glaring out of an emaciated face, they burned with a sick intensity. Gil had seen that look before. It had been in the eyes of his mother many years before.

Gil worked desperately to get free of the wire, his eyes moving back and forth between the crazed man and his weapon lying a few feet away. His hands were slippery with blood from the wire cuts. Jennifer stood shivering in the clutch of the man's arm, while his hand pulled viciously at the wire. His right held an automatic pistol leveled at the Detective's face. It was like staring into the mouth of a viper, ready to strike.

"What should I call you? Mel, Annie, Charles?" Gil quickly choked out. His training had included a session with one of the Department's Hostage Negotiating Team members, who had said that if you got someone talking, they were less likely to act. For the moment it seemed to work. The freakish figure paused. Instead of the sound of a shot, Gil heard a small voice answer his question. It wasn't Jennifer.

The answer seemed to come from nowhere, because the man's mouth didn't move, and the voice was the sound of a puppet, a ventriloquist figure's voice.

"You should call him the 'Master,' but it doesn't matter, because he won't speak with you."

"Then who is speaking?" Gil asked, desperately searching for a way out of the situation.

"Melvin, of course," the voice replied, as the man in the dress scowled. "I am the only one he can't control."

"Then why don't you stop him from hurting people?" Gil asked, feeling like the psychiatrist in The Three Faces of Eve.

"Oh, just because he can't control me, doesn't mean that I can control him. Besides, he doesn't want to hurt anyone," the small voice explained. "He believes that he is doing them a favor when he releases them."

"Maybe they don't want to be released," the Detective was arguing, when a creaking sound drew attention to the fire door. Then everything happened at once.

A gun barrel appeared in the crack of the door. The crazed ventriloquist raised his weapon and fired. The shots were wild but created a deafening racket which Gil instantly realized would work in his favor. Mel was facing the door, firing, which forced him to loosen his grip on Jennifer. She managed to pull out of his grasp, which in turn, caused him to lose hold on the wire choking Gil. The Detective reached out for the girl, grabbed her, and wrapping his body over hers, rolled around the corner, down the stairs. He cracked his head, knees, and shoulders against unyielding concrete. Every extended or bony spot was bruised, but no bullets plowed into his body. He was quickly at the next landing, out of the line of fire. Jennifer was crying and holding her wrist like it was broken. He shoved her behind him, while he pulled his pistol from its ankle holster.

The sound of footsteps echoed from above. Mel was going up again. Frank called through the door.

"Gil! Are you okay? Is it clear?"

"I'm okay!" he shouted, wondering how true it was, "I've got Jennifer."

Gil worked his way back up to the landing, opened the door and gave Frank the girl. He retrieved his Steyr GB before starting back up the stairs.

He was halfway up the next flight, when he heard a splashing sound. Each landing was equipped with a fire hose coupling. Apparently, Mel had opened the valve a floor above. In moments water started cascading down the steps and poured from above, a dirty shower. At first, it was merely a bother, soaking the Detective's clothing and hair while forming puddles which soaked his shoes. But soon the volume increased. Gil realized that the man above was opening the valve at each floor.

As he reached the tenth level, Beach found himself fighting through a current that clutched at his ankles and battered him from above. At least three valves were blasting cascades of water from higher floors, before he reached the first open one and spun the circular handle to close it off. He must have been losing ground, because the volume was just as bad or worse when he moved upward again. Now it was like pushing through a waterfall, a pummeling cataract that slammed into his face and body, slowing him still further.

He had to keep going. Now that Frank was with Jennifer, Gil was the only one who could stop the killer. He shook his head, water flying like a long-haired dog coming out of a lake. He drove on, toward the eleventh-floor landing.

There was an architectural variation at this level of the building, the step-down construction of the next "wedding-cake" layer which resulted in a different arrangement of the landing. To the right, the stairs continued upward, but on the left, instead of door and wall, there were several steps leading down to a short landing. In the landing there were a utilities closet and telephone company switching panel, then the fire door that opened out from the main building corridor. This limited space, recessed from the stairwell but sealed off by fire-rated closures, had filled with water, to form a pool of brackish water, with cigarette butts and other filth floating in it. Leery of this pool, and half blinded by the cascading torrents from above, Gil didn't see the storage cabinet on the landing itself, or the figure huddled behind it, until the ghoulish form jumped him. Something sharp slashed Gil's shoulder, sending pain lancing through him. The two men grappled at each other as they fell back and down into the filthy water, blood now mixing with dirt and dust and garbage in a disgusting soup.

Gil managed to clasp his assailant's knife hand in his own left, though he vaguely realized that the man was right-handed, and the contest wasn't going to be equal. The struggling bodies submerged, bloody lace and wig hair swirling into the hellish mix.

Gil felt something wrap around his face, binding and suffocating. He felt panic tearing at his mind, as the demented man/woman tore at his body. He felt himself losing the battle for control, as he lost his strength. There seemed to be soggy terrycloth cutting off his breath, the figure above him a woman larger than life, with a short lethal blade flashing and dripping with his own life blood. The filthy water in which he was submerged had the taste of salt and smell of rotting seaweed. Burning shafts of pain shot through his chest and arms, from wounds present and past.

He surfaced for a moment, only to see the shiny blade, a clam-knife ready to plunge into his heaving chest. He heard a voice calling him. It was his mother. She had searched and finally found him. His vision darkened as he felt himself being drawn into the pool of sewage, the dark place where she had gone and was now taking him.

His strength was at its end. He began releasing his grip on the hand holding the knife. It was time to let go. It was time to stop the struggle. It was time to find release.

Chapter

51

Saturday, 4:19 p.m.

The Master was waiting behind the cabinet for the Detective to turn the corner. It would have been easy to blow him away with the gun, but that would not have pleased the forces of the universe. There had been enough long-distance violence. The final cosmic struggle had to be face-to-face, hand-to-hand, blade-to-flesh. When the end came, it would be a true Release, with the Master lapping up the adversary's life-force like water in the desert. He felt committed to the struggle ahead yet was concerned about his power.

The Detective had managed to prevent him from Releasing the girl. His adversary seemed to have more magic, more power than expected. He should not have been able to mount all those stairs and push through the rush of water as he was doing. Only a supernatural being could do that, he feared. The Master was also concerned that his own power was not at its peak. He chose this area for his stand, largely because his legs would not take him any further. They were only his physical being, but he would have to use that to channel his power against the enemy forces. It was better to move quickly, while his body still served.

The Master assumed invisibility, waiting until the enemy came around the corner of the landing. Then he launched himself through the air onto the man, slashing with his blade in one combined motion. He felt the satisfying resistance of flesh being parted by steel, and then the shock of the cold water as they tumbled into the dirty pool. It didn't take long to gain the upper hand. The man's spirit was weak. At first, Mel whispered to his enemy of mastery and release, undermining his resolve and weakening his last shreds of hope. He could see defeat in the detective's eyes.

"I will Release you," he growled. "It's all over. Don't fight anymore. Accept the peace." They were the same words the Master had spoken before as he ended someone's earthly struggle, but this time, they were even more meaningful.

Mel was ready to stab the blade into the Detective's heart as he sensed the man's force flowing out, a preliminary leakage that previewed the outpouring of his life that would follow momentarily. The grip holding back his hand and blade began to weaken, the resistance lessening. The point began a slow downward plunge, his weakening opponent's eyes fixed on the glistening steel.

Then something changed. The Detective's eyes lost their unfocused look of surrender, centering on the knife. There was a blink of something like recognition. The grip on Mel's wrist tightened.

A wave of force seemed to flow into the man, and with a mighty howl, he surged upward, throwing the Performer back. Now bellowing something, the adversary struck out with his legs, which found vulnerable flesh. The Performer's body betrayed him once again, as a foot smashed into his groin. He felt bile rising in his throat. His legs buckled, and he went down. He felt himself being pushed back against the steps leading down into the dirty pool.

His head slammed into the concrete, fogging his vision as the impact stunned him.

It could not be. The Master could not be vanquished. Yet he felt himself losing all strength as a fist smashed into his cheek, and another, and another. Then he gagged, as a cold, oily piece of metal was forced into his mouth. It was a gun. He could taste grease and smell the acrid odor of gun powder. The hand holding the gun shook with emotion, and he knew that the trigger was being pulled.

The spark of recognition was almost too late. Gil was in the process of finally giving in to the voice of capitulation, the one that says it is too hard to go on. Gil was choosing to surrender to that voice, when another voice intervened. The hideous creature pushing him down into the murky liquid seemed to be speaking in his mother's tones.

"It's over and you are out of my life," she screamed, the short clam-knife poised to stab again. "You are my problem! It's all your fault! You are evil! You are bad!"

In his choking, exhausted, oxygen-depleted state, memory merged with reality, and he couldn't tell if he was being killed by his mother, a nightmare figure come to life, or a being of flesh and blood. It hardly mattered. In any case he would be dead, and the struggle would be over. He longed to say "Yes" to the voice calling him.

"I will release you. It's all over. You don't have to fight anymore," the voice called. "Come to me and I will give you peace."

The only peace he could remember knowing for years was during a few short hours with Pilar. It was a fragment of that memory, and her name, that broke through the mixture of pain, confusion, and exhaustion. He had a visual flash of Pilar, lying on a hospital bed, tied down in Gulliver fashion by a myriad of small lines, tubes keeping her alive. The figure shoving a knife toward his chest was not his mother. It was the one who had hurt Pilar.

Out of some hidden reservoir, came a surge of energy. It was a potent mixture of anger, protest, and need. He focused on the knife descending toward his chest, noticing its curved blade. That couldn't be. Clam-knifes aren't curved, they are short, straight, triangular blades. This one wasn't like that at all. The clam-knife wasn't real, it was part of the memories. It was part of a past which no longer could claim him. The wet cloth clinging to him was not terrycloth at all, but soggy, stained lace and there were many awful odors, but none of them was that of shellfish.

While he moved to confront the present situation, a part of his mind was instantaneously making the final connections to understand his nightmares and fragmented memories. On that terrifying day long ago. His mother had cut herself, trying to open clams. In his childish lack of understanding, he had laughed at her cry of pain. He remembered it now. It couldn't have been just that incident. She must have been close to the edge of insanity for a long time. But the wound and her helpless embarrassment further irritated by his childhood laughter must have been the last straw, the thing that pushed her over, for she turned on him then, the short blade in her hand, blood on the terrycloth robe and madness in her eyes.

The same kind of eyes were staring at him now, but they were not those of his mother. They were the eyes of a madman who had tried to kill Pilar and might do so if Gil gave up now. It was someone that wanted to steal their life together, their chance at happiness.

"NO!" he bellowed, bending in the water so that his powerful legs were under him, then giving a desperate push, "NO! You can't have her. You can't have me! You can't have US!"

The expression in the berserk eyes wildly staring at him changed from victory to doubt, and then fear, as Gil shoved him back, and slammed him down, a knee thudding into the man's groin. The Detective swung his fist and smashed it into the bizarrely painted face, then pulled back and slammed it down again and again, watching water and blood and mucus fly at the blows. His hand found his gun, and brought it to the hideous face, shoving it between teeth into the man's mouth. His finger tightened on the trigger, obeying the red tide of feeling.

Then he stopped.

His finger halted its fatal pull.

No one stepped in to restrain him. He just stopped.

Why?

He had come to his boundary...

He marveled to find it there. For so many years he had believed that there was no line his anger would not cross. It had shackled him with a fear that both held him back and drove him.

But Pilar had been right. He didn't yearn for it. He hated the killing rage, and did not want it as his master. It was not really the color of his soul. Finally, he knew he could let it go. It was not worth his self-respect, or his love.

Gil pulled the gun out of the man's mouth. He grabbed handcuffs from his belt, slapping them on the bony wrists. Then he shoved the abject figure into a sitting position against the wall of the landing. The man's expression was stonily blank.

There was a pounding sound, as the fire door in the hall was shoved open a crack, allowing water to pour through the gap like a dam's sluice gate. The opening widened, and several police officers led by Frank Terranova came pushing through, guns in firing position, cursing at the water flowing over their shoes.

Gil sagged against the wall, his face a mask of exhaustion, though a deep satisfaction helped warm his wet shivering frame. There were yells from some of the cops, congratulations and praise. They held back as Gil and Frank shook hands, then grasped each other in a bear hug.

One could be excused, if they assumed the chaos was ended.

A tiny tinkling sound barely caught Gil's attention. Glancing at the handcuffed madman, he saw a smile that should not have been there. It struck a wrong note in the situation that made the Detective realize he had just heard a small metallic clink. He looked from the lunatic grin on the man's face, to the concrete floor and saw the safety release pin of a hand grenade, lying there. Detached.

It happened so fast; he didn't have time to think. Somehow the madman had been armed with a grenade, probably hooked to his belt. There had been no time for a body search. Now the crazed lunatic got his hands on it, managing to pull the pin. In a microsecond, Gil understood. There was no question of trying to disarm the man, find the grenade and wrest it free. There wasn't even time to try to save him. The body of the grenade must be hidden behind his back. The only question was whether they would join him in the deadly blast. Gil had no intention of doing so.

The instant he saw the smile and the pin, he yelled, "Grenade!" At the same time, he launched himself toward Frank. His lunge bounced them against the open metal door and into the cluster of cops watching from partly behind it. The force of his leap carried him through the opening, along with Frank and a couple of others. He looked back to see Mel rising and starting toward them. The door was a safety exit that swung outward, into the landing area. With no one holding it, the heavy metal started swinging back toward the closed position. The blast, when it came, slammed the door the rest of the way shut, delaying the inevitable sickening moment when they would have to see the carnage in the landing on the other side of the door. The frame held but showed signs of buckling from the force of the blast in the stairwell. A splatter of red dripped from the wall. Blood had sprayed through the last crack before the door had completed its closing.

Frank helped Gil to his feet, before giving him a visual once-over. They stared at each other for long moments.

"I'm not sure whether we just lost one killer, or several," Frank said thoughtfully.

"I don't know," Gil replied thoughtfully. "But whatever he was, I think he was lost a long time ago."

Gil's legs began shaking, and he almost went down again.

"Where's Jennifer?"

"One of the guys has her, don't worry." Frank grabbed his partner's arm and pulled it over his shoulder. He looked at Gil with an expression that was too serious to be a smile, but with a hint of humor in it.

"Boy, you look like shit!"

"Yeah, well right now, the only difference between me and a bucket of shit... is the bucket."

They laughed the laughter of post-battle release, tinged with leftover fear and the gratitude of survivors.

"C'mon, let's get somebody else to finish this up,' Frank said. "By the way, I got some good news, Gil."

"I could use a little. What is it?"

"There was a message for you from a Dr. Poole. She said you might want to come down to the hospital. Pilar is starting to respond and seems to know what's going on."

"What the hell? I thought the doctor said there would be plenty of advance warning!" Gil blurted out, upset at the thought that she would wake without seeing him there.

"Yeah, well, what do doctors know, anyway," Frank laughed. "Look, Gil, you did what you had do. Pilar's just going to be glad to see you. The doc says her quick response is a real good sign, and makes a full recovery likely."

"Thank God!"

"I didn't think you believed in God," Frank kidded him.

"Yeah, well that's how much you know," Gil grinned back, laughing. His smile was a bit tired, but it was natural, it was a real. It widened as he saw a uniformed cop appear with Jennifer in tow.

Slowly, he kneeled, spreading his arms to the girl. She was favoring her wrist, but moved into his embrace, using the other limb to return the hug. After a long squeeze, Gil laboriously rose, took her good hand in his and started limping away. As he moved down the hallway, even injuries and exhaustion didn't prevent a hint of bounce to his step.

CHAPTER 52

Three months later ... Saturday afternoon

The heat of the sun was like a blanket, wrapping Pilar in a cocoon of warmth and well-being. She raised herself from a bench at the foot of the stadium stairs. She had walked all the way from the parking lot, without resting. Now, after a breather, she would start one complete revolution of the oval that she managed to walk three times a week. There were bad days as well as good ones, but she could see the steady progress when she looked back over weeks of effort. She still had little memory of the first days after she had been shot. Perhaps that was just as well. There was a lot of pain and confusion that had slowly dispersed over time, along with other things. The first solid memory she had after coming out of the fog, was of Gil-dear sweet Gil, tears in his eyes, kneeling at her bedside, kissing her hand.

There he was, now, out on the track—thickly muscled legs extending from athletic shorts. He was jogging slowly around the track, waving at her every now and then. He started up the long line of stairs on the opposite side of the covered bleachers. After climbing the first flight he paused. Two figures appeared out of the adjacent tunnel ... one adult, one child.

She recognized Tom Tyler next to little Anne Marie, in matching jogging suits. Last week she and Gil had attended the Tyler's celebration party when the adoption of the orphaned girl had been finalized. It was interesting how the names of Ann Marie, and her new mother, Mary Anne, were so similar. Anyone not knowing the history of either, would think they were naturally related. The previously childless couple were clearly ecstatic that arrangements had been made for the adoption. Tom had shortened Anne Marie to "A.M." and spoke to the child in private moments as "our Morning Star." The little girl was out of her cast for two months now. She had almost full use of her legs again.

Pilar thought about the future. She wondered if there would be children in it for her and Gil. Then again, Jennifer and her mother had become so much a part of their family, she felt almost like they already had one. Perhaps, if they had difficulty, they might follow the Tylers' lead and consider adoption one day. For now, it was a pleasure just to see Gil be the best uncle a child ever had and herself accepted as "Aunt Pilar."

She saw Gil and his companions walk back down the stairway, laughing and talking. Then the three of them broke into a slow trot around the track, the two men going easy to allow the girl to keep up. As they came around to the spot where Pilar was limping along, Gil detached himself from the group and walked by her side for a few strides.

"Easy does it, my lady. You're doing fine."

"Oh, go on. You don't need to walk with me. I know you want to be out there exhausting yourself."

"Exhaustion is fine," he laughed, "but I'll take walking with the lady I love, any day. You might as well get used to it, 'cause you're going to be walking with me the rest of your life."

They stopped, and she turned, receiving his kiss on her forehead, another on her lips. She turned back to the track, nodding at a pedestal water fountain a quarter of the way around.

"Want to bet I can reach that bubbler, before you make it one time around the track?"

"I wouldn't bet anything against that stubborn will of yours, but if the price is right, I might bite."

"How about dinner for two and a wild night in the waterbed?"

"And if I lose?"

"You will have to pay MY price."

"Which is...?"

"Dinner for two and a wild night in the waterbed.

"I like the stakes."

Pilar moved first, pulling away in a determined slog a determined slog toward the water fountain. Gil gave a whoop and took off like a kid.

For people putting out tremendous physical energy, they had unusually big smiles.

www.ingramcontent.com/pod-product-compliance
Lightning Source LLC
LaVergne TN
LVHW021758060526
838201LV00058B/3145